Praise for *Azur Like It*

"To dismiss it as chick-lit would be a shame . . .
Fans of her writing know that Holden's skill, wit, and
aplomb make her a stand-out in the oft-sugary genre."
—*Gotham* magazine

"[A] breezy read." —*Entertainment Weekly*

"[A] gleeful jumble of Brit-style slapstick, puns,
and sly wit. Quite a treat." —*Kirkus Reviews*

Wendy Holden is the internationally bestselling author of five
novels, including *Farm Fatale* and *Gossip Hound* (available
from Plume). She lives in London and Derbyshire with her
husband and two children.

Also by Wendy Holden

Simply Divine

Bad Heir Day

Gossip Hound

Farm Fatale

Azur Like It

THE WIVES OF BATH

Wendy Holden

A PLUME BOOK

PLUME
Published by Penguin Group
Penguin Group (USA) Inc., 375 Hudson Street, New York, New York 10014, USA
Penguin Group (Canada), 10 Alcorn Avenue, Toronto, Ontario, Canada M4V 3B2,
(a division of Pearson Penguin Canada Inc.)
Penguin Books Ltd., 80 Strand, London WC2R 0RL, England
Penguin Ireland, 25 St. Stephen's Green, Dublin 2,
Ireland (a division of Penguin Books Ltd.)
Penguin Group (Australia), 250 Camberwell Road, Camberwell, Victoria 3124,
Australia (a division of Pearson Australia Group Pty. Ltd.)
Penguin Books India Pvt. Ltd., 11 Community Centre, Panchsheel Park,
New Delhi – 110 017, India
Penguin Group (NZ), cnr Airborne and Rosedale Roads, Albany,
Auckland 1310, New Zealand (a division of Pearson New Zealand Ltd.)
Penguin Books (South Africa) (Pty.) Ltd., 24 Sturdee Avenue,
Rosebank, Johannesburg 2196, South Africa

Penguin Books Ltd., Registered Offices: 80 Strand, London WC2R 0RL, England

Published by Plume, a member of Penguin Group (USA) Inc. Previously published
in Great Britain by Headline Publishing, Ltd.

First American Printing, May 2005
10 9 8 7 6 5 4 3 2 1

 REGISTERED TRADEMARK—MARCA REGISTRADA

CIP data is available.
ISBN 0-452-28589-5

Printed in the United States of America
Set in Garamond Light

PUBLISHER'S NOTE
This is a work of fiction. Names, characters, places, and incidents either are the
product of the author's imagination or are used fictitiously, and any resemblance
to actual persons, living or dead, business establishments, events, or locales is entirely coincidental.

For Isabella

THE
WIVES
OF
BATH

CHAPTER
1

Hugo peeled his face from the white-coated chest of an exceptionally pretty woman. His rush through the hospital was such that he had failed to consider that the corner he was heading for might have someone coming round it.

"Sorry," he grinned at her, thinking that, actually, he wasn't sorry at all. It wasn't every evening he got to bury his nose in something as luscious as . . . he squinted at her badge . . . Dr. M. Watson, Consultant Pediatrician.

"Don't worry," the doctor replied slightly frostily.

"You're not really called Dr. Watson, are you?" Hugo looked her up and down flirtatiously, taking in the glossy black hair and large dark eyes. Confidently he waited for his own handsome face and commanding height to have their usual effect on a woman. To his surprise, he waited in vain.

"Are you looking for somewhere in particular?" the doctor asked. Her manner was polite but no-nonsense.

"I'm here for a class." Hugo maintained his expectant smile. She'd crack eventually. They always did. "A prenatal class."

Dr. Watson did not crack, however. Instead, she gave him directions. After several more twists through the gray linoleum maze, Hugo finally found the door he was in search of.

He knocked and opened it to find Amanda sitting tense and

annoyed amid a horseshoe of people, an empty orange plastic chair next to her.

"Sorry I'm late," Hugo muttered.

In front of the horseshoe stood a thin-faced woman with wire-framed glasses and a bright, toothy smile. There was, Hugo thought, something over-eager, manic even, about the way her eyes shone through her lenses.

"Goot evening," she said. "My name is Lotti. Yes, you are late, but bedder late than never, as you say in this country, I think?"

Dutch, Hugo guessed, as, bracelets rattling on her outstretched arms, the woman came toward him. He found himself bustled to a table and asked his name, which was then written on a badge and stuck on his lapel. Thus labeled, Hugo was free to stumble to the seat beside his wife.

He looked swiftly about him. The sight of so many pregnant women made him nervous. Their stomachs looked strained beyond endurance, about to burst any second. He imagined a huge cannon bang: a twenty-one-gun salute.

Lotti beamed round at the horseshoe. "It's goot to see you all here tonight. You know, I hope you find these classes useful, not just for information about baby and birthing, but also to make frens? You know, couples who meet at these classes sometimes stay frens for years."

Hugo stared fixedly at the floor. Nothing made his toes curl like forced social interaction. Like that bit in church when you had to offer each other a sign of peace.

"Now," Lotti instructed, lenses glinting, "I'd like everyone to stand up one by one and introduce yourselfs to the class. Please!" She gestured at the person nearest, who rose to her feet.

This woman's name badge read "Mel." She was short and pugnacious-looking, with cropped gray hair. Hugo's glance flicked over her to rest approvingly on the woman she was next to: a very pretty, very pregnant redhead, with creamy skin, faraway eyes and an air of dreamy gentleness. She looked vulnerable, he thought. This must be why her mother was with her.

"I'm Mel," the gray-haired woman announced, glancing dismissively down at her name badge as if to acknowledge she was stating the obvious. She gestured to the redhead. "And this is Saskia. My partner."

"That's great, Mel," Lotti beamed. "And can you tell the class what you do?"

"Saskia's a Home Office pathologist. I'm an organic gardener."

"Baby's sure going to be lucky with the vegetables, ha ha. Nothing out of the jars in your house, ha ha."

"No," said Mel shortly, and sat down.

Next it was Amanda's turn. She bounced up, despite her bump, a dazzling, red-lipsticked grin stretched rigidly across her face. "My name is Amanda Fine," she breathily declared. "Although it is more likely you'll have heard of me in my professional capacity. As Amanda Hardwick." She paused expectantly.

"Are you that woman off *NYPD Blue?*" a thickset man next to Saskia eventually hazarded. Amanda tightened her lips. "I'm *quite* a well-known journalist," she corrected him, as Hugo felt his fists tighten and his toes ball up with embarrassment. "*Very* well known in the States. But I don't suppose," she added, looking round disparagingly, "that anyone here ever gets *Style* magazine."

"I do, sometimes," offered a woman with heavy makeup, shiny skin, a large nose and wild brown hair. Her name badge read "Laura." "You mean the one that comes with the *Sunday Times?*"

"No," Amanda said freezingly. "I do *not* mean that one. I mean the extremely prestigious and influential American one of the same name."

Hugo was surprised at the mention of the magazine. Earlier that year, Amanda had resigned from *Style*—and in rather mys-

terious circumstances. On principle, she had told him. A dis-
agreement with the legal department or something. He hadn't
realized until then she had had any principles. Her complete
lack of scruples had been one of her attractions, initially.

Lotti's voice broke into his thoughts. "Well, it's all very interesting anyway, Amanda. Thank you."

Amanda sat down and gave Hugo a bad-tempered nudge.
She was, he saw, staring at his lapel. Dismayed, he now saw
that, positioned at a drunken angle on his suit, the crumpled
white name badge read "Yogi." Lotti had obviously misheard
"Hugo." But you probably didn't get many Hugos in Holland.

"Yogi!" Lotti trilled, inadvertently rubbing it in. "Your turn
now, please."

Crossly, Hugo got to his feet. He had assumed that the covert
glances from the rest of the class, particularly from the women,
had been approving and possibly flirtatious. The realization he
was the object of amusement was both unusual and unpleasant.
"Erm, well," he began uncomfortably. "The first thing I should
say is that this badge isn't strictly accurate. My name's not Yogi."

"Shpeak up, Yogi!" urged Lotti from the front. "We can't
hear you!"

"My name's not Yogi," Hugo bleated. "It's Hugo—Hugo
Fine." Bloody hell. Why hadn't he just stayed in the pub and
ignored his mobile? Amanda had rung even as he raised the
pint glass to his lips, demanding to know why he wasn't in the
prenatal class.

"I understand you've recently moved from London, Yogi,"
Lotti steamrollered on. "Would you like to tell us why?"

Good question, Hugo thought. The same one he asked
himself most mornings. He suppressed a sigh and affected
breeziness. "Oh, you know. All the usual stuff. Better quality
of life and all that."

"And so much better for children," Amanda energetically interrupted from beside him. "Family life in the country, we
thought. Real life. Quality time."

There was a murmur of agreement from the others at this.

"Dandling angelic infants in the dappled sunlight under the apple blossom, that sort of thing." Amanda flashed her red grimace again.

The murmur stuttered slightly. There were glances of surprise.

"So we're both thrilled to be here," Amanda finished, as graciously as a visiting Royal. "*Aren't* we, darling?"

Hugo flinched at her violent nudge and nodded faintly.

In point of fact, and as Amanda well knew, he was not at all thrilled to be here. He had resisted fiercely her idea of moving out of London and into the countryside. An urbanite to the core, he had a terror of the deep middle of nowhere with its black nights and awful stillness. But Amanda, once pregnant, had insisted that her city days were over.

The compromise was Bath. As well as halfway house between big city and rolling ruraldom, it had the additional benefit of being somewhere Hugo had actually heard of. It also had good London train links, not that he used them. He had imagined commuting to his old job as a real estate agent in Islington, but his wife, it turned out, had decided *his* city days were over as well.

As a result he was now the wage slave of one Neil Dustard, boss of a small Bath property firm. He had seemed reasonable enough at first; the only agent Hugo had applied to that had taken him out to the pub to discuss prospects. At the time this had seemed evidence of the sort of laid-back friendliness that corresponded to brilliance in business.

What it turned out to be was evidence of the alcoholism already hinted at by Neil's red face. As a result of which his character was as unstable as his company, which Hugo soon discovered to be as mired in lack of ideas as it was in lack of ambition. And he was mired there too, now. Bugger Amanda, for making him move here. And bugger himself, for letting her.

There was a commotion at the class door as a man came in. Lotti trained her glasses on him. "Hi. Welcome. Come in.

You're a bit late, but never mind." She bustled over to do the business with the name badges.

"We had to wait for a bus," the man said defensively.

The newcomer was, Hugo realized, extravagantly hand-some. From the Cherokee cheekbones to the dark hair curling carelessly round the base of the muscular neck, his were the type of film-hero good looks that aroused resentment in the most relaxed of men. And Hugo, standing up amid sniggering strangers, sporting a silly name badge, was feeling far from laid back at the moment.

"A *bus?*" echoed Amanda disdainfully.

The long-haired man looked at her. "We don't do cars," he said witheringly. "We believe they're damaging to the planet."

Lotti glanced delightedly up from her sheet of stickers. "Hey, me too. I don't do cars either. I bicycle everywhere." She brandished her marker at the bus fan. "What's your name?"

"Jake. My wife, Alice, is here too, but she's in the loo throwing up at the moment." He grinned at the women. "Guess you know how it is, eh, girls?"

Hugo's stomach tensed in dislike at the easy populism. The women, however, looked charmed. There was a sympathetic murmur from all except Amanda, who looked disgusted. She did not, Hugo knew, appreciate being reminded of preg-nancy's less glamorous aspects.

Jake was now looking at Hugo. Or, more precisely, his name badge. There was a mocking gleam in his eye. "Yogi, huh? As in Bear or as in Maharishi Mahesh?"

"Neither," Hugo replied icily, suddenly loathing him. "My name is actually Hugo. I'm not sure Lotti heard properly."

Lotti was now fixing Jake's badge onto his broad chest. Her manner was half investiture, half flirtation and entirely distracted.

"Do go on, Yogi," she gasped, flushed. "You were saying what is it you do."

Hugo shifted to his other foot. "I'm a real estate agent."

Was that a snort coming from Jake's direction? He looked

challengingly at the new arrival. But Jake avoided his gaze, seemingly absorbed in somewhat sneering contemplation of Hugo's pinstriped suit.

"Thank you, Yogi. You can sit down now." Lotti's glasses flashed speculatively around before being drawn magnetically back to Jake. "Jake," she fluttered. "Why don't you tell us a little about yourself?"

Jake, who had sat down, rose slowly up again. There was a stirring among the women as he unfolded himself to his full impressive height. Hugo noted with irritation how confidently he stood in his battered lumberjack shirt and scruffy jeans. He seemed at ease to an almost aggressive extent, rolling gently but constantly from one foot to the other.

"I'd just like to say, before we start," Jake looked round with an intense, deep-set gaze, "that I, for one, am not here just for decoration. I think we fathers should take an active part in everything to do with the birth. I mean, we're mothers too, in a way, and I personally don't have a problem with feeling that."

Ecstasy lit Lotti's face. "That's right, Jake," she gasped, eyes brimming behind her glasses. "If only more men felt like you."

Nauseous, Hugo thought, was the only way to describe how he personally felt. Sliding a glance round the room, he divined similar sentiments in the other men present. Their expressions ranged from miserable to murderous.

The women, however, were audibly sighing with admiration. And none more so than Lotti. "Tell us what you do, Jake," she invited.

"I run a magazine."

"But that's marvellous!" Lotti threw out an excited arm in Amanda's direction. "Amanda here was just telling us about the magazine she works on."

Jake looked Amanda doubtfully up and down. "Can't imagine it's the same sort of thing. Yours is all celebrities, sex and makeup, right?"

"Sounds great," interrupted Laura, evidently anxious to atone for her *Sunday Times* gaffe.

Amanda favored her with a tight smile. "It's a glossy, if that's what you mean," she told Jake. "Is yours a glossy?"

He shook his lustrous locks. "Not likely. It's printed on eco-sustainable paper. It's a recycling magazine."

"A cycling magazine!" exclaimed Lotti in delight.

"*Re*-cycling," Jake's Calvin Klein–ad perfect brows drew together in irritation. "It's called *Get Trashed!* Available from health-food shops, Soil Association–approved organic greengrocers and by subscription from me." He looked around challengingly.

"Recycling!" Lotti clasped her hands together. "A very important subject. Isn't it, everyone?"

Heads nodded, Hugo's included. For what it was worth, he had religiously washed out his bottles and cans and posted them through the appropriate holes in the recycling container near their old flat. Once, after a particularly lavish party, Amanda had written to the council suggesting they provide containers with holes for magnums. So far as he knew, she had never received a reply.

"Our latest issue," Jake informed the class, "shows you how to build a house made entirely of reusable waste."

Hugo snorted and tried to turn it into a cough. He was rewarded with a bright smile from Lotti. "You know, Yogi, maybe you ought to get together with Jake. You're a real esh-tate agent, right?" Her emphasis was on "esht" and "agent."

"A house made of reusable waste?" Hugo mused as politely as he could manage. "I'm not sure Dunn and Dustard have handled anything like that before."

"And I don't think they're likely to," Jake returned smartly. "Unless you accept your commission in LETs, that is."

"In what?" Hugo asked, his polite tones now under some strain.

Jake's expression was pained and impatient. "Local Exchange Tokens. Another of our interests is phasing out conventional payment methods in favor of trading skills. Or benefits in kind."

"I'd have to get back to you on that."

Next to introduce himself was stocky Jim, who had imagined Amanda to be in *NYPD Blue*. He was a carpenter originally from St. Helens.

"How marvellous," gushed Amanda. "Is that in the Caribbean?"

Jim looked at her in amazement. "Merseyside."

Next came Laura. Hugo looked at her with interest. Besides thick makeup, she had a wide gap between her front teeth, giving her smile a bawdy appearance. She was wearing a lot of hot pink. Hugo wondered where her other half was.

"He's, er, too busy to come," Laura admitted when Lotti brightly asked the same question.

"No father of a baby should be too busy to come," Jake opined loudly. "It's his duty."

"Fergus works in advertising in London," Laura snapped back. Jake rolled his deep-set eyes in disgust.

The door opened and a blonde woman came in. The room rippled with interest as it realized that this, presumably, was Jake's wife. The one who, also presumably, had been in the loo all this time.

She was, Hugo decided, rather less glamorous than her partner. She was thin, despite her pregnancy, and lanky. Cleanliness seemed her most distinguishing feature. She looked almost carbolically well scrubbed in maternity jeans and a white T-shirt, with a long, calm face completely devoid of makeup. She looked, Hugo thought, extremely earnest.

Yet however understated it seemed to him, the woman's appearance had had an electric effect on someone else in the room. Amanda, beside him, was breathing short and fast. "It *can't* be," he heard her hiss to herself.

"My wife, Alice," Jake was announcing. "Feeling better?" he asked her solicitously.

Not exactly, Hugo guessed, puzzled. For Alice was staring at Amanda, her calm face registering unpleasant shock.

Lotti had picked up none of the drama. "Tell us about yourself," she beamed toothily at Alice. "Are you working at the moment?"

Hugo heard Amanda breathing heavily. He sensed that she was very interested in Alice's answer. Frankly, after this build-up, he was interested himself.

"N-no," Alice stuttered. Then, recovering, she added in a clear, soft voice. "But until recently I was in the legal department of a New York magazine company."

Hugo's head exploded with the pealing of loud bells. So that was the connection. *Style* magazine. Was this mousy woman, then, involved in Amanda's mysterious resignation? With her scrubbed face and mild air, she hardly looked the type to take on his formidable wife.

Lotti was looking expectantly round the class. "OK. Right. Now we all know each other, let's get down to business. Does everyone here know what a uterus looks like?"

CHAPTER
2

Standing at the bus stop after the class, Alice and Jake watched Amanda and Hugo's gleaming four-wheel drive sweep by. Behind the tinted panes, the white blur of Amanda's face stared contemptuously out.

"*How* does that woman know you?" Jake asked. "Seems to hate your guts, for some reason."

"I think she does," Alice admitted, hoping Jake would not probe further. It hardly seemed possible Amanda Hardwick was having a baby in exactly the same place and at the exact same time as she was.

"So what happened?" Jake asked as the bus, with its customary obduracy, failed to materialize.

Alice groaned. "She was the one involved in that libel case. The one I packed the job at Intercorp in over."

In the orange sulphur lamplight, Jake's eyes widened in recognition. *That was her?*

Alice nodded. "But in a funny way," she said consideringly, "she did me a favor." She squeezed Jake's hand. "I would never have met you if it hadn't been for Amanda Hardwick. If she'd been just one tiny bit less horrible, I'd probably have stayed in New York."

As Jake looked at his watch and peered, frowning, at the

timetable mounted on the bus stop, Alice's thoughts returned
to the fateful fortnight when her life was changed forever. It
had all started when Sherry, her assistant, had knocked at her
office door.

Sherry was pregnant. She was stroking her bump and smiling dreamily through the glass. Alice beckoned her in.

"What's up?"

"Brant wants a word," Sherry smiled toothily.

"Oh. Right." Brant was head of the Intercorp legal team and
her boss. Alice rose from her desk.

Sherry paused. "And I'd like one too, if that's OK."

"Sure. Fire away."

"Is it OK if I take the afternoon off to go to my breastfeeding support class?"

Alice hesitated. "But you know I've got that conference call
with Europe this afternoon. It's important you're here to make
sure all the international dial-ins work."

Sherry's pixie face fell. "Oh, it doesn't matter," she sighed
martyrishly. "I guess that if you're not pregnant, or not a
mother, you just wouldn't understand."

"I guess not," Alice said, trying not to be hurt or offended.
Pregnant women could be so bloody *patronizing*. Along with
everyone else, they assumed her childless state to be her choice.

If only, Alice thought, it was that simple. Yes, she was
thirty-six, unmarried and child-free. But that didn't make her a
baby-hating careerist. Alice had, in fact, always imagined that,
at some stage, she would be a mother. She had certainly imagined being one by her current stage. But it hadn't happened.
Among the cards destiny had dealt her, the marriage-baby one
just hadn't turned up.

So while other women her age brought up families, Alice
had simply carried on working. She was now wealthy, successful and enviably free from commitment or responsibility.
And while she was vaguely aware this wasn't everything in
life, it was surely a reasonable option.

She got up to go to Brant's.

It was obvious from his face that there was trouble. His expression, habitually concerned, looked more so even than usual. He regarded Alice gravely through thick horn-rimmed spectacles.

"What's up?" she asked.

"Amanda Hardwick," Brant said shortly.

"Oh. Shit."

"You could put it that way. But I'm hoping you can sort it out."

"No time. I'm up to my eyes in that recipe case."

Brant looked blank.

"You remember," Alice prompted. "That cake where readers were told to put in fifty cups of whisky instead of five. There are a lot of angry people out there. And a lot with very bad hangovers. I've been working late nights to sort it all out."

This was no exaggeration, as the shadows beneath her eyes attested. But late nights were nothing new at the Intercorp Magazine Company and the glint in Brant's glasses was steely. "Someone else can take that over. Amanda Hardwick's English, and handling English is your speciality."

"Thanks a bunch," Alice muttered. New York, as Brant well knew, was full of English people, many of whom he dealt with every day of his life. It was just an excuse to give her the short straw. And as straws went, Amanda Hardwick was about the shortest.

Amanda was Intercorp's most celebrated or notorious journalist, depending on which way you looked at it. She wrote mostly for the flagship publication, *Style*. Despite being based in London, where she was rumored to have a husband, she seemed to be a constant presence in New York. Her fame, so far as Alice could see, sprang from her extreme nastiness to any celebrity foolish enough to agree to one of her interviews. The fact that so many did represented, Alice supposed, the triumph of hope over experience. Either that or the terminal stupidity of the famous.

However, Amanda's latest victim, a celebrated actor, was, it seemed, threatening to sue *Style* on ten different counts.

"How come it got this far?" Alice demanded. As Brant's deputy, she was entitled to get cross with him on occasion. "Did no one up here have a look at the piece?"

Brant shrugged. "Look, Alice, it's in your hands, OK? If anyone can get us off this hook, you can. You've done it before."

Alice rolled her tired eyes. It infuriated her that so much of her time, energy and expertise had been spent saving Amanda Hardwick's neck. Thanks to her efforts, and despite the proximity of Amanda's interviews to the wind and knuckle, the only retributions so far were some strongly worded letters of warning from affronted celebrities' lawyers. Yet achieving this outcome had required all Alice's diplomacy and legal dexterity; she groaned inwardly at the thought of repeating the feat yet again.

Alice worked on the Hardwick piece for the rest of the morning. It was, as Brant had intimated, a disaster. *Style* really had done it this time. Alice had arranged to see its most notorious contributor that afternoon in order to find out what could be salvaged. She doubted it was much. Shoving the offending documents into her desk, she dragged herself out for coffee and a bagel.

In the café, she carried her cardboard tray over to a table by the window. Lying on it was a copy of the *New York Times,* open at the Weddings/Celebrations page.

Alice flicked an eye over it as she ate. Among the flotsam and jetsam washed up on this week's matrimonial shores was a bride who had founded "a humor Web site for people with one Jewish parent." Two male doctors were "celebrating their partnership." A voice-over artist was marrying a trumpet player and a cardiologist was marrying a hematologist-oncologist. Whatever that was. The most interesting union, Alice thought, was the New Haven automobile princess who, in a classic "Uptown Girl" scenario, had married a local carpenter, son of a builder and a supermarket worker. Alice wondered what the bride's fearsome-sounding parents, clearly east coast royalty, made of it all. And especially what they made of the bridegroom's mother and father.

She chewed a fingernail contemplatively and imagined her own entry on the page: "Miss Alice Lamorna Duffield, daughter of Mr. and Mrs. James Duffield of Madron, Cornwall, and deputy chief legal adviser to the Intercorp Magazine Company, was married last evening to . . ."

Who? Someone who sounded like a firm of solicitors, if the men on the rest of the page were anything to go by. Grayling Hotchkiss. Bradford Todd. Pulling a face, Alice got up to go back to work.

Later that afternoon, a short blonde strutted into her office. Her head seemed to rise straight out of a large white cleavage and her red-lipsticked mouth wore a sulky, defensive expression.

"Would you like some coffee?" Alice offered. No harm, she thought, in being civil.

Amanda Hardwick clearly thought otherwise. She put both hands on a pair of plump hips. "Just how long is this going to take?" she demanded.

"Long enough for coffee."

"Oh, for Christ's sake. I'll have a skinny latte," the blonde huffed.

"Sorry," Sherry said. "The machine only does filter."

Amanda Hardwick fixed her with a cold eye. "So you'll just have to go down to Dean & Deluca and get me a latte, won't you?"

Sherry gaped. The coffee bar, as everyone present knew, was seventy-four floors down and two street crossings away. "I'm, like, six months *pregnant?*" Sherry said, pointing with both hands at her bump.

Amanda stared coolly back. "I think," she said witheringly, "that you're confusing me with somebody who gives a toss."

"Sherry hasn't got time to go and fetch one," Alice cut in hastily. "It's filter or nothing, I'm afraid."

After some pouting and protests, filter was accepted. The meeting began.

"I'll run through the contested items," Alice gestured at the article, which she had highlighted in various places. "The first concerns your claim that your subject dyes his hair and has had several facelifts."

"He does," snapped Amanda Hardwick. "He has."

"Do you have proof?"

"Yes."

This answer was a pleasant surprise. Hope rose in Alice that the case was salvageable after all. "Great. So what's your proof?"

Amanda Hardwick pressed her thin red lips together. "I don't need *proof* proof. You've only got to look at him."

Alice flexed her fingers. "I see. Well, *he* says his hair isn't dyed and his face is the one he was born with. So the onus is on you to prove otherwise."

"*What?* This is pathetic. I can't believe you've dragged me up here to tell me this."

"So that's a no then, is it?" Alice enquired calmly. "You have no evidence on that point?"

Furious silence greeted this.

"And then," Alice moved her finger down the page, "there's your allegation that he suffers from a sex addiction and takes recreational drugs."

Amanda jumped up and clamped a hand melodramatically to her forehead. "Oh, please. I can't believe I'm hearing this. Get with the program, will you? All Hollywood knows *that's* true."

"I'm afraid that won't stand up as evidence in a court of law," Alice said gravely. "Or will all Hollywood come into the witness box?"

"He sniffed all the way through the interview. What more proof do you want?"

"That could have been a cold. Did he admit to you in the interview that he was a drug-taking sex addict? Or . . ." Alice ran her digit down several more paragraphs, "that his two young children aren't his at all and their father is actually Brad Pitt?"

Christ. The more you read, the more unbelievable this interview was.

"All Hollywood knows that as well," Amanda said defiantly.

Alice propped her chin up on one hand and stared wearily at Amanda. "Quite apart from any immediate legal implications, have you any idea of the devastating effect this sort of rumor can have on a family? Those are *children* you're talking about. Little kids. But old enough to understand. This sort of thing can ruin lives."

Amanda looked scornful. "What is this obsession with kids round here?" she snarled. "What are you, the fucking Mothers' Union?"

"I'm just pointing out," Alice said calmly, "that these are vulnerable youngsters you're writing about. The courts won't like it."

"What do I care about some effing celebrity kids?" Amanda snarled. "Or any kids, come to that? Kids, schmids. Anyone who has them deserves all they've got coming to them."

Alice regarded her levelly. The baby-hating career bitch personified, she thought.

Amanda leaned over the table, giving Alice a grandstand view of her cleavage. "Look, baby," she spat, "you do realize who you're dealing with here? I'm Intercorp's star writer, OK? And who the hell are you? Some jumped-up goody-goody drone pen-pusher in the effing legal department, that's what."

Who just happens to have saved your skin more times than you've had hot dinners, Alice thought savagely. She restrained the urge to fling her desk lamp, keyboard and computer screen at the woman in front of her and instead folded her hands composedly. She spoke calmly. "These are serious allegations and he's going to sue. All I'm trying to do is establish what evidence you have. So far, to be honest, it doesn't look like much."

It was at this charged point that Sherry came in bearing a tray of freshly brewed filter coffee. As she put a cup and saucer down by Amanda's elbow, the elbow shot out. The cup and its contents were propelled all over Sherry. Alice gasped. She had no doubt that the action was deliberate.

"So sorry," purred Amanda, eyes wide in mock shock. "So clumsy of me. But that's the problem with these cups, isn't it? No lids! Would have been so much better if you'd got the latte after all."

She got up, seized her handbag, blew them a kiss and strode out.

"You OK?" asked Alice.

Sherry looked up from scrubbing frantically at her skirt with a handful of tissues and nodded.

Alice banged her head against her desk in frustration. "Jesus. Who'd be a magazine lawyer?"

Sherry stared at her in concern. "You know, you need a break. You've been working your ass off lately."

"I know I have," Alice muttered into her desk. "But where would I go? I haven't the energy to organize anything. And it's not," she added miserably, "as if I've got anyone to go with, either."

"You should get out more," Sherry advised. "Meet people."

"No time." Alice rubbed her eyes. But she knew, and knew Sherry knew too, that this was an excuse. She had, in fact, opted out of the New York dating scene. It was too competitive, too serious. Dates here were like job interviews, usually for jobs one wasn't certain one wanted.

Moreover, Manhattan Man seemed completely to believe the publicity about his scarcity value. Even the ugly ones with rampant halitosis were convinced that somewhere in the city were at least ten stunning women desperate to marry them.

Alice's gaze slipped to the papers Sherry was scrubbing her skirt with. What she had assumed to be tissue now looked suspiciously like the advice the outside attorney had sent for the whisky cake case.

"Gee, sorry," Sherry grinned. "My brain's just all over at the moment."

The telephone rang. Sherry disappeared to answer it. "Your mother," she announced over the intercom.

Alice snatched the receiver up gratefully. Her mother. One shard of sanity in a mad, fractured world. "Hi, Mum."

"Hello, darling. Now listen. I've got some news for you."

Alice listened. Her stomach twisted with dismay. "But, Mum, I can't just drop everything because Sally's getting married."

"But she's your cousin, darling. You used to be very close."

"Yes, but I haven't really seen her since the Bay City Rollers were in the charts."

"Who?"

"Never mind, Mum. I just mean the last time Sally and I got together we were wearing flares and platform shoes."

"That sounds," her mother said briskly, "a vast improvement on what Sally wears now. Her hair is blue, apparently."

Alice smiled. She had heard her cousin had developed hippie tendencies, no doubt as a reaction to her straitlaced and bossy mother. Sally's recent career, to the reported despair of Alice's Aunt Frances, had featured stints as a face-painter and community juggler, the latter post, to Sally's father's disgust, being sponsored by a liberal-minded local council. Who she might be marrying defied speculation.

But speculate, Alice decided, was the most she planned to do.

"I'm sorry, Mum," she said resolutely. "Too busy."

Alice's mother was not one to give up easily. "Come *on*, darling. Time you took a break from that high-flying career of yours. The family would love to see you." The command, for so it undoubtedly was, rolled from Cornwall, under the Atlantic and up to Alice's seventy-fourth-floor Madison Avenue office. "You could do with a holiday, I'm sure."

Alice hesitated. High-flying career? Never, thanks to Amanda Hardwick, had she felt quite so professionally low. Or quite so in need of time off. But was this the pick-up she needed?

"Do come, darling." Her mother had changed tack and was now wheedling. "Aunt Frances particularly wants you to. She's really rather devastated about the wedding, you know. The groom's called Bo and he's in an anarchist circus."

Alice smothered a snigger. Just as she had suspected. "What's an anarchist circus?"

"They do things with dustbin lids and old car engines."

"What's wrong with that?" Alice was teasing her mother. But her query was also genuine; as an extremely fair person and a lawyer to boot, she deplored condemnation without proper trial. "Those sorts of circuses are very trendy. They make a fortune, some of them."

"Not this one, I can assure you. Still, at least his father was a vice admiral. That, and the fact she's persuaded them to marry in a church is about the only thing that's keeping Frances going."

Alice scrunched her free hand into her mouth. She mustn't laugh. The situation was obviously extremely serious.

"Because there's the baby as well, of course," Alice's mother added.

"Baby? Sal's pregnant?"

"Darling, you just have to come," her mother urged. "Seeing Sally about to pop might make even *you* feel broody at last!"

Alice, irritated, did not reply.

"Well?" The Cornwall end clearly wanted closure.

"I don't know, Mum." But Alice felt her resolve cracking. Apart from anything else, the wedding had definite comic potential. "Sally's timing could hardly be worse," she demurred, as a feeble last stand at resistance.

"Frances's sentiments exactly, darling. Now when can we expect you at the airport?"

CHAPTER
3

ARMANI-ED AND MANOLO-ED OUTSIDE THE CHURCH ON THE WEDding day, Alice felt glad she had come home. She had forgotten just how beautiful England could be. And the West Country in particular. Today was a picture postcard from Somerset: blue skies, snowdrops, glossily new-leaved hedges and a lovely old village of fudge-colored stone.

Adding to her good mood was the unusual, agreeable sensation of standing out rather glamorously from the crowd. Generally, Alice had little interest in fashion, yet, working where she did, she disregarded it at her peril. She had settled on a style that was less dressing to impress than dressing to pass muster; fortunately her long body, thoughtful oval face, blonde hair cropped neatly to chin length and straight-backed, authoritative walk were sartorial short cuts in themselves. Although her tailored cream suit and sharp heels wouldn't have raised a postboy's eyebrow at Intercorp, they looked quite dazzlingly chic here. Admittedly, there was little competition.

Alice filed into the cool gloom of the church and took a pew next to her parents. In front was Aunt Frances. Her fuchsia flowered hat shook violently from time to time as emotion threatened to overwhelm her.

Alice had been looking forward to seeing Bo, the controversial groom. But he was not, as expected, nervously ring-twisting at the front of the church.

"It's ridiculous," Aunt Frances snarled over her shoulder to Alice's mother. "It's the *bride* that should be late."

"Look on the bright side," Alice's mother whispered back. "He might have had second thoughts."

The hat stopped shaking. Aunt Frances turned round with the look of someone reprieved at the last minute from a death sentence.

The murmur of conversation was by now loud enough to drown the stumbling fingers of the village organist. Then came a silence so sharp it was as if everyone had been turned off at the mains. This was followed by a strange, unsteady, clunking noise.

Alice, glancing over her shoulder, saw a man with dread-locks, a patchwork waistcoat and an insane grin coming up the aisle on stilts. There was a strangled gasp from the pew in front. When Alice looked in her aunt's direction, the fuchsia flowers were once again shaking furiously.

"Here Comes the Bride" suddenly struck up, and a beam-ing Sally appeared in the aisle. She wore a pointy hat swathed in white silky fabric and a green medieval-style gown, which, gathered in at the breasts, flowed outward and over a vast pregnancy bump.

Aunt Frances now seemed beyond emotion. She stared, lost, at Uncle Tommy, on whose arm Sally was draped. Uncle Tommy, dwarfed on the one side by the stilted Bo, and on the other by his daughter's wimple, looked desolately back at his wife.

The vicar stepped forward, cleared his throat and stretched upward on tiptoe with the loudly whispered request that Bo lower himself.

"Not as easy as it looks, mate," was Bo's cheerful reply. "But bring us over that table and I'll see what I can do." "That table" being the altar in the antechapel, the vicar, eyes bulging, looked elsewhere for a dismounting block. After some moments, he found one in the shape of the organist's stool and the bridegroom was returned to earth. The organist played on standing up throughout, and in noticeably improved fashion.

The service proceeded to its usual conclusion—both Frances and Tommy visibly restraining themselves during the "just cause or impediment" section. Bo and Sally issued forth from the church beneath a guard of honor of fire-eaters drawn, Alice assumed, from the ranks of the anarchist circus.

The reception was held in a field and featured a marquee bar, jugglers, more fire-eaters and, a discreet distance from the main attractions, a "head tent," which Aunt Frances had been persuaded was a hospital facility for those who had drunk too much.

"Great, isn't it?" a man's voice next to Alice said softly.

She jumped. She squinted at the person who had spoken. It was difficult to see what he looked like, his head being between her and the lowering sun. She could, however, make out broad, muscular shoulders, longish, rather wild, dark hair and a wide, white smile.

As he moved his head, the sun struck at a different angle. It revealed a face straight from Botticelli: fine nose, full lips, sharp cheekbones.

"Hello," Alice forced out through her suddenly dry throat.

His eyes, thick-fringed by black lashes, were narrow, green and piercing. She felt held in their beam, and that the beam was sweeping the ocean bottom of her soul.

"Hello."

His wide-lapelled brown pinstripe suit set off his wild hair to glamorous effect. He looked, Alice thought, like a rock star meeting his accountant, or a model off a Fifth Avenue billboard. It seemed unlikely that Sally, being a crusty, had friends in the fashion business. But you never knew.

"Versace?" She nodded at the suit. She was on shaky ground with designers, but prepared to give it a try.

His teeth flashed. "Scope."

"Scope?" Some happening new English design team, no doubt.

"Second-hand shop. It's the disability charity."

Alice flushed, feeling foolish.

He held out a large brown hand. "I'm Jake, by the way." His eyes danced as he looked at her.

"I'm, um . . . Alice."

"And what do you do . . . Alice?" As his tongue caressed the "l," she saw its red tip flick out from between his lips.

She tore her eyes away. "Company lawyer in a glossy magazine firm."

"What does that mean?"

Alice wasn't sure it meant anything. It was meaning increasingly less to her, at any rate. Reluctantly, she explained.

He rubbed his chin with a forefinger. "It's about making sure some celeb doesn't get a payout because someone from Intercorp's papped their penis?"

"Basically, yes."

"Or about killing yourself trying to save some flaky journalist who can't be bothered to check her facts?"

"That's about the size of it."

"It sounds awful," Jake said baldly.

"It is." She twiddled her empty champagne glass unhappily.

"So what are you doing it for then?"

"You tell me," Alice said gloomily.

"I'd rather get another drink."

Jake took a bottle of champagne from the bar and led Alice outside. He drew her some distance from the crowd and the tents, to a group of trees whose branches hung low and screening.

He took off his jacket and spread it on the grass. Alice, mindful of her cream suit, was grateful for this. There was a calming, thickening sensation in her head as the fizzy liquid flooded her stomach.

A bonfire had been lit and rippled against the gathering dusk like a ragged red flag.

Alice smiled at Jake and held out her glass. But the hand holding the bottle hesitated. "Don't you feel wasted?" he asked her.

"I'm definitely starting to feel woozy," she confessed as he filled the glass.

"Not that sort of wasted." His tone was serious. "I mean what you were saying about your job. Don't you want to do something more worthwhile with your time?"

"Like what?" Alice said defensively. "What do you do?"

"I run a recycling magazine."

"Do you? I thought you were a model. Something in fashion, anyway." Too late, blushing, Alice realized this was as good as admitting she considered him drop-dead gorgeous. But Jake, snorting, didn't seem to have registered a compliment.

"All those glossies have affected your brain," he told her.

"Probably. But—a recycling magazine? That's, um, *great.*"

He shot her a swift, speculative look. "Interested in recycling, are you?"

Alice wasn't sure that "interested" was quite the word. It wasn't a subject she had devoted a great deal of thought to. But she sensed that to say so would offend. "Well, it's important, isn't it?" she hedged.

"You bet it is. But not enough people think so." He grinned ruefully into the fire. "It's slowly catching on, but there's a long way to go." His eyes gleamed. "We'll get there, though. We have to. For everyone's sake."

"It must be great," Alice said enviously, "to do something you really believe in for a living."

He looked at her through long firelit eyes. "Well, you could too, you know. You're a free agent. A single girl—am I right?"

"Is it that obvious?"

"Not in the least. As soon as I saw you I was looking around for the lucky guy."

"You're too kind."

Jake ignored her ironic tone. "So what I'm saying is, you can do what you like. You're, ahem, unattached. Earning big bucks, I bet . . ." He looked at her for confirmation. Alice did not bother to deny it. Yet the fact her salary was large had somehow lost its excitement. Along with everything else concerning work.

"With nothing to spend it on but," he glanced at her spike heels, "shoes."

Alice laughed.

"So, come on. You've got dosh galore. You could easily afford to take some time out. Think about what you really want to do with your life."

"You seem to have it all worked out for me," she teased. "What if this isn't the right time?"

"We never recognize the right time until it's too late," Jake said gravely. "You need to live more in the moment."

He topped up her glass again. Alice felt her brain start to thump. They were both silent for a while.

"And kids?" Jake asked lightly. "Where do they fit in? Oh, don't tell me." His voice had become mocking. "Let me guess. There's no room in your busy, kick-ass, work-obsessed life. You're one of those typical career—"

"No I'm *not*," Alice snapped, sitting up angrily. "And you know what? I'm sick of people thinking that I am. I've always wanted children. *Always.*"

"So what are you waiting for?" His voice was gentle now.

Alice stared at her hands. "Oh God. I don't know. Nothing in particular. Or lots of things. Like the right man. It's not simple." She looked despairingly back toward the bonfire.

Alice realized that Jake was watching her. The ridges of his cheekbones reflected the flickering firelight. His eyes glowed wolfishly.

"Don't you ever think about giving New York up?" he asked softly. "Coming home?"

"Why are you so interested?"

He grinned. "Selfish reasons. Because you're gorgeous and I fancy you rotten."

Alice's mouth dropped open.

He refilled her glass. At the touch of his hand she felt a current, faint but definite, pass between them. She jerked her hand away in panic.

"Did you feel that?" he whispered.

Alice's heart was speeding. She looked accusingly at the glass.

"It's nothing to do with *that*," Jake said with a throaty laugh. "Look at me."

Alice looked. There was no mistaking the message in those eyes. It was the oldest in the world, designed through centuries of evolution to be impossible to misunderstand. She forced herself to look away. This couldn't be happening.

He moved his face toward hers. She could almost taste his breath. Her eyes started to close of their own volition and she felt her tongue tingle, her mouth water and her lips twitch to be kissed. So this was what pure animal attraction was like. She'd never believed it existed outside the movies.

"I don't see the point of beating about the bush," he murmured. "If you like someone, you should tell them. We don't have time on this planet to mess about. It's a waste to do otherwise and I hate waste. Of all descriptions."

As his face approached hers again Alice felt herself pulling toward him, a helpless iron filing before a powerful and very sexy magnet.

He pressed her hard into the grass with his kiss. "Don't go back to bloody New York," he ordered.

* * *

Alice did go back, however. She went back, as intended, the very next day. She had, after all, a life and career there; which, while not all they might have been, were not going to be knocked off course by a wedding reception snog, however pleasant. And the snog with Jake had been very pleasant. The best ever, in fact. And, in fact, rather more than a snog.

Her face warmed at the memory. He'd laid on the grass watching her as, repeatedly, she'd got dressed. Then, just as she fixed the last button and crease, he would pull her down, kiss off her lipstick and push up her skirt.

Night after New York night, Alice relived their encounter. At odd moments during the day his words would come back to her. "You could easily afford to take some time out . . . think about what you really want to do with your life . . . live more in the moment. And kids? Where do they fit in? What are you waiting for?"

Increasingly, Alice found herself gazing at babies. Suddenly they seemed to be everywhere. Had Fifth Avenue always been full of fashionable mothers pushing offspring in designer infantwear? Every magazine she looked through seemed alive with beautiful families. Even the billboards bounced with babies.

Meanwhile, at work, the fallout from the Amanda Hardwick article showed no signs of letting up. Nor did Brant.

"You're slipping, Duffield," he ungenerously observed one morning, waving the latest threatening missive from the actor's lawyers.

"I'm doing my best."

"Well, do it better."

Alice smarted. She *was* doing her best, goddammit. But why the hell, really, was she bothering? Where was the fun? Where was the bloody point? Did she really want this boss? This job? This city? That elegant little minimalist mortgageless flat, even, with its enviable position on Central Park? The train of thought Jake had started seemed as impossible to stop as the court case against *Style*.

Nor was this Alice's only preoccupation. Her period had been due within days of Sally's wedding. But she had been back almost a week and it had not yet arrived. There was, in addition, an unusual tenderness in her breasts. It was only when the nausea started that the impossible, the unthinkable seemed even vaguely probable. But how could it be? Jake had worn a condom.

When the line in the "Pregnant" box showed triumphantly blue, Alice felt first of all a tremendous numbness. This was replaced almost immediately by a huge, near-heart-bursting surge of delight.

Admittedly, it would have been nice to have the choice. To have planned the pregnancy with the father. But frankly, given her age and her ovaries, that was trivial. Was she not unbelievably fortunate to have been given such a chance? Not until now, actually staring at the line that indicated her baby, did Alice realize how desperately she had wanted one. And how hard she had tried to repress what had seemed an impossible dream.

Alice carried her glowing secret everywhere. She surged with energy; even the prospect of coping with the different, difficult stages alone did not deter her. She had money enough to cushion her from most things and making decisions by herself was something she was used to. She would cope. But there was one thing that worried her.

"You say you met him at Sally's wedding?" From three thousand miles away, Alice's mother sounded uncertain. "I don't remember him."

"You might have gone by then," Alice admitted. "Or maybe you were somewhere else in the party."

"And you didn't get his address at the time? Not like you, darling. You're normally so organized."

Alice smiled wryly at her end. There had been nothing organized about the frenzied coupling behind the screening tree branches.

"What did you say you wanted him for?" her mother asked.

Alice took a deep breath and tried to sound casual. "Just a small, er, legal matter, Mum." Hopefully the word "legal" would forestall further questions until she was ready to supply the real answers. Keen as her mother was to have grandchildren, she would hardly have envisaged this.

"*Legal* matter?"

"Yes, but only a very small one. A very, very small one," Alice said, with perfect truth. "Anyway, Mum, the point is that I thought Aunt Frances might get his number or address for me. She could ask Sally and Bo."

"They've gone to a vegan yoga camp in the Shetlands on honeymoon. Apparently it's got a birthing tent, whatever that is, for when Sally finally goes into labor. Can you imagine?"

"No," said Alice, not wanting to steal her mother's thunder. In fact, she could very well imagine. The world was full of nutty camps. And, as Intercorp's magazines faithfully recorded, legions of nutty celebrities who went to them. "But Aunt Frances can get in touch with them there, can't she?"

"I don't think impure elements from the outside world are allowed," Alice's mother said. "That's what they told Frances when she tried to ring. She was very offended."

Alice racked her brains. "Jake runs a recycling magazine. It'll be based in the West Country, although I'm not sure where. You might be able to track him down through the phone book."

"I can try. What's this magazine called?"

"Ah." Alice slapped her forehead in frustration. "Forgot to ask."

Her mother sighed. "I'll do my best."

But Mrs. Duffield's best, and Alice's own searches on the Internet, came to nothing.

Alice felt, on the whole, a kind of relief. She had tried and her conscience was clear. She had wanted only to let him know, but the fact he wasn't to be involved was probably a good thing. Less complicated, less messy.

So it was to be just the two of them together, her and the baby. Alice lay awake at nights and tried to imagine it. She was, after all, to be a mother. She would, after all, have a baby.

CHAPTER
4

"He's taking us to court?" Amanda Hardwick repeated at the London end of the phone.

"Yes," Alice replied with a calmness she did not feel. "You're going to have to go in the witness box." She drove her nails into her palms with frustration. The last chance of salvation was gone. The actor had refused a generous out-of-court settlement. He was, Alice recognized, hellbent on making Intercorp suffer as publicly and humiliatingly as he had presumably suffered himself. And, considering what had been written, she could hardly blame him.

"Fine," trilled the person who had written it. "I can wear my new black Dior."

Alice groaned. Time, she decided, to bring this nonsense to an end. "It won't make any difference, I'm afraid. We're going to lose anyway. The only question is—how badly."

"Lose? We're going to *lose?*"

"Yes. So what you and I need to do now is work out what you're going to say in order to get the damages down."

"You're saying *I've* got to help *you* get the damages down?"

"That's right. It should be possible if—"

"Hang on a minute," bawled Amanda. "You're the fucking

legal department. It's your job to sort this out, not mine. What sort of a useless shmuck are you?"

"Now look—" Alice prepared to present Amanda with a few home truths. The first being that, had she not written a tissue of lies in the first place, they would not be in this situation.

"No, *you* look, Miss Goody Bloody Two-Shoes. Just because you're a shit lawyer about to lose a court case, don't expect *me* to bail you out."

Click. Burr. Amanda's end had gone dead. Alice stared at the receiver in her hand. She was tempted to hurl it at the wall. Yet anger and stress were not good for the baby. Closing her eyes, Alice tilted her head back and gulped down several steadying mouthfuls of air instead.

"Hey there. Didn't realize you'd taken up transcendental breathing."

Hearing his voice, familiar yet still strange, she jerked her head violently up. She blinked away the tears of frustration still shining in her eyes. Incredibly, it was true. He really was there. Dazzlingly handsome, dazzlingly smiling, so dazzlingly tall he filled the door frame, his arms blooming with dazzlingly red roses. Alice's mouth fell open. *Jake.*

"He says he knows you," Sherry piped anxiously from behind. "He just came in. I couldn't stop him."

Alice half rose to her feet, then sank back into her chair. Her head whirled. "It's OK. I do know him. Thanks, Sherry. Could you . . . er . . ."

"Shut the door? Sure." As the huge bunch of flowers moved forward, Sherry retreated, grinning and making huge thumbs-up signs as she did so.

Alice looked at Jake. He looked back at her over the roses.

"What are you doing here?" she gasped. "How did you find me?"

"I heard that you were looking for me. Through the grapevine," he said through the roses. "Your aunt told some friends of Sally and Bo's, whom I happened to bump into. I had to come and make sure you weren't trying to sue me or anything."

"*Sue* you?" Alice exclaimed.

The eyes over the blooms were creased with amusement. "Well, you never know. Apparently you wanted to talk about something legal. And you being a lawyer and all that. And considering what we got up to at the wedding . . ."

Alice reached hurriedly to switch off the intercom that connected her to Sherry. She hadn't the slightest doubt that her assistant was listening.

"So?" He was smiling expectantly at her. "Go on. Shoot. What is it? Sexual assault? Failure to keep your stomach lined with alcohol-absorbing sandwiches? Not that there were any from what I could see."

"Sit down." Alice felt suddenly nervous. It was no small thing to tell a virtual stranger they were to be linked to you for all eternity by a cluster of cells.

The knuckles clutching the rose stems went white as she told him. His eyes widened with amazement. He did not, however, say anything. There was an awful silence. "Well?" Alice whispered eventually. "What do you think? Don't worry, I'm not after you for maintenance. I'll look after the baby myself . . ."

But he had tossed the flowers aside now and was dancing round the office, whooping, whirling, his hair streaming with delight.

"So you're pleased then?" Alice gasped, almost perspiring with relief.

His strong brown hand slapped the table for emphasis. "Pleased? Christ, it's not every day you find out you're going to be a father."

Then, much to the frustration of Sherry, who had crossed from her desk to see what the noise was, he winked at her, locked the door, pulled down the blinds and pulled Alice toward him.

"We can't!" Alice gasped, as he pushed her floorward. "Not *here*." But, it turned out, they could. And did.

Jake stayed for a few more days. As they walked through Greenwich Village, he waxed a good deal less lyrical about the historic house-fronts and bijou ambience than he did about his environmental magazine, *Get Trashed!* Alice listened, half admiring, half scared as he outlined the fate awaiting the planet if people didn't get their recycling act together soon. So persuasive was he, so passionately committed to his cause, that Alice felt the first stir of outrage herself as she surveyed the polluted urban landscape all around her. Listening to him talk, she felt like a churchgoer beneath the pulpit of a wildly charismatic priest.

The more time they spent together, the more Alice realized that she had never met anyone who really believed in anything before. Let alone lived, as Jake so obviously did, by its principles.

"There's a reason for everything," he had said about the baby. Was the reason she had become so unexpectedly pregnant been to save her from the meaningless life she was living and give her selfish, shallow existence some much-needed depth? As Jake's visit drew to an end, Alice became increasingly convinced that it was.

* * *

Jake proposed on his final day, in a boat in Central Park. Alice felt she was in an ad or a fashion shoot. The scene—a soft, sunny morning with a head-turningly handsome man staring besottedly at her against one of the most famous backgrounds in the world—had an unreal edge. It was surely too romantic to be true.

"But you hardly know me," she pointed out. "It's all a bit whirlwind, isn't it?"

"Some things are, Alice. But then, some things are just . . . right. Feel right."

Alice stared at the water. "It's a bit sudden."

"And perhaps that's for a reason," Jake said gently. "You need to go with the flow, Alice."

Alice trailed a hand in the lake. The flow felt cool and silky between her fingers.

What doubts, after all, did she have? He had flown over in a heartbeat without even knowing she was pregnant and had no qualms about taking full responsibility when he did. How many men would have done that?

And there was his ideological commitment. She loved him for his concern, his energy, his belief, the way he tossed back his hair and his eyes blazed. It kindled a dormant idealism she had not realized she possessed. Life with Jake—and the baby, of course—would have real meaning. It would be significant, useful, and a dramatic contrast to the trivial world of New York glossy magazine publishing. Not to mention that of New York legal back-stabbing . . . Time, Alice thought, to get out of the writ race.

Last but not least, there was the matter of Jake's looks. How many men were as handsome or could bring her to the point of ecstasy with a few strokes of a sensitive, knowing hand?

What more, ultimately, did she want?

"I suppose it's all been a bit much," she confessed eventually. "All these surprises. It's very complicated."

"It is if you want to look at it that way." He reached for her face and lifted it to his. His eyes were radiant with sincerity. "But as far as I'm concerned, the rest of my life is at the disposal of you and the baby. What's so complicated about that?"

"Nothing," Alice admitted after a pause.

"So resign tomorrow."

* * *

Through hooded, half-open eyes, the head of Human Resources looked Alice up and down.

"Sure is a shame you're going," the HHR drawled. "You

were earmarked for great things here. Youngest deputy ever in the legal department and all that. You're sure ya wanna pack it all in? Because we sure don't wanna lose ya. We can fix you up with an apartment. Daycare. Whatever."

Alice forcibly turned her head from side to side.

The HHR raised an eyebrow and smiled slightly. "Well, honey, if it doesn't work out . . ."

"Doesn't work out?" Alice was indignant. "Why wouldn't it work out?"

The HHR opened her hands. "Hey, ya gotta face it. Motherhood might not be your thing. It ain't everyone's. And if it ain't yours, there's always a desk for you here. Remember that."

"It's very generous of you," Alice said stiffly, offended. Of course motherhood was her thing. She was having a baby, wasn't she? It would have to be her thing, and forever from now on.

"Generous!" The HHR snorted. "You're joking, aren'tcha? We ain't being generous. Just reflecting a proportion of what you save us every year in libel actions. Even if you don't win 'em all."

Alice burned at this reminder of her one professional failure. "Yes, well, I'm certainly not going to miss Amanda Hardwick." Never seeing that wretched woman again was one of the greatest benefits of leaving New York. Her doubts about having made the right decision receded.

The HHR raised an eyebrow. "Hey, we're none of us gonna miss her, believe me."

"She's leaving?" Alice stared in amazement.

"Got the chop, didn't she? After her latest screw-up in *Style* magazine. That case you were working on—one too many for the guys upstairs." The HHR stabbed a purple-tipped finger upward in the direction of the executive floors. "She's dead meat round here, let me tell ya."

"No!" Alice felt a smile pull at the corners of her mouth. She had hated the fact that Intercorp would lose the case. But if Amanda Hardwick went down with the ship, well, that was different. She had gotten what was coming to her at last. "I hadn't heard that."

"She only found out herself ten minutes ago."

CHAPTER

5

AMANDA REACHED FOR THE SMALL BOTTLE OF WARMISH SCREW-TOP airline wine. Pouring it into her plastic glass, she tried not to reflect on the chilled champagne she knew was currently being served in first class. Economy was torture. How did people stand it?

She glugged back the wine and cursed that long-faced beanpole bitch of a lawyer who'd lost the case and killed the goose that laid the golden eggs. If she'd concentrated more on what she was supposed to be doing, done her bloody job properly in other words, I, Amanda thought, wouldn't be in this mess now. Damn her. Damn her to hell.

She gulped more wine and began to flick through some magazines. Her gut twisted with envy at the unrelenting display, page after page, of shiny-haired women with white teeth, fabulous figures, stunning homes and, presumably, wealth beyond the dreams of avarice. Many of them had beautiful children clasped in their arms, and were running happily with them about their gardens, or else bouncing up and down with them on one of those vast, round trampolines that were obviously this year's must-have accessory.

Apart from the children themselves, of course. Amanda narrowed her eyes in thought. It was obvious from the pages before her that children were more fashionable even than trampolines at the moment. At a subconscious level she knew this already; she'd been in enough *Style* features meetings when it was discussed, after all. Not that she had listened. Babies, shmabies, or so she had always thought. Boring, noisy, smelly and sick all over your Marc Jacobs. As for pregnancy, it not only prevented you from having fun, but interfered with your career and lost you power and money. Basically, motherhood was for losers.

But was it? Had she been too hasty? From the evidence of these glossies, Amanda concluded, babies looked more than bearable. They didn't, after all, stop you having fun—the world seemed to abound with luxury hotels complete with nannies to look after them while parents hit the swim-up champagne bar. Nor did they stop you having nice things—on the contrary. Amanda devoured details of the baby gifts a certain pregnant supermodel had received from celebrity friends. Baby Dior outfits, a monogrammed bathrobe, Pucci print Babygros, pink suede moccasins, a Ralph Lauren hat and mitts in lavender merino wool. Plus a pair of baby Tod's driving shoes in sky blue!

That settled it.

Amanda, who saw the world as a box of chocolates from which she always got first pick, hated to think she was missing out on anything. She needed to get in on this one. And fast.

Amanda thrust a shaking hand in the air as a harassed stewardess trundled past. "More wine," she barked.

The bottle was even warmer than the one before. But Amanda hardly noticed as she sloshed it into her glass. Her thoughts were all about her husband. Was Hugo, she wondered, father material?

All the basics were there, she supposed. He was good-looking in just the way she liked—tall, neat-featured and with luxurious dark hair. He kept middle-age spread at arm's length with energetic squash sessions and as a consequence had the type of lean, muscled torso that rose without a shred of spare fat from the waistbands of his tailored pinstriped trousers. It also looked very good against white sheets on Sunday mornings.

He was an efficient breadwinner too, she had to give him that. He was the most successful employee of the real estate agents he worked for. Amanda could almost overlook the company's embarrassing name—J. Bond, Special (Real Estate) Agent, 007 Islington High Street, for God's sake—because of the constant stream of champagne cases, complimentary weekends away and sports cars on loan as rewards for Hugo's excelling performance targets. There were bonuses too.

But the money did not go far. Hugo, who enjoyed living up to his firm's image of tongue-in-cheek suave, was very fond of his Savile Row suits and handmade Jermyn Street shoes. He had almost as many costly designer face products in the bathroom cabinet as she did. Then there were all his gadgets—the mobile phone you could make an entire movie on, the iPod, the cutting-edge electronic personal organizer . . .

Amanda finished the wine and plonked her plastic cup down decisively. Well, that would all have to stop now there was a baby on the way. How else were those junior J. P. Tod's to be paid for?

The baby, Amanda realized, also raised the question of the house. The house they did not have, as opposed to the flat that they did. Despite Hugo's access to the best and the brightest properties in London their own place was crap, frankly. Their third-floor apartment was all wrong for a child. You couldn't swing a kitten round it, let alone a baby. There was nowhere to pitch a huge circular trampoline. The visions of big-housed familial loveliness in the magazines diverged on a number of fronts from the reality of Amanda and Hugo's living conditions. Basically, they'd have to move.

So where should they live? Amanda's gaze dropped to the

magazines again. Most of the pictured happy families dwelt in rural, parklanded splendor without a tower block or overhead cable in sight. The family in *Harpers & Queen* stood before a vast cream-painted mansion against which, with their white clothes and gleaming blond hair, they were actually barely visible. "The country's the only place for children if you ask me," enthused the father, a Lord Fairbourne. "Clean air, lots of space and a better quality of life. We're really awfully lucky."

She had never, up until now, imagined herself more than a credit card's toss from Harvey Nichols. But the country had obvious advantages, including removing her far from the London magazine industry tom-toms. Which, being what they were, would even now be beating out the news that Amanda Hardwick had come a spectacular cropper. Well, they could all eff off, frankly. Careers—how over were they? The smart money was on motherhood and nesting.

Amanda stretched—as best she could, given the space restrictions—and congratulated herself on sorting out the whole of their future in fifteen minutes or less. She could hardly wait to tell Hugo about it all.

*   *   *

That very moment, in the offices of J. Bond, Special (Real Estate) Agent, 007 Islington High Street, the champagne corks were popping. The James Bond theme tune, as always on triumphal occasions, was roaring from the corporate ghettoblaster.

"Congratulations, old boy." Toby from Leases and Lettings raised a plastic cup of warmish yellow fizz in Hugo's direction. "The supersalesman triumphs yet again. So the Aston stays, I take it."

It was a standing joke within the office that the Aston Martin awarded each month, for a month, to whoever had exceeded their sales targets, had been parked outside Hugo's flat since the incentive had been introduced. Or perhaps standing joke was not quite the phrase, especially among Bond staff who relied on public transport.

The sale had been a triumph, there was no doubt about it. His reputation as Bond's most dynamic salesman was not only assured, but enhanced. No one could have sold that place but him. It had taken every trick in the book, gone to both the bridge and the wire, pushed the envelope and any other metaphor that one cared to employ to convince the portly, young and rather pompous barrister that the unconverted former office was the dream home he wanted to spend one and a half million pounds on. Hugo wished Amanda was not still in New York. He could hardly wait to tell her. Of course, he could always call her. But that wasn't the same.

He needed to see her. They really had to spend more time together; make something solid out of what was starting to feel worryingly impermanent. Her stateside commitments meant they had been apart even more than usual lately, which had given him unwelcome opportunities to consider their relationship. Without her forceful physical presence to remind him, it was, for example, disturbingly easy to start wondering why they had gotten married at all.

Their affair had been hasty and scattered, fitted in between her trips round the world for *Style* magazine. He had fallen for her flashy glamour, and she, he suspected, for what women usually fell for in him; his honed-to-perfection brand of floppy-haired, chisel-featured, slightly sleazy patrician charm.

The sex, on the whole, had ticked the "experimental" box. Usually after Amanda had read or been told something about the erotic predilections of someone famous she admired. The result of one of these encounters had been his drunken Valentine's Day proposal in the whirlpool bath of a country house hotel he couldn't now remember the name of. But there had been no doubts on the wedding day. He had been happy enough to walk Amanda down between the two banks of chairs in the restaurant of the fashionable London club that had been converted into a chapel for the occasion. She had looked wonderful, her brass-bright hair caught up with summer flowers, her dress a heavy satin Empire-line number straight out of *My Fair Lady*. Her something old had been some antique earrings he had given her, her something new some crazily expensive underwear. The something borrowed, he recalled, had been a friend's pearl necklace, which had later in the evening become something lost, and the friend an ex-friend. He couldn't remember the something blue.

Unless it was how he felt now.

* * *

The Heathrow arrivals door sprung open. Amanda, laden with luggage, stomped crossly through. For the first time in years there would be no Intercorp-financed driver holding her misspelled name up on a card.

Gritting her teeth, she stuck her bags on the escalator going down to the Heathrow Express. By now she had thought through the baby scenario so often she could practically feel the fetus move. Hugo, of course, had not thought about it at all. He had some significant catching up to do before he shared her point of view. She planned to speed up the process with a little subtle persuasion. Surprise was to be her weapon. Or one of them. He had no idea she was coming home, largely because, between HR department interviews and the rush to JFK, she had no time—or indeed inclination—to tell him of the ignominious way her Intercorp career had ended. Now Amanda saw this oversight as an advantage.

By the end of the afternoon, she was ready. Courtesy of her not-yet-canceled corporate credit card she had had a facial, a seaweed body wrap, a Dead Sea scrub, her hair and nails done and her teeth blasted.

Then she had hit the shops. To one used to summoning from the designers whatever she wanted to wear and then conveniently forgetting to return it, this had obviously been a comedown. But Amanda, magnificently overcoming the humiliation, had tracked down the highest pair of heels ever seen and descended with a growl of triumph on a plunging red sequinned gown with tight waist and slits up the sides.

Now, from the top floor window of the flat, Amanda saw Hugo's Aston Martin draw to a halt outside. She checked herself in the mirror and draped herself across the sofa. What a surprise for him this would be.

His key scrabbled at the door. Amanda stretched her mouth and rolled her eyes to rid herself of any set facial expressions. This was her moment.

He opened the door. The first thing he saw was a shapely leg in a cartoonishly high heel extend upward from the back of the sofa. "Daaaaarling!" drawled Amanda's voice.

"*Bloody hell.*" Hugo entered the sitting room, approached the sofa and stopped in astonishment. "When did *you* get back?" Amanda slid him a sluttish look from under her lashes. Then, fiddling with her hair with one hand, she ran the other down what, thanks to the heels, appeared impossibly long legs.

"You never said you were coming . . ." Hugo swallowed and stopped. Her cleavage was nothing less than a chasm. Pale, creamy and faintly shaking, it looked as if a man could fall down it and be lost for ever. Hugo, looking at it and licking his lips, felt he would like to be that man.

As Amanda slowly parted her legs and flicked aside the red sequins to reveal a complete absence of underwear, Hugo felt his head spin. "God, I've missed you," he growled.

A strap tumbled down one creamy shoulder. One forefinger circling an exposed nipple, Amanda stretched red and shining lips in a lazy smile. "And I you," she breathed huskily. "And I've got the best news. Darling, something's going to happen to make our marriage complete. To draw us together, closer than we've ever been before."

"Great," said Hugo, who was intending to get close at the earliest possible moment. "What's going to happen?"

Amanda clasped her hands together and summoned a dewy look to her eyes. "Darling. Hugo. We're going to have . . . a baby."

"A *baby*?" Hugo echoed. Gone were the fuzzy effects of the champagne. His head, suddenly, had a bell-like clarity. His vision was so sharp he could have flown a night fighter. He stared at Amanda in amazement. "But I had no idea . . . I mean . . . oh God." He sank, shocked, to his knees in front of her, gobbling air as he searched for the right words. "It's just that I didn't realize we were even trying—"

"We weren't," Amanda cut in. "But we are now." She pulled him toward that chasm of a cleavage.

Hugo, disappearing into it, felt bewilderment mingle with his lust. He had never suspected her to have a maternal bone in her body.

"Motherhood," Amanda declared throatily, grinding her breasts into his mouth, "is the one box on my life experience sheet that I haven't ticked yet."

She pushed him back and stood up. As he remained kneeling, she placed one of her stilettos in the center of his chest. She forced him down, down against the polished wooden floor of the sitting room and began to unzip his trousers.

"After all," she added, "I've been there, done it, stayed in the same celebrity compound as Bruce Willis at the Turks and Caicos spa resort and got the Stella McCartney T-shirt."

"Eh?" said Hugo.

"Never mind," said Amanda, lowering her head, "I mean that now I want *more*."

Hugo wanted more too.

"I've had all the excitement," Amanda growled, as, with a matador flick of her side-slit skirt, she lowered herself on to him.

Hugo snapped his eyes open indignantly, "What do you mean you've had all the excitement? We've been married less than a year. What about the best being yet to come and all that?"

"I mean," Amanda gasped, her voice leaping several octaves, "I've had all the great life experiences. I've stayed at Sandy Lane, flown Concorde, dined with Tony Blair."

"Tony Blair?" Hugo yelped. He had not realized dinner with Tony Blair was a great life experience, particularly the dinner Amanda had attended. Prawn cocktail and rubber chicken as one of a cast of media thousands, from what he'd gathered.

"The point is," Amanda threw her head back as she rode him, "that what I want now is the greatest life experience of all. Babies."

As he thrust upward beneath her, Hugo tried not to think about babies. Or, rather, think about what he thought about them. That they were sick on you and cried. That they stopped you going out at night and kept you up instead. That if he ever wanted to sing "The Wheels on the Bus" to some two-year-old, he had plenty of godchildren. He presided at christenings these days with the same regularity he had appeared as best man a decade ago.

"You see," Amanda panted, lashing her head from side to side now, "it's all very well for you. Men," she added, with an expert jerk of her pelvis, "can wait."

No they can't, Hugo thought wildly, his need rising swiftly and unstoppably.

"But I don't have that luxury. I'm thirty-five. A few years from now I'll have ovaries like walnuts. Do you want to be fifty and childless?" She raised herself slightly, as if to clamber off him. Damn her, he thought, squirming with frustration. She'd developed to an art form that trick of stopping just before the crucial moment. No end of treats and presents had been quite literally screwed out of him this way.

Beneath her, Hugo moaned. He had no idea. He knew that he liked being thirty-six and childless, but he was prepared to believe this might change. As Amanda lowered herself once more, he wondered what exactly he was letting himself in for. Fatherhood. It was a big question. And one to which he was unsure he had the answer.

CHaPTeR
6

H UGO SHIFTED IN HIS SEAT. THE CHAIRS WERE HARD, THE ROOM was hot and these prenatal classes always seemed to last forever. Tonight seemed the longest yet.

It had kicked off with Lotti asking all the women present to stand up and point out the location of their pubic bones. Matters had not improved since.

Lotti was now showing the class a plastic oblong pierced with different-sized holes. It looked just like a giant pasta measurer to Hugo until the midwife explained that the smallest, barely visible hole was the normal size of the opening of the cervix. "And this," she added, rotating her forefinger within the biggest circle, "is the ten centimeters Mum needs to dilate to before Baby can be born."

There were a few gasps at this. Hugo leaned forward in horror. "It's not humanly possible!" he exclaimed, realizing too late that he had spoken aloud.

"Evidence that it is is all around you," Jake remarked smartly.

Hugo ignored him. His first impression of Jake as smug and objectionable had only increased with subsequent meetings. And then there was that ghastly, simpering wife looking adoringly up at him. From what Amanda—frothing with rage—had told him about Alice since the first class, he realized that his initial view of her as scrubbed and innocent-looking had been wrong. Her serene expression, it seemed, was a veneer beneath which lurked a skilled plotter and vicious back-stabber.

A hand went up on the left-hand side of the horseshoe. "Excuse me," asked a woman called Martha, who habitually took copious notes. "But are we going to learn anything about what to do with the baby once it gets out? Nappy-changing and all that stuff?"

There was a murmur of agreement at this. The expression on Lotti's face, however, was pure incomprehension. "The mitwifes show you that," she said.

"But aren't you a midwife?" asked Martha.

"Yesh."

"So why don't you show us?"

"Because this is prenatal class," Lotti explained with elaborate patience. "We are here concerned with the birth only. That stuff you talk about, it's postnatal. After birth."

"I understand," said Martha. She looked round the class. "But it would still help us all to know in advance."

"Speak for yourself," Amanda said haughtily. "I'm having a maternity nurse."

There was a disgusted snort from Jake. Laura, meanwhile, looked envious. "Get you!" she exclaimed. "Wish I was having one."

Amanda preened. "Great, isn't it? She'll be coming for six weeks from when the baby is born."

"That'll cost," remarked Jim from St. Helens.

Amanda continued, "And I'm having an elective Cesarean. At the *Cavendish*," she added, with emphasis.

Hugo's heart sank. He had been trying not to think about the Cavendish. He could understand the maternity nurse. He could understand Amanda buying designer satin maternity bras—the standard sort were, as she said, too repellent for words. (But did she really need ten?) He had even been prepared to indulge her "nesting" instinct; too late had he realized this was a euphemism for ordering all the most expensive home furnishings she could lay her computer mouse on. Number four Fitzherbert Place must, Hugo thought despairingly, be the priciest nest ever built.

He had also gone along with—and to—these private pre-natal classes when Amanda had refused to attend NHS ones. But he had always disputed, and still did, that she needed to have the baby at a private maternity hospital. In vain had he explained it was the last straw—well, more of a bale, really—that would break the back of their bank balance.

"Elective Cesarean?" Lotti was regarding Amanda as a vicar might regard a lost soul. "Well, of course it is your choice not to have a natural birth," she said sorrowfully.

"You bet it is," Amanda retorted. "I don't fancy being doubly incontinent and I've found my pelvic floor quite useful over the years."

Lotti looked hurt.

"We've put on our birth plan that we're having the baby naturally. At home," Jake piped up.

Lotti nodded delightedly.

Hugo winced. Home births sounded hideously messy. On the other hand, they probably had certain cost advantages over the Cavendish.

"Are you having any pain relief *at all?*" The gap-toothed Laura peered round at Alice. She had an even more revealing top on this week. Her husband, Hugo had already noticed, remained absent.

"Research has shown that it's bad for the baby," Jake told her swiftly.

Laura eyed him. "I was asking Alice. She's the one who's pregnant."

"We don't see it like that," Jake said calmly. "We're taking equal responsibility throughout, so we think of it as us both being pregnant."

Christ Jesus, Hugo thought. If there were such a thing as an earnestometer, it would go right off the dial at this point.

Alice smiled at Laura. "No, I'm not having pain relief. Not if I can help it."

"Well, the best of bleeding British to you in that case. As it were." Laura sat back in her seat. "Personally, I'm having every form of pain relief going."

"Good for you," applauded Amanda.

Lotti looked anxiously at Laura. "You're sure about this? You might not need it," she cautioned. "Breathing exshershises can be really very useful in reducing pain . . ."

"Is that right?" asked Laura in tones of withering disbelief.

Lotti looked at her watch. "We have fifteen minutes left," she announced, beaming toothily again. She flung out a pair of sinewy forearms. "Over to you. This is the point in the class in which we exchange ideas."

Hugo stiffened. This sounded dangerous.

"What sort of ideas?" Amanda asked suspiciously.

"Worries," Lotti smiled.

Hugo flinched. Worries? Was it that obvious?

"Everyone," said Lotti, "is now free to tell the rest of the class about any aspect of birthing they are concerned about. Air their anxieties, you know? It's all perfectly natural. And goot to do it in this situation, where we are all in the same ship together."

"Boat," snapped Amanda.

Lotti's good nature came Teflon-coated. She was impervious to insult. She smiled at Amanda. "Boat, yes. You are right. So." She looked expectantly at the class. "You tell me your consherns and I try to give you honest answers."

Hugo wondered which aspect was more terrifying: his worries, or Lotti's honest answers.

Thick silence fell on the class.

Lotti pulled a quizzical face. "There is no one here with consherns they would like to share with the class in a relashed, intimate and trushting environment?"

Further silence.

Then someone broke it. "Sex," drawled a voice. It was Laura who had spoken.

"Sexsh?" Lotti repeated doubtfully.

There was a titter. Hugo, meanwhile, eyed Laura warily. If only she and Amanda had not hit it off quite so well after the first prenatal class. Subsequent sessions had revealed Laura to be a rampant attention-seeker who clearly got no attention from her ever-absent husband. There was, Hugo felt, something un-stable and rather desperate about her. She slid him nakedly provocative looks at every opportunity and, though a natural flirt himself, he felt uncomfortable around her. Amanda, on the other hand, clearly felt the opposite. In Laura she had found the perfect accomplice for long afternoons having prenatal spa treatments at Bath's leading health club. During which, it seemed, sex was high on Laura's conversational agenda.

"I mean, how soon can we have sex again?" Laura continued.

Lotti beamed. "Oh, I see. Well, I'm glad you asked me that question Laura. Actually, intercourse can be resumed after sev-eral weeks if the birth is uncomplicaded."

"Several weeks!" gasped Martha.

"That's right!" beamed Lotti. "The vagina can recover re-markably quickly."

Silence again. "Anything else?" Lotti paused. Then she smiled. "Well, how about it if I ask you all some questions?"

Hugo riveted his gaze to his shoes.

"How do you feel about becoming a daddy?" she asked someone.

Him. With horror, Hugo realized she was asking *him*. The sixty-four-thousand-dollar question, coming straight out of left field. His heart thundered. His hands were twisting together. He opened his mouth and closed it. Then opened it again.

"Er . . . being a daddy . . ." he said uncertainly. He paused for what seemed like hours. "To be honest, I'm not sure," he blurted.

"Not sure?"

He caught Jake's scornful eye and Amanda's furious one. Lotti was adjusting her glasses and peering at him as if he were a specimen in a laboratory. Fear swept him like wildfire. Why in God's name had he said that?

"I mean not sure in a great way, obviously," Hugo stammered, desperately clawing back what lost ground he could. And perhaps this *was* how he felt. Perhaps he would grow to love the baby after it was born and he could actually see it as a person, not just a lifestyle-cramping and expensive theory.

Lotti had moved swiftly on. She looked about for the next questionee. "What about *you*, Jake? How do *you* feel?"

As if, Hugo thought sourly, we can't guess. He braced himself for the inevitable.

Jake beamed dazzlingly. "There's nothing we're looking forward to more than parenthood. Is there, darling?" He squeezed Alice's slim hand, which was already linked in his. "We can't wait to welcome our little one onto the planet. However appallingly exploited and abused that planet is at the moment."

CHAPTER
7

A LICE LOVED COMBE ON SIGHT. JAKE'S VILLAGE CONSISTED OF A medieval church, thatched pub and tiny half-timbered cottages—of which his was one—dotted about the green.

It was, admittedly, rather further from Bath than Alice had imagined. Nor had she anticipated that, thanks to Jake's principled objection to all cars, the city would be reachable only by bus. Or buses; getting to the prenatal class involved two.

There were other surprises as well. Such as the extent to which Jake lived and breathed his environmentalist beliefs at home. Alice was amazed at the ingenious uses to which Jake put the many articles he picked up from dumps, Dumpsters or his own household rubbish.

Eager to support him and anxious to show herself a worthy ideological consort, she was swift to agree that old colanders screwed to the ceiling made attractive and effective lightshades. Although she privately considered the metal variety prettier than the plastic ones. Records with the middles knocked out and made into picture frames looked very striking too, and the ex-television in the sitting room made an excellent aquarium. As Jake said, "There's always something to see on the telly in this house."

Despite such excitements, Alice found country life quieter

than expected. While she wouldn't have objected to the odd glass of wine, Jake was worried about possible fetal alcohol syndrome, and so the pub, which offered the village's only social stimulus, was more or less out of bounds. But there was always plenty to do at home.

Checking the *Get Trashed!* page proofs before they went to the printers, for example. The letters section particularly made fascinating reading.

"Listen to this," she urged Jake as they sat over the proofs one evening. " 'In my part of China, we only get about twenty-five days of true blue sky a year. Blue sky good for laundry, so when gray takes over, I think: these pants won't dry by sundown, I'll have to wait till tomorrow to do wash. I feel degradation of environment through my pants.' " Alice giggled.

Jake's face, however, remained utterly straight. "What's so funny?" he asked. "He's concerned about the changing weather patterns. As we all should be, if we had any sense."

The evenings there was no proofreading were filled with other pursuits. Writing letters to multinationals demanding more earth-friendly practices or less wasteful packaging was one at which Alice, with her lawyer's flair for menacing paragraphs, proved particularly adept.

Otherwise, she and Jake would sit at the kitchen table recycling salvaged items. His quest for ever more inventive uses for household waste—it was his proud boast he put out only one black rubbish bag a month, as did the *Get Trashed!* office—was, Alice found, an absorbing way to pass the peaceful country evenings. They made keyrings out of old shower curtain rings, or twisted the wire from old spiral-bound notebooks into coat hangers.

"The wire from an average notebook is up to nine feet long," Jake would tell her as they worked. "Just think about it, Al."

Alice gazed into his impassioned, handsome face and thought about it. She also thought about him and the nobility of his cause. Her conviction that he brought meaning to her existence was one of the many reasons why she loved him. And, of course, he had brought meaning to her body too. Preparing to produce a child, it was finally fulfilling its potential as well.

* * *

The only serpent in Alice's Eden was that her mother and Jake not only did not hit it off, but would probably like to hit each other. Mrs. Duffield's first visit to Combe was not a success.

Her first shock was to find that Jake's cottage, instead of being called Honeysuckle, Apple Blossom or something similarly picturesque, went by the more striking name of the Old Morgue.

"You mean . . . they stored dead bodies here?" she gasped to her daughter.

Alice shrugged. "So what? It's reusing an old building in a way that makes sense. And the rent is cheap at least."

Her mother looked at her in concern. "Surely money's not an issue with you, darling? You must have lots of savings, especially now you've sold the New York flat."

Alice paused. It was true that the flat sale had left her with a sizable sum that her share of the Old Morgue rent barely dented. On the other hand, the loan she had given Jake to prop up the eternally cash-strapped *Get Trashed!* had made a small hole. Not that she minded; it was she who had pressed the money on him, after all, once the extent to which the magazine was struggling had been revealed. While in theory it survived on subscribers, at the moment they seemed on thin ground.

Of course, as expected, he had resisted her money at first. "I can't accept it," he insisted.

"But I want to give it to you. I want to do something useful with it at last."

Jake's face had lit up in an ecstatic beam of acceptance. "Al, you're an angel."

"Don't be silly. It's just sitting there otherwise. And it's not just my money, anyway. We're married now, remember."

Yet the double-quick Manhattan register-office service had been over in the blink of an eye and was in fact quite hard to remember. Rather more unforgettable had been the hurt in her mother's voice when she was told. Fortunately, the additional news about the impending grandchild had taken away some of the sting, as had the revelation that Alice was returning to England.

But, as Mrs. Duffield's visit proved, this new proximity was not without its problems.

"Darling," her mother exclaimed now, coming in from examining the Old Morgue's garden. "There's the most ghastly pile of festering rubbish on your lawn. It's just by the back door and it's absolutely covered in flies. Don't you think you should move it?"

Alice took a deep breath. "Actually, Mum, it's not a pile of rubbish. It's Jake's, erm, wormery."

"Wormery?" Her mother looked appalled. "You mean . . . there are *worms* under there?"

"Yes. About three thousand of them. They came by post . . ."

"Post!"

". . . and they eat our kitchen waste. Recycling organic matter by feeding kitchen waste to worms is one of the most ecologically sound things you can do."

"I see." Mrs. Duffield swallowed hard. "Well. If you don't mind me saying so, darling, they don't seem to have eaten very much of it."

"It takes about six months for a wormery to really get going," Alice said defensively. "They like their food to be slightly rotten before they tackle it. We have to give them plenty of worm treat as well."

She did not add that they too had been concerned at the worms' apparent lack of appetite and Jake had called the

Worm Hotline to investigate the problem. She doubted her mother was ready to discover a worm hotline existed. She was still getting over it herself.

"Six months!" Mrs. Duffield's face was a mask of horror. "But won't they escape and wriggle into the kitchen? Won't they attract vermin? Won't they *smell?* And, darling, what about the *baby?* It won't be good for it, surely, having them all wriggling around." She screwed up her face.

"Jake says it will be very educational for the baby," Alice said firmly. "He wants to make the garden a biodiversity haven for wildlife."

The next crisis concerned tableware.

"What's this doing on the table, darling?" Mrs. Duffield whispered at dinnertime when Jake was out of the room. She was waving half of the cardboard center of a toilet roll at her daughter.

"It's a napkin ring, Mum." Alice looked brightly at her mother over her lentil soup. "It's Tip of the Month in *Get Trashed!* Great, isn't it?" She tore a piece of bread from the tubular loaves Jake baked by pushing the dough into erstwhile bean cans.

Alice's mother turned her attention to the former cottage cheese containers serving as soup dishes. "I suppose those are Jake's idea as well."

Alice felt irritated. "Come on, Mum. You don't need bone china. Wouldn't you rather save the planet?"

Yet a planet where rinsed-out plastic milk containers became on-table water jugs was not, she knew, a planet her mother had any interest in saving. This was, after all, a woman who had lovingly preserved every piece of the Crown Derby dinner service she had received as a wedding present forty years ago.

She least of all appreciated having to bathe after Jake in his "gravy" because the cottage rules forbade wasting water.

"He's rationing it extra sternly at the moment," Alice explained, "because of the birthing pool."

Mrs. Duffield's face tightened. "Birthing pool?"

"That's right," Jake said, lowering his copy of *Complete Rubbish, Get Trashed!*'s bitter rival. "It's in the birth plan."

"Birth plan?"

"You write down how you want the birth to be and show it to the hospital," Alice enlightened her.

"I'm not sure they had such things in my day," Mrs. Duffield said. "The only plan, as I remember it, was that you went into the hospital and the baby came out."

"Would you like to see it?" Jake asked, faintly provocatively. Alice stared at him in anguish. Part of her had been hoping this subject would never come up. Her mother was sure to disapprove, especially as the plan was mainly Jake's. In the end, given his clearly strong feelings on how their baby should arrive, it had seemed easiest if he drew it up himself.

"I'll get it for you, Mum," she said reluctantly. She went to a corner of the room and rummaged in the cardboard box that served her as both desk and filing cabinet. She passed a sheet of paper to her mother.

" 'Our wish is for a home birth, and one as natural as possible,' " Mrs. Duffield read aloud. She looked up at Alice. "Darling, are you sure? First births can be tricky, you know."

"We're sure," Jake answered.

Mrs. Duffield lowered her head over the paper again. " 'We will listen to Alice's body and respond to its needs.' " She adjusted her bifocals. " 'We do not require gas and air, pethidine and, above all, no epidural. Alice will spend the early stages of labor in her own bed, then, as delivery gets closer, transfer to the shower curtain . . .' *Shower curtain?*" She looked up in horror. "Darling, you're not having the baby standing up in the bath. Surely?"

"Of course not," Jake said impatiently. "The shower curtain will be taped to the floor to catch any—"

"I see," Mrs. Duffield hastily interrupted. She returned to the birthing plan. " 'Soothing whale music will create a co-

cooning atmosphere and throughout the labor Alice will enjoy the facility of a birthing pool . . .' "

"And there it is," Jake said triumphantly, pointing to where the box containing the apparatus, rented from an earth-friendly lifestyle center some weeks ago, stood against the wall of the sitting room.

* * *

Hugo swung onto the motorway and cruised down the fast lane in the Toyota. This damned family four-wheel-drive Amanda had made him buy felt like a tank in comparison to the Aston Martin. Which, in the medium term, he was unlikely to be enjoying again; Neil didn't go in for metropolitan-style sales incentives. "We don't pay London salaries here, you know," he had warned. Except to yourself, Hugo had thought.

God, he missed London. But it would be almost worth having left it to see Neil's face when he told him he'd sold the rotting station house on the old branch line now reserved for nuclear waste or some such spoil of industry.

As he reentered the city, his mobile began to shriek with missed call warnings. No one had left a message, however; something and nothing, Hugo assumed. There would probably be a message at the office, but that was his second stop. First was a café and a takeout bacon sandwich.

Hugo was starving, but then he always was these days. Strange food cravings assailed him at even stranger times. It was, he supposed, nerves as the baby's arrival grew more imminent. During the last few weeks it had been him, rather than Amanda, who got up in the middle of the night for peanut butter and banana sandwiches, washed down with full-cream milk. It was having an expansive effect on his normally lanky six-foot-two frame.

Hugo got to the café to find the lunchtime queue in full swing. It was a full twenty minutes later that, reeking of frying bacon, he reached Dunn and Dustard. No sooner had he entered than a pinstriped explosion burst from Neil's office.

"Where the fuck have you been?" demanded the managing director.

Hugo, now at his desk and tearing into his bacon sandwich, looked up, unsurprised. Investing every minute of the day with as much drama as possible was all part of Neil's self-importance. Hugo smiled at his boss. What he was about to tell him should prick that self-importance right where it hurt.

"We rang you about four hundred times on your mobile," Neil ranted. "You never picked up."

"Couldn't. Miles out of range. Selling that station house, remember?" Hugo spoke through a savory mouthful of bacon and tomato. He felt deep satisfaction. Was there a better flavor combination in the world? He grinned at Neil, preparing to reveal the great news. Surely his use of the word "selling" had been a clue.

"You won't be smiling in a minute," Neil said grimly. "The West Country General rang. They say Amanda's gone into labor."

Somewhere far below, Hugo heard a soft thump. It was the bacon sandwich falling out of his hand onto his desk.

"Labor?" he repeated. "Amanda? She can't be. She's at home. The new kitchen's being fitted today." He paled. The thought of the new kitchen was almost as frightening as the birth, frankly. Amanda had insisted on the most expensive kitchen known to man, complete with hand-carved cabinets and chandeliers. What was incredible—apart from the price— was the fact that she had no interest whatsoever in cooking.

"They definitely said it was Amanda." Neil was obviously delighted at the impact his words were having. He handed Hugo a Post-it note on which the hospital's telephone number was scrawled.

"Can't be. She's having an elective Cesarean at the Cavendish in a fortnight." Hugo fought to sound firm and remain calm.

Neil shrugged. Hugo seized the phone—on which the bacon sandwich had partly fallen—and dialed the hospital. Getting through to the necessary department took some time. A midwife eventually answered, said that she would check, then put the receiver down. Hugo heard her footsteps dying into the distance. After what seemed hours, during which Hugo peeled tomato off the receiver, the footsteps returned.

"Your wife is currently three centimeters dilated."

Hugo remembered Lotti's pasta measurer and winced. "No, there's been a mistake," he insisted. "You've got the wrong person."

"Is your wife's name Amanda Hardwick?"

A warm surge of blood filled Hugo's face. "Er, yes. Yes, it is."

"Well, she was brought here late this morning. In labor."

"But the baby's not supposed to be born yet," Hugo wailed.

There came from the other end what sounded like a snigger. "Babies don't always do what they're supposed to," said the midwife. "As you may be about to find out."

* * *

"Ow," bellowed Amanda. "Ow. Ow. OW!"

The pain she was in was unbelievable. No one had warned her it would be as bad as this. It was so bad that she'd had to abandon making notes for a first-person, as-it-happens piece about giving birth. *Vogue*, she had thought, was bound to be interested.

She had intended the piece to be amusing and had managed the first few lines. "Considering the comfort-challenging design faults of pregnancy—bowels below baby, stomach in throat and so on—it's quite incredible the human race has survived as long as it has . . . Ow!"

Amanda could no longer see anything amusing about it. She wasn't terribly sure about the survival bit either.

Almost as unbelievable and unamusing as the pain was the fact Carinthia was arriving two weeks early. Amanda loathed people who came early. It was rude, unfashionable, caught you on the hop and, worst of all, implied they had nothing better to do. The sort of people Amanda prized always had something better to do. They were powerful and busy, with lots of calls on their time. If, as was intended, Carinthia was going to grow up to be one of them, she had better start mending her ways.

"OW!!!" yelled Amanda, as another mighty spasm crushed her pelvis. It was like the worst period in the world, or, rather, all the periods she had ever had occurring simultaneously. "Look," she gasped at the midwife through watering eyes. "Get me a fucking epidural, will you? Now. This minute."

The placid and pretty Chinese midwife was checking the printout of the baby's heartbeat. She looked calmly at Amanda. "You have to dilate to four centimeters. So far you are three."

"THREE?" yelled Amanda. "But I've been at it for *hours*. I'm being split in fucking half here. What are you, some sort of sadist?"

"We can't give epidural before four centimeters dilated," said the midwife, whose name, according to her badge, was Una.

"Well, I *might* be four now," bellowed Amanda, as another spasm gripped her. "If you could be arsed to look. As it were."

Una checked her watch. "I looked thirty seconds ago." She walked toward the door.

"Where are you going?" bawled Amanda, lunging toward her in a vaguely preventative gesture and almost falling off the bed. "What about my bloody Cesarean?"

Una folded her neat arms. "Doctor say Cesarean not needed."

Amanda sat as bolt upright as her condition would allow. "*Not needed?*" she bellowed, aghast. "But I'm too posh to push."

This powerful argument left Una unmoved. "Is dangerous operation. Only do if medical necessity."

"But this is a medical necessity," shrieked Amanda. Was that great lump in her stomach really going to come out of her front bottom? It was impossible. It would kill her. "I'm in *agony*."

Una nodded. "But you not dilated enough. I back in ten minutes. You ready for epidural by then."

As the door closed, Amanda let out a scream of frustration that wasn't entirely due to the pain. It was due to the Cavendish maternity hospital too.

Amanda had been in the hallway at Fitzherbert Place, shouting at the workmen fitting her new luxury kitchen, when the first twinges struck. As the twinges deepened and lengthened to cramps, she fled to the phone and called Hugo. When, to her apoplectic fury, his mobile did not pick up, she dialed the Cavendish.

All of their operators were busy. After listening to the whole of Vivaldi's *Four Seasons* apparently performed on a stylophone at the bottom of a dustbin, Amanda was still glaring at the telephone dial. Halfway through *Music for the Royal Fireworks*, an operator came on the line.

"What do you mean you can't admit me today?" Amanda yelled sixty seconds later. "I'm coming in for a fucking elective Cesarean."

"Yes, madam, indeed you are. But the operation is booked for two weeks' time."

"So?" raged Amanda. "The baby's early. You're just going to have to do it today, that's all."

"I'm afraid that's impossible, madam."

"So what the fuck am I supposed to do?" bellowed Amanda.

"Madam, if you could just calm down and stop swearing . . ."

"Calm down?"

"Madam, I must ask you to remember that extreme emotion is inadvisable in pregnant mothers," said the receptionist in her unengaged monotone. "It may precipitate the birth."

"Well, it's a bit late for that now," Amanda snarled, thinking longingly of the glossy brochure photographs of the hospital's private suites. The four-poster beds, whose damask curtains and magnificent carving concealed touch-of-a-button adjustable mattresses and more state-of-the-art equipment than NASA could dream of. The vintage-champagne-filled minibars. The huge, luxury-hotel-style bathrooms with hot tubs and miles of marble. "Look," she gasped urgently as the cramps struck again, "you've got to get an ambulance here—I mean, one of your chauffeurs. You send chauffeurs, don't you? That's part of the deal, isn't it, a luxury limo with medical assistance on board?"

"Indeed it is, madam, for those with the right coverage."

"Coverage?" Amanda said suspiciously. "What do you mean?"

"Madam, can I ask you if you took out the Cavendish Hospital's Early Bird Insurance Package?"

"The what?" yelped Amanda in mid-spasm.

"I've got your details up on the screen now, madam," went the monotonous singsong, "but you only seem to have taken out the Standard Delivery Package."

Amanda vaguely remembered arguing with Hugo about this. He had pointed out that the Early Bird coverage would more than double the cost of her Cavendish care. And as it was obviously quite impossible a child of hers would be early, Amanda had dropped the idea. Sod Hugo. She might have known it would be all his bloody fault.

"So you're saying that, despite the fact I'm booked into your hospital and I've paid an effing fortune for it, you can't—won't, rather—give me any treatment at all?" she said slowly.

"The Basic Delivery Package does not cover a patient for early arrivals," the receptionist confirmed. "Have you got the number of your local hospital?"

Amanda, now lying grumpily on the damask-free NHS hospital bed, succumbed to another spasm and tried not to remember what had happened next. The journey to West Country General in the kitchen fitters' van. Asking them to take her, just after she'd accused them of bodging, incompetence and fraud, was bad enough. But the bumpy ride on the grubby van seat was another dimension of discomfort altogether. Hardly the limousine arrival she had imagined. And paid for, dammit.

"Ow!!!" she screamed, as the worst pain so far gripped her body. "OOWWWW!! AAAARRGGHH!!"

* * *

Hugo rushed frantically about in the bowels of the West Country General, clutching an increasingly wilted bunch of petrol-station flowers. Why the hell, he wondered, wasn't Amanda in the Cavendish? She'd made enough fuss about the place. That she'd had a last-minute economy drive seemed unlikely.

"Ooof!" Hugo was suddenly, conclusively, winded. He opened his eyes to realize that the person he had run into was the beautiful pediatrician, Dr. Watson.

"You again," she said icily.

Hugo stared back desperately. "Birthing center?" he gasped.

The doctor was instantly all professional solicitude. She pointed an elegant finger. "That way. Up the stairs and round to the right. Your baby, is it?"

Hugo nodded.

Dr. Watson smiled. "Good luck. I'll probably see you later. I check all the newborns."

Hugo felt suddenly, wildly glad that she was checking the newborns. Rushing in the direction indicated, he turned yet another blazingly striplit corner to find—at last, at glorious last—the words "Jane Austen Birthing Suite" on a sign above a double door. Dashing toward it, Hugo desperately hoped he had not Missed It. But only because Amanda would be cross if he had. In his heart, Hugo had no desire to watch the birth. Least of all from the batting end, as Neil insisted on calling it. "Stick to the bowling end, that's my advice," he had yelled as Hugo left the office. Hugo intended to do just that.

Finally, he had got to where the action was. He felt tight with anxiety. Please God, he prayed, as he rarely did, let everything be all right with Amanda and the baby.

He cannoned through the double doors of the Jane Austen Birthing Suite. The dull-eyed security guard on the other side looked up, startled, as something tall, pinstriped and agitated appeared in his midst.

"I've come to see my wife," Hugo squeaked through a throat dry with tension. "She's called Amanda Hardwick. She's in here having a baby." He looked expectantly at the guard, but congratulations, recognition even, came there none.

The guard, whose twelve-hour shift was finally coming to an end, yawned. He ran his finger slowly down a clipboard. "Oh yeah," he drawled eventually, without looking up. "You in the wrong place. You expected in Bereavement Suite."

There was a gasp of horror from Hugo.

The guard looked up to see the tall, pinstriped man seem to hang briefly in the air before crashing down like a felled tree.

CHAPTER
8

IT WAS DARK WHEN ALICE WOKE. SHE KNEW IMMEDIATELY AND IN-stinctively that the dull, period-like pains were the baby coming. A day or two early, but clearly on its way. She felt a surge of excitement, followed by dread. This was it.

She lay there, deliberating. Should she wake Jake? She turned her head and looked lovingly at his handsome profile, reluctant to acquaint him with his coming responsibilities. Let him dream on for a little while longer.

The pains were, anyway, faint and widely spaced. The real action, Alice recalled from the prenatal class, began only when they were strong and frequent. She hoped that strong was not a euphemism for painful. It was not that she was fainthearted. She agreed wholeheartedly with Jake that pain relief was self-ish as, though it might make her feel better, it could also harm the baby. But now that the actual, raw, medically unaided mo-ment was on her, she flinched at the prospect of hours of un-ending agony.

Ouch. That was a sharp one. Alice's eyes watered with the sudden pain. Were the contractions coming slightly quicker now?

"Jake!" she whispered. "I think the baby's on its way."

"Uh?" Jake shot up in bed. "It can't be. It's not due yet."

"Well, it's coming, ready or not," Alice replied, more calmly than she felt. The contractions were faster now. And stronger, which, unfortunately, did mean painful.

"Shit." Jake ran two hands through his bed-tousled hair. "I haven't got the birthing pool built yet. But don't worry. I'll sort it." He was now bounding about the room stark naked. His penis and testicles were swinging agitatedly. "Stay there," he urged her. "It'll all be OK, I promise."

"I know." Alice smiled up at him as he pulled on a T-shirt and bounded down the rickety stair.

Five minutes later, she was struggling to her feet. It had occurred to her that Jake might need help with constructing the birthing pool. It had looked very complicated on the box. She levered herself up and made her way down to the sitting room where, in the quarter-light of the coming dawn, she found Jake looking cross amid a sea of cardboard, Styrofoam and shiny plastic slabs.

"Is it tricky?" she asked fearfully.

"Not just that," Jake huffed. "It's supposed to be ecologically friendly—and look at this." He held up one of the pieces of Styrofoam. "How rainforest-destroying can you get?"

As the pain gripped her in its vice and squeezed mightily, Alice closed her eyes. She arched her back and let the long, low moan of agony escape. Then she felt Jake's twitching, sweating hand on her brow.

"Oh, Al, sweet, don't worry . . ."

"Have you called the midwives?" she gasped. "I think it's probably time they came round."

He leaped to his feet, alarm in his eyes, and rushed to the phone. Alice, meanwhile, tried to ease the pain with a turn around the tiny kitchen. The sink was full of unwashed jars and tins destined for a new recycled identity, presumably somewhere within the household. Alice squirted some Palmolive over them and began to run the hot tap, only to discover that no hot water came out of it. Horror clutched her. Surely the heater hadn't picked this morning of all mornings to pack up again. Didn't it realize there was a birthing pool to fill?

"The midwives are calling back," Jake announced when she returned to the sitting room. He was on his knees among the birthing pool pieces again. Alice shuddered, imagining it erect and full of freezing water.

"How are you feeling?" Jake asked solicitously.

Alice forced a smile. "Better," she croaked, breathing more calmly as the contraction eased.

"You're sure?"

"Yes. Can I do anything to help?"

"Just lie on the sofa and keep calm."

"No, I mean something practical," Alice insisted. She was determined not to appear to be wallowing in her pain. That would be selfish and, as Jake repeatedly said, neither he nor the planet had time for selfish people.

She plucked the birthing pool leaflet gently out of his hand and looked at it. It was full of complicated line drawings of panels, arrows and bolts. In the final one a huge-stomached woman, sitting in the completed hexagonal construction, contemplated the head of an infant emerging from between her wide-open thighs.

"Well, if you *really* want to make a start on that," Jake said, evidently relieved, "I'll go and find the garden hose."

"Garden hose?"

"To fill the pool."

"Er, Jake, the water . . ."

But he had left the room. The telephone rang. Clutching her stomach, Alice clumsily made her way toward it.

"This is the Jane Austen Birthing Center at West Country General Hospital."

There followed a minute or two of explanation.

"I see," Alice said slowly. "And you're quite sure about this? The situation's not likely to change?"

"I'm afraid not," the other end confirmed.

Alice sank despairingly to the floor. Tears of terror swelled in her eyes. Oh God. Could this nightmare really be happening?

Then an idea struck her.

"Are you all right, madam?" the other end asked anxiously.

Alice was silent. She was busy processing the astonishing, wonderful, rescuing possibility that had just occurred to her. "Er, hang on a moment," she murmured. Could her calculations be right? Please God, let them be right. No, she was sure she was right.

Frankly, she'd better be. "Actually," Alice told the hospital, "don't worry. I've got another plan." She rang off and dialed a number before another contraction kicked in.

A few minutes later, Jake reentered the sitting room, brandishing a dusty garden hose. "Found the whale music as well," he added, triumphantly waving a cassette.

"That's fantastic," Alice told him. "But actually," she said gently, "we won't be needing it."

He looked appalled. "Why not? Do you want to listen to something else?"

"I won't need it because I'm going to the hospital."

Jake took a sharp, indignant breath. "But, Al, we agreed. Home birth. The midwives come here. We're going to listen to your body and take it all from there."

"But my body," Alice groaned, "is saying it needs to be in a hospital. Now."

"A hospital's not in the birth plan," Jake said stubbornly.

"Fuck the birth plan!" Alice shrieked suddenly, finding being reasonable while in torture-chamber-level pain finally beyond her. She closed her eyes to shut out Jake's shocked expression. "The hospital can't send any midwives," she added, apologetically.

Jake's face darkened with fury. "What do you mean they can't send any bloody midwives? They're a fucking hospital, aren't they?" He leaped for the phone, which lay on Alice's thighs.

Her hand tightened over the receiver. "Look, there's no point arguing with them," she muttered, feeling the sweat start to trickle down her forehead. "The problem is that you need two midwives for a home birth, and they can't spare two tonight. They're too busy. So I'm going to hospital."

"To the West Country General?"

"Well I could go there, but I'm not," Alice gasped as the agony struck again. "They're obviously run off their feet at the moment."

"Where, then?"

"Somewhere . . . ow . . . called the Cavendish."

Jake's face drained of all its ruddy outdoor color. "The private hospital? The one where that arse of a real estate agent and his stuck-up wife are going?"

Alice, fists clenched tightly, looked at Jake incomprehendingly. She vaguely remembered Amanda Hardwick saying something about the Cavendish, but she was now in too much pain to care.

"It's like this," groaned Alice, gearing up to one final, huge effort at explanation. "My Intercorp private health insurance is valid to the end of the year. It covers everything. I rang them and they recommended I go to the Cavendish. It's the nearest, the newest and the best-equipped maternity hospital around and they'll take me immediately. My policy even covers me for this package they have called Early Bird, for people whose babies come before they're supposed to." She flopped back, exhausted by the effort of speech, before rallying for one last time. "They're sending a limo-ambulance for me now."

* * *

The birth, Amanda thought, had hardly been pleasant, although matters had dramatically picked up following the epidural. Carinthia had appeared soon afterward. In textbook fashion too, give or take a couple of stitches. She hated to admit it, but Una was right. A Cesarean had not been necessary.

The only non-textbook aspect of Carinthia's birth was that the baby was not, after all, Carinthia. That small, beautiful, flattering version of herself conclusively failed to materialize.

"Baby boy," Una had said, plonking a gory lump on Amanda's stomach. Amanda stared at it.

It wasn't the blonde cherub she had imagined. It was dark, wizened, and with unpleasant purple-red skin. In addition, something about its slimily bent angles reminded her of giblets and she was glad when Una took it away to clean it up.

Amanda had tried at an earlier stage to bag one of the few private recovery rooms, but they were allocated on a first-born-first-served basis. Amanda's labor having been twelve hours at the final count, she'd been conclusively pipped at the post. But in the end, she'd had the last laugh. She'd kicked up such a fuss that the hospital had allotted her the only private vacant room they had available. Which strictly speaking had another use altogether.

＊　＊　＊

"It was a bit of a shock, that's all, being told to go to the Bereavement Suite," Hugo bleated as Una ministered some hot sweet tea.

Amanda was far from pleased. The fact that Hugo had not made it for the birth was infuriating. To give birth alone was frankly embarrassing. As if one was a single mother or something. But then, Amanda thought bitterly, perhaps that was preferable to having a husband who turned up in the state that Hugo had. In a wheelchair, with his head bandaged and an aluminum vomit bowl on his knee.

One heard of husbands getting squeamish in delivery rooms, but Hugo was the first she'd known to collapse before he even got there.

"But I thought you were both dead." Slumped in his wheelchair, Hugo relived the horror of the moment.

"Well, we're not," Amanda had briskly pointed out. "Now pass me my mobile, will you? I'm phoning the Cavendish."

"You're not supposed to use mobiles in hospitals . . ." Hugo's voice trailed away. There was no point arguing with Amanda in this mood. In any mood, come to that.

Hours later Amanda stared up, satisfied, into the canopy of a Cavendish four-poster. The phone call it had taken to achieve this was admittedly long and terse. She had threatened the Cavendish's director with an unfavorable mention in the birthing piece she was writing for *Vogue* if he didn't allow her to convalesce there, at least. She could not imagine why this obvious and simple route hadn't occurred to her before. Pregnancy clearly fuddled the brain. Thank God she wasn't pregnant any more.

As Amanda sighed happily and tapped away on the Internet-connected laptop that was all part of the Cavendish service, Hugo, sitting in a tapestry-patterned wing chair in the huge bay window, lowered his copy of *The Times*.

"What are you doing?" he asked. "You're not working, surely? You've just had a baby. What about quality time dandling angelic infants in the dappled sunlight under the apple blossom?"

"Oh, for Christ's sake, it's hardly the weather for it." Amanda threw an impatient hand in the direction of the sleet-streaked window. "Look, I'm just checking my e-mail, OK? But while I'm at it, I'll firm up Nurse Harris's arrival time. She's due tomorrow. Mary-poppins.co.uk," she muttered to herself, typing in the maternity nurse agency's e-mail address.

Hugo glanced apprehensively at the cot. The baby was asleep, although he had little faith in this state of affairs continuing. A mere few hours' acquaintance had revealed in the child a tendency to go off like a bomb at any moment. Like mother, like son, Hugo supposed. He wondered in what way, if any, the child resembled him. Not in looks, or at least not so far. The baby was scrunched, purple and terrifyingly fragile-looking. The only remarkable resemblance it bore, so far as Hugo could see, was to a baby.

Hugo knew that to think this was a terrible failing. Becoming a father was famously one of the great life experiences. Men burst into tears when they first saw their offspring and were filled with an overwhelming sense of wonder. Yet Hugo's main sensation in the hours that followed the birth was that of terminal uselessness.

There seemed nothing he could do, no role he could play. When the baby was awake, Amanda and her two assigned Cavendish nurses were occupied with it to such an extent that Hugo never got a look-in, and hardly a look. The only time he had tried to bond with his son had been in the full public glare of these ancillary personnel and he had not known what to do or to say. The baby had screamed the whole time he had held it, which had not helped. The mewling, cat-like cries upset Hugo and made him want to wail too.

So now he sat in the chair pretending to read the paper, but in reality scouring the corners of his heart for some trace of fatherly feeling. His joy, so far, was mainly attributable to the fact that the baby was not called Carinthia. Amanda had apparently once known someone glamorous with this name, but it was nonetheless that of a province of Austria and a ridiculous thing to call a child. You wouldn't get Austrians calling their offspring Humberside. Fortunately the baby had provided the solution by being a boy.

This had, of course, left the question of what he would be called. Amanda was working on this with the help of *Names for Leaders*, a smartly bound and complimentary volume provided as another part of the Cavendish service. The names all seemed impossibly elaborate and were, Hugo suspected, pitched with deliberation and cringeworthy accuracy at the aspirations of Cavendish clients. The boys' section, for example, included such horrors as Merlin, Vercingetorix and Ezekiel, all of which Amanda loved. Plain English names like James and John, which Hugo liked, were nowhere to be seen.

The baby stirred. Contrary to expectations, it did not erupt in a yell. It snuffled a bit then seemed to go back to sleep.

"Thank God," Amanda muttered from the bed. "He's chewing my nipples to shreds." She already hated breastfeeding. There had been a sharp exchange of words when one of the nurses, instructing Amanda in the proper procedure, had advised her to "get into a comfortable position."

"Comfortable position?" Amanda had yelled, outraged. "I've had my arse ripped open and my tits feel like rugby balls. There's no such thing as a comfortable position."

Hugo knew that a free bar was all part of the Cavendish service. He had seen the large lounge downstairs when they arrived. He recalled the flickering fire, beams, squashy leather sofas and, no doubt, as many cut-glass tumblers of whisky and soda as you could force down your gullet.

He silently folded the newspaper and contemplated the scene before him. Amanda was nodding over her laptop and Merlin-Vercingetorix-Ezekiel was sleeping, well, like a baby. Hugo rose gently from his easy chair. He'd only be ten minutes. It wasn't as if anyone would miss him.

He made his way down the sweeping baronial staircase and into the lounge. The faint smell of antiseptic could be detected among the potpourri and cigars. The cigars were free too, Hugo realized, helping himself to a fine-looking Romeo y Julieta. How did the saying go? A baby was only a baby. But a good cigar was a smoke.

He perched on a swivel stool, placed his elbows on the polished copper surface of the cocktail bar and stared at the drinks menu. There was a theme here, he realized, although he was not sure that it was appropriate.

C-Breeze was top of the list, followed by Puerpal Haze, Forceps Flip, Dr. Tom Collins and Twin Martini. Perhaps worse were the cocktails whose names had not been tampered with, but to which the context of the clinic lent hideous new meaning. Slow Comfortable Screw and Screaming Orgasm, for example, both of which, judging from the frank gynecological details of the birth Amanda had supplied him with, seemed some distance away at the moment. As for Bloody Mary . . . Grimacing, Hugo put the menu down and asked the barman for a stiff whisky and soda.

As, with grateful reverence, he took the first mouthful, he was aware of another pair of elbows arriving next to him. Checked, lumberjack-shirted elbows.

"Champagne, zurr?" slurred the barman in what struck Hugo as a highly bogus Continental accent. "Cocktail, zurr?"

"No, thanks. Got any, like, organic carrot juice?" asked a voice Hugo recognized. His insides shrank. It *couldn't* be. They were having a bloody home birth, weren't they? What the hell was he doing here? Hugo stared fiercely at the cut-crystal bottom of his whisky tumbler.

"Carrot juice?" repeated the barman, surprised. "I don't theenk so, zurr."

"Well, water then?" The customer was evidently put out. "Reverse-filtered, obviously."

"I theenk we might have a bottle of water somewhere," the barman said doubtfully. After bending and burrowing under the bar, he re-emerged empty-handed. "Sorry, zurr. Most of the gentlemen who come down here, zey are wanting alcohol. Cigars. You know, for celebration."

The newcomer waved his arms energetically to rid the air of Hugo's cigar smoke. "Well, not all of us want to celebrate by poisoning our livers and igniting phallic symbols to the detriment of the atmosphere."

Hugo sensed that his neighbor had now turned and was looking at him. "Hey," he said. "If it isn't Yogi!"

"Hello, Jake," Hugo forced out through a face rigid with dislike. "Didn't realize you were here. What happened to the home birth?"

"Baby came day before yesterday. Slightly before schedule." Jake looked momentarily irritated. "But hey, that's Mother Nature for you, no?" he added, recovering his customary jauntiness.

"How do you mean, 'slightly before schedule'?" Hugo sensed something Jake didn't especially want to talk about.

"Er . . . emergency Cesarean. Things got a bit complicated."

"Emergency Cesarean!" Hugo exclaimed. So the all-natural organic couple had had the most hi-tech, unnatural delivery imaginable.

"You were having a Cesarean too, right?" Jake hit back defensively.

"No, actually Amanda had a vaginal delivery." Hugo savored the sensation of having scored a point.

"You wan' tomato juice, sir?" interrupted the barman, hopefully brandishing a small red bottle at Jake.

Jake looked at him suspiciously. "Is it GM?"

"Sorry, no. Ees Schweppes."

Jake settled on a glass of milk.

"So. Congratulations." Jake lifted his over-burdened glass.

"Thanks. Congratulations to you too."

"Fantastic, isn't it, fatherhood?" Jake punched the air with one of his sinewy brown forearms. Hugo nodded briefly.

"Best feeling in the world," Jake added.

"Yes."

"Nothing like it, eh?" Jake took a sip. "Just—incredible. So—moving. So—amazing."

Hugo nodded at the barman for a refill, almost certain now that Jake was deliberately winding him up.

"I don't mind telling you, I cried," Jake said.

Hugo said nothing. Jake's dig, if dig it was, had hit home. Why hadn't he felt like that? The only excuse he could think of was that the knockout blow to his chin had temporarily suspended all normal emotion.

"I mean, the moment the baby came out . . ." Jake shook his locks in wonder, ". . . just the best moment of my life. You were there, yeah?"

"Didn't quite make it," Hugo muttered into his whisky and soda. As soon as he had admitted this he wondered why he had. It would have been so easy to lie, to have not presented Jake with such an easy target.

"Didn't make it?" Jake's voice was all triumphant amazement. "God, I wouldn't have missed it for the world. I was there *every minute.*"

Hugo, both defensive and drunk, felt the overwhelming urge to knock Jake off his swivel stool. Instead, he pushed his empty glass toward the barman again. "Comfortable here, isn't it?" he observed.

"Can't wait to see the back of the place myself. We're going home today."

"Today? Bit early, isn't it, if Alice only had her Cesarean the day before yesterday?"

Jake shrugged. "We want to get Baby home, get on with family living, all of us together." His teeth flashed with eager enthusiasm.

Hugo thought glumly of home life with Amanda and Merlin-Vercingetorix. He could not easily imagine it.

"Anyway." Jake drained the milk, slipped off the stool and punched Hugo playfully on the shoulder. "Gotta get going. See you around, Yogi."

"The name's Hugo," Hugo winced at the force of the blow. "And not if I see you first," he muttered through gritted teeth.

CHAPTER
9

ALICE ADORED HER NEW DAUGHTER. FROM THE FIRST MINUTE SHE held Rosa, a powerful tide of emotion crashed through her in which swirled love, relief, awe and a determination to protect this tiny creature for whose existence she, with Jake, was entirely responsible. Her first impressions of motherhood were that it was everything she had imagined, but more so. All the clichés were true. She had never thought it possible to love anything this much.

"Now you know how I feel about recycling," Jake grinned from the bedside when she told him this.

Alice laughed uproariously. How could she have thought, as she occasionally did, that Jake might lack a sense of humor? She felt she was drowning in happiness. "I can't believe it," she sighed ecstatically to Jake, clutching the warm bundle of baby close. "Just think, I almost missed out on this altogether."

"Like I said, Al, it happened for a reason," Jake assured her with a gentle smile.

"Darling!" The door of Alice's private room flew open to admit her parents. A nanosecond later, Alice was enveloped in her mother's scented hug.

"Did you get my roses, darling?" Mrs. Duffield asked, after

exclaiming delightedly over her new granddaughter. "Frances sent some too."

Alice was surprised. She had not received any flowers. "What a shame," she lamented. "Roses are my favorites." And the reason, moreover, that Rosa was called Rosa. Or Ro, as Jake shortened it to, just as he abbreviated Alice herself to Al. This habit, she knew, irritated her mother, who could not understand, as she put it, why he could not go that extra syllable mile.

Underlying her indignation was her suspicion that Jake had not only failed to give Alice any flowers, but also any other token marking the arrival of the baby. She was wrong in this assumption, but only because Alice had, reluctantly, judged it best not to show her mother the recycled toothbrush, which, stripped of its bristles, bent with the aid of hot water and painted with rather shaky stars, made what Jake, presenting it to her, had described as a "birthing bracelet."

Alice's mother decided to change the subject. "About Rosa's christening," she said brightly. "If you would like to, you could use our garden. It's perfect in the summer—we could have a champagne reception. A marquee even."

"Your mother's dying to buy a hat," Alice's father chuckled.

His wife tapped his hand playfully. "Shush. But seriously," she looked at Jake and Alice, "I'm sure the vicar at St. Enodoc's would love to do the service. Alice was christened there, after all."

The offer, Alice knew, was a very attractive one. A party in her parents' vast and pretty garden, tumbling with honeysuckle, orange blossom and general summer glory. Plus a service at the exquisite medieval gray stone church on the hill above their Cornish village, where to walk out on the porch was to enjoy a breathtaking view over fields to the distant sea. Her mother, Alice knew, had cherished hopes that she would be married there some day. Hopes that she had evidently now transferred to the next best thing.

And hopes that, Alice feared, would unfortunately have to be dashed. "Er, the thing is, Mum," she began uncomfortably.

"We're not planning a christening as such," Jake interrupted.

"You're not?" Mrs. Duffield blinked.

"Although we haven't ruled out some form of humanist ceremony," Jake added brightly.

Alice's parents looked nonplussed. "Humanist?" echoed Mr. Duffield. "Isn't she Church of England?"

"Actually," Alice explained gently, "when we filled in Rosa's religion on the hospital form, we didn't put C of E."

"Oh." Her mother, while obviously disappointed, was trying her best to look bright and interested. "So what *did* you put?"

"Pagan," said Jake proudly.

Alice's mother spluttered. Her father blinked. The conversation switched to the weather, giving Jake an opportunity to share the latest depressing intelligence concerning greenhouse emissions.

"Funny, isn't it?" Alice mused after her parents had gone.

"What is?" There was, so far as Jake was concerned, nothing remotely amusing about the Duffields.

"The flowers. Funny that she sent them and they never got delivered."

"Actually," he said lightly, "they did get delivered."

"They did?"

"But you were asleep when they came so I thought I'd take them down to the local Action on Addiction drop-in center."

Alice blinked. "*Where?* Why? Why did you do that?"

"Because they would have meant nothing to you and everything to them."

"They would have meant something to me," Alice said quietly, wondering what bouquets of roses would mean to recovering drug addicts anyway. Or perhaps not so recovering drug addicts, who knew?

Jake gave her his most dazzling smile. "Come on, Al. You're

in the lap of luxury here and what have they got? Nothing. It would have been selfish to do anything else."

Alice immediately felt guilty. Jake was so much greater and more generous a spirit than she was. Feeling unworthy in comparison was becoming a familiar sensation.

But still, secretly, she regretted the loss of the roses. Alice loved flowers and wished they could grow some in their own garden, but all horticultural efforts were restricted to Jake's organic vegetable-raising. This had not been successful so far. No more successful than the wormery which, for all the hotline's assurances, did not seem in the least to be settling down and eating. Had they, Alice wondered, been sold the world's only known colony of anorexic earthworms?

*   *   *

As Amanda showed no inclination to leave the Cavendish, it fell to Hugo to welcome Nurse Harris to Fitzherbert Place on the day set for her arrival. The woman waiting outside Number Four's as-yet-unpainted front door was solid, foursquare, tall and broad, with thick calves, big hands, and a face, Hugo thought, straight out of some particularly bleak period drama.

"You must be Nurse Harris," he said, hoping she would contradict him and turn out to be someone from the council or the local Methodist church. To his disappointment, however, she nodded a brisk affirmative.

She had the air of having been born in uniform. She also had the air of being accustomed to better things. On first seeing her bedroom at Fitzherbert Place, with the deep crack on one wall and the damp stain on the other, Nurse Harris looked round wordlessly, gave a deep, disapproving sniff and remarked, "It wasn't like this at Lord Fairbourne's."

Asking what it was like would, Hugo realized, be folly of the highest order. But asking was not necessary. Ten minutes after Nurse Harris's arrival he knew that it was like a luxurious, self-contained flat in the east wing of Fairbourne Hall. And what Fairbourne Hall was like was a large cream-painted stately home set amid rolling parkland. A structurally iffy terrace house it was not. Albeit, thanks to Amanda, a terrace house with a Hollywood kitchen installed by Bath's most expensive fitters.

Just who the hell, Hugo wondered, was Lord Fairbourne, anyway? Amanda, he recalled, had read about him in some magazine or other and been profoundly impressed. She had been determined to track down the very maternity nurse he had used. Not for the first time Hugo cursed his wife's reading habits.

"Not dark enough," was Nurse Harris's verdict on the nursery. "You must install blackout blinds and curtains with light-proof linings *immediately* if Baby is to get the sleep he needs."

"Oh, right," said Hugo, wondering where all this equipment was going to come from. It was clearly required on the double.

"I don't mind telling you . . ." Nurse Harris offered in what unexpectedly promised to be a moment of constructive suggestion.

"What?" asked Hugo.

"I had *exactly* the same problem when I arrived at the home of, *ahem* . . ." In hushed tones, Nurse Harris spoke the name of a very famous rock star. "*He* hadn't got blackout blinds either."

Hugo felt encouraged to be in such glamorous blindless company. "So what did he do?"

"Called Harrods *immediately* and got someone to come round and put it all up. It was no expense spared in *their* house." Nurse Harris's rather boiled-looking eyes swiveled disapprovingly about. They settled on the largely exposed bottom of Gary, the painter recently engaged by Amanda to paint what she called "the master bedroom" and landing in heritage colors. Hugo disliked the dull blue currently being applied to the landing. It was, he had realized after considerable effort of memory, the exact shade of the covers of math exercise books at school.

Hugo nervously rubbed his hands. "Harrods." That sounded expensive.

"Don't worry," said Gary, looking up. "I've got the answer, squire."

Hugo was surprised that Gary had been listening. He certainly never seemed to when being given instructions.

"What if," Gary offered in his oddly high, squeaky voice, "I just paint all the kiddo's windows black? A coat of black on the outside and you won't be able to see a thing, squire, let me tell you. No need for blackout whatsits."

Hugo looked at him in amazement. "That's a very good idea, Gary." He turned to the maternity nurse. "What do you think, Nurse Harris?" He accompanied the query with his most dazzling smile. Battleaxe she may be, but he'd crack her.

Nurse Harris, however, appeared to be that woman. "Well, it's certainly unorthodox. But if it's really the best you can do . . ." She pursed her lips. It went without saying that such a thing would never have happened at Lord Fairbourne's.

"Now, on another matter, Mr. Fine," Nurse Harris said sternly. "I'm going to explain my routines to you. It's vitally important that they are adhered to. There are specific times for sleeping, eating—"

"Sounds great," Hugo interrupted encouragingly, turning the charm up as far as it would go. He wasn't beaten yet, not by a long chalk. "We all need some discipline round here."

Nurse Harris frowned. "Mr. Fine, the routine of which I am speaking applies to Mrs. Fine and Baby. I am not proposing to supervise anyone else in the family."

Nurse Harris's routines, pinned up with great speed all over the baby's nursery walls, made Hugo's head spin whenever he looked at them. His son was supposed to wake on the dot at 6:45, be bathed, dressed and breastfed by Amanda, spend two hours playing and then return to bed for forty-five minutes. His next feeding was at 10:30, after which he would be engaged in a variety of activities until his lunchtime sleep. Given his commitments, it seemed to Hugo surprising that the baby didn't have his own personal assistant. Perhaps it was no bad thing he was still in the Cavendish with his mother. Considering the schedule awaiting him when he came out, he needed to rest while he could.

*   *   *

Alice didn't want to leave the Cavendish any more than Amanda did. She adored being warm and comfortable, in a proper bed that was not on the floor, drinking out of proper glassware and eating from china plates. She hadn't realized how much she had missed these things, yet resisted letting Jake know this. He was sure to deplore such self-indulgence— and with good reason.

Back in the Old Morgue, Alice tried not to notice the contrast. Or the heaps of detritus in the kitchen, the latest results of Jake's "foraging." She tried desperately not to mind when, as she opened her underwear drawer, a group of fruit flies, refugees from the ever-more-rotting wormery, flew out.

Instead, she concentrated on the positive. Such as the changing table made by Jake from recycled milk crates. Whenever Alice was tempted to think it was a bit wobbly and slightly too low, she immediately asked herself how many fathers would bother to build their firstborn such a thing. It was hard to think of a more touching expression of paternal devotion, combined, of course, with commitment to the planet.

Another such miracle was Rosa's sleeping hammock, constructed along authentic American Indian lines from sacking, rope and some old clothes pins Jake had found in the cottage garden. Alice's secret worry, that it was a rather tenuous construction, was one she kept to herself.

Despite such conscience-calming equipment, Rosa proved

a restless sleeper. Night after night Alice lay in the dark and listened to her mewling before finally bursting out into a full-blown, nerve-shattering bawl. Dragging herself out of bed, Alice would wince at the still-tender Cesarean scar.

"Everything OK?" Jake said sleepily, as tonight, as usual, Alice crossed the bedroom to the hammock.

"Fine. She just needs changing." Alice held her daughter close and took her into the bathroom where she laid her gingerly down on the recycled milk crates.

As she set about the pins and undoing the nappy, Jake appeared at the door. "Just watch her while I rinse this out, would you?" Alice asked.

She had accepted without question Jake's suggestion that they use terry nappies instead of disposable ones. That any other course would be monumentally self-indulgent. Terries were fiddly, they were difficult, they were bulky and they involved three rather unpleasant buckets (or recycled catering-size margarine tubs) standing around at all times in the kitchen. But at least they weren't adding to a landfill mountain comprising four percent of the total household waste in the whole of Britain.

These statistics Alice would repeat like a mantra as she stood, as now, with the freezing water from the toilet flush streaming over her reddened hands, watching the green effluvia dislodge from the sodden, grayish material she held. Sometimes, as now, it took more than two flushes, and long minutes' waiting in between while the temperamental cistern filled back up again. Eventually, Alice handed Jake the partially clean nappy to take downstairs to add to the soaking bucket while she began the thankless task of putting a new one on the still yelling baby.

Despite the nappy change, Rosa's roars were harder and more urgent than ever. It was clear that something else was wrong.

"I think she's hungry," Alice guessed. "I'll just take her

downstairs and feed her. Shush, darling," she whispered into the baby's warm head.

"I'll come down with you," Jake offered.

"Really, you don't have to. No point us both being up. Better if you go back to bed."

"No, I'm coming too. I'll make you a cup of tea."

She smiled at him. Had any new father ever been so considerate?

Downstairs, Jake guided Alice toward an orange-box armchair. She lowered herself carefully and began the struggle to unite baby to nipple.

"Has she latched on yet?" Jake called from the kitchen. Alice felt her heart swell with loving pride. How many other fathers not only knew but used the correct terminology? "Yes," she called softly back, trying to keep the wince out of her voice.

The main thing was that the crying had stopped, even if the agony in her breasts had started. It sometimes seemed to Alice that childbirth—its immediate aftermath, at least—was the constant swapping of one uncomfortable experience for another.

"Damn, we've run out of milk," she heard Jake mutter under his breath.

Alice looked down at Rosa and hoped she hadn't done the same. That was the problem with breastfeeding: it was impossible to tell. Even after Rosa had fed for hours, or what seemed like hours, she often spent the rest of the night screaming, apparently starving. Alice hoped this would not be the case tonight.

"You know," she said conversationally to Jake as he came into the sitting room with two cups of milkless greenish water, "I'm beginning to wonder whether bottle-feeding Rosa might not be an idea."

"Bottle-feeding?" Jake repeated. Alice detected an ominous note in his voice.

"Oh, not with formula, obviously," she said hurriedly. "I

mean breast milk. You can express it into bottles with a breast pump, so it wouldn't make any difference to Rosa. And my poor old savaged dugs could recover," she added, grinning.

Jake dropped on his haunches before her and took her hands. "Al," he said persuasively, "don't you see it's the thin end of the wedge? If you start giving Ro one bottle, it'll be five a day of formula before you know it."

Alice gave a surprised laugh. "Of course it won't. It's just that one of the midwives mentioned that it was a good idea to introduce bottles at the end of the fourth week. Any later and Rosa might reject them."

"Midwives!" Jake scoffed. "They're all in the pay of the baby milk companies."

"Oh, Jake. I'm sure that's not true. And surely the occasional bottle won't do any harm? At least then I'd know what she was getting."

His smile was gentle but his eyes had a steely glint. "Don't you think it's a bit selfish to put your comfort above what's best for Ro? Breast is best." Jake bent his head forward and kissed her breast. She gasped softly. It was amazing, after the battering her body had received, how he could still set it jangling with desire. With the lightest of touches. Of looks, even.

"Go back to bed," Alice murmured.

He pulled at her hand. "Only if you come with me." He had, she saw, that New York look in his eye. Smoldering, suggestive and thoroughly thrilling.

"I can't." Alice gestured at Rosa with her free hand. "She's not finished yet."

"OK," Jake nuzzled her neck. She shuddered with pleasure. "All I'm trying to do is support you. You do know that, don't you?"

Alice nodded, the tears springing suddenly to her tired and heavy eyes.

"You are happy, aren't you darling?" He was looking at her intently.

"Of course I'm happy."

"You don't regret giving up the rat race? Coming here to live with me?" A hank of long dark hair had dropped fetchingly into his eyes, its end touching his lips and making her stomach twist with longing.

She shook her head, sniffed again and smiled. "'Course not." She gathered the contentedly suckling Rosa closer to her. "How could I?"

"Good. I'm happy too, darling." He kissed her lingeringly on the lips. "And if you try harder with the breastfeeding, I'll be happier still."

*   *   *

In Fitzherbert Place, Hugo opened an eye. In the midnight dark, something was stirring. It was the baby. Or Theo, as they—or rather Amanda—had finally decided to call him. In vain had Hugo pointed out that he had been at school with a Theo, who, thanks to his lack of academic distinction, was widely known as Thicko. Hugo, who had hardly set the examiners on fire himself, feared the same fate for his son.

His ear strained into nothingness. Theo seemed to have gone back to sleep. Hugo, intending to do the same, burrowed thankfully back beneath the duvet.

Beside him, Amanda was sleeping like the proverbial log. Odd how he, rather than she, was always the one to wake up when the baby did. On the other hand, Amanda, these days, always slept with earplugs.

"But you won't be able to hear Theo crying," Hugo had objected.

"Exactly," said Amanda, squishing the foam rubber cylinders into her ears. "That's the point."

"But you're his mother."

"Yes, and you're his father. And Nurse Harris is his maternity nurse." With that, Amanda had turned over and pulled the duvet over her head.

Waaaaahhh! The high-pitched, indignant roar had begun again. Hugo never failed to be amazed that something as small as a baby could make such a huge noise. He jerked upright and looked at the clock: 2:37 A.M. He nudged Amanda.

She fiddled in her ear and removed one of the grubby plugs he was growing accustomed, but disgusted, to finding all over the bedroom floor and in the bed. "What's up?" she snarled.

"Theo. He's crying."

"Oh, for fuck's sake," Amanda snapped. "What the fuck's the fucking matter with him *now?*"

"He's a fucking baby, Amanda. That's what's the fucking matter with him."

"What's that fucking old bat doing then?" Amanda demanded furiously. "She's supposed to fucking see to him in the fucking night."

"Fuck knows," groaned Hugo.

Had the old bat even heard Theo? She usually did, it had to be said. Whenever Theo had gone off, as Hugo thought of it, in the past, the cries had almost immediately subsided amid the efficient sounds of doors softly opening and closing. But perhaps Nurse Harris was in a particularly deep sleep.

Bugger it, 2:38 A.M. was a sod of an hour to be getting up. And as Amanda clearly wasn't, he obviously was. As, cringing, Hugo peeled back the covers, the chill of the bedroom swept across his chest, which was bare like the rest of him. He had always slept in the nude, the better to be ready for action, as he had joked to various girlfriends through the years. Although now, practically celibate in the frozen depths of the country, he was beginning to wonder why he bothered. Lotti's assurances to Laura that sex could be resumed within weeks clearly did not apply in his case.

"I used to have a healthy sex life," he had moaned to Amanda a couple of nights ago.

"Oh, yeah? Who with?" she had snapped back.

WAAAAHHHHHH!!! As Amanda, sealed aurally against the world, had by now gone back to sleep, Hugo swung his legs out of bed. It was like submerging oneself in an agonizingly cold sea. Hugging his chest for warmth, he stumbled out of the bedroom and made his way upstairs to the third floor. At the nursery doorway, he grabbed the handle, pushed the door open, and froze. Froze even more than, in his completely naked state, he was doing already.

The nursery light was on. Bent over Theo's cot in the corner of the room was a familiar broad back. As Hugo stared, rooted in horror to the spot, the back turned and he was skewered in a bulging, boiled, horrified gaze. "Mr. Fine!" gasped Nurse Harris, a large hand flying to her chest.

Hugo turned and fled. But not before registering an astonishing fact. Nurse Harris, even at quarter to three in the morning, was wearing, not the candlewick and curlers one might have expected, but full dress uniform.

As Hugo skidded back down the stairs, he could hear Nurse Harris exclaiming to herself in tones of deep disgust. Quite what she was saying, he could not make out. But it seemed likely Lord Fairbourne came into it.

CHAPTER
10

CHRISTMAS WAS NOW APPROACHING AND ALICE FELT AS EXCITED AS a child. She had always been moved by the festive season. But the first Christmas with their baby would be so special it made her eyes prick just to think about it.

Special was certainly one way of describing their Christmas decorations. The homemade, undyed, recyclable cardboard tree was hung with blown lightbulbs salvaged from a Dumpster in which the stripped-out contents of an office had been thrown. "Baubles!" Jake had announced triumphantly, arriving back with a bulging plastic bag. Alice had seized them eagerly, imagining them the real, fragile, glittering thing. It had been hard to disguise her disappointment when they weren't, but she had tried to be pleased for the sake of the planet. And anyway, when hung, they covered up some of the grease stains on the cardboard.

Alice's contribution to the cardboard tree was to cut out images from old Christmas cards apparently salvaged from last year's rubbish.

She could not help contrasting this with the *King's College Christmas* tape and glasses of champagne traditionally accompanying her parents' tree-trimming. She dreaded them seeing Jake's. They wouldn't understand, she knew. Yet see it they would, for, despite her best efforts to discourage them, they were coming to stay over Christmas.

"We want to be with our new grandchild, darling," Mrs. Duffield had said, sounding hurt but determined as Alice tried yet again to put her off.

And if the tree was unlikely to impress them, the presents would still less. To Jake and herself the gifts were things of beauty, wrapped according to the most rigid of recycling principles as expounded in the festive issue of *Get Trashed!* Some were packed inside cereal boxes, and some stuffed into Jake's beloved toilet-roll tubes. All were wrapped around with toilet paper and decorated with ribbons made from the shiny insides of potato-chip bags.

But her parents *should* appreciate them, Alice thought crossly. It was their moral duty to. Didn't they realize how selfish they were being, perpetuating an endless grasping materialist culture that was slowly strangling the planet to death?

She resolved that when the time came to unwrap her own presents she would give an ecstatic reception to the bracelet made from old shoelaces her husband had just completed, and the abstract sculpture he was making on the kitchen table from the entrails of some redundant machine or other. *That* would show them.

*   *   *

In the foyer of the Bath boutique hotel where they had stopped for a break in their Christmas shopping, Hugo and Amanda sat sipping cappuccinos. Both were staring, unseeing, at the gold-sprayed apples heaped in a gold-sprayed urn that formed the establishment's take on the festive season. Both were lost in their own thoughts.

Amanda was thinking how much better life was when Theo was safely at home with Nurse Harris. The novelty of motherhood had worn off weeks ago. If she were honest, it wore off the afternoon he was born.

What all the fuss was about, she could not imagine. As anticlimaxes went, being a mother was the biggest ever. Hanging around the house all day waiting for her nipples to be attacked was an intensely dull way to spend her time.

She had, she now accepted, been overly optimistic about babies. There was nothing particularly fascinating about them; two days after bringing Theo home she'd been bored out of her mind. Perhaps it would have been easier if he wasn't so ugly and had been closer to the blond, blue-eyed cherub of her imagination. But Theo was skinny and dark like a monkey. Even though his hair was now turning fairer, it had a worrying ginger tinge.

Sitting in the hotel bar drinking her coffee, Amanda remembered the glossy magazines she had read on the plane from New York. Those visions of glamorous parenthood to which she had responded with such high hopes. The vast houses. The endless gardens. The happy, carefree, fulfilled mothers clutching exquisite infants. She could see now that, at the very least, those women were richer than she, and had more help. At worst, the features had all been complete lies. But why was that a surprise? She of all people should have known that the lifestyles peddled by magazines were fantasies. What a bloody idiot she had been.

*   *   *

Hugo too was thinking about work. Neil was champing at the bit to have him back at Dunn and Dustard. His paternity leave was about to expire and he was needed. Things were busy; there had, apparently, been an unexpected pre-Christmas rush on houses.

Hugo was secretly relieved his time at home was nearly over. Although he would never have admitted it to anyone, he felt no nearer to his son than he had when Theo first was born. This was due mostly to the fact that Nurse Harris seemed to dominate his every waking moment, ever ready to snatch her charge from inadequate parental hands. On one rare occasion, Hugo had taken Theo, bundled in a blanket, outside to show him the snow on the trees. Within seconds, Nurse Harris had shot out, grabbed the baby and disappeared back inside, muttering darkly about infant pneumonia.

"Come on. So much Christmas shopping, so little time!" Amanda poked Hugo painfully in the thigh with her high, sharp heel. "Next stop's the spa. I'm booking some pre-Christmas postnatal de-stressers."

Hugo wondered, with a maternity nurse to run everything, how stressful Amanda's postnatal period had actually been. Amanda's attention, however, was now focused on a large-nosed woman in a tight fuchsia suit at the lobby reception desk. She stiffened with excitement and half stood up, one hand clamping her napkin to her knees and the other waving wildly. "Laura! Over here!"

Laura whipped round on hearing her name. "Well, if it isn't you two!" she declared in the ringing foghorn voice he remembered from the prenatal classes. Laura's cleavage, Hugo saw as she tottered over, was still her most distinguishing feature. Predatory as ever, it threatened to burst the moorings of her suit buttons.

Laura enveloped Amanda in a heavily scented hug. As her chin rested on Amanda's tailored shoulder, she gave Hugo an emphatic wink. "Haven't seen you for a while," she drawled through a thickly lipsticked smile. "Where have you been hiding, handsome?"

"I've been busy," Hugo said shortly.

"With the baby, I suppose." Laura sat down, crossed her black-stockinged legs, produced a packet of cigarettes and lit one. "Bloody hell, I envy you," she said to Amanda. "Fergus can't be bothered to do anything with Django."

"Django?" Hugo repeated.

"What a wonderful name; you are clever," Amanda exclaimed. "Funnily enough, it was among the ones I was considering for Theo."

Hugo stared. He hadn't realized things had been *that* close.

Laura leaned over and ground her cigarette out in the ashtray. "Look, I'll give you a ring. I'd better go now. No, no, don't get up." She swayed to her feet, tugging down the short, tight skirt and loudly kissed Amanda. "See you around, gorgeous," she murmured throatily to Hugo as, kissing him too, she bent so far over him he could see the tips of her nipples.

As she clacked off across the marble, they gazed after her, Hugo with relief to see the back of her, Amanda with blazing curiosity.

"She's meeting someone," she murmured, craning her neck to look. "A man," she added excitedly. "Sort of blond and big. Very good-looking." A largish crowd was now filling the previously empty lobby, so it was difficult to be sure, between the bodies, who Laura was disappearing with toward the elevators. But in the light of what she had just said, it seemed unlikely it was Fergus.

* * *

When, finally, Hugo cranked on the emergency brake outside Fitzherbert Place, he felt unusually relieved to see it. The afternoon's shopping had been long, boring, crowded and alternately stifling hot and freezing cold as Amanda insisted on going in and out of what seemed like every single store. In the course of it, Hugo had decided that he hated Christmas, hated Bath and hated especially being Amanda's parcel-bearer, which meant attempting to walk along while laden like a gift-shop window and not fall over even though everyone he passed seemed to be trying to knock him off his feet.

In the kitchen, most unexpectedly, was a welcoming committee.

"Nurse Harris!" Amanda exclaimed, peeling her gloves off. "Are you cold, or something?"

Nurse Harris's coat, neatly belted over her uniform, was sitting on one of the Marie Antoinette chairs beneath the chandelier. The severity of her appearance only accentuated, Hugo thought, the room's ridiculous opulence. Kitchens were supposed to be functional places. Theirs looked like a ballroom with cookers.

A large brown suitcase, obviously packed, sat on the floor at Nurse Harris's side. "No," she said shortly. "I'm not cold."

"Well, it's very useful that you're here," Amanda said briskly, trotting over the Indian stone floor in her heels. "You can help Hugo carry the parcels in."

Nurse Harris raised her chin in an affronted manner. "I'm waiting for a taxi."

Amanda stopped dead in her tracks. "What?"

"A taxi?" Hugo echoed. "Are you going somewhere, Nurse Harris?"

"I am leaving this establishment, Mr. Fine."

"Hang on, hang on." Hugo held up both hands in panic. "*Why* are you leaving, Nurse Harris?"

Nurse Harris turned boiled, affronted eyes in his direction. "I'd rather not say, Mr. Fine. Not in front of Mrs. Fine, anyway."

"*Why* can't you say it in front of me?" Amanda demanded.

Hugo blushed to the roots of his hair. Oh God. He might have known Amanda would find out about the nursery incident sooner or later. He should have told her straight away. But the whole experience had been excruciating and he was sure she would only have laughed.

Nurse Harris said nothing, just stared accusingly at beet-faced Hugo.

As she did the calculations, the smile faded from Amanda's face. "*You?*" She looked aghast at Hugo. "And . . . *her?*"

"It's not what you think," Hugo assured her, panicked.

"No employer of mine," Nurse Harris thundered, "has had the extreme bad manners to show themselves *naked* to me before."

"*Naked?!*" Amanda screeched. Her head snapped from Nurse Harris to Hugo. "Bloody hell. Just can't keep it in your trousers, can you?"

"Look," Hugo pleaded. "I wasn't up to anything. You've got it wrong. What happened was a mistake."

"The oldest fucking line in the book," spat Amanda.

"I got up in the night to see to Theo," Hugo persevered desperately. "He was crying. I, um, couldn't find my pajamas. I didn't know Nurse Harris was there."

"A likely story," yelled Amanda.

"Please, darling. You've got to believe me."

The rattling sound of a taxi could be heard coming up the road. Seconds later, the lights flashed through the window. Nurse Harris stood up.

Amanda gripped a chair back. "You can't go," she informed Nurse Harris.

Nurse Harris bent and closed one large, thick-fingered hand round the handle of her suitcase.

"Is there nothing we can do to persuade you to stay?" Amanda's voice was hoarse with emotion. She was trying, Hugo realized, to appeal to Nurse Harris's soft side. He doubted this would work. Nurse Harris didn't have a soft side.

"Nothing whatsoever," the nurse confirmed. "This very lunchtime I accepted a post with," she dropped her voice to name a member of the Royal Family. "I'm a tolerant woman, Mrs. Fine . . ."

"You'll have to be if everything one hears about *them* is true," snapped Amanda furiously. She glowered at Hugo. "*Now* look what you've done," she shouted. "This is all your bloody fault."

"But nonetheless," Nurse Harris continued, looking disdainfully round the kitchen, "this isn't at *all* the sort of thing I'm used to. I can tell you, it wouldn't have—"

"Happened at Lord Fairbourne's," Hugo groaned as Nurse Harris picked up her suitcase, opened the door and stalked out into the night.

CHAPTER
11

"HAPPY CHRISTMAS, EVERYONE." JAKE PLACED A LARGE PLASTIC bowl of steaming sprouts down on the lunch table.

The three people sitting at it exchanged strained smiles. There was a definite atmosphere, although not, as Alice had feared, because of the presents. These had not yet been opened.

The point at issue was that Alice's parents, on arrival at their Bath hotel, had discovered that their reserved suite had been canceled and something smaller and cheaper booked in its place. It had then been discovered that Jake had done the rebooking.

"But why, Jake?" Alice remonstrated, her ear still hot from the angry telephone call from her mother.

"They didn't need a room that size." Jake spoke without a hint of apology. "And I gave the difference in price to the homeless."

But doing the "right thing," as Jake called it, had moved on since then. On Christmas Day, it meant jollying everyone along and preventing any awkward moments. Fortunately, her parents seemed determined to make similar efforts.

"That's a very nice bowl," Alice's mother remarked, looking at the sprouts.

Jake flashed all his teeth at Mrs. Duffield. "Glad you like it. It used to be the front of an old washing machine."

"How terribly clever of you to think of doing that with your old machine!"

"Oh, it wasn't ours," Jake said breezily. "I found it on the landfill and brought it home. It was a waste, leaving it where it was."

"How interesting," Mrs. Duffield muttered into the napkin with which she was delicately dabbing the corners of her mouth and which, had she known it, was cut from one of Jake's old T-shirts.

There was a silence as the sprouts were ladled out using the cup from the top of an erstwhile Thermos, the bottom of which stood as a vase in the center of the table with a bunch of greenery in it.

Everyone picked up the plastic knives and forks routinely collected by Jake from any fast food outlet he happened to be passing.

"Beer?" Jake offered Alice's father.

"Thank you." Mr. Duffield looked doubtfully at the former gasoline container from which a weak brown stream of liquid was issuing into the jam jar by his plate. He picked up the jar and tasted it gingerly. "Home brew, is it?"

Jake nodded vigorously. "Best way to thwart the multinationals. Brew it in the bath."

Alice's father made no comment. Particularly he made no comment about having worked in a legal capacity for a despised beer multinational for many years.

Alice slid him a grateful yet defensive glance. That her parents thought their son-in-law rude was obvious. But what they didn't understand was that Jake was an idealist.

"In the bath?" Mrs. Duffield echoed in horror. "What do you use to wash poor Rosa if the bath's full of beer?"

"Not the *upstairs* bath." Jake grinned at her. "The one in the garden I got from the dump."

Alice's mother looked puzzled. "I didn't see a bath in the garden."

"It's round the back," Alice muttered.

"Although I must say you've got plenty of old loos and sinks outside the *front* door," Mr. Duffield remarked jovially. "I counted about fifteen altogether. Are you storing them for someone? Or just planning five or six new bathrooms?"

Jake looked horrified at the suggestion. "They're reclaimed."

"Jake's using some of the loos as planters," Alice added loyally.

The meal continued in silence.

"How's the magazine going?" Alice's father asked Jake, after a while. "Booming, I should think. Everyone's very green these days."

Alice clenched her buttocks slightly. The magazine was a touchy subject at the moment.

"Nowhere near as green as they should be," Jake said sourly. "Which is why, since you ask, the mag's not doing as well as *it* should be. People have yet to catch up with the *Get Trashed!* take on eco responsibility."

"I see." Alice's father was nodding gravely. "So you've got to water down the message to suit them, you mean? I can see that would be annoying."

Jake's eyes flashed. "Of course I'm not watering down the message. If anything, I'm doing the opposite. People need a kick up the arse about the planet. We've got to show the way, whether people want to hear about it or not."

"But if your magazine's not selling . . ." Alice's mother faltered.

". . . how are you managing to, um . . ." Alice's father faltered too.

"Pay myself?" Jake enquired archly. "And the staff and the printers?"

"Well . . . yes."

Jake dug a reclaimed plastic fork fiercely into a sprout. "I'm managing, thanks." The fork snapped.

Alice did not look at him. She thought of her gradually dwindling bank balance he was managing on and hoped her parents would change the subject.

"Delicious sprouts," remarked Alice's mother.

"Sprouts? Glad you like them!" Jake, jauntiness restored, proffered some more. "All homegrown and totally organic. We can't wait for Ro to get on to solids, can we, Al? She's going to have such fantastic food."

"That's right." Alice looked at the green spheres on her plate. Or, rather, the former frisbee which served as one. Picking them in the freezing cold had been ghastly, particularly when the means they grew by was taken into consideration.

"You grew them yourself? How clever of you," Mrs. Duffield made a determined effort at brightness. "How *is* the garden these days? Worms getting on well, are they?"

Alice sighed. The worms were doing as badly as ever. The fact that Jake had another obsession in the garden—his vegetable patch—had, she hoped, been an opportunity to take them to the nearest bait shop. But he had rumbled her plans at the last minute.

Her heart sank as she heard Jake begin to describe his Yin-and-Yang vegetable patch. "The Yin side's mostly white vegetables, turnips, onions and so on. Whereas the Yang is darker—beets, that kind of thing. And sprouts, of course." Sprouts, of course, being the only thing that actually grew, Alice thought. Yin and Yang or no Yin and Yang.

Mrs. Duffield was nodding. Alice could almost see the hope rising within her that here, at last, was something she and her difficult son-in-law could have a conversation about.

"And what sort of fertilizer do you use?" she asked.

"Fertilizer?" Jake grinned. "The original and best fertilizer on the market."

"Ooh, do tell," urged Mrs. Duffield. "I'm always looking for good ones. Not blood, fish and bone, then?"

"Human sewage," Jake beamed. "Cheap, easy, accessible and frankly unbeatable. And planet-friendly, obviously."

There was an exploding noise. Alice's father had spat out his Brussels sprouts into his napkin. His face was puce with disgust as he laid the bundle on the plastic surface of the shower curtain that, having failed to make an appearance at Rosa's birth, was now doing service as a festive tablecloth.

Alice's mother looked at her daughter in horror. "Excuse me," she muttered, pushing back her chair and thundering upstairs to the bathroom.

*   *   *

At Fitzherbert Place, things for Hugo were going every bit as badly. Take this morning, for example. Amanda had come storming into the bathroom and let rip, Christmas or no Christmas.

"What the hell do you think you're doing?" she had demanded.

"Changing Theo's nappy," Hugo said crossly. "What does it look like?"

"It looks like my bloody face cream!" Amanda yelled, grabbing the small white tube out of Hugo's hand. She shook it at him. "Have you any idea how much this costs?"

Hugo sighed. He had been unable to find normal nappy cream and was improvising.

"This," growled Amanda, still brandishing the tube, "is a special skin treatment. It plumps out lines and adds radiance."

"Well, if it's any comfort," Hugo retorted, "Theo's bottom looks very radiant."

"You're useless," exploded Amanda.

"Hello Pot, meet Kettle," snapped back Hugo.

Nurse Harris's departure had revealed more than Hugo in the nude. It had also exposed the fact that neither he nor Amanda had the first idea about even basic baby care. Neither knew his or her way around a nappy, and they were constantly losing count of the scoops when mixing the bottles of formula. But whether Theo was being under- or overfed seemed to make no difference. He cried all the same, all the time.

Following Amanda's own nappy-changing attempts after lunch, Theo appeared looking traumatized in some lopsided Pampers and the present-opening began. Hugo received a book called *Brain Child—How Smart Parents Make Smart Kids,* from his wife. She, meanwhile, received one from Laura, a novel called *Faux Pas.* "It's about a girl with father issues, apparently," she said, reading the blurb on the back. Hugo made a mental note to read it. He had a few father issues himself.

"Happy Christmas!" he said as the champagne cork exploded with a violence that made the baby jump almost out of his bouncer. His bottom lip trembled and he burst into tears.

"Oh, shit," said Hugo impatiently, more to himself than Theo.

"Well, it's hardly his bloody fault," Amanda pointed out savagely. "Get his first Christmas Day off with a bang, why don't you?"

"I'm going to miss this." He grinned ironically at Amanda as Theo roared on.

She looked up from sloshing more wine into her glass. "What do you mean?"

"When I get back into the hamster wheel." Hugo rolled his eyes in mock despair. "Back to the grindstone. Work."

"Oh, that reminds me." Amanda gave him a dazzling smile. Hugo's insides twinged in warning. "What?"

"I've got a job."

Hugo blinked. He raised his hand. "Hang on a minute. Stop. Rewind. What do you mean," he said, slowly, "you've got a job?"

"Anne Dexter's been sacked from *Class* and they've asked me to step in. Temporarily at first, but they're going to see how it goes."

She punched the air with triumph. "I'm an editor!"

"But you never told me about this!" Hugo exclaimed. "I mean . . ."

"When did it happen?" Amanda leaped in. "Christmas Eve. Yesterday."

"No, not that. How . . ."

"Much are they going to pay me? *Lots!*" Amanda shrieked. Theo, who had briefly stopped crying, started to wail again.

"Not that," Hugo said, more forcibly. "What I was trying to say is—who's going to look after Theo?"

Amanda opened wide astonished eyes. "I hope you're not imagining," she said with a disbelieving titter, "that *I'm* staying out in the sticks changing nappies? A woman of my caliber? With the talents I've got to offer the world?"

"But you're Theo's mother!" Hugo exclaimed. "What about . . . ?" What about, he was going to challenge, all the declarations about motherhood being the ultimate career and the best job satisfaction available? But, quite suddenly, he found himself speechless. The carpet had been whipped so utterly from under him that he felt almost physically winded.

"Yes, I *am* his mother." Amanda's face had the appearance of a cornered rodent. "*And you're his bloody father.*"

"But," Hugo yelled, recovering slightly, "*I've* got to go back to work. My paternity leave expires next week."

"Tough," Amanda said lightly. She raised her champagne glass triumphantly. "I've done my bit. I had him. Over to you, buddy."

* * *

Meanwhile, at the Old Morgue, the gloom that had begun with the hotel bookings and deepened over the fertilizer showed no signs of lifting now everyone was gathering beside the recycled cardboard tree for the present opening.

Alice watched tensely as her mother began to pick apart the toilet paper covering her gift. "I suppose," she said brightly, "we should be grateful this hasn't been used before as well!"

As her father exploded with mirth, Alice did not dare look at Jake.

"It's made from an old computer keyboard," she eagerly told her mother, who was releasing from its confines the chunky ring featuring her initials.

"How lovely," said Mrs. Duffield in strained tones. She slipped it on beside her Garrard diamonds and stretched her hand out to admire the effect.

Alice's father, meanwhile, who detested gardening, was staring nonplussed at his waterproof garden-kneeler made from strips of old wallpaper.

They had bought Jake some Umberto Eco novels. "Joke, you see," Alice's mother urged him. "Eco—get it? You being an environmentalist and all that."

But Jake was not smiling. His brow clenched as he examined the bleached paper the books were printed on; he was, Alice knew, calculating the exact amount of tree involved.

Alice had warned her parents not to bring too many presents for her. She saw now that they had circumvented this by buying a very small number of great value. She tried to suppress her thrilled excitement over her cashmere dressing gown for fear of offending Jake. But Jake was offended anyway over the flashing, talking Minnie Mouse Alice's parents had brought their granddaughter and which Rosa, now up after her lunchtime sleep, adored on sight.

Later, in the bathroom, Alice was changing Rosa when her mother slipped in. "Can I have a word, darling?"

Alice's heart sank. She had sensed this was coming and had been trying to avoid the word all afternoon.

"Darling, I know he means well," Mrs. Duffield predictably began.

"He doesn't only mean well," Alice attacked immediately. "He does well too. He practices what he preaches."

Alice's mother put a restraining hand—now minus the computer-key ring—on her arm. "No need to be so defensive. Honestly, darling, you're such a teenager sometimes. I only want to ask a question. You might be able to help me understand."

"What's the question?" Alice grumpily pulled the terry over Rosa's leg rather tighter than was necessary. The baby squeaked in protest.

"Those bathtubs, loos and sinks piled in the garden. And the washing machine. And all the rubbish inside the house as well."

"Jake's waste transfer stations, you mean?" Alice conscientiously employed her husband's preferred euphemism.

"I was just wondering about them."

"Wondering what about them?"

Mrs. Duffield took a deep breath, "Surely it's one thing, and one very laudable thing too, to recycle one's own household rubbish. Most people try and do it to a certain extent. But, darling, isn't it entirely another to go out, collect lots of rubbish from somewhere else and bring it all home?"

Alice rebutted the accusation immediately. "You don't understand, Mum. Jake runs a recycling magazine and he's got to—"

"Yes, dear. Practice what he preaches, I know. But bringing all that junk in from elsewhere is a bit excessive, don't you think? I just wondered," her mother continued gently, "is Jake trying to recycle, not just his own rubbish, but that of the entire world?"

Alice was silent.

"And some of the things he recycles, darling." Mrs. Duffield shook her neatly bouffanted pepper-and-salt head. "That Christmas cake . . ."

Alice tensed. Admittedly, the uncertain, broken squiggles that, with the aid of a former toothpaste tube rinsed out and with its end cut off, Jake had piped over the wholemeal vegan Christmas cake were not particularly beautiful.

"Darling, how exactly is that going to save the planet? How many times a year, apart from Christmas, does one actually use a cake-icer, and isn't it worth investing in a nice metal one that would last and do a good job rather than—"

"Mother, that's enough." Alice picked up Rosa and headed out of the bathroom. Before she could, Mrs. Duffield caught her by the arm. Her smile had vanished.

"Alice, it's *not* enough." The gentle tones had turned serious. "And you can't just storm off in the middle of a discussion. Apart from being a grown-up, you're a lawyer. A professional logician. You're trained to listen to both sides of an argument. Why can't you hear me out?"

Alice looked at her mother resentfully. In her arms, Rosa began to mew and wriggle.

"Alice, your father and I are worried about you."

"Worried? There's nothing to be worried about. I've never been happier in my life," Alice said scornfully.

Her mother looked down, biting her lip. "Darling, of course we're glad you're, er, so happy. It's just that some things make us—well—wonder. You know, you used to be such a career woman—high-powered, happy—"

"I wasn't happy," Alice rebutted fiercely. "At the time I met Jake I'd never been so miserable in my life."

Mrs. Duffield raised an eyebrow. "Well then—you were doing your own thing. And doing it very well—"

"I've got a different career now," Alice snapped, jiggling Rosa in her arms. "A *much* more important and rewarding one."

"And that's great, darling, really it is. Rosa *is* adorable." Her grandmother looked at her fondly.

"So what's the problem?" Alice demanded.

Mrs. Duffield hesitated. She put out an arm and pulled at Rosa's nappy. "Well, this sort of thing, for a start. I know terries are planet friendly, but they're not very life friendly. Believe me, I remember. And it's much worse for you, being restricted to only four."

"Er, three actually," mumbled Alice. Any more, Jake had decided, would be profligate.

Mrs. Duffield rolled her eyes. "Why make being a new mother even more difficult than it is? There are lots of convenient green whatsits around. I've been doing some research." Rummaging in the pocket of her neat fawn slacks, she produced a catalog and held it out to her daughter.

The thought of her mother researching—no doubt with enormous difficulty—the unfamiliar area of earth-friendly baby bottom products was touching. Nonetheless, Alice let indignation get the better of her. She took the catalog abruptly and laid it on the changing table. "Terries are fine, Mum. They're not that difficult."

"And then there's the breastfeeding thing." Mrs. Duffield looked pleadingly at her daughter. "The odd bottle would help *so* much. Formula's not poison, you know."

"Jake thinks it is," Alice muttered.

"Well, it isn't. You're living proof that it isn't. You were on it from two weeks old."

Alice looked up in surprise. "Was I?"

"Yes," said her mother firmly. "And what exactly did he mean about Rosa and solids? He's surely not going to have you slaving away making everything she eats out of the . . . *garden?*" She swallowed and edged a hand up her throat.

"Of course not." In truth, Alice had no idea what Jake had meant. Or what solids might mean. She'd been too tired to think about it. But they surely couldn't be worse than the endless agonizing struggle with breastfeeding.

Her mother looked doubtful. "Well, just remember, you can get jars of organic baby food now. You must do everything you can to make it easier for yourself, darling. You look exhausted."

"I'm *not* exhausted." Alice felt her eyeballs weighing heavy and aching in their sockets. But she was determined not to let slip a single word that was not loyal to Jake.

"There's no need to pretend," her mother said gently. "Believe me, I can see what you see in him. Jake is quite extraordinarily handsome."

Alice gave her a faint, proud smile. "He is, isn't he?"

"I think he's probably one of the best-looking men I've ever seen. And with a very powerful personality as well. But, darling, don't you think your and Jake's lifestyle is, well, a bit extreme? I'm all for recycling, darling—who isn't? But I really think Jake takes it too far. No one could live the way he wants them to, although you're trying your very best, admittedly." She looked sadly at the milk crate changing table before meeting Alice's eyes again. "I hate to say this, darling, but it's almost as if you've been brainwashed."

Alice was white with anger. "How dare you? How I live my life is no business of yours."

Mrs. Duffield had tears in her eyes. "I know. And I wouldn't have said anything. Except that I love you, and your father loves you. Believe me, darling, I would much rather have said nothing. But we're both worried about what's happening to you."

"Well don't. Worry about the planet instead." Clutching Rosa closely to her, Alice marched out of the bathroom. If her mother was unable to understand the finer points of Jake's crusade against rubbish, the fault lay in her. Not him.

CHAPTER
12

"I DON'T KNOW WHY YOU'RE SCREAMING," HUGO MUTTERED, stumbling into the nursery at God only knew what hour of the night.

Why, Hugo thought, was the one place he himself was so desperate to be—bed—such anathema to his son? What was so wrong with lying down and being warm and comfortable? This lack of logic seemed only to widen the gulf between them.

After half an hour of fruitless pacing up and down in the cold, the frustrated and exhausted Hugo decided to stick Theo back in his cot and ignore the wails as best he could. The baby, however, had other plans. Obviously sensing such a plot was afoot, he shot out a chubby arm and wrenched off Hugo's glasses.

This had become a favorite trick of Theo's of late, albeit one he could only employ when his father was not wearing his contact lenses. He was good at seizing his chances, however, and now, with his defenses down, Hugo was easily outmaneuvered. The glasses clattered to the floor and in the dim illumination of the night-light Hugo was completely unable to see where they had gone. As he crawled around on all fours on the hard boards of the nursery floor, Theo, now back in his cot, roared triumphantly on.

"Shit!"

The night-light bulb blew out. Thanks to the black-painted windows, the way out was now impossible to see. Hugo stepped on a plastic turtle belonging to his son, shot across the floor at a terrifying velocity and crashed head first into Theo's chest of drawers. Head throbbing, he crawled across the nursery floor, feeling his way through the booby traps formed by scattered toys.

Theo screamed on. It was obvious that he wasn't going back to sleep. Hugo dragged his wrist toward himself and saw that it was quarter to six. As the baby, quite clearly, had started his day, Hugo miserably accepted the inevitable. "Time for bottle and bath, Theo," he announced with all the cheer he could muster.

Hugo had long since stopped looking to Amanda for help. Up at dawn and down the road shortly afterward in the gleaming BMW supplied by the magazine company, his wife had neither time nor interest for anything other than her new job.

"Your turn now," she told Hugo baldly. "It's up to you to look after him. By yourself."

Almost the first decision Hugo made by himself was that he absolutely could not look after Theo. Not without professional back-up and certainly not full time; he was as determined as ever to return to work. And as, after the Nurse Harris experience, the idea of live-in help filled him with dread, he decided to seek it from a nursery.

Finding the right one had taken time, however. This was not because Hugo was looking for perfection. He was merely looking for somewhere that wasn't full. Chicklets was the only one in the whole of Bath that had places available for babies this side of Theo's twenty-first birthday, albeit only mornings.

This was a blow to Hugo's plans, not least because it meant working for Dunn and Dustard part-time. Arranging this, Hugo knew, would be far from easy. Neil's dinosaur views on family matters had been aired more than once in the office. His best hope, Hugo calculated, was to schedule a meeting with his boss after one of his typically liquid lunches.

"He wouldn't have a free slot in the afternoon, would he?" Hugo wheedled Neil's secretary Shuna over the phone in as syrupy a voice as he could manage. He doubted this would have much effect, but he persevered. He had realized soon after starting at Dunn and Dustard that Shuna, whose contempt for the human race seemed general, reserved particular loathing for him. Her hostility made sense after Neil let slip that her boyfriend had applied for Hugo's job.

"He's free at half past nine in the morning tomorrow," she snapped. "But that's it. Take it or leave it."

"I'll take it, thank you Shuna," Hugo said with every appearance of contentment. Inside, however, he despaired. The optimum bear-with-a-sore-head slot was his.

Half past nine in the morning was, in addition, a time Theo was guaranteed to be awake. Very much awake; bouncing-off-the-walls awake, in fact. Which was unfortunate, as Theo would have to come to the meeting. Hugo could hardly leave him in the house by himself.

Next day at nine thirty-five on the dot, Hugo arrived at his erstwhile and hopefully future part-time workplace with a wriggling baby under his arm and a number of smears on his lapel which Shuna made a point of staring at as he passed her desk.

"Come in," Neil said, every bit as grumpily as Hugo had feared. Slumped, bloodshot and crumpled over his desk, he looked at Theo with horror. "He's not going to yell, is he? I've got a hell of a headache."

"I don't think so," Hugo said, more confidently than he felt. Fortunately the baby, fascinated into silence by the novel sights and smells of the first office he had ever encountered, was less interested in making trouble than he was in the depressed weeping fig in a dusty pot by Neil's desk. Hugo sat down and struggled to keep his keen-to-explore son in his lap while he outlined his plan for returning to work.

"So basically," he finished, "mornings only would be fantastic."

Neil rubbed his red, bristly face and looked doubtful. "I don't hold with part-timers," he grumped. "What's this all about anyway? I thought you were the shit-hot salesman with the lethal charm, not the househusband in the handknit sweater." He stared at Theo, who was wriggling on Hugo's pinstriped knee. "Didn't realize you were so politically correct," he added disapprovingly.

Hugo sighed, grasping the baby around the waist to stop him lunging at the plant leaves he so clearly longed to rip off. "It's nothing to do with political correctness," he said loudly over Theo's protests. "Or handknit sweaters. It's to do with the fact Theo can only go to nursery in the mornings. And the fact Amanda's in London all day every day."

"That woman's wiping the floor with you. You should tell her, Fine."

Hugo did not bother to say that he had, in fact, aired his concerns to Amanda. That she hadn't been interested in hearing them would not, he sensed, raise him in Neil's estimation. Besides, he was desperate to stop Theo making any more noise. He rummaged in his pocket for a pacifier, praying he had remembered to put one in. He hadn't.

"I'll have to think about it," said Neil.

"Well, can you think about it now? Otherwise I'm afraid I'll have to look elsewhere." Desperation had made Hugo bold. His tired nerves, he knew, would not stand another interview elsewhere accompanied by Theo. Attracted by the glitter, the baby was now swiping in the direction of Neil's paperweight.

It was a gamble. Neil shot him a look. Hugo's ears filled with fizzing tension.

Theo, he realized, had stopped wriggling. His face was now bright red and his entire small being concentrated on some huge straining effort. Oh God, thought Hugo. Not here. Not now. But already wafting up into his nostrils was that familiar, pungent scent. Within seconds, he knew, the entire office would reek of it. For more reasons than just one he needed a quick decision out of Neil.

"I *suppose* we could make an exception," Neil said, after what seemed to Hugo like hours. "Not every firm would. Most wouldn't, in fact. But I *suppose* we could make it work."

Hugo felt a powerful flood of relief. "Thanks, Neil," he said humbly, repenting the unflattering thoughts he had entertained about this man in the past. Neil was decent after all. "That's great."

"At a lower hourly rate, of course. To reflect the lower overall commitment." There was a sly look on his boss's face.

Hugo bit back his indignation. *Bastard.* In the time he'd been at Dunn and Dustard, he'd moved more houses than you could shake a surveyor's report at. Lower commitment? How bloody *dare* Neil, the drunken, lazy . . .

He thanked his boss calmly, however. It seemed to him he had little choice. Apart from wanting to keep a toe in the water of adult existence—even if it was only *this* water—he needed whatever money could be brought in at the moment. The bills Amanda had racked up at Fitzherbert Place were horrendous, Nurse Harris had not yet been paid and the nursery fees, even for mornings only, were considerable. It would, in addition, be some time before Amanda's new salary reached the household. If it ever did.

"God," said Neil, as Hugo and Theo prepared to leave his office. "What's that awful stink? Drains or something?"

"Smells like it," said Hugo, exiting hurriedly. "I'd get them seen to if I were you."

*   *   *

Theo's first day at Chicklets dawned a particularly wet one. Rain so hard it sounded like a concert audience clapping hammered the windows of Fitzherbert Place. As he set off late despite his efforts not to be, Hugo thought thankfully of

Chicklets' car park, adjacent to the nursery's front steps. They should at least escape a soaking.

His previous visits to Chicklets not having been this early in the morning, Hugo was unprepared for the volume of traffic about. In particular the Panzer division of vast, gleaming people carriers that greeted him as he turned into the nursery street. It was like encountering a military convoy head on in the wrong direction.

Aggressively revving, hazard lights flashing, radios thumping, manned by wild-eyed women whose height seemed in inverse proportion to the hugeness of their vehicles, the Range Rovers, Land Cruisers and SUVs of all other imaginable types blocked the road and the sidewalks for what seemed at least half a mile. The nursery car park was clearly out of the question.

Hugo looked doubtfully out at the streaming rain. Then, glancing at the dashboard clock, his doubts scattered. He was fifteen minutes late for work. Like it or not, he and Theo would have to swim their way to Chicklets.

With a stab of joyful relief, Hugo remembered he had, some days ago in a fit of efficiency, put the fold-up baby buggy in the trunk. A conveyance, moreover, that came with its own rain protection.

"Don't worry," he assured Theo. "We'll have you covered up in a flash." Dragging the plastics out of their protective covering, Hugo shook them out and stared at them. Contrary to his confident expectations, there was no indication as to which hook, tape or stud went where. Not for the first time he suspected the hand of a baby-hating sadist in the manufacture of child-related equipment.

As the rain intensified, so did Theo's howls. Kneeling down on the pavement, the wet soaking into his trousers, Hugo wanted to howl too as he struggled despairingly with the recalcitrant strips of Velcro and apparently mate-less studs and holes. To add insult to injury, the buggy's fold-out canopy, theoretically forming a weatherproof roof over the infant's head, kept falling off its side attachments and hanging drunkenly over Theo's face.

Hugo miserably imagined the uninspiring picture he must present to these mothers. Fumbling, crumpled, clueless, cruel, even, with Theo screaming like a banshee against the unaccustomed wet. The very essence of paternal uselessness, in fact. A *man*, for God's sake. Trying to care for a baby on his own. What the hell, they were no doubt wondering, did he think he was doing?

And it was, Hugo thought, tugging once more at the Velcro with the cold, raw hands of an Arctic fisherman, a good question.

"Can I help?" The voice, above his head, was as sonorous as that of the Angel Gabriel. He looked up into the face of a red-haired woman with a handsome, if harassed, lean face. He registered with amazement that humor and sympathy, rather than contempt and disgust, were twitching about her mouth.

She crouched down. "You slip these loops over the handles first. Then you stick the studs at the bottom through here. Then slip it over and . . . *voilà!*" Within seconds, it seemed, Theo was snugly encased in plastic. A flood of gratitude more substantial even than the shower swept over Hugo.

"You Chicklets?" the woman asked. "Me too," she smiled as he nodded. She stuck out a wet hand. "I'm Barbara. I must say, it's great to see a man doing all this."

"But not very well," Hugo said apologetically.

"More than a lot of men bother doing, believe me." Barbara flashed a rueful smile at him. "Must dash, anyway. Work." She rolled her eyes. "Nice to meet you . . . er . . ."

"Hugo. And, er, thanks . . ." As he stammered his gratitude to her retreating back, he realized the rain was easing. Indeed, it had almost stopped. He could even feel the sun on his back. The plastic had been fitted just in time to be removed.

With Theo now steaming up under his covering, Hugo pressed hurriedly on to Chicklets. The place was a hubbub of people; the corridor crammed with mothers rushing to drop off their children and race off to work before the nine o'clock deadline. Adding to the frantic, almost hysterical atmosphere was the fact everyone was expected to slip electric-blue plastic galoshes over their shoes before entering any of the children's rooms.

The idea, Hugo gathered from the large information notice taped to the baby room entrance, was to safeguard the infants by keeping their surroundings clean. The much greater potential damage to the babies if their parents fell over while trying to snap galoshes on while holding them didn't seem to give rise for concern.

In the baby room, a capable-looking nursery assistant seized Theo from Hugo. "Go now and don't make a fuss," she instructed. "Particularly on the first day." With a mixture of relief and, unexpectedly, something like muscles tearing around his heart, Hugo turned his back and plunged out.

On the nursery steps, where he had left the buggy, he now faced the reverse struggle of folding it all up again. He was just congratulating himself on the remarkable speed with which he had removed the plastic and restored everything to its original golf bag shape when he realized he had closed the handles around his ankle. He tugged, but to no avail. He lifted his knee and shook it, but the parental ball and chain held fast. "Fuck it," muttered Hugo. "I'm the Mr. bloody Bean of parenting."

"*Hi*, handsome!"

Her. Complete with plunging cleavage and full makeup, despite the early hour.

"Hello, Laura," Hugo said stiffly, jiggling his trapped leg agitatedly. "How are you?"

"All the better for seeing *you*, sexy. It's been *ages*." She wiggled her hips at him. "So what's a gorgeous guy like you doing in a place like this?"

"Trying to get out of it," Hugo said irritably, shaking his leg again.

Laura looked down and burst into loud laughter. "Hugo! You're stuck!"

"I had noticed."

She squatted down—with difficulty, given the tightness of her jeans. Amid a great deal of cleavage-heaving and what seemed rather unnecessary pressing of her face against his groin, she managed to un-concertina the back of the buggy and release him. She pouted up at him, batting her eyelashes.

"Thanks," Hugo said, grasping the buggy handles. "I'd better be off now."

Laura, however, seemed determined to delay him. "Didn't know your boy had started *here*," she grinned, smoothing her hot-pink tracksuit top over skintight denim hips. She had a talent, Hugo noticed, for making the most innocent remark appear a double entendre.

"He's starting today." Hugo flinched as she started picking Weetabix crust off his collar. It was too intimate a gesture for that time in the morning—for any time, come to that.

"Django's here too," she said. "When he's not off with conjunctivitis."

Hugo had no idea what conjuctivitis was. It sounded like an East European tennis player to him. He glanced at his watch. "Look, Laura, much as I'd like to stay here all day talking—"

"You've got work to go to, sure."

"Yes."

He started to walk down the steps. Laura walked with him, twining her arm through his.

"Fancy a coffee?" she suggested. "There's a good place just round the corner."

"Er, like I just said, I've got to go to work. Sorry."

"Oh, *go on*. Just a quick one."

Hugo, looking into her eyes and about to refuse, saw

something there that he was not expecting. Something beyond mere flirtation. Something begging and desperate. His surprise made him pause.

"Please?" Laura said, in a small voice.

"Oh, OK then." The words were out before he could stop them. But what the hell? He was so late already he may as well be really late. Besides, he was under an obligation to her, thanks to that wretched bloody sabotage buggy. And having a coffee with her now would at least save him having to have one with her in the future. "Just a very quick one, though. I've got to get to the office."

"Have you gone back to the real estate agents'?" Laura asked as they went down the nursery steps.

"Yes."

"The same one? Dunn and whatsit?"

"Yes."

"Only Amanda told me during our last spa session that you were going to be a househusband. We had quite a laugh, imagining you naked in a frilly pinny waving a feather duster."

"Did you?" Hugo said stiffly. He could imagine the scene all too well. The spa one, that was. The other he preferred not to think about.

"Oh yes." Laura dug him suggestively in the ribs. "I could quite see you hoovering in the nude and knocking back the Baileys. I imagine," she added, low and throaty, "that you'd look rather gorgeous."

Hugo now bitterly regretted the moment of compassionate madness that had led to him agreeing to this coffee. He resolved to get it over with as soon as possible.

"When's Amanda coming back?" Laura's elbows were spread out on the table and spread out on top of those was her cleavage. Quite a few of the male customers had slid sidelong glances at it already.

"Coming back? Er . . ." Trust her to ask him the ultimate unanswerable question. For how was he to know? Amanda had rung last night to say she'd been working so late at the office she was going to stay at the company's Soho flat. She might, she hinted, be doing the same tonight. And possibly tomorrow as well. "But you'll be fine holding the fort with Theo, won't you?" she had trilled. "Frankly, sweetie, you'd better be. You're going to have to get used to it. I might be going to New York next week."

"But . . ." Hugo had protested, aghast. Too late. Click. Burr. Amanda had gone.

"Later this week," he told Laura firmly. "She's very busy with work."

Laura's thickly mascaraed lashes fluttered downwards. "Work! Lucky her. Must be nice."

"Why must it be nice?" Hugo asked glumly, remembering how late he was.

"Having some sort of meaning to your life." Laura's mood had switched abruptly. Her tone now was bitter.

Hugo wasn't sure what Laura meant, or that he necessarily wanted to know. Sensing dark, deep waters, he picked up his cup and drained as much of those dark, slightly scalding, waters as he could, anxious to make his escape as quickly as possible.

Laura jerked her chin up and sniffed. Her eyes, Hugo saw, were swimming with tears.

"What's the matter?" he asked reluctantly.

She shook her head. "Nothing." He was tempted for a second to take her at her word. To say "oh, okay then," and get up and go. Instead, he found himself patting her hand and saying, "Well it doesn't look like nothing. You're crying. Come on. Tell me what's wrong."

"No one told me it would be like this," Laura gulped.

"But I thought you liked it. I imagined you must come here a lot."

She flung him an impatient look. "Not the café, for Christ's sake. Having a fucking baby." She bit her lip. Her face crumpled and reddened.

Shit. He'd been right about the deep waters. Oh why hadn't he escaped when he had the chance? Sitting on the minimalist iron seat, Hugo clenched his buttocks with frustration. "How do you mean?" he hedged. "Not that bad, is it?" Laura, after all, was a woman. She was bound to have a better grip on things than him.

Laura's head was now slumped onto her elbows. She spoke in a dreary monotone. "Depends what you mean by not bad. Sitting in my bathrobe for days on end on my own. Too knackered to get dressed because the baby keeps me awake all night. Only ever seeing the milkman. Listening to shit plays on Radio Four about invisible housewives and Scottish submariners while I feed Django for hours and hours and *hours*. Stuffing myself with leftover Christmas chocolates and panicking whenever I lose the Gina Ford book. Feeling angry all the time. Going completely fucking mad, basically." She slipped a hand round to her back pocket and pulled out a pack of cigarettes.

"But what about Fergus?" Hugo asked.

Laura cackled. "What about him? *Got a big campaign on at the moment, yeah?*" She imitated what was presumably his voice. Even from this Hugo gathered it was harsh, brusque and accustomed to getting its own way. She inhaled savagely on her cigarette.

"What campaigns does he work on?" The sooner they reentered shallower, more general waters, the sooner he could get away.

Laura exhaled in a great angry rush. "His main clients are anti dog-poo products for people's gardens. He sits in his office all day thinking up names like Doo Don't, Shit Happens and Piss Off My Lawn."

"Can't you get a nanny to help?" Hugo's eyes darted to his watch.

"Nannies?" Laura snorted. She touched the top of her head. "Had them up to here already. The secret smokers, the ones who smash up the car, the ones who won't do laundry, the ones who get stroppy if Django's sick on them, the ones who shag Fergus, on the few occasions he's actually here . . ."

"Shag Fergus?"

Laura nodded, eyes screwed up against the smoke. "Fergus is one of those men who think monogamy's some sort of wood."

Hugo remembered the man Laura had been with in the hotel foyer at Christmas. He did not comment.

"So now I'm trying Chicklets," Laura groaned. "Sticking him in a nursery for a few hours so I can try and get my head together. Hey. Enough of my moaning. Why don't you come round for a drink some time? We could have some fun." An eyelid lowered in a lascivious wink.

Hugo's stomach tensed in alarm. He got up from the table, drained his cup and rummaged in his pocket from some change. "Um, sure," he said, sticking a five-pound note down on the table. "But if you'll excuse me, I've really got to go to work now."

CHAPTER
13

"IT'S WRONG TO SEE IT AS A CHORE, AL," JAKE SAID, GIVING HER his most dazzlingly charming and persuasive smile. "It's a privilege. A joy. You should want to give Ro the best possible nutritional start in life. Any good mother would."

"And I do, of course I do," Alice said desperately, smiling bravely back while her heart sank into the mire.

How foolish she had been to imagine her feeding problems would be over now Rosa had started on solids. Twenty ounces of breast milk a day were somehow still to be squeezed out. In addition Jake was now insisting Rosa must eat nothing but home-cooked baby food made with organic vegetables. Home-cooked by herself.

That this was entirely in line with her mother's prediction was maddening. But nowhere near as maddening as trying to make it. Alice, who had never been keen on cooking, hated every minute. There had to be easier ways to ensure Rosa got her vitamins and minerals.

"Sure there is," Jake said easily. "You just need a good recipe book, that's all. There's bound to be a good organic vegetarian or vegan baby cookbook. In fact, I'm sure I read about one in the *Guardian* the other week. *Ultimate Organic Baby Food Made Fun*, or something. Yeah, that was it.

Had fantastic recipes for making bechamel sauce with breast milk."

Alice gulped. "I was thinking," she ventured, remembering what her mother had said, "more along the lines of organic jar food for babies."

Jake looked disgusted. "Rosa isn't eating gloop from supermarkets."

"I don't mean all the time," Alice backtracked. "I'm talking about *organic* gloop, anyway."

Jake's beautiful face was stony. "I don't see what the problem is," he said. "Why can't you make it yourself? You've got all the time in the world."

"Actually," Alice corrected him, "I don't have *that* much time, as it happens."

"Why not?"

"The breastfeeding, for a start," Alice pointed out. "That still takes hours. And changing Rosa's terry nappies takes time. And then there's the proofreading for *Get Trashed!* Not to mention that bit of bookkeeping."

"I didn't realize you didn't want to help," Jake said huffily. "I thought you believed in recycling as much as I do."

"Of course I do, and, honestly, I don't mind helping," Alice said earnestly. "All I'm saying is that when I'm not doing any of that—which I am most of the day to be honest—I'd rather play with Rosa than slave over a hot food mill. I just think," she persisted, "that it does no harm to give Rosa the occasional jar. Or make her something that doesn't involve redecorating the kitchen afterward."

Jake's gaze was accusing, mixed with just the right amount of guilt-inducing disappointment. Alice felt her shoulders droop in defeat. "OK. I'll go and get a cookbook."

Looking on the bright side, a trip into town would probably do her good. Being stuck in the Old Morgue trying to concoct edible organic vegetarian baby food was making her stir crazy. In more senses than just one.

* * *

Neil, it was soon clear, intended to get his pound of flesh from the new part-time deal. What Hugo had once taken a day to do, he was now expected to achieve in a morning. Including, as before, all Dunn and Dustard's most challenging cases.

"Tricky little number for you here, Fine," Neil announced one day. "Couple who want a property in Bath."

"What's so tricky about that?" Hugo asked absently. He was trying to work out how, during the busy morning ahead, he could fit in a visit to a bookshop. Baby manuals, he was hoping, would lighten his childcare darkness.

Neil placed a piece of paper on Hugo's desk. "They've sent through a few, um, *conditions*. They refuse to buy property from anyone who's been divorced, that has a number three in its address or has a front door any other color than green."

Hugo rubbed his tired eyes. "Bloody ridiculous."

Neil frowned. "I'm not asking you for your opinion, Fine. I'm asking you to find it for them."

"Sure, Neil," Hugo said hurriedly. Pungent opinions and personal feelings were, he remembered, a luxury he could no longer afford.

Later that morning he showed an elderly couple round a bungalow called, incredibly, "Osokozi." Osougly, more like, Hugo thought, spotting the hideous brown-painted unicorns atop each gatepost. Despite its appearance and extortionate price, the couple seemed genuinely interested in the property.

The old lady turned to him with rheumy, trusting eyes. "Do you think you'd buy it, if you were us?"

Hugo hesitated. Coughing up for this place would clearly wipe out the couple's life savings. On the other hand, what was that to him? There was no room for emotion in this business. Let it in and you were lost.

"You bet I would," he said, flashing her his most persuasive grin. "Matter of fact, I was thinking of putting an offer in myself."

Lying to the old couple felt oddly difficult. At least, not as easy as it once would have been. But *caveat emptor,* and all that. Selling was his job. He could not allow himself to go soft on people at the very time his income was so unprecedentedly necessary. He had another mouth to feed now, although not a mouth that seemed particularly interested in being fed. He was definitely getting the mealtimes wrong. The sooner he got a childcare book, the better.

One of Osokozi's few virtues was its ease of access to the town center. Hugo shot into the first bookshop he came across, where an assistant of etiolated Pre-Raphaelite appearance directed him toward the Baby and Toddler section. Hugo rounded the indicated corner and reeled at what he saw. He was, admittedly, looking for advice, but not quite in this quantity.

Advice stretched from floor to ceiling, shelf upon black ash shelf of doctors, psychologists and "child care experts" of every hue. Literally. There was mile after mile of neon and pastel spines, none of which bore the title he wanted. *How to Put on Nappies, Feed and Other Basic Skills for the Terminally Clueless Parent* did not seem to be among the books on offer.

Pulling out *What Happens During the First Year,* Hugo discovered that a baby of Theo's age "should be able to pay attention to a raisin" and "make a wet razzing sound." His stomach rushed with panic. What was a wet razzing sound exactly? Had he ever even bothered presenting Theo with a raisin to pay attention to? Or any other piece of dried fruit for that matter? The hell he had. He was an appalling parent. The worst.

Miserably, he pulled out some books about feeding routines, threw himself down on the black plastic sofa and prepared to learn.

Hearing someone else come into the section, Hugo looked up. To his surprise, he recognized the newcomer.

He felt an initial jolt of dislike. It was Alice. Earnest, well-scrubbed Alice, wife of the unspeakable Jake, and the woman who had single-handedly ruined Amanda's American career. Although, admittedly, he didn't feel quite as indignant about that as he used to.

Alice did not look at the man in the book section. She turned her back quickly, hoping her red eyes had not been spotted. Quite unexpectedly, on the bus, she had burst into tears of frustration and exhaustion. And all because Jake had asked, as she left the Old Morgue, whether she could pick up some baking soda.

"Why?" Alice had asked. "I'm not baking anything."

"No, but it's very versatile as a cleaning agent," Jake had smiled. "It's about time we took a more ethical approach to housework."

Alice had looked back at him blankly.

"You can add it to white vinegar and it deodorizes carpets, cleans drains and scrubs stainless steel, all without damaging the planet in the way conventional cleaning products do." He'd pulled a face. "Doesn't the thought of all that bleach swilling around in our sewers worry you?" Alice thought it worried her much less than trying to clean the bathroom with vinegar.

Because, of course, the doing of the housework with baking soda and vinegar would obviously fall to her. It was this miserable prospect that had upset her on the bus. She was exhausted from a tiring night with Rosa, her bruised breasts flared with pain whenever she moved and her bones ached insistently as if she was coming down with flu which, given Jake's ever-more-restrictive approach to having the heating on, seemed probable. Alice, sitting at the bus's rear clutching a now peaceful Rosa, felt the tears slide silently down her cheeks. She had cried all the way into town. Only now, just outside the book shop, had she succeeded in stopping.

Hugo watched Alice covertly. A baby in a sling, he noted,

was sleeping peacefully on her chest. Whatever his reservations about Alice, it was hard not to be impressed with that.

And her baby, from what he could see, was not only clean and pacifier-less but had its hair brushed as well. This, too, struck Hugo as amazing. Never, before he had been in charge of a baby, had he regarded women with under-control infants as anything more than the way things should be. But now he knew the amount of effort involved in getting a child washed, dressed, changed, invariably changed again, fed, dressed again after the feed and finally ready to go out, not to mention sorting oneself out into the bargain.

But then, he reminded himself, if anyone was going to be triumphantly on top of things, it *would* be the ghastly, earnest Alice. The earnest Alice with a fist of steel too, if Amanda's venomous accounts held true of how this woman had held not only the entire Intercorp legal department but most of the company's writers in her pedantic, creativity-crushing thrall.

True, he thought, staring at her still profile, the megalomaniac aspect was not obvious. But, no doubt, all the more dangerous for that. Certainly, just like her execrable husband, she exuded an air of complete control, confidence and capability. Look at her now, leafing through—for God's sake—*Ultimate Organic Baby Food Made Fun*.

He felt a crushing sense of inadequacy. He himself, after all, could barely manage to heat up a baby food jar without burning the contents. Depressed, he looked down at the books spread across his knee.

Then, floating into his ears, came a soft sound. A sniff. He glanced immediately toward Alice. God, yes, her shoulders were shaking. Alice, earnest, goody-goody ghastly Alice, was *crying*. Weeping into *Ultimate Organic Baby Food Made Fun*.

Clearly not that much fun.

Books thumped to the floor as Hugo leaped to his feet in concern. "Are you OK?" Stupid question. She would hardly be howling in a bookshop if she was.

"Here. Use this." Hugo handed over a crumpled ball of linen formerly a smart monogrammed handkerchief presented to him by Amanda. "It's clean," he added. He'd now got the hang of the washing machine. But ironing was still some years off.

He looked politely away as Alice blew her nose. He was puzzled. Her behavior was not at all consistent with what he knew about her. Evil people did not break down in tears. Nor did smug goody-goodies.

"Sit down," he urged her, hurriedly scraping the rest of the books to the side of the squashy black sofa. She pushed some hair out of her face and glanced at him in bleary embarrassment.

"Excuse me saying so," Hugo said, "but I think we've met before. Weren't you in the prenatal classes at the West Country General?"

Alice nodded, surprised. She did not recognize him, and was amazed he recognized her. These days, she barely recognized herself. As she hadn't seen the inside of a hair salon for months, her blonde hair now sported long, mousy roots and spent most of its time in a ponytail. And it had been months since she had even seen her makeup bag; no doubt, by now, it had made its way to the drugs shelter. Bare-faced had felt strange at first. But after Jake insisted he loved her natural look best, there seemed little point bothering with full war paint.

"Hugo," he said, shooting out a hand. "Hugo Fine."

"Oh, I remember," Alice said, realizing with dismay that this knight with the kind words and clean hanky was the real estate agent husband of the unspeakable Amanda Hardwick. Amazement followed the dismay. He looked entirely different to what she remembered. Formerly suave, he now needed a shave. His erstwhile smoothness was crumpled and curled at the edges. His eyes were bloodshot and swollen with large purple sacs of exhaustion. His skin was dry and stubbly, and he had a haunted, desperate look.

"Oily bastard," she remembered Jake saying. He had, she recalled, loathed him on the spot for reasons she didn't quite understand. He, after all, had not suffered at the hands of the Hardwick.

But the only oil in sight now was on Hugo's evidently unwashed hair. His formerly posh suit was crumpled and also stained; around the shoulders and lapels especially. A baby, obviously. She knew he and Amanda had had theirs; Jake had met up with him by accident, in the Cavendish hospital bar of all places. "Drinking his own weight in whisky and smoking like a crematorium," Jake had reported scornfully.

Recognizing in Hugo all the signs of frazzled parenthood, Alice could not help a lurch of sympathy. She suppressed it immediately. The fact he was a harassed parent didn't make him any less unpleasant. Which of course he was; anyone who lived with Amanda Hardwick had to be.

Lovely skin, Hugo was thinking. Motherhood had added no long-term surplus to the lithe frame clearly evident even under the bulky coat. And tears made those clear blue eyes bigger and clearer than ever. And, close up, that long oval face had the serenity of a medieval angel. She didn't look evil, not in the least.

She did look suspicious, it had to be said. He supposed this was understandable. He was, after all, Mr. Amanda Hardwick, and there was no reason to suppose Alice felt any differently about Amanda than Amanda felt about her. Or than he felt about Jake, and vice versa.

Yet even so, the wish that he and Alice could be friends was expanding rapidly within him. Its root was not sympathy for her tears, nor even appreciation of her looks, but the fact that Alice clearly knew her way around a baby. He, on the other hand, didn't.

"I'd better be going," Alice said. She placed a hand protectively over the baby in its sling.

Hugo racked his brains for a reason to detain her. "So you had the baby," he said conversationally.

"Yes." Alice looked surprised.

Hugo felt himself reddening. What help was he going to ask for, anyway? Where did he start? "Er . . . how old is he?"

"She," Alice said abruptly, wanting to cut this conversation short. Unlike Hugo, she had no hidden agenda for wanting to stay and talk.

"Oh, sorry. Silly me. *Ahem*. So how old is *she*?"

"Four months."

"Same age as mine. Mine's a *he* as it happens. Called, um, Theo."

Her eyes slid to the pile of books beside him. "I'm on a bit of a learning curve," Hugo confessed sheepishly. "My wife's, ahem, away at the moment. I'm in charge, and not doing very well, to be honest."

"I've got to go," she said sharply.

Oh, well. He'd tried. But she plainly didn't want to be friends, and why should she? Given her relations with Amanda, it was surprising she still stood there.

He gestured at the books. "Which of these would *you* buy? If you were an utterly hopeless, clueless, totally crap parent who did everything as badly as possible?"

As he finished the sentence, his smile was shaking. The misery, confusion, fear and sleeplessness of the past few days and nights had finally caught up with him, To his horror, Hugo felt his bottom lip tremble and his eyes well.

"Because," Hugo sniffed, throwing himself completely on her mercy, "I'm just lost, to be honest." He snatched the top book off the pile and opened it at random. " 'Are we *really* listening to our children?' " he read from it. He looked blearily up at her. "Well, frankly, I am. Every night for hours on end, to be precise."

To his surprise, Alice giggled. It was a giggle utterly unlike Amanda's habitual titter. It was a warm, gurgling peal that made the world seem suddenly a better, brighter place. "What problems are you having, exactly?" she asked.

"Um, well, it's difficult to be specific . . ."

"You mean everything's the problem?"

"You certainly could say that there are a few, er, challenges."

"He's not sleeping?" Alice guessed.

"Er, no." Theo's near-insomnia was one of many problems, of course. But it would do for starters.

"The thing to do," Alice said, "is try and keep him awake as much as possible during the day. That's what I've been doing with this one," she patted the back of her baby's sling, "and it seems to work. They sleep at night then. It's obvious, really, I suppose."

Hugo nodded. "That makes sense. Theo does tend to snore all day and party all night. Although now he goes to nursery in the morning."

"Well, that should help keep him awake." Alice shoved *Ultimate Organic Baby Food Made Fun* under her arm. "Good luck, anyway. I've got to go."

He could think of no further questions to keep her.

CHAPTER
14

THE NOVELTY OF COMING TO CHICKLETS HAD CLEARLY WORN OFF for Theo. This morning, like yesterday and the day before, the baby stiffened and whimpered as soon as he caught sight of the nursery building.

"Separation anxiety," one of the nursery staff said briskly. "He'll get over it."

Hugo wished he could be so sure. Theo must really hate the nursery if he seriously wanted to stay with his father. It wasn't as if they had much fun together. Theo seemed to spend most of the time crying while he, in turn, tried to understand what he was crying about.

"Come on, darling," he muttered now to his roaring son. "Don't be like this. Not today of all days."

An important meeting was scheduled for half an hour after he got in to work. Some clients selling a portfolio of Victorian brewery buildings were holding a beauty contest among local real estate agencies. This morning was Dunn and Dustard's turn to audition. Neil, Hugo knew, was desperate for them to be appointed sole agent for the sale. Industrial heritage buildings of exactly this sort were in demand among the many young media and technology companies currently mushrooming in Bath. It wasn't exactly the King's Cross redevelopment phenomenon, but probably the nearest Bath came to it, and Hugo felt something of the old excitement in his loins at the prospect.

He couldn't afford to be late for the meeting. "I'm depending on you to impress them," Neil had warned. "I've told them we'll get our best shit-hot ex-London supersalesman to screw the last penny out of any potential buyer. I've built up your charm and powers of persuasion. You've got to get in there and knock them dead."

As, now, they mounted the nursery steps and Theo threw his body into a rigid block of screaming protest, Hugo groaned in despair. How the hell was anyone supposed to cope with this, let alone think about work at the same time?

He noticed one of the mothers, Sue, teetering toward the entrance. Like Theo, her baby was thrashing and yelling as if it was being murdered.

"Hello," Hugo shouted. "You all right?" he added, noticing that her face had a distinct green tinge.

She shook her head. "Stomach bug. I've been throwing up all night."

"You should be in bed," Hugo told her as they entered the building.

Sue gave a hollow laugh. " 'Course I should. But who'd take Hamish to nursery if I was? And I can't miss work. I've had so much time off recently with *his* various illnesses they're going to sack me if I'm off any more."

Guiltily, Hugo realized that he wasn't the only parent with problems. Even Alice, for all her efficiency, had been crying about something.

"Having a baby and holding a job down is a bloody nightmare," Sue said as they reached the baby room entrance. "Employers are so unsympathetic if you've got children. I ask myself all the time if it's worth it. The bloody job only just covers the fees anyway."

"It's a struggle," Hugo concurred. The camaraderie he felt

with Chicklets' working mothers was not something he had ever anticipated. And yet there was something grimly enjoyable about it. They were all in the same boat, and a stormy boat at that.

"I'd better go," Sue said, gulping. "If I'm lucky I'll make it to the loo before I'm sick again."

Having deposited his son and returned to the car, Hugo felt sick with guilt. Theo's separation anxiety was a nightmare, exposing as it did the writhing pythons of guilt and general incompetence that lurked below the surface of his parenting attempts. What was he doing wrong? He wished he could ask Alice. Was there a way he could contrive to see her? There was so much he didn't know.

A sudden glance at the car clock was followed by the jerk of his foot on the accelerator pedal. He was going to be later than he'd thought for this bloody meeting.

"They started five minutes ago," reported Shuna with satisfaction as he passed her desk.

Hugo ignored her, knocked on the closed door of Neil's office and went in. A woman in beige and a gray-suited man with a ratty, Oswald Mosley look sat side by side before Neil's desk.

Neil's red face glowed blue from the screen of the laptop into which he was peering, presumably to give an air of cutting-edge efficiency. He glared at Hugo as he entered.

". . . depends entirely on the salesman," Oswald Mosley was explaining in a grating voice. "This is a very particular project requiring a very particular type of man. Someone who'll be at ease with the sort of client we're hoping to attract—trendy London migrants, mostly. We're looking for someone who combines knowledge and skill with charm, persuasion and sophistication. Appearance is of the utmost importance . . ."

"Look no further," Neil boomed. "Here he is, the man of the moment, right in the nick of time. Been out shaking up the property market already, eh, Hugo, even at this time in the morning?"

Hugo realized this was a prompt. "Er, yes. Yes. Absolutely."

"You see? This is your guy. The man never sleeps," Neil grinned at the couple in front of him. "Eats, breathes and even shits selling."

Hugo summoned up his best, most confidence-inspiring and persuasive property-selling smile. He was aware, however, as he trained it on the clients, that they were not looking at it. They were, for some reason, looking at his feet.

Neil was looking at his feet as well. A freezing feeling now crawled down Hugo's spine. Had he forgotten to clean his shoes, or something?

Hugo, too, now looked at his feet to see that each of his size eleven Church's was partially concealed by a plastic cover of electric blue. He was still wearing the galoshes from the nursery.

At half past twelve Hugo looked at his watch. A visit to Sainsbury's was urgently required before picking Theo up from Chicklets. There were no jars in the cupboard and the small cartons of ready-made formula milk—he'd long stopped trying to count the scoops of the powdered variety—had run out as well.

Oh, and God, there was the cake to buy. As posters had been reminding everyone for weeks, Chicklets was about to hold a fundraising bake sale to which all parents were expected to contribute. Hugo had got the strong impression that if he didn't, the baby would get it.

Rain spattered on the windscreen as he entered the supermarket car park. The last space in the Parent and Child spaces near the door had just been taken. He watched furiously as a large family of four exited their Escort, both enormously fat sons well into their twenties. Hugo thought of his tiny son being carried in the rain from the other side of the car park and saw boiling, furious red.

"Excuse me!" he shouted, winding down his window. "That space is for people *with babies.*"

The mother, a round-faced woman in tracksuit bottoms, turned around. "So what?" she blasted back. "Oi've got my kids with me, haven't Oi?"

"Well, aren't you being a bit inconsiderate?" Hugo challenged. "Those spaces are designed so people with babies in supermarket carts can unload them more easily. And they're nearer the shop door."

For a moment, he could hardly believe what he was saying. Hugo Fine, former lad about town, now militant moutheroffer at supermarket parking space abusers. A parent with attitude, no less. But why not? This sort of selfishness was simply intolerable. Especially if Theo had to suffer for it.

"Yeah, and so what's it to you?" yelled the woman's large, doughy husband. "Oi don't see no kids in your car."

Hugo whipped around to check Theo's car seat. It was empty. Sick panic surged within him until he remembered that of course it would be. Theo was still at Chicklets, waiting to be picked up.

Inside, Hugo stared at the wall of nappies, spirits sagging at the prospect of buying another large and expensive collection of the impossible-to-fit objects. This morning's attempt had, even by his own standards, been disgraceful.

He shoved some Pampers in his basket and moved on to the baby food. As usual, to save time choosing, he began to work his way along the shelf, piling every second jar into his basket.

As he reached the end of the row, a woman walked past. She was tall, slim and blonde, with a long, thoughtful face and wide eyes peering anxiously at a shopping list. A wellbehaved baby peeped out of the sling around her neck.

"Alice!" Hugo exclaimed, in a rush of delight.

Her basket, he saw, was groaning with fresh vegetables. No doubt this was connected with *Ultimate Organic Baby Food Made Fun*. He looked at his own basket, groaning with jars, and gave her a guilty grin. "You put me to shame."

"What?" asked Alice distractedly.

"Cooking all those vegetables for your baby. I'm impressed."

"They're not all for Rosa, actually. Some are for a dinner party tonight."

Hugo stared at her in amazed admiration. Not only did this woman have her child under control, she entertained as well.

"A dinner party. What fun," he said lamely. He could hardly remember the last one he had been to. It was somewhere back in the mists of time, when he had lived in that mythical place called London and had had some sort of life.

"Should be," Alice smiled. "Jake's asked a few of his *Get Trashed!* people round. His magazine," she added, as Hugo looked blank.

Hugo remembered the ultra-worthy-sounding recycling organ Jake allegedly ran. "Great," he nodded, hoping he sounded sincere.

He was, he realized, wasting an opportunity. Here in front of him was Alice, the most capable parent on earth and a positive font of baby knowledge. And what was he talking to her about? Some boring eco-beanfeast involving her evangelist loon of a husband.

"Er . . ." He looked toward the café by the supermarket entrance. "Would you . . . er . . . like a cup of coffee?" His tired mind suddenly fizzed with possibilities. He could ask her about the sleep issue again; maybe even move on to the nappy one.

"I'd love to," Alice said politely. "But I haven't really got time."

"I can throw a cake in too," Hugo pleaded.

Alice couldn't help grinning. "Sorry." She heaved her basket up to hip level. "Some other time."

Miserably, he watched Alice walk away. Then his heart soared as, unexpectedly, she stopped and turned. Had she changed her mind? Was the thought of a shot of caffeine before blanching all those mung beans more than she could resist, after all?

"Any idea where the organic miso is?" asked Alice.

"Sorry." Hugo shook his head. And he was sorry. Sorry about resigning himself to years and years of not having the slightest clue what to do with Theo. To a lifetime of sleepless nights, separation anxiety and, of course, risible nappy-changing.

Then he noticed something small and brown lying on the lino floor in front of him. A purse, it looked like. Alice's purse?

He leaped on it like a starving man might leap on a plate of fish and chips. Alice's purse! Surely it was Alice's purse. At least now, with this demonstrating his honesty and good intent, he might be able to ask for her phone number.

Brandishing the precious small leather object, he strode to the end of the aisle where the checkouts were. Alice was in the Baskets Only. She was standing beside a harvest festival pile of vegetables on the conveyor belt and slapping her pockets with panic. The checkout assistant, as was her privilege on such occasions, looked on with expressionless lack of sympathy.

"I think," Hugo called as he approached, "you're going to need this." He held up the purse—which he was praying hard was Alice's.

She beamed at him with tears in her eyes.

"Oh God, thanks," she breathed, visibly drooping with relief as she handed her card to the assistant. "You've saved my life."

"My pleasure," Hugo smiled. "You look like you've had a bit of a shock. Still sure you don't want a coffee?"

Doubt flickered across Alice's face.

"Seeing as how I've saved your life," Hugo prompted. He hated to twist her arm, but desperate times meant desperate measures.

Alice smiled at him. It was a no-holds-barred smile. Caught in its soft, full beam, Hugo felt a ripple in his groin. "I'd love to," Alice said. "I can't now, though. But if you like I could meet you here in a couple of days. Friday?"

CHAPTER

15

"IS THIS REVERSE-OSMOSIS DEIONIZED WATER WE'RE DRINKING?" The deputy editor of *Get Trashed!* was waving his jam jar in a demanding sort of way.

To her surprise Alice realized he was waving it at her. His tone was unexpectedly brusque; rather rude, in fact. Especially given he was a guest in her house and they had only just been introduced. As the editor's wife, she had anticipated more respect, but perhaps everyone was equal in the eco-community. She was determined not to seem offended, however. Her role, tonight, was to help Jake host the evening and make it a brilliant success.

"I'm not sure what you mean," she said about the water. "But it's out of the tap, if that helps."

The deputy editor, whose name was Joss, raised his eyebrows in unimpressed fashion. "Oh, well. If it isn't ROD, it isn't," he said with bad grace. "Is there any more in that tap, anyway?"

"Steady on," joked a weaselly someone Alice remembered to be the layout person. "Reservoir levels are dangerously low as it is."

There were some guffaws at this. Alice laughed too, anxious to show willing. She wanted to enjoy the dinner party, despite her secret worries about her cooking and the ridiculously short notice Jake had given her to get the food together. Tofu kebabs, mung bean salad and chickpea flan had stretched her meager culinary skills to the limit. She had her doubts about the flan, especially. But she would have doubted chickpea flan even if Nigella Lawson had made it.

A movement caught her eye. Jake was waving the ex–petrol container water pitcher at her. It was clear that she was expected to go and fill it up. She looked back, annoyed but trying not to show it. Why couldn't he be water monitor? She'd done her bit: the shopping and food. Now that the guests had arrived and were mingling in the sitting room, sipping organic mulled wine from jam jars and recycled mouthwash containers, she had been looking forward to a little social stimulation. Not yet more servitude.

She ignored him and smiled at Joss. "Planning any holidays this year?" she asked, wheeling out an admittedly far from original conversational gambit. But one had to start somewhere.

"WOOF," said Joss.

"Sorry?" She jumped. Why was Joss barking?

"Worldwide Opportunities on Organic Farms," Joss elucidated impatiently in his nasal whine. "I joined in ninety-five. I've been on working holidays in Bosnia, Tibet and Slovenia, as well as Wales and Albania. I can say 'That couch grass needs to be got rid of' in seven different languages."

"Gosh," said Alice, trying hard to look impressed. "But don't you, um, ever, you know, fancy something a little less . . . arduous? Flying off to some beach or something?"

Joss's large nostrils flared with disgust. They now looked, Alice thought, big enough to crawl up.

"Did you know," he asked her, "that the carbon emissions from one transatlantic flight negate all the recycling you do?"

"Er . . ." began Alice, who didn't.

"Before WOOF," Joss interrupted, "I used to go on walking

holidays. And even then, when I just took the train, I had to plant at least *one* tree in a sustainable forest afterward to neutralize all the carbon I produced—"

"Excuse me," Alice broke in. "I think Jake's asking me to go and get some more water."

"Yes, but can you ever be strong-willed enough to watch ads on television without them subverting your shopping habits?" someone was saying to someone else as she passed them en route to the kitchen.

It seemed impossible that Jake's colleagues could always be so deadly serious about everything. Perhaps they just took time to warm up. Unsurprisingly, given the temperatures in the Old Morgue. And Jake had mentioned heat was rationed in the *Get Trashed!* office as well.

Besides Joss, the guests comprised the weasely layout person and the assistant editor, a messy aubergine-haired beanpole called Jessamy.

Alice had been surprised when Jessamy shuffled in to the cottage. She had not realized Jake had women on his staff. He had never mentioned any.

Jessamy, it turned out, supplemented her *Get Trashed!* paycheck by working as a goat psychologist.

"How *fascinating*," Alice gushed, unsure what else to say.

Jessamy looked her up and down, the suspicion she was being mocked clear in her eyes. "So what do *you* do?" she demanded.

Alice was flustered for a second. It was the first time she had been asked this question socially since resigning from her high-flying job at Intercorp. But what of it? Her job now was a million times more important. "I'm a mother," she said proudly.

Jessamy's top lip lifted slightly in scorn. "I know *that*, obviously. But Jake's a father, and he manages to be an editor too." She shot him a glance that could only be described as adoring. Alice was not surprised at this. Naturally Jessamy adored Jake. He was adorable, as well as off-the-scale good-looking. Which, reassuringly for Alice, Jessamy herself wasn't, not particularly.

"But what do you do besides *mothering?*" Jessamy pressed.

Alice kept calm. People were famously incapable of imagining what mothers did all day. Jake himself was a case in point, and he was Rosa's father. She smiled at Jessamy. "Well, I do some odds and ends for *Get Trashed!*, obviously."

"That can't take up all your time."

Alice felt irritated, but maintained her smile. "You'd be surprised. There isn't time to do much else, to be honest."

Jessamy lifted her chin. "It's probably just bad organization."

Alice stared furiously at the floor. How dare this woman speak to her in this way? Was she aware she only had a job at all thanks to her subsidies? Without the income from Alice's New York flat sale, now severely eroded, *Get Trashed!* wouldn't even exist. "Excuse me," she said in strangled tones. "I thought I heard Rosa crying upstairs."

She hadn't, of course. But she needed an opportunity to slip into the bathroom and collect herself. Closing the door behind her, she recoiled at the smell of the new vinegar-and-baking-soda cleaning routine. The place stank like a fish-and-chip shop.

She took a deep breath and peered at her reflection.

The eco-friendly regime Jake insisted on was, she glumly concluded, doing absolutely nothing for her skin. Having feasted luxuriously on Clarins for so many years, it was objecting fiercely to its new diet of vegetable soap and water. Jake's recent ban on deodorant was another challenge; Alice hated to think that other people could smell her. But she rarely met other people these days so perhaps it didn't matter. And the crowd downstairs, anyway, were pretty whiffy themselves.

She looked at her clothes. She had worn her old jeans until they wore out and were replaced by tracksuit bottoms with holes Jake had foraged from some Dumpster. Her mother's voice floated into her memory. "You used to have such lovely clothes . . ."

When she returned to the sitting room it was to discover Jake's staff gathered about him in a tight knot. A debate about what *Get Trashed!* should feature as its next Tip of the Month was in full swing.

"Those underarm deodorant rollers," Jessamy suggested. "There's got to be a good use for those."

Alice joined the group eagerly. A creative discussion was a luxury she had not enjoyed for some time. "If you painted them, they'd make great skittles for a bowling alley," she suggested. Really, the idea was rather brilliant when you thought about it. And much easier and more fun than most of the *Get Trashed!* tips she'd seen.

Joss looked at her from over the bridge of his nose. "I don't think so."

"Why not?" Alice smiled at Jake, expecting encouragement.

But her husband's face, to her surprise, bore unmistakable signs of embarrassment. "Al, I'm not sure you really get it," he said.

"Get what?"

"*Get Trashed!* You see, it's more than a magazine. It's a way of thinking."

"A way of *life*," Jessamy stressed.

"Look," Joss said, in his nasal voice. "Let's move on, shall we? The other thing we were going to discuss was whether or not we should go down the celebrity path. Have a star interview."

Jessamy pulled a disgusted face. "What, and be just like everybody else? We deal in real issues, you know. We live in the real world. We have real ethics. Real beliefs."

"I agree with Jessamy," Jake stated. For this, Alice noticed, he received another adoring look from his assistant editor. "Having celebrities would just be lowering ourselves. We exist to heighten people's consciousness, not cater to the lowest common denominator."

Joss looked annoyed. "I'm not saying I *want* celebs," he grumped. "I'm just making the point that they help with circulation. Get sales up."

"That's right," Alice chipped in boldly. But why shouldn't she say what she thought? After all she almost entirely funded this magazine. She might not be allowed an opinion on Tip of the Month, but surely she was on this. "It might help to have a famous face on the cover."

Jake looked irritated. "Oh, really? And which one do you suggest?"

Alice stared at him, puzzled and hurt.

"We need," Joss said, "some celebrity who's particularly associated with rubbish."

"Easy!" Alice clapped her hands.

"Is it?" Jessamy asked frostily.

"Of course," Alice beamed. "There can't be a single celebrity who hasn't been up to their ears in complete rubbish at some time or other."

The *Get Trashed!* editorial board looked at each other. "This is no place for flippancy," said Jessamy crossly.

"Look, Al, this is an editorial meeting we're holding here," Jake added in detached tones. "You're probably better off in the kitchen for the moment."

Alice was so taken aback she could hardly speak. "I'm *terribly* sorry," she said with freezing politeness. "I thought this was a dinner party."

"It is," Jake said easily. "The other guests aren't here yet. I just asked the guys a bit earlier to thrash out a few ideas over some drinks. There isn't any more of that mulled wine, is there?"

In the kitchen, Alice furiously put more wine on to warm. She deliberately chose a bottle her father had brought at Christmas and which had been shoved under the sink by Jake because it wasn't organic. It was, however, a first-class Bordeaux, which was a terrible waste to ruin with mulled wine herbs. But the mildly naughty thrill of watching everyone drink it would be compensation for that. And she could have an unadulterated glass or two of it while the mulled stuff warmed.

As a knock sounded on the front door, she wondered who the other guests would be. Hopefully the new blood would be better value. These hopes were dashed as soon as Alice saw it. None of the new blood looked as if it had any blood at all.

The newcomers comprised, Alice gathered, what her husband grandly called his "panel of editorial advisers."

"This is Dr. Enoch Scarthin," Jake beamed. "He's our soil erosion expert." Dr. Scarthin, Alice thought, looked pretty eroded himself. He was a wizened, squinting wraith, with pitted, yellow skin. "And this," Jake clapped a frog-like man with bulging eyes on the back, "is J. Larry Tabasco. He's our global warming prophet."

As they finally sat down at the table, Alice, with a sense of inevitability, found herself between Mr. Tabasco and Dr. Scarthin. "Sort of a rock and a hot place," she joked. They both looked blankly back at her.

Sipping copious quantities of wine, she allowed her mind to wander in and out of the various discussions. No one seemed to be listening to anyone else.

". . . yes, but we know that the high consumption Western lifestyle generates a huge amount of household waste—28.2 million tons in Britain every year, 1.2 tons from every home . . ." shouted someone.

". . . restrict traditional waste-disposal methods—incineration and landfill—because of their adverse effects on the environment," yelled someone else.

"Organic household waste should be composted, instead of allowing it to rot in landfill sites where it generates potent greenhouse gases such as methane . . ." boomed another.

Alice realized, as the evening progressed, that she had been overly hasty in condemning Jessamy for asking what she did all day. It was the only question she would be asked about herself all evening. The only intimation, in fact, anyone considered her a member of the party. The assumption of everyone else, including Jake, seemed to be that she was there in the capacity of waitress.

It was around the seaweed pudding mark that Alice started seeing double and began to sway in her orange-box seat. Across the table, Jake was listening intently as Jessamy reeled off a list of annual tonages, all the while gazing adoringly into his eyes. Beside her, the soil analyst was expounding erosion theories, while Joss, picking his teeth, looked fascinated. Alice put her hand over her mouth to press back the laughter she felt bubbling relentlessly up. Everyone looked so serious.

On her other side, the global warmer was getting heated. "The position," he was intoning, eyes half-closed, "is far, far more dangerous than anyone would like to think."

Alice hiccuped. She gave the prophet a glassy grin. "Oh really?" she slurred. "Actually, *actually*, I'd like to think the danger is more dangerously imminent than the most dangerous thing anyone could think of . . . *hic.*" She reached for the petrol water container and waved it unsteadily in his face. "More reverse-thrust deionized whatsit, Professor?" Then, spurred helplessly on by the sight of his outraged face, she dissolved into hysterical giggles.

There was a shocked silence.

"Al!" thundered Jake.

In the ensuing silence, a high, whining sound from overhead could be heard. Rosa had woken up and was demanding attention.

"Al," Jake repeated.

She met his gaze and did not move. She felt like shouting defiantly that he should go, Rosa was his daughter too. But then her eyes dropped to the chickpea flan and she thought better of it. She got up from the table and left the room.

As she mounted the stairs, she heard the stir of conversation. "Sorry about that," Jake muttered. Then he dropped his voice still further ". . . can't expect much else . . . used to work for a glossy magazine company . . ." was all Alice could make out. But it was enough. In the bedroom, she held the baby to her, burning with indignation. How bloody *dare* he? Saving face in front of his colleagues was no excuse. He was her husband, and his first loyalty was to her. And Rosa.

* * *

By the time Hugo finally arrived at work, he felt as if he had been awake for several days and had overcome more challenges than the Fellowship of the Ring. He reflected wistfully on the days when his most pressing early morning appointment was a long session on the loo with yesterday's papers.

He rummaged through his work pile. This was a depressing business, given the number of problems Neil had landed him with recently. Lurking just below the top of the heap was the list from the demanding couple unwilling to buy a house without a green door or with a number three in the address. And only from a guaranteed non-divorcee.

There had to be a way round this somehow. The guaranteed non-divorcee was the trickiest bit. How could one go rummaging through the wreckage of clients' personal lives to find out that sort of thing?

He pulled out some of the other papers on the problem pile. Among them was Firth House, a property in one of Bath's most prestigious Georgian terraces that was proving slow to sell, thanks to the colossal price being demanded for it by the owner. This was an architect called Tarquin, who was the most flamboyantly gay person Hugo had ever met.

Hugo smiled faintly, remembering Tarquin mincing theatrically around the house during the assessment. His smile broadened. An idea was forming in his head. Could two tricky-to-solve birds be killed with one stone? He picked up the telephone.

"Tarquin?"

"*C'est moi*, sweetie. Who's this? Oh, the *divine* Hugo. How absolutely lovely. Tell me, darling, have you sold my little bolt hole yet, or not?"

"Well, I've got someone who might be interested. But I need to ask you a few things first."

"How unutterably exciting. Fire away, scrumptious one."

"Firth House. Has it got a number of any sort?"

"Well, it used to, darling, but I thought numbers were just *so* dull. So I named it after the heavenly Colin and his delicious bottom in *Pride and Prejudice*. Rather clever, don't you think, this being Bath and all that?"

"What was the number?" Hugo asked, crossing his fingers.

"Sweet one, I'll have to check. But actually, I think it's seventy-eight or something utterly yawnworthy like that. Seventy something, anyway."

Hugo punched the air. Two out of three, at a stroke. "Tarquin?"

"Yes, oh godlike one?"

"How do you feel about painting your front door green?"

Tarquin, it transpired, felt just fine about it. Hugo replaced the receiver feeling even better. Immediately the phone rang again.

"Is that Mr. Fine?" asked a fluting, birdlike voice.

"Yes."

"It's Mrs. Grimbley here."

Grimbley, *Grimbley* . . . oh, *yes*. The picky house-hunting couple. Half of it, anyway. He sat up excitedly in his chair.

"Hello, Mrs. Grimbley," he greeted her cheerily. "You've chosen a very good time to ring, as it happens. I think I may have found you exactly the property you want. With a green door, without a three in the number and owned *most definitely* by a guaranteed non-divorcee."

"How very exciting, Mr. Fine," exclaimed Mrs. Grimbley. "Because we think we've narrowed it down as well."

"How do you mean?" Hugo asked carefully.

"We had a dream last night that the house we must have was a little detached cottage with a red front door. It was number forty-two and had an apple tree in the garden. We thought you'd like to know. We thought it would make your job *so* much easier."

Putting the phone down, Hugo tried valiantly to concentrate on the only cheering prospect currently visible on his horizon. Which was meeting Alice at lunchtime in the supermarket.

CHAPTER
16

Aᴸɪᴄᴇ ʜᴀᴅ ɴᴏ ɪɴᴛᴇɴᴛɪᴏɴ ᴏꜰ ᴍᴇᴇᴛɪɴɢ Hᴜɢᴏ, ʜᴏᴡᴇᴠᴇʀ. Aᴅᴍɪᴛ-
tedly she had allowed herself to be charmed in both the
bookshop and the supermarket. But as soon as she had left
she had remembered he was husband to the vile Amanda
Hardwick and not, therefore, someone she could feasibly be
friends with.

Alice forced from her thoughts Hugo's look of tired defeat
in the bookshop, his returning her purse in the supermarket
and his touching desperation to have coffee. She was *not*
meeting him. Even though she had promised and she always
kept her promises. But in this case it was impossible.

And so, as the morning of the meeting ticked by, Alice determinedly mushed vegetables for Rosa and vowed not to stir
from the Old Morgue. From time to time she looked up from
this loathed task to see through the kitchen window that the
early rain had stopped and the clouds were parting to reveal
a sky of brilliant blue.

It *would* be a good day for an outing. And Rosa, currently
mewling on the kitchen floor, clearly dissatisfied with the
sand-filled Evian bottle Jake had given her, *adored* bus
rides . . .

But that, Alice thought, reining herself in, was just tough. The

Amanda factor wasn't the only reason that meeting Hugo was impossible. There was the Jake one too; while the precise reason for Jake's loathing of Hugo remained a mystery, Alice suspected that, fundamentally, it was Hugo on sight in the prenatal classes; perhaps, Alice guessed, because he seemed the opposite of everything Jake stood for. It was certainly hard to imagine Hugo insisting on politically correct nursery rhymes. Or growing vegetables in human sewage. Or showing his wife up in public . . . Alice forced herself from this train of thought. The point was that meeting Hugo behind Jake's back would be a betrayal. As Jake's wife, such a move was out of the question.

Or it had been, until the *Get Trashed!* dinner party. Alice's thoughts returned swiftly and resentfully to what she had overhead Jake saying as she went upstairs. He had not spoken a word—of apology or otherwise—about the dinner since, not even as they cleaned up the following morning. But for Alice the memory festered, burning in her gut like undigested chickpea flan. While she was aware that she hadn't behaved terribly well herself, the way he had treated her was difficult to forget.

Alice looked out of the kitchen window again. It was a bright blue and gold day. An outing was almost unbearably tempting. But if Jake found out she had met Hugo he would be furious. Yet what right, given his recent behavior, did he have to be angry about anything?

On the other hand, could she let petty point-scoring over her own husband be reason to have coffee with Amanda Hardwick's?

Seconds later, Alice was wiping her hands and reaching for her own and Rosa's coats.

Hugo stood apprehensively at the entrance to the supermarket café. He'd been here fifteen minutes and there was no sign of Alice.

His initial mood of buoyant optimism was being gradually replaced by a crushing sense of disappointment. He had unthinkingly trusted that Alice would turn up, but this struck him as more and more unlikely. She was married to Jake, who vehemently disliked him, and he was married to Amanda, who Alice seemed to view in much the same light.

He was about to turn away and trudge back to the supermarket car park when he saw someone tall and fair walking rapidly toward him. It was a woman holding a baby. It was Alice.

Ten minutes later, sitting opposite her over a cup of supermarket cappuccino, Hugo felt things weren't going quite as well as he had hoped. Conversation, to say the least, was stilted.

Alice's baby Rosa—or was it Rosie?—was staring at him in an unnerving fashion. He raised his eyebrows at her, stuck out his tongue and waggled his ears. The baby started to cry. As she jiggled her comfortingly up and down, Alice smiled at Hugo awkwardly.

Mortified, Hugo stopped the sideshow. "So. Ahem. Rosie's four months old, did you say?"

"Rosa." She looked at him over the rim of the huge, thick, coffee cup. "And, actually, she's five months, now."

"Oh God, of course, the same age as Theo." Hugo clapped his palm to his head. The coffee from the cup in his other hand slopped over the rim and down his wrist. He felt the tepid brown stream run stickily into the bend in his elbow. Damn. Another shirt ruined and he had no idea how to get stains out.

Silence fell again. Alice started pulling her coat and bag toward her. "Well, thanks for the coffee," she smiled. "I must be going."

Under the table, Hugo twisted his hands in anguish. Here she was, sitting in front of him, the answer to all his problems. But somehow he could not frame the questions. His confidence in dealing with women, once as natural as breathing, was gone. What the hell, Hugo wondered, has happened to me?

Yet this was his one chance. Once Alice walked out he would never see her again. He rose from the table, hands spread imploringly on the glaring blue Formica surface.

"Don't go. Please. It's just that . . . well . . . there's something I'd like to ask you."

"What?"

Hugo shot her a wild glance. "I was wondering," he said hoarsely, "whether you might know how to . . ."

"How to what?"

"How to . . . um." He cleared his throat. "How to put a nappy on."

Alice, who had started to stand up, abruptly sat down. Her eyes, already wide, grew wider still and rounder as she looked at him. "A nappy? You're asking me how to put a *nappy* on?"

"Er, well, yes. Exactly that. On a baby, obviously," Hugo added hurriedly, before wishing he hadn't. If she hadn't thought him a pervert before, she probably did now.

"You've got a five-month-old baby and you don't know how to put a nappy on?" Alice shook her head in amazement.

"I know it sounds ridiculous," Hugo said, embarrassed. "But the thing is, we had a maternity nurse and I suppose I never really learned the skills. And neither did Amanda."

"So what about the maternity nurse?" Alice asked, not particularly sympathetically. "Can't she help? Can't you get her back for a couple of weeks to show you the ropes? *Again?*"

"Er, well, she's not around any more. She left in, er, rather a hurry. The Royal Family needed her or something."

Despite her disapproval, Alice giggled. "The Royal Family?" she repeated, disbelievingly.

"To be honest, I think she was glad to see the back of us." Encouraged, Hugo told Alice the story of Nurse Harris's arrival and the endless references to Lord Fairbourne. As she giggled again, Hugo felt, quite out of the blue, that he would do anything to make her giggle more.

"Amanda had insisted she wanted to stay at home and look after the baby," he began. "She said it would be a pleasure, that it was the ultimate important job and nothing she had ever done in her career had ever come close . . ." He stopped.

Alice raised an eyebrow. "Go on," she said.

Hugo went on. Reality, he explained, had set in. Amanda had realized that babies woke up at all times of the night, screamed for no reason, and, more worryingly, for real reasons too. That they vomited, filled nappies, bit, scratched, farted and were far from always being docile and adorable. At which point she had, abruptly and utterly, lost interest. She took the first job she was offered and now she was away rather a lot.

"So you see," he summarized, trying to sound as unselfpitying as possible, "that's my position. My wife's away all the time and suddenly I'm in charge of a baby and frankly . . ." he paused, raking a coffee-sticky hand through messy dark hair, "frankly, I've no idea what to do with him. He sleeps all day and he yells all night and . . ." Hugo rubbed his eyes, "from bathing him to putting him to bed and everything in between seems to be a disaster. I mean, I don't want to make it sound as if I don't love my son, because I do, or at least I *suppose* I do . . ."

"You only *suppose*?" Alice echoed, shocked. Her hand moved to caress Rosa's head.

Hugo shrugged helplessly. "I know that sounds awful, but Theo hasn't really taken to being with just me all that well and . . ." he blinked at Alice in despair, "I suppose what I mean is that if I knew what to do with him, we'd have a better relationship. There's this horrible situation with the nursery, for a start." He explained about the separation anxiety.

Alice nodded. "But what do they say when you ring up?"

"Ring up?" Hugo's eyes were wide. "What do you mean, ring up?"

"Well, during the day. To see how he's doing."

He could not believe her matter-of-factness. Ring up? Did she realize what she was saying? "I never have," he shuddered. "I'm not sure I'd dare."

"But why not? You're a parent. A paying client. You have the right to ask questions."

"I suppose so." This revolutionary thought had never occurred to Hugo.

"My guess," Alice swished her coffee around the bottom of its cup, "is that Theo is fine the minute you go out of the baby room. He's just trying to manipulate you. All babies do it."

"Do they?"

"Well, how is he when you fetch him? Crying?"

Hugo shook his head.

"There you go then," Alice said briskly. "I'd put money on it that he's absolutely fine when you're not there."

"Do you really think so?" Hugo felt a wild rush of relief. His eyes, Alice saw with a pang, shone with emotion.

"Why don't you ask them when you go and pick him up?" she suggested. A glowing sensation was spreading through her now. It was, she realized, a long time since she had felt needed, and that her advice and opinion counted for something.

"Shit!" she suddenly exclaimed.

Hugo nodded resignedly. "Well, I can hardly blame you for saying that. I deserve it."

"No, I mean shit, look at the time." Alice waved her wrist at him. "I have to go. It takes ages to get back on the bus."

"The bus?" Hugo looked amazed. "Oh, of course. You only do public transport." He tried to speak without irony. "I remember from the prenatal classes. But surely it makes sense for you to have a car *now*? You're miles from anywhere with a baby."

"Cars are bad for the ecosystem," Alice muttered.

"Yes, and I've seen that bus to Bath that goes through

Combe," Hugo answered. "That exhaust hanging off the back of it's bad for the ecosystem as well. And surely it's bad for your spinal column to carry all that shopping *and* a baby."

Alice wished he would stop this particular line of argument. Her mother held identical views on the subject and it was hard to deny their logic. Hugo's face, however, had changed. He was looking at her aghast.

"The nappies!" he stuttered. "You said you'd show me how to put them on."

"Nappies. Yes," Alice bit her lip. "Er, well, I could demonstrate on Rosa, I suppose. The only problem is that there's not really the time. Not if I'm going to make the bus."

"Look, why don't I give you a lift? I'm going back into Bath anyway. I can take you to the bus station. Or home, if you like. Anywhere," he pleaded, eyes wide with desperation.

"The bus station's fine," Alice said. She smiled reassuringly at Hugo. "Come on then."

But Hugo's face had fallen again.

"What's the matter?" Alice asked.

"Do you use disposables?" he asked. "Even they're beyond me."

To his surprise, a guilty blush had crept over Alice's face. "Erm, well," she said. "As a matter of fact I have started to use the occasional disposable." She cleared her throat. "Just in emergencies, obviously."

"Of course," Hugo nodded gravely. Alice flashed him a conspiratorial smile. "So let's hit the baby-changing room."

Having dropped Alice off at the bus station, Hugo drove away on air. He was finally an initiate into the cult of correct nappy-fitting.

He needed to practice, of course, but there was no shortage of opportunity for that. And in case of real difficulty, he had managed to get Alice's telephone number.

"I'm sure I won't need to ring you," he had persuaded. "But it would be wonderful, just in case."

As he drove away, he watched her slight figure receding in the side mirror. While it was reassuring that he could call her about Theo, he was aware that he wanted more than that. The person he wanted her to focus on was not only his son, but himself.

He barely saw the road in front. Instead, that slow smile, that fair hair, those wide, surprised blue eyes floated before him. He wondered if her bus had come yet. He wondered, with a suddenness that made him swerve, what it would be like to kiss her, to lift that fine hair and pull that angelic face to his.

At Chicklets, he had more reason than ever to thank her. The baby room staff, once he asked them, confirmed that, so far as Theo's separation sufferings went, he was dry-eyed and eating Weetabix within minutes of his father's departure. Hugo's burden of guilt and unhappiness lifted like a hot-air balloon.

"Mr. Fine? Can I have a word?"

Hugo froze. "Uh . . . yes. Of course."

The Rottweiler, otherwise known as the nursery head, trotted briskly up to where Hugo stood in the corridor. She scrutinized Theo, who had now started to whimper. The corners of her small mouth pressed down in disapproval. She shook her head. "Mr. Fine. We can't have this."

"Have what?" gasped Hugo. "Look, he can't help it. It's separation anxiety . . . he's a bit sensitive at the moment."

"Not that. I'm talking about *this*." The Rottweiler pulled at Theo's trousers. "This is how you dressed him this morning. The trousers were on back to front, for a start."

So they were, Hugo saw. The pockets were facing the wrong way. But why did babies need pockets anyway?

He switched on his most charming smile. Time to dig out the renowned Fine magic and get the old bat on side. "To be honest," he said, dusting off his most melting look, "it's a miracle those trousers are on at all. Trying to dress Theo's like, well, wrestling with an octopus, ha ha . . ."

The Rottweiler held up a hand. "Mr. Fine. If you please. I run a nursery used by over fifty parents of small children. They all manage to dress them perfectly adequately."

Hugo was stung by the unfairness. He was a man, struggling by himself. Surely she could cut him some slack? He watched with trepidation as the Rottweiler fingered the slack on Theo's top or, to be more precise, the slack at the bottom, which hung down with two unmatched buttons on it. And which corresponded to the slack at the top with two vacant unbuttoned holes. "We were in a bit of a hurry and—" Hugo blustered.

"Not only have you not bothered to do this up properly," the Rottweiler accused, "but this item is on backwards as well. It's meant to button up the back."

Oh, for Christ's sake. How the hell was he expected to know that? The damned shirt hadn't come with a map. Didn't the woman realize how long it had taken to do up the buttons, however badly, in the first place?

"Mr. Fine." The Rottweiler folded her arms and stared him squarely in the face. "That children are presented neatly by their parents is one of Chicklets' most basic rules. As, having read the prospectus, you will know."

Hugo's shoulders slumped. In point of fact, he had not read the prospectus. It was, no doubt, lurking beneath one of the piles of paper that now rose like Manhattan in every room of Fitzherbert Place.

"I'm sorry," he muttered.

But the Rottweiler had not finished yet. "There is a reason for this rule, Mr. Fine. It encourages tidiness and cleanliness, as well as respect for others and the institution. Turning up with your child looking disheveled not only suggests the opposite, but suggests neglect of the child itself."

The flash of anger Hugo felt surprised him with its violence. "Are you saying I'm neglecting my son?"

The Rottweiler pursed her lips. "I am merely warning you that further transgressions of Chicklets' rules will be viewed in the dimmest of lights."

Hugo's fury was replaced by a sudden wave of terror. He remembered how utterly, already, he had come to depend on the nursery routine to give structure and stimulation to Theo and allow him to work.

"And there's one other thing," the Rottweiler said.

Hugo's heart plummeted. "There is?"

The Rottweiler eyed him sternly. "Is Theo up to date with his shots?"

Hugo was relieved to be able to nod with confidence. This was one aspect of childcare he'd been particularly careful to observe, with the help of reminder notes from the health visitor. "Absolutely. The next one's coming up soon."

The Rottweiler looked satisfied. "Good. There've been a couple of nasty rashes around in the nursery. But Theo should have no problems in that case."

As they left the nursery, Theo gave vent to his frustration by means of a sustained, piercing wail. Hugo did not blame him in the least. On the contrary, he wanted to join him. The noise intensified as Hugo tried to persuade the resisting infant into the car seat.

"I sure wouldn't be making that noise if you were holding *me*," purred someone behind them.

Laura was slinking across the car park as if coming onstage at the Moulin Rouge. Theo, rather unexpectedly, immediately stopped screaming and stared at her in amazement. Possibly, Hugo thought, because he had not seen that amount of lipstick before on anyone anywhere. Not even on his mother, who in any case must be becoming a distant memory by now.

"Amanda around?" Laura picked up uncannily on his train of thought.

"Er . . . No. I'm not exactly sure when she's coming back, either."

Laura's eyes lit up. "So she's left you all by yourself?" She ran her tongue suggestively across her teeth. "So why don't you come over for a drink sometime?"

"That's very kind." Hugo glared meaningfully through the open back door at his son. Never would an attack of separation anxiety have been so welcome. But the baby just stared on silently at Laura.

"I think he likes me." Laura pressed close to Hugo as she waved to Theo. "But then, he's a man. Most men do. Apart from bloody Fergus, that is," she added venomously. "Come on then," she urged. "Let's make a date."

Hugo shrank back, floundering for an excuse. "Er, the thing is . . ." He paused, then bent into the back of the car. Silently apologizing to Theo, he pinched the baby hard on the thigh. "I'm sorry," he gasped as the child gave a loud screech of protest. "But he's terribly tired. I'd really better take him home."

CHAPTER
17

"COME ON, DARLING," ALICE COAXED ROSA, PUSHING A SPOONFUL of beet, okra and sweet potato mush at her daughter's mouth. Rosa's red lips, however, were obdurately closed against the pink-gray slop and would, Alice suspected, remain that way. "Just a taste. It's not as bad as it looks. *It couldn't be,*" she added under her breath.

When Rosa was done eating, Alice took her up into the bedroom and laid her down. While thankful the child was now too large to fit in the hammock, she was less delighted with the substitute, a cot Jake had made by taking the lid off an old ottoman he had found—where else?—on a dump. Alice had scrubbed the box out several times but it still, she thought, sniffing it critically, had an unpleasant, musty smell.

Rosa nonetheless seemed happy in it, so Alice went into the bathroom to wash vegetable purée off her clothes. She tried not to look at the ottoman lid. This, with its hideous dusty-pink padded Dralon surface, had been put into service strengthening the top of the by-now-so-clearly-collapsing-even-Jake-could-not-ignore-it changing table. Alice felt irritated every time she looked at it and considered what grubs and insects might be living beneath the lid's dusty pink surface. How long it had been on the dump before Jake "found" it did not bear thinking about.

Her eye met the bathroom cupboard. Or, rather, the former wooden wine container mounted on the wall, which did the same job. It was full mainly of Jake's clutter, some from before she moved in. Occasionally she had thought about tidying it out, but had abandoned the idea in favor of something more pressing. Now, however, seemed the perfect time. Alice opened the door, which promptly fell off. She looked at the crammed shelves. Drawing the bathroom trash bin—a former paint tin—over, she began to clear them.

She was absorbed in her task when someone behind her said "Hey, there," in a low, suggestive growl.

Alice jumped as Jake snaked muscled arms around her waist and moved his hands up to caress her breasts. As he turned her head to his she stiffened. "I'm sorry, Jake. I'm not really in the mood."

"You were always in the mood *once*," he reminded her grumpily.

"I know. I probably will be later."

"Bloody hell!" Jake exclaimed. She realized that this was not an exclamation of anticipation. He wasn't talking about sex any more. His eye had caught the trash bin and what she had thrown in it. "That's perfectly good stuff!" He was yanking out a tube of cucumber face cream.

"Jake, it's *not* good stuff. I bought it as an emergency in some village shop in Wales about five years ago. It's always been rubbish and now's the time to get rid of it."

"But can't you use it for something else?" His eyes were wide with panic. "It's cucumber, is it? Can't we use it for . . . I don't know . . . salad dressing?"

"Jake, it's face cream. You can't *eat* it."

He was no longer listening. He had delved into the trash bin again and was looking anguished as he brought out a small, half-opened foil packet. "You're not throwing *these* away, are you?"

Alice swallowed. "These" had not been a particularly pleasant discovery. "Jake, they're condoms."

"So?"

"*Used* condoms." He must, she assumed, have put them back as a hideous mistake.

His expression did not change. "Yes?"

"But they've been put back in the *cupboard*." Alice felt a thrum, like an engine, start to build in her feet. "Jake, surely you're not telling me that you keep *used condoms*. That you *recycle* them?"

"Nothing wrong with that," he said defensively. "They're clean. I just rinse them out and they're as good as new."

"Good as new for what?" Alice croaked. Then the tension in her stomach eased as she realized that—of course—he must be talking about one of his reclaimed-junk sculptures. He must at some time have used them in his art. Very Jake and Dinos Chapman.

"You're asking what they're good for?" A wide, suggestive smile split Jake's face. "What do *you* think?"

"You're joking!" Alice felt her legs about to buckle. She fumbled behind her for the wall.

Jake's expression had become defiant. "I'm not joking. It makes sense. The condom industry has a lot to answer for. Those poor trees suffer agonies when they're bled for the rubber."

"Did you use a recycled condom when . . . when you met me?" Alice's heart was pounding so hard she could hardly hear her own voice.

"Um, yes, probably."

"What?" she rasped. It was the blithe, casual way he said it that appalled her. Hot tears burned behind her eyes.

"It's not impossible," he added. His voice was bouncy, almost self-congratulatory. As if he expected to be praised for such an admirable economy.

Alice felt about to burst. Her life had changed entirely because of this. She had given everything up when presented with the *fait accompli* of pregnancy. And although she had done it gladly, who was to say what her reaction would have been if she'd been given the choice? Quite possibly, having a child following a one-teatime-stand at a wedding would not have struck her as the answer to her problems. Certainly, she had been at her wits' end with Intercorp. But, as the head of Human Resources had said at the time, a week's holiday and a change of job could easily have been the solution.

Alice had never understood, not really, how she had become pregnant when Jake had been using a condom. But she did now. Condoms were not, of course, ever one-hundred-percent reliable. But they were a damn sight more so when new, and not rinsed-out used ones of questionable vintage. Possibly with more holes than those bloody colanders he had nailed to all the ceilings.

Accidents happened—Alice accepted that. One had to live with them. But what had happened to her was no accident. He had known, as she hadn't, that the protection being used during that first, passionate encounter, was almost certainly inadequate. He had sacrificed her power to determine her own future to his determination to recycle even the ludicrously, inadvisably, ridiculously unrecyclable.

She could hear her own voice in her memory, wondering over and over again at the way motherhood had come about so unexpectedly. And Jake's invariable reply: "Things like this happen for a reason."

Her fists clenched. Now, of course, she knew what that reason was. He had put the interests of a group of trees—a group of fucking *trees*—before her own.

She finally raised her eyes to meet his. "You bastard," she said simply. "You stupid, fucking, irresponsible *bastard*."

CHAPTER
18

Now that he'd cut four teeth Theo had, Hugo thought, the most adorable smile. He stared at it, hypnotized, unable for a moment to get on with the daily business of preparing for work and nursery.

He watched his son crawling swiftly off and leaped to get to the top of the stairs before Theo did. What strength there was in those solid little legs. He would be walking soon at this rate. Hugo felt his eyes prick as he imagined his son tottering toward him in that drunken, bow-legged, saddle-sore way that babies had. And Theo talking, which must surely happen sooner or later.

"Come on." He picked up his son and felt the small chubby legs grip his hip. They fitted well together these days, he and Theo. Better than they had. As he held the baby close, Hugo felt something else. Something squishy in the bottom region. Reluctantly, he returned to the bathroom and the baby changing unit.

The telephone rang as he finished the nappy change. Hugo went to answer it, returning to the kitchen with the portable handset and putting it on speakerphone as he shoved some toast under the grill.

"Are you signing with him?" demanded a testy female voice.

"*Amanda?*"

Both he and Theo stared at the handset in amazement.

"Well, don't sound so surprised. I am his mother, you know."

"Actually, I was beginning to forget," Hugo muttered under his breath as Theo hurled a piece of crumpet that hit him square in the suit jacket. He reached for one of the baby-wipes with which the house was littered and rubbed frantically at the stain.

"What was that you just said?"

"Nothing. It's an awful line. Am I *singing* with him, did you say? Well, a bit, I suppose. He prefers Elvis, though."

"*Signing.* Not singing, you idiot. Babies who sign have an IQ twelve to fourteen points higher by the age of seven compared to children who don't and—"

"Amanda! Where are you? What the hell are you talking about?" Hugo squinted at the wall, as if this would improve his hearing.

"New York. And I'm calling to ask whether my son is being given the opportunity to improve his brain by using the latest powerful but effective child development technique, namely signing."

Hugo drew shuddering breath as he realized that Amanda, having been absent and incommunicado for weeks on end, was actually calling with parental advice.

It was, he knew, vital not to express the anger he felt in front of Theo. Listening to your parents fighting was powerful child development of another sort altogether. "What is this signing?" Hugo asked through gritted teeth, rubbing harder at his suit to work off his irritation.

"I can't believe you've never heard of it," Amanda snapped. "Isn't he doing it at nursery, for Christ's sake? Everyone here is. God, the UK is just *so* backward. OK, well, the sign for milk is like milking a cow, right? You squeeze your fist and make this sign before you give Theo milk and then Theo will do it back when he wants milk—"

"Excuse me," Hugo interrupted with freezing politeness, "but if Theo wants milk, I know all about it, believe me. He doesn't have to make any signs. He just yells."

"That's because he's frustrated," Amanda cut in. "He's disempowered because he's preverbal."

"Come again?"

"Very young children lack the motor skills to produce speech but they do have the ability to sign." She sounded, Hugo thought, as if she was reading it off the back of a box. "You can't start too early . . . girls routinely outperform boys in school."

"Amanda. Hang on. Theo is five months old."

"Yes. Exactly. You'd better buck up and get signing if he's going to be on *University Challenge*."

"What?"

"Hang on." There was a muffled discussion on the other end of the line. "I've got to go," Amanda said imperiously. "Must dash and talk about Estée Lauder. Have you got it yet, by the way?"

"Got what?" Hugo sniffed. There was a definite smell of burning in the air. He looked around with panic at the grill. Black smoke was pouring out of it.

"That stuff I sent. Look, I'll talk to you later."

"What stuff . . . ?" The line went dead. As Hugo dragged forth the incinerated bread, there came a hammering at the door, accompanied by the revving of an engine. Knowing of old the dangers of leaving the baby in his high chair, Hugo threw both grill and toast into the sink, lifted Theo out, put him abruptly down on the floor and gave him his car keys to play with before hurrying along the hall passage.

"This number four?" bellowed the man in the brown United Parcel Service uniform. "Got a delivery for you."

"But I wasn't expecting anything." Hugo glanced anxiously over his shoulder down the hallway. Was Theo where he had left him?

The deliveryman strode around to the back of the van and flung open the doors. "Help me down with this lot, can you?"

"I can't. I've got a baby inside." Inside the bloody oven by now, probably. Or putting his tongue into the electric sockets.

"Won't take a minute. 'Ere you are, squire."

"*Umph.*" Hugo reeled under the weight of the huge, heavy cardboard boxes being thrown his way. "Look, there's been a mistake."

The deliveryman consulted his notes. "Nah. No mistake. Delivery to four Fitzherbert Place, this says."

"But what is it?"

The deliveryman squinted at the clipboard. "Trouble with these things is you can't read the writing . . . oh, 'ere we go. It's a Hideaway Hollow."

"A what?"

"Don' arse me. A Hideaway Hollow, whatever that is."

Hugo's distracted ears strained for Theo. He could hear nothing. No doubt he was halfway up the stairs by now. Or lying at the bottom in a crumpled heap. Desperately, he looked at the labels on the boxes. "Tree house, it says here," he said wildly. "It's a tree house."

"Well, there you are then," said the man in brown. "It's a tree 'ouse."

"But I haven't ordered a tree house . . . oh, sod it. Never mind. Where do I sign?"

As the van roared off, Hugo shot back inside. To his vast relief, Theo was still sitting on the floor, chewing happily on the keys to the Toyota. Picking him up, Hugo went outside and tried with one hand to drag the heavy cardboard parcels off the pavement and up the front step. Who the hell had sent this ludicrous contraption and, more to the point, why?

Opening the first of the parcels, Hugo found a small gold envelope on which was typed, in loopy, foreign-looking typing, the word "Theo." Inside was a note from Amanda. It was scented and printed with pastel balloons.

My darling Theo, Hugo read disbelievingly. *Here's a little present for you! Your Hideaway Hollow! I hope you like it. Brooklyn Beckham's got one exactly the same—they cost £8,000 and are hand-carved from real wood, not nasty plastic! From a Scandinavian redwood tree, apparently! I bet none of your friends have got one! You can only get them at Harrods. Get Daddy to put it up for you. And get him to help you send a thank-you letter to that lovely Mr. Fayed. See you soon, my darling. Your loving Mommy.*

A series of increasingly bizarre gifts followed where the tree house had led. A huge, barking toy dog came one week, a mini-biohazard suit from a shop near Ground Zero the next, "because you never know" the note attached had said.

One thing he certainly didn't know, Hugo thought, was when Amanda was coming back. Or whether. Her absences stretched from one week to the next with no fixed date for her return. No doubt these stupid and extravagant presents were intended to compensate Theo for this. He, meanwhile, Hugo thought crossly, was clearly expected just to carry on regardless.

His irritation peaked the morning he opened the door to go to nursery and found, staring him in the face, a well-built man with his fist raised. "What the hell . . ." Hugo began.

"Sorry mate," said the man in a broad Cockney accent. "Was about to knock."

Behind him, half on the pavement, was a large pink and purple van bearing the star-festooned logo "Twinkledreams."

"I'm 'ere to do the ceiling," the man informed him.

Hugo stared. "I don't understand. What ceiling?"

"You jokin' me? The one in the baby's nursery, o' course. Now look 'ere, I've come all the way from Kensin'ton. If this is some sort o' bleedin' joke—"

"Look," Hugo cut in. "I don't know what you're talking

about. And I'm in a hurry, so . . ." He was about to disappear back into the house and shut the door behind him when his mobile shrilled.

With difficulty he fished it out, and with even more difficulty stopped Theo grabbing it. "Amanda."

"Just checking to see if it's here."

Hugo exhaled hotly through his nose in annoyance. "What the hell have you sent now?"

"A Twinkledreams ceiling."

So that was what it was. Another insane bequest from across the Atlantic. "We don't want a bloody Twinkledreams ceiling. Whatever that may be."

"I can't believe you've never heard of them. Or maybe I can," Amanda sighed martyrishly. "Anyway, they're very trendy. The projectors built into the walls change the sky on the ceiling from dawn to dusk while Baby sleeps. Oh, and the stars twinkle."

"But what's the point if it all happens when Theo's asleep?"

"He never sleeps," Amanda said authoritatively.

"He does now," Hugo returned triumphantly.

"Well, whatever," Amanda snapped. "Everyone who's anyone's baby's got one. They cost twenty thousand pounds. Don't you think that's lovely?"

"Twenty thousand?"

There was a shrill of laughter from the other end. "You don't think *I'm* paying for it, do you? Woman in my position? Hardly, sweetie. By the way, the photographer's not there yet, is he?"

"Photographer? Amanda, would you mind explaining just what the hell is going on?"

Theo's bedroom, complete with new fiber-optic ceiling, was, it seemed, to be featured in a prominent US interiors magazine. The ceiling company had supplied it free in exchange for publicity. As soon as she had explained this, Amanda hung up. Hugo watched helplessly as the Twinkledreams representative picked up his tool bag and went past into the hall.

His mobile rang again. He answered it crossly, expecting more Amanda. He did not, at first, recognize the woman's voice on the other end. It was muffled and nasal, as if the speaker had a bad cold.

"Hugo?" it sniffed.

"Alice?" Hugo immediately forgot all about Twinkledreams. The goddess of parenting, with her serene face and dreamy blue eyes, was phoning . . . *him?* What tremendous stroke of luck was this?

"Can we meet for a drink?" Alice asked. "I've had some, er, bad news."

"Erm-God-yes-absolutely-of-course-no-problem-when?"

"Now?"

"Yeah. Great." A date with Alice! It was unbelievable. His morning was suddenly looking up. Much as, in bemusement at his ceiling, Theo would shortly be doing.

"Couldn't be better. I've just got to drop Theo off at nursery and I'm all yours."

"Don't you have to go to work?"

"Well, yes. But not straight away." This was not true. He was supposed to do a show-round in half an hour on the other side of Bath. But, he reasoned to himself, it was only a couple of Saab-driving tossers looking for a second home in the country. He could easily ring them and rearrange it. "Where do you want to meet? There's a café near the—"

"Café?" Alice said contemptuously. "I don't want *coffee*. I know it's only half-past eight, but I want a *drink*. And a pretty fucking stiff one, if it's all the same to you."

*   *   *

"You're *joking*," Hugo gasped as, one hour and several drinks later, Alice reached the climax of her tale. "He'd been recycling the *condoms?*"

Hugo was amazed. His low opinion of Jake had turned out to be a flattering overestimation.

"I can't believe it," he said eventually, shaking his head slowly. "He sounds straight out of one of those weird religious sects they have in the States, where the women obey their menfolk no matter how reactionary and repressive they are. Know what I mean?"

"I have an idea," Alice said tightly.

"Oh God, of course you do. How stupid of me."

Alice covered her face. "How stupid of *me*, you mean. I can't believe what I've been putting up with. It's all so obvious now. My mother was absolutely right. She said he was brainwashing me." She shook her head. "Why did I put up with it? *Why?*"

Hugo shrugged. "Love?" he suggested, coloring slightly. "It's the oldest excuse in the book, obviously. But it's still the best. I mean, look at me. I thought I was in love with Amanda . . ." He stopped, appalled. Mentioning Amanda in front of Alice was never a good idea.

But Alice was considering. "Love." She smiled ruefully. "Yes. I *was* in love. Very much." Her face softened as she looked at the baby asleep in her lap. "And I still am," she added, extending a finger to touch Rosa's peachy cheek.

"With *Jake*?" Hugo was horrified.

"I was talking about Rosa. I don't know how I feel about Jake at the moment."

"Well I must say I bloody do." Hugo told her indignantly. "Not that it's my business of course," he added a second later.

There followed one of those awkward silences Hugo remembered from the supermarket café. He searched for a way to break it.

"We'd better have something to eat," he suggested. "Soak all this booze up. What do you fancy?" He peered at the bar menu.

"I don't care," Alice said. Then a defiant light blazed in her eyes. "Oh, actually, I do. Just for once, I'd like the most mass-produced internationally corporate hamburger imaginable, with gobs of synthetic cheese and tomato ketchup, served in a white roll made of bleached flour inside an ozone-layer-destroying Styrofoam container."

"Coming up," grinned Hugo, waving for a waiter. "Fancy another drink?"

"Are you sure you've got time?" Alice met his smile with a shy one of her own. "Thanks for listening," she added. "It's made me feel—well—*better,* telling you about it. You see, I'm a bit like you with Theo. There's no one else I can really talk to."

Looking into her sad, sincere face, Hugo felt like ice cream on a hot August pavement. Rescuing his reputation at Dunn and Dustard could not have seemed less important. "My appointment can wait," he heard himself saying.

The waiter arrived with the drinks.

"What's it like being a real estate agent?" Alice asked, seizing both her gin and the opportunity to change the subject.

Hugo shrugged. "OK, I suppose. You get out and about."

She looked at him wryly. "Jake says real estate agents spend their whole time lying. Forcing people into deals that plunge them into debt, all for the sake of houses that aren't worth living in."

"He really is a ray of sunshine, isn't he?" Hugo said crossly.

Alice picked at a bowl of vegetable chips. Up until now, Hugo had assumed they were potpourri. "I wonder if these are organic," she mused.

"Shouldn't think so."

"Great." She took a handful and smiled at him. "Yes, well, quite apart from what Jake says, can you honestly say that every single house you sell is as marvellous as you make it out to be?"

"A lot of the ones around here are very nice," Hugo insisted.

"So real estate agenting's not a lying profession?" Alice teased.

"Not at all—well, sometimes I suppose," Hugo confessed. "Oh, look," he said thankfully. "Here comes the food."

And that's not the only thing, he thought in horror a second later, as a big-nosed woman with high heels clacked toward them across the lobby floor.

"Hewwwwwgooooo!" exclaimed Laura, enveloping him in an elaborate kiss. He could feel, rather than see, Alice's amazement.

"Hello, Laura," he muttered, extracting himself from her cleavage. "Fancy meeting you here! This is Alice," he said hurriedly, wondering why he felt so defensive. It wasn't as if he and Alice were there for the purpose Laura had been. And was again, for all he knew. "She was at the same prenatal class as us," he added.

"Really?" Laura, a proprietorial hand still on Hugo's shoulder, scrutinized Alice closely. "Can't say I remember."

Alice got to her feet, slightly unsteadily. "I'd better be going."

"But you haven't eaten your burger," Hugo pointed out in despair.

"Haven't time. Rosa's going to wake up in a minute."

"Don't worry, it won't go to waste." Laura had picked up the ketchup-slathered bun and was stuffing it into her face. "Mm. Delicious."

"Bye, then." Hugo's eyes were beaming messages into Alice's, none of which she appeared to receive. She looked back blankly.

"What's that?" Laura squawked suddenly, pointing at the handles of Rosa's buggy. And, specifically, at the large white bag stretched across them. "I know this sounds far-fetched and they're probably the most stylish buggy carryall going, but they look just like maternity knickers with the legholes sewn up."

"That's exactly what they are," Alice muttered, blushing. "They're recycled."

Laura frowned for a split second, then waved the burger in excitement. "Oh, of course! I remember you now. You were that mad environmentalist who was going to have a home birth on a shower curtain."

CHAPTER
19

THE FOLLOWING MORNING, HUGO DROVE THEO INTO BATH TO THE health center. While he was not looking forward to watching his son being stabbed with a needle, it was difficult not to feel cheerful. It *was* an absolutely beautiful day.

As he parked and carried Theo to the health center, Hugo found himself admiring the Georgian buildings en route. He registered, with a prick of surprise, that there was a space of a good few minutes before he started to reckon what each structure was worth. And what, were he selling it, he could hope to cream off in commission. Was the habit of a lifetime weakening? Was he finally appreciating architecture for its own sake?

Certainly he had found himself, recently, even admiring the contours of Fitzherbert Place. The house had a definite grace, despite the enormous amount of work it needed. But Hugo had now quietly abandoned Amanda's plans for refurbishment. Seeing them through involved not only time and money, but inclination. Neither he nor Theo cared if an ever-largening stain accompanied them most of the way up the staircase.

His mobile shrilled as he registered Theo at the reception desk. The possibility that it was Alice leapt wildly in his mind, to be swiftly and cruelly followed by the discovery that it was Neil. Sounding very angry. As he carried the writhing baby into the waiting area, Hugo felt his benevolent mood leak away.

"Where the fuck are you, may I ask?" Neil demanded.

"At the health center. Theo's having a shot."

"Oh, for Christ's sake. Don't bother telling us, will you? Why don't you just become a full-time nanny and have bloody done with it?"

"I did tell you about it. Or Shuna, at any rate. She put it in the diary."

"You knew about this, did you, Shuna?" Neil yelled at his secretary. "Fine's bloody baby getting a shot? In the diary is it . . . *no*? He *didn't* tell you? You didn't tell her, Fine," Neil announced, returning to the receiver.

Hugo fought to keep patient. "Well, she obviously forgot." His ear caught Theo being announced over the doctor's intercom. "I've got to go. I'll be in later. After I've dropped him off at nursery."

"Nursery? *Nursery?*!" Neil was expostulating as Hugo turned the phone off.

Hugo reached Dunn and Dustard with a cold sense of dread in his stomach. Yet, most unexpectedly, Neil actually smiled as he came in. An assessment request, it turned out, had come through half an hour ago, from someone in one of Bath's nicest areas. They had asked for Hugo personally. "They say they've heard you're very good," Neil added, raising an eyebrow.

Hugo turned his attention to the notes concerning the assessment. He whistled. "Wow."

"Quite something, eh, Fine?" Neil grunted.

"You bet. Must be the most tasteless place I've ever seen. 'The house is called Leather, after the nightclub the owners met in,' " Hugo quoted from the notes.

"Yeah, but the guide price is two million. Get that on our books and we stand to make some serious money. And you stand to redeem yourself, Fine. The owner's expecting you tomorrow, by the way."

The next day, Hugo parked in the road outside Leather. As he remembered to do only rarely these days, he checked his appearance in the mirror. He was relieved he had. There was some salvage work to be done.

He wiped himself down as best he could, raked his hair with his hands and smoothed his eyebrows with his thumbs. Then he swung his legs out of the car, squared his shoulders and set off for the house.

In contrast with—or defiance of—the gracious Georgian houses neighboring it, Leather was of a type best described as contemporary. Its enormously high boundary wall was of brash, golden, brilliantly new stone. Its gates, as expected, were electronic, and as they swung slowly open to reveal the boxy, glassy house at the end of the curving drive, Hugo stood for a minute, stunned. It was even worse in reality than it had sounded on paper. Even London, at its lurid worst, seemed restrained compared to this.

He crunched up the dazzlingly orange paved brick drive to the front door. The tune that pealed out as he rang the doorbell reminded him unpleasantly of a turgid rock anthem called "The Wind Beneath My Wings." But surely that was a little farfetched. Even for a house called Leather.

The shape visible through the glass doorway was singing something as it approached. "You're the wind beneath my-hiy wings," it declared in a husky vibrato as it opened the door.

"Laura!" Hugo clutched the folders under his arm in panic.

"Hi, sexy! Is that a tape measure in your pocket or are you just pleased to see me?"

It wasn't just the line that was bad. The clothes weren't too good either. She lounged against the door frame in a near-transparent red chiffon negligée, every available edge of which seemed to be trimmed with marabou feathers.

He struggled hard to feel relaxed rather than alarmed. Laura routinely dressed like a Bangkok ladyboy, so this was probably nothing out of the ordinary.

"I didn't realize this was your place," he remarked with as much ease as he could muster. Although, he supposed, if there was one person in the whole of Bath he might imagine lived in Leather, it would be Laura. "What a coincidence!" he added, knowing perfectly well it was nothing of the kind. So it was she who had requested his services in particular. Was it merely an excuse to see him? Was there the remotest chance that she was serious about this sale?

"Isn't it just?" Laura beamed back.

"Especially as," Hugo said pleasantly, "you never mentioned you were putting it up for sale when we met at the nursery."

"Must have slipped my mind." She turned and beckoned him to follow her.

He looked around for as long as he possibly could before reluctantly returning his gaze to Laura. In addition to the usual plastering of makeup, she wore red satin high-heeled mules to match the negligée.

"Like it?" She put her hands on her hips and pushed her breasts forward.

Hugo paused, on the horns of a dilemma. To say yes would obviously mean trouble, while a no would just as obviously annoy. Yet the slight chance the house really was up for sale was not one he could afford to endanger. He settled for what he hoped was a polite but noncommittal grunt.

"Want a drink?" Laura purred.

"Yes, please." Hugo jumped at the chance to inject some normality into the scenario. "Coffee would be great."

Laura bent over to open the fridge despite the fact its handle was on a level with her elbow. That negligée left nothing to the imagination. You could see up to her tonsils. Averting his eyes, Hugo brought them back a few seconds later to see Laura holding, not the carton of milk he had expected, but a bottle of champagne. Before he could say anything she had prised off the cage and was handling the cork in a highly suggestive manner.

"Oh." Hugo smiled uncertainly. "That sort of drink." His eyes slid to the kitchen clock. It was not yet ten.

Nonetheless, he accepted the bulky cut-crystal glass Laura smilingly passed him. "Your husband around?" he asked casually, fervently hoping so. Fergus sounded horrible, but less so than being alone with his wife.

Laura's smile snapped off. *"Him?"* she spat. "He's casting a commercial in Sweden. *If* you get my meaning."

"Oh. Right."

"He doesn't fancy me anymore." Laura's lip suddenly trembled and her head started to wobble. She clutched his arm, nails boring in through his jacket fabric. "Don't *you* fancy me, Hugo?" she asked plaintively. "Aren't I attractive?"

Hugo sighed. Another tactical cul de sac to extricate himself from. "Fergus can't possibly mean it," he said evasively. "It must be his idea of a joke."

"Joke!" Laura exclaimed furiously. "Know what he said to me the other night?" Her champagne glass, he noticed, was almost empty already.

"We were lying in bed and he was doing the usual—"

"Well, there you are," Hugo interrupted triumphantly. "He was doing the usual. What more proof do you need that he finds you attractive?"

"When I say the usual," Laura's eyes flashed over the rim of her glass, "I mean that he was banging on as usual about how important he was. And so I said, 'Well, of course, I only do a *little* job. Looking after Django and all that.' Just to see what he'd say."

"And what did he say?"

"He said 'mm.' He *agreed*!"

"Mmm," said Hugo. He corrected himself hastily. "I mean, er, oh dear."

She burst into tears, flinging herself, sobbing, on to Hugo's chest. He felt the sooty tears soaking into his pristine white shirt and her hot, panting breath and damp skin. Her heavy perfume made his head swim. Tuberose. A smell that always made him feel he was gasping for air. He thought fleetingly of Alice, who, he imagined, never smelled of anything but soap.

She raised her streaked face, eyes tragic. "I don't have any friends in Bath. Apart from Amanda, of course, and she's buggered off and left me." She was wiping her nose on the backs of her hands.

Join the club, thought Hugo.

Suddenly, the megawatt smile was back on again. She sidled up very close. He stiffened.

"Still," she purred, running her hands down her hips, "at least I haven't let myself go. Have I, Hugo?"

He swallowed. "Er, no. No, not at all."

"Not like that hippy from the prenatal class you were with the other day," Laura tittered. "What does she think she looks like? Not a scrap of slap and hair like straw. Shame, though. She'd probably scrub up well if she bothered."

Indignation swept Hugo. How dare she talk this way about Alice?

"I saw you from the other side of the foyer." Laura nudged him meaningfully. "And I thought, way hey, what's naughty old Hugo up to then? But I have to say I was a little bit disappointed when I saw it was *her*. Or do I mean relieved?"

"I don't follow," Hugo said stiffly.

"Do I have to spell it out? I thought you were up to—well, *you know*—but then I realized, when I saw *her*, that you couldn't possibly be! I mean, you're married to Amanda. Miss Well-Groomed Glossy 2005. You don't have affairs with tramps."

Tramps! If anyone round here was a tramp . . . Hugo bit back a furious defense of Alice and fished out his notebook. The sooner he did the assessment, the sooner he could get out.

"What are you doing?" Laura breathed, tracing the line of his cheekbone with a finger.

"Taking notes for the house details. The brochure, you know."

"Why?" She was ruffling his hair now.

"Well, there's usually a brochure when a house like this is being sold."

"Is there?" She giggled.

"Yes." Gently yet determinedly, he detached her hand from his head. He fought his instinct to turn on his heel and run. He needed this commission. "So," he said brightly, "this is the kitchen. What about the rest of the place?"

She stuck out a teasing lower lip. "Refill?" She brandished the champagne bottle.

"I'm all right, thanks."

"Oh, for God's sake. Live a little." She tipped some into his own nearly full glass and slopped a lot into her empty one. She looked at him quizzically. "OK then," she said resignedly. "This way." He followed her out into the hallway.

"Oops!" she exclaimed, clacking to a halt and picking up a small black remote control that lay on a mirror-topped side-table. She pointed it at the corner of the room. "Best deactivate the security system, eh?"

"Security system throughout," Hugo said loudly, making notes in a businesslike fashion.

Laura started her bottom-wiggling ascent of a sweeping Plexiglass staircase best described, Hugo thought, as *Gone With the Wind* meets *Star Wars*. Could he put that in the brochure? She went up remarkably quickly, given her heels. When he got to the top, there was no sign of her.

"Laura?" he called.

"Come and find me!" sang out the teasing reply.

He followed the direction of the voice down a white-painted, cream-carpeted corridor featuring about six identical, wide white doors with Perspex globes for handles. Only one was ajar.

"Laura?" he repeated, outside it.

"In he-yah!" she trilled.

When, some time later, he could bear to think about this scene, Hugo supposed he was asking for it. He should have known, given the morning's run-up, given Laura's history in general, exactly what lay behind that bedroom door. He should have acknowledged what was glaringly obvious: that her reason for calling him to the house had nothing to do with selling it. Ultimately, he should have faked some call from the office and beaten a hasty retreat.

But he did none of these things. Instead, he pushed open the bedroom door.

It was worse than he had feared. Laura, naked apart from the red silk mules, lay in the center of a large, rumpled, purple four-poster. Her knees were up and her legs were spread wide in an attitude reminding Hugo unpleasantly of the birthing position in Lotti's videos. The white flesh of her breasts spilled over the hands that pushed rhythmically upward and outward toward him. She was gyrating her pelvis and moaning.

"Come and get it, big boy," she murmured. "You know you want it."

Oh fuck, thought Hugo. Or, rather, the opposite. He had never seen anything less erotic in his life. The atmosphere in the room was suffocating. The curtains were pulled, the heat was intense and the scent of tuberose overwhelming.

Desperately, he tried to get a grip on the situation. "Er, look, Laura. I mean, it's very good of you to offer, but the thing is . . ."

As he stood on, rooted to the spot, Laura's come-hither looks darkened to annoyance. "Well! What are you waiting for?"

"Er, I'm, you know, well, there's Amanda . . ."

"Amanda!" She rolled across the bed and slid off the end toward him. Her mouth was distorted in a big red sneer. "She doesn't give a flying fuck about you. Otherwise why isn't she here?"

It was a neat summary of his situation. He could hardly have put it better himself. "Erm, well, even so, technically at least, I'm a married man."

"So what?" Laura shot back. "I'm a married woman."

"I'm a father," Hugo argued.

"I'm a mother," she countered.

Hugo backed away. "Laura, I really don't think this is a good idea."

"Why not?" she growled, approaching him like a lioness might her prey. Her unruly hair had clumped over her face and her breasts swung heavily from side to side. "Don't I turn you on? You said I was attractive."

"You are attractive. But . . ."

Her head flew up, dislodging the hair. "Are you saying," Laura accused, "that you don't fancy me?"

"Er . . . hang on, that's my phone." Never had he scrambled for it so eagerly.

"Leave it!" Laura commanded.

"I can't," Hugo had spotted Chicklets' number on the screen. "It's Theo's nursery. It could be anything."

"It'll be something and nothing. Always bloody is. They're always sending Django home with conjunctivitis. I just clean him up, put white foundation powder over the red bits around his eyes and send him back."

Never, Hugo thought, pressing the little green phone icon, had he been so glad to hear from the Rottweiler.

His relief lasted approximately three seconds.

The Rottweiler, as ever, was crisp, to the point and terrifying. "Mr. Fine, I would be grateful if you could come and get Theo immediately. He has a suspect rash on his chest."

"But he was fine when I left him."

"That may be so. But he isn't now."

"Well, don't you know what this rash is? He had a shot yesterday. It's probably a reaction to that."

"Mr. Fine, we are a nursery, not a hospital accident and emergency department."

The mere mention of such places sent a chill through Hugo. "But don't you have someone there who knows about . . . that sort of thing?" Surely, with the fees they charged? It seemed amazing that they could just ring up and suddenly all the responsibility was the parent's.

"Mr. Fine, I repeat, we are a nursery. Not a sanitorium. And we would be most grateful if you came and removed your son. Now." *Click. Burr.*

Hugo stared at the mobile, his bewilderment mixed with a growing terror.

"Hewwwwgoooo!" Laura mewed at him from the bed. She was rubbing herself up against the bedpost, one hand pushing her breasts toward him. "I *need* you," she lowed through pouting lips.

Distractedly, he stared at her. In the light of what he had just heard, the situation he was now in seemed more unreal and absurd than ever. "You don't need *me*, Laura," he said slowly. "What you need is . . . I don't know. Therapy or something."

"Therapy?!" Her eyes flashed fire. "How fucking dare you?"

"Because it's true," Hugo said quietly, walking out of the room.

Her outraged howl followed him down the slippery glass staircase. "Therapy! Me? I'm not the kind of woman who needs therapy! There's nothing fucking wrong with me. You'll be sorry you said that. *Bastard*."

CHAPTER
20

A T CHICKLETS, THEO WAS CRYING. "HE'S NOT QUITE HIMSELF," THE nursery assistant remarked as she pushed up Theo's onesie to reveal a handful of faint red spots.

At the sight of them, Hugo felt faint with relief. Only now did he realize he had been expecting something akin to bubonic plague. "They don't look so bad," he said.

"You never know with rashes," the assistant replied equivocally.

The baby's spots, so far as Hugo could see, did not get worse through the afternoon. At bedtime, Theo, most unusually, did not protest either at being taken upstairs or laid down on the changing table for his pajamas and new bedtime nappy. He did not even wail for his pacifier, which Hugo was especially pleased about. While pacifiers had been an essential part of life when Amanda had first left, and were still vital in getting Theo off to sleep, Chicklets did not approve of them. Hugo himself had a love-hate relationship with them— while grateful for the peace they provided, he deplored the way they made Theo look like Hannibal Lecter, wings of plastic spreading out on either side of his face.

But as he undressed Theo, the possible reason for the baby's uncharacteristically placid mood became instantly, hideously obvious. The pale red spots which had sprinkled Theo's stomach and chest had changed. They had multiplied a hundredfold and glared out a dark and angry crimson, raised slightly from the skin. They looked, Hugo thought, like flocked wallpaper. The meningitis poster in the doctor's office flashed horribly into his mind.

For a few seconds, he was too terrified to move, as if, somehow, by keeping still, he would maintain control of the situation. He dithered, baby-wipe in hand, before suddenly snapping into action and, stuffing Theo under his arm, flinging himself downstairs to the phone. With trembling hand, he called the doctor's office.

The recorded voice of the receptionist advised him in warm, West Country tones that the health center was now closed. It recommended that he call NHS Direct. Flustered by this unexpected turn of events, Hugo had to call back twice to get the number accurately, then punched it on to the keypad with shaking hand. Eventually, someone came on the line and asked for his address.

"My baby's got a rash," Hugo croaked. What the hell did his address have to do with it?

"We'll get to that. Could I just have your postcode? And your date of birth."

"But he might have fucking meningitis," Hugo yelled. Under his arm, Theo began to cry.

"The sooner you give me your details, sir, the sooner someone will be able to call you back."

Hugo was aghast. "Call me back? Can't I talk to you about it?"

"I'm one of the operators. A nurse or doctor will call you back."

"And how long's that going to take?"

"Hopefully not longer than ten minutes. Now if you'll just give me your postcode . . ."

Hugo slammed the phone down in panic. Ten minutes! He

wasn't sure how fast meningitis acted, but he knew it didn't hang about. Theo's little life could have been snuffed out by then. Hugo clasped his by now screaming son to his chest, wrapping him in the folds of the suit jacket he was still wearing from this morning. He felt like crying himself and only by a supreme effort of will managed not to.

Instead, he paced up and down, trying to calm the riot in his brain. He should, he knew, ring Amanda. She was Theo's mother. She had a right to know what was happening. She might, he hoped as he stabbed the keypad, have some idea what to do.

"Hi, Amanda Hardwick here," said her mobile's answerphone. "Sorry I can't come to the phone right now, but if you leave a message . . ."

The panic in Hugo's head was a whirling blizzard. He wanted to run amok and scream. But he couldn't. He had to hold on, for Theo's sake. The baby's life might depend on the decisions he made now. Hugo breathed in deeply—so deeply it made his head spin. Then it came to him. Alice. Of course. He could ring Alice.

*　　*　　*

Alice was upstairs when she heard the phone ring, putting Rosa to bed in the ottoman. Jake, at home on account of the rubbish still apparently filling his office, went to answer it.

"Alice?" she heard him say suspiciously. "She's here, yes."

Against her better judgment, Alice thought grimly. In the white heat of her first, furious anger following the condom discovery, she had been ready to leave and take Rosa with her. On the back of the humiliation of the dinner party, it was the last straw. Then her native good sense had kicked in. Emotional grand gestures, tempting though they were, often resulted in repenting at leisure. She wasn't making decisions for herself alone; Rosa's best interests were the most important thing.

A factor, minor but not insignificant, in her eventual decision to stay was that Jake seemed genuinely sorry for his actions. It was the first time Alice had heard him either apologize or admit that he was wrong.

"It was stupid of me, I know," Jake had groaned, his handsome face creased with regret. "I honestly didn't think the condom would have a hole in. I hadn't used it that much before, honestly."

Alice winced.

He tried another tack. "And of course your human rights are more important than those of the rubber trees."

"Jake, trees don't have human rights as such. They're *trees*."

"But if you'd just tell me who's calling . . ." Jake's voice, irritated, floated up from downstairs. Still on the phone, Alice realized, returning from her daydream. But hadn't whoever it was rung for her? Indignantly, she went to the top of the stairs to listen. "So you say you're a friend of hers, sure," Jake was saying. "But *who shall I tell her's calling?*"

Hugo, at the other end, hadn't expected to have to get through Alice's security system first. That, after the unbelievable condom business, Jake was still around was an unpleasant surprise. "Tell her it's a friend," he repeated stubbornly.

"Yes, but *what* friend?" The jaunty, slightly whiny voice had a ring of insistent steel in it. Jake would, Hugo knew, put the phone down in an instant if he knew his identity. The thought of this happening with Theo possibly dying in the background brought him to the edge of murderous frenzy. With a superhuman effort, he tried to calm down.

"Just put her on, will you? It's an emergency."

There was a distrustful silence. Hugo sensed he was about to be cut off. Then, miraculously, in the background, he heard Alice's voice. She must have just come into the room. He felt like yelling to attract her attention, but realized this would be futile.

"Someone for me, is it?" he heard her ask.

There was a crashing noise as Jake handed the receiver over.

"Hello?"

"Oh Alice," Hugo gasped, "thank God you're there. You've got to help me, I don't know what's wrong with him, he's—"

Alice frowned. "Who *is* this?"

"It's Hugo."

"Hugo?"

Alice felt her face glow red. Her heart raced at the memory of their last meeting. The things she had said. The amount she had drunk. What he must have thought of her.

On the other side of the room, Jake stiffened with hostility at the name. "*Him!* What does *he* want?"

"What's the matter?" Alice asked, doing her best to ignore her husband. She sensed immediately that this was not a social call.

"Theo. He's got a rash," Hugo whimpered. "It looks bad, Alice."

"How bad? Have you done the glass test?"

"Glass test?"

"*What's going on?*" demanded Jake agitatedly, closing in on Alice and the phone.

"You press a clear glass over the spots," Alice instructed while trying to bat Jake away. "If they fade, it's not meningitis. If they don't fade, it is. Try it. I'll stay on the line while you do."

At Hugo's end, the phone clattered to the floor. She heard him rummaging in cupboards, cursing, then the smash of several glasses falling. Throughout, in the background, was the high, keening note of a crying baby. She bit her lip.

Jake was gesturing angrily in her face again. Again she tried to make him go away. "He's in trouble," she hissed. "His baby's ill . . ." She stopped as, at the other end of the phone, a scraping and bumping announced that Hugo had snatched it up again. "All our glasses are cut crystal," he howled. "Amanda didn't seem to buy anything else, bugger her."

"But you must have *something*. Not even an old jam jar?" Alice's gaze trailed around her own sitting room. Jam jars were all she could see—used as candle holders, filled with earth and used as doorstops, standing on the mantelpiece collecting coins, corks and bits of scrap paper.

"He's a waste of time, Al!" Jake snarled. Suddenly, he snatched at the telephone.

Furiously, Alice slapped him away.

"Found one," Hugo gasped, returning to the phone. "Used to have a really horrid scented candle in it," he added, with the pointlessness of panic. "Right. What did you say I should do now?"

"Press it against the spots. If they fade on contact, they're not meningitis."

In the background, Theo's crying changed key and became harder, more desperate. Alice's fists curled with tension. When Hugo came back to the phone his voice was cracked and barely audible. It was clear he was on the verge of weeping.

"Alice, I can't bloody tell if it's fading or not. I've tried, but I just can't. I'm too fucking scared to think straight."

"Hugo, calm down," Alice said gently. "It's a hard thing to do, I know, but it's important. Have you called the doctor?"

"I've rung both the doctor and NHS bloody Direct. The office was closed and NHS Direct was useless."

Alice considered for exactly half a second. "Right. *Here's* what you do. Call an ambulance now. Then wrap Theo up warmly. And give me your address. I'll be right over."

She put the phone down to find Jake glaring in hot-eyed indignation. "His *address?* You're going over there?"

"Yes, and before you ask, I'm not hanging around for a bus either. I'm going to go to the pub. Someone there will take me. It's an emergency. He's on his own with an ill baby and he needs help."

"Well, you've just told him to call an ambulance," Jake

snapped. "He'll get plenty of help from them. And at the same time steal it from someone who really needs it."

"What's that supposed to mean?" Alice was buttoning her coat with swift fingers.

"You should only call ambulances in *real* emergencies," Jake said piously.

"And what makes you think this isn't one?" Alice asked coldly as she reached for the doorknob. "The baby has a bad rash by the sound of it. If it's meningitis he might die if he doesn't get to hospital soon."

* * *

Hugo, waiting for the ambulance, had the sensation of time dragging and flying at the same time. It seemed like hours before he heard the engine outside, yet, according to the kitchen's fake-rococo clock, only eight minutes had elapsed between him placing the 999 call and a green-boiler-suited man and woman arriving at his door.

"This the little fella?" asked the burly man kindly, looking at Theo. The baby's cries had subsided now to exhausted moans. Hugh nodded, his eyes pricking and a painful feeling coursing the inside of his nose. "Right," said the paramedic. "Let's have a look at him."

Hugo handed his son over and shakily locked up Fitzherbert Place. He climbed into the back of the ambulance to find the burly man examining Theo's chest. "Real bobby dazzler this is," he remarked cheerfully of the flock wallpaper.

"Is it dangerous?" Hugo asked jumpily.

The burly man did not look up. "You never know with rashes," he said evasively. "Or babies. It's best to be safe. Right. Let's get to the hospital." The ambulanceman knocked a signal on the screen dividing the back from the driver's section. The woman was at the wheel, Hugo realized, surprised. He'd always imagined all that high-speed, wailing-siren stuff to be the work of men.

Just as the burly man pulled the doors shut, there was a mighty banging on the other side of them. He pushed them open to reveal Alice, wide-eyed, dishevelled and panting. "Wait for me," she gasped, climbing in. "Is Theo all right?" she asked Hugo, placing a chill hand on his.

"Er . . ." Hugo looked fearfully at the ambulanceman. There were no clues in the broad face. "I'm not sure."

"We're taking him in," the ambulanceman said. "It's best to check."

"And how are you?" Alice looked in concern at Hugo. He tried to smile, despite his trembling lip, thundering heart and looming hysterical tears.

"You're the child's mother, I take it," the ambulanceman remarked to Alice.

"No. Just an . . . er, friend." Alice grinned awkwardly at Hugo. He squeezed her fingers gratefully, not trusting himself to speak.

He was aware as never before of the vulnerability and complexity of the tiny body laid so lightly on his own, and of his utter helplessness in the face of Theo's illness. He could not escape the black center of his ragged, heightened impressions; the possibility that his son might die. Hugo could see it all now: the small white coffin, the empty cot, the deserted high chair, still spattered, like the rest of the kitchen, in mashed banana from teatime. Theo's clothes still dirty in the laundry basket; his last filled nappies in the dustbin, even. He closed his eyes, clutched the baby closer and felt he was going to die himself.

Alice, he sensed, had an idea of what he was going through. Her hand remained on his while she questioned the ambulanceman about his work.

". . . What do we think is a real waste of time? Well, the biggest drain on our resources is picking up drunks," he was saying. "You wouldn't believe it. People come out of the pub, fall over and ring us up."

With an effort, Hugo tuned in to Alice's conversation. The sound of her voice both reassured and distracted him.

"We're here!" the ambulancewoman called from the front.

Hugo felt a jolt of mixed shock, fear and relief. The doors at the back of the ambulance were opened and he and Theo were unstrapped. Within seconds they had been hurried under the red and white Emergency sign into the blaze of light that was the hospital.

CHAPTER
21

"Oh, thank God," Hugo croaked, the tears welling and spilling over as he looked into Dr. Watson's lovely face. "Thank *you.*"

The pediatrician handed Theo back. The baby was now happily chewing on a biscuit and looked brighter than he had all evening. "So there's no need to worry," the doctor said. "We've had a good look at him. It looks quite dramatic, I know, but it's really only a viral infection. He could have picked it up anywhere. From the floor, from putting his hands in his mouth, anything."

"I'm so sorry," Hugo bent his head. "I've been wasting your time. It was just that it looked so . . . *awful.*" He blinked hard.

"Don't worry, Mr. Fine." Dr. Watson tossed back her shining spill of hair. "It was a quiet evening, as it happens. And it's better to be safe than sorry, eh?" She chucked Theo under his busy, biscuit-encrusted chin. "He'll fight it off himself, probably pretty soon, as it looks as if this is the high point. The spots may even have gone by tomorrow, if you're lucky . . . Oh, excuse me." She looked down at the pager at her waist. "I'd better go. Good night."

And off she went in her white coat, disappearing down the

brilliantly lit white corridor like, Hugo thought, those visions of heaven people have from time to time.

He kissed the top of Theo's head and looked at Alice. Her eyes, he noticed before she quickly glanced away, looked wet as well. "I don't know how to thank you," he said quietly. "I don't know what I would have done."

Alice linked her arm through his. "Oh, shush. Come on. Let's call a minicab from reception and take Theo back to bed." She had no intention of returning immediately to the Old Morgue. There was certain to be an inquisition from Jake and what had happened was none of his business. Moreover his behavior about the phone call had been appalling, and had seemed even more so after what the ambulanceman had said. She was, in short, disgusted with him.

"You're coming back with me?" Hugo asked in delight.

"I want to see you both settled." As she smiled at him, Hugo felt his knees weaken for reasons that had nothing to do with Theo.

*   *   *

In the kitchen at Fitzherbert Place, Alice stared at the shepherdesses painted on the cupboard doors. This had to be Amanda Hardwick's work. Overlaid, it was equally obvious, with Theo's. The effect of all that pastel and carving spattered in mashed banana was quite surreal.

"Sorry about the mess," Hugo muttered. "I haven't had the chance to chisel it all off yet."

Alice smiled. "You've had other things to worry about."

"You could say that," he smiled, hugging the now-sleeping baby carefully and close. He beckoned her into the sitting room. "Sit down while I put Theo to bed. Help yourself to drinks—there are some around somewhere." He wondered where, exactly. Amanda had once kept a well-stocked cocktail tray, but he had drunk it dry long since, right down to the blue Curaçao. He had a feeling there were some dusty cans of Budweiser around, maybe in the cupboard under the sink.

Bugger. He really wasn't very well prepared. Probably he should have got the cab driver to stop at the liquor store. But it would hardly have looked good, being picked up from hospital with a baby only to stock up on booze at the first opportunity.

Once in the nursery, Hugo settled Theo comfortably in his cot. The baby sank into sleep with a grateful sigh, a tiny sound that flooded his father with tenderness and relief. He stood there for a moment stroking the unconscious little head. The moment Theo was tucked up in bed was always his favorite of the day, and not only because things were quiet at last. It was also to do with the gratitude and pride he felt at being able to provide his baby with a safe, warm haven. Tonight, after the hideous evening they had suffered, it felt more special than ever. He tiptoed away feeling simultaneously as if he would burst with love, and more tired than ever before in his life.

Heading for the door, Hugo stumbled over something big and soft. It was, he realized, the hideous, battery-operated barking dog that was one of Amanda's many ludicrous presents.

The dog was huge and its bark, activated from several inches away by a sensor on its nose, was terrifyingly realistic and aggressive. The only way to stop the noise was to flick the switch at the back, which Hugo had done exactly five minutes after unwrapping it. Theo was adept at turning the wretched beast back on, but for the moment, thankfully, it seemed quiet enough.

He made his way back down to the sitting room and Alice. She sat there, smiling and patient, on the edge of the sofa. She looked tired, but still lovely. Lovelier, he thought, because the reasons she looked tired were lovely in themselves.

"Right," Hugo grinned, rubbing his hands together. "Drink. Oh, and supper. You must be starving." His own stomach was tying itself in knots of hunger.

"Can I help?" Alice bounced up.

"No, really. Leave it to me. You've done enough helping for one night."

Hugo wasn't just being polite. He was playing for time. He did not want Alice, who he wanted so desperately to impress, to see he had no idea what he was going to cook. That he couldn't cook. That he had nothing to cook with. Who was he kidding even trying? His eye caught the well-worn menu of the Taj Mahal stuck behind the telephone. Should he ring for takeout? All those cartons and paper bags with the grease showing through, though. Not very sexy.

He rummaged in the cupboards. Ah, *there* were the cans of Budweiser. Three left. He hoped, rather against hope, that she liked lager. There was nothing else apart from a musty box of herbal teabags left by Amanda.

Hugo detached one of the cans, rubbed the top against his trousers to remove the dust and pulled the ring off as discreetly as he could. Carefully, he poured it into a cut-crystal gin-and-tonic glass and took it to Alice.

"Thanks very much." Alice sipped it gingerly. Lager. Her least favorite drink in the world. Apart from that stuff made of grass, which Jake had brought back once and which was supposed to have amazing cleansing properties. She'd thought at the time that she could have drunk Lemon Joy and got the same result less disgustingly.

Hugo fled back into the kitchen. After a frantic search he unearthed a half-finished package of dried penne. A start. All he needed now was sauce.

There was none, of course. A tin of sardines, a tin of chickpeas and a packet of bayleaves was all Hugo could find. In the cupboard there were a couple of jars of Theo's baby food. The outlook was bleak.

Doubtless there was some amazing and delicious recipe involving bayleaves, chickpeas and sardines, but he was damned if he knew what it was. Whereas—his eyes slid to the baby food jars—were there not distinct possibilities here?

No. He couldn't possibly. On the other hand . . .

Hugo examined one of the jars. Organic tomato and mozzarella flavor pasta. Well, what could be more suitable? Mix it in with the penne, and Alice would never know. He rattled around for a couple of pans, emptied the baby food into one, stuck the pasta water on to boil in the other and started to look for some plates. For the first time that evening he began to whistle.

"Supper!" he called, not long afterward. Bringing the plates through to the sitting room, he beamed.

"That was quick," Alice remarked, impressed, as she took the plate he handed her.

"Just a little something I rustled up," Hugo smirked modestly.

Alice, sampling the pasta, detected a strange taste, thick, blunt, bland. She was, however, too polite to comment.

They had their feet companionably up on the sitting-room coffee table. It would, Hugo realized, be the ideal opportunity to ask Alice how things were with Jake. That he had answered the phone had not been a good sign, and the mystery of what he was still doing in her cottage—in her life at all—troubled Hugo. Yet he shied away from the subject. He had suffered enough trauma for one evening and he feared the answer.

"Is that Theo I can hear?" Her ears, ever-attuned to infant cries of distress, had picked something up on the floor above.

Hugo, midway to the kitchen with his plates, stopped and dumped them abruptly on the floor. He flew up the stairs two at a time. Alice heard him enter the nursery and murmur something reassuring to Theo, who instantly stopped crying.

She decided to make herself useful until he came down. Picking up the heap of plates from the carpet, she carried them into the kitchen where, on the counter next to the cooker, she saw the empty jar of baby food with the red-stained pan beside it. She stared in disbelief. Could it be possible that he'd mixed it with . . .

Just then, an ear-splitting series of barks exploded somewhere above her. Theo screamed in terror. There was banging, crashing and what sounded like a struggle. It sounded as if the biggest, loudest, most savage dog in the world was loose in Theo's nursery.

The plates slid out of Alice's arms and into the sink with a smash. She shot up the stairs. On the top landing Hugo was emerging from the baby's room. He seemed remarkably free of bloodstains. Under his arm he carried what looked like a large soft toy. He looked sheepish.

"What happened?" she hissed as he closed the nursery door behind him.

Hugo shook the toy. "This bloody dog Amanda sent. Fell over it earlier and must have switched the sodding thing back on somehow. It goes ape—or rather dog—if you come within a few inches of it."

Alice looked at the dog. Its ears hung askew and its expression was comically doleful. It looked as if it had got the worst of the fight. Then she looked at Hugo. She thought of the tell-tale pan and empty jar in the kitchen.

Alice felt a pulling at the corners of her mouth. The pulling got harder. She began to giggle and shake. Hugo, after an initial stare of surprise, started to grin as well.

Alice, trying not to squeal with laughter, pressed her hand tightly to her mouth and went swiftly back downstairs. Hugo followed closely. Very closely. In the darkness at the bottom, he turned her toward him and gently pulled her face to his.

He kissed her for a long time. As he pulled her body closer, she yielded eagerly, sighing and twisting in pleasure as his tongue probed deeper and his exploring fingers edged up her shirt.

He pressed her backward and downward. On the carpet, he explored her, slowly, luxuriously, deliciously.

"Oh Alice," Hugo groaned. He felt all the tension and misery, not only of this evening, but all the weeks and months before, flowing out of him. As his hand slipped beneath the waistband of her trousers, he felt her stiffen in resistance, then relax. Her stomach, he saw, pressing his lips to it, was smooth and taut, the warm skin stretched over her hipbones like a teenager's. Only a neat scar, faded now, hinted that a child had once grown here.

Alice, trembling with pleasure, stretched her arms above her head as he pushed downwards, to the white cotton underwear he had somehow suspected she would wear . . .

"*Woof!* Woof! Woof! *Woof!*"

His eyes snapped open.

"Bugger." He struggled on to his elbow "Bloody dog must have switched itself on again." He looked at her in despair. Her eyes were creased with laughter. What a clown she must think him.

The toy was, he knew, probably broken. He had given it a good kicking earlier, after all. "Woof! Woof!" There it went again. And, fuguing with it now, the high, plaintive sound of a woken-up Theo.

Alice scrambled to her feet and pulled her jeans up her long, pale legs. She began buttoning her shirt. She tucked a piece of hair behind an ear and gave him an awkward smile. "I'd better be going."

"Sure," Hugo grimaced, cursing the dog. Talk about caninus interruptus.

"Have you got a minicab number?"

"Of course. Hang on." Miserably, he went into the kitchen. There were, he knew, some taxi firms on the Taj Mahal menu.

"I'll call it while you sort out Theo and the, erm, dog," Alice suggested, coming in behind him. Panicked, Hugo lunged for the counter beside the cooker to conceal the evidence of the baby food jar.

She put a hand on his arm. "Don't worry. I've already seen it. It doesn't matter."

Wordless, cringing, he passed her the menu and dashed up-stairs to settle his son.

"Bye, then," Alice waved from the cab as he prepared to shut her in. "Thanks for supper."

He looked at her in anguish. Supper! After all she'd done for him tonight, one of the lowest evenings of his life, didn't she deserve better than a can of warm lager and some ancient pasta mixed with baby food?

"Can I see you again?" he asked. "I'd love to take you out to dinner—you know—properly. To thank you."

"There's no need. Honestly."

"But I want to," Hugo insisted. "Really, I do. What about next weekend?"

"OK." She gave him her gut-twisting, slow burn of a smile. "That would be lovely. But you know, it really wasn't a prob-lem, helping you. I was just glad I could. And if there's any-thing else, just call me."

He waved until the taillights of the taxi had vanished around the corner. Then he went back inside, seized the dog and marched it out to the dustbin at the back. "That's you fin-ished," he snarled at it, clanging the lid down on top. The dog, however, had other ideas. Throughout the night, Hugo was woken up intermittently by the sound of wild barking with an additional metallic echo. Thank God, he thought, as he settled back to sleep each time, it was trash day tomorrow.

CHAPTER
22

HUGO DROVE TO WORK NEXT DAY WITH A LIGHT HEART. THEO'S spots had miraculously disappeared, just as Dr. Watson said they might. Almost more miraculously, Chicklets had accepted him back without a murmur.

The morning was clear and sunny, lending sparkle to the grass and highlighting the wealth of detail on the buildings. Hugo admired elegantly spare railings, gleaming brassware and shining glass in many-paned windows. The stone glittered with a thousand unnameable minerals. Unnameable by him, at least.

Hugo admired all this partly to stop himself thinking about Alice as he drove. Remembering his mouth around her nipple, he had already hit the curb twice. And he feared the memory of her white cotton underwear in heavy commuter traffic. For the sake of his car if nothing else, the dog's intervention had been a godsend.

"Don't know what you're so bloody pleased about," snapped Neil as Hugo arrived, whistling, at Dunn and Dustard. Hugo looked in surprise at his boss's long face.

"What's up?" he asked.

"What's up?" Neil repeated incredulously. *"What's up?"* His piggy eyes flashed. "What the hell happened at Leather?" he raged.

Hugo's head, which had been full of the freshness of Alice, now flooded with the depravity of Laura, stark naked and legs splayed in that suffocatingly perfumed room. He felt a sickening jolt. The entire episode had slipped his mind. An entire lifetime seemed to have passed between then and now.

"You might well look like that," Neil barked. "You know we've lost it, obviously."

"Lost what?"

"Leather. The owner rang after you'd gone, saying that everything she'd heard about you was obviously wrong and that you were the most unprofessional agent she had ever met."

Hugo felt the blood drain from his face.

"She's taking the house off our books," Neil fumed. "She'll be giving it straight to one of our rivals, obviously."

Hugo remembered Laura bawling after him down the stairs: "There's nothing fucking wrong with me. You'll be sorry you said that." So this was how she was making him sorry. By threatening his job.

He took a deep breath. "Look, Neil. Nothing's lost. That woman's got no intention of selling that house. She's bullshitting."

"Oh yeah?" Neil's hot little eyes were screwed challengingly on Hugo's. "And how do you know?"

"I just know." Hugo was aware how weak this sounded. "Trust me," he added.

Neil gave Hugo a level look. Then he exploded. "Trust *you?*" he thundered, head and neck swelling like a bullfrog's. "You must be fucking joking, Fine. You came here full of yourself as some shit-hot London real estate agent and, frankly, shit is what you've been. Everything you've touched lately has turned to it. We were going to cream off the commission from those warehouse buildings until you turned up with bags on your shoes. Then there was that dog business. And as for this bloody house—the client had even asked for you *by name.* What more of a head start could you hope for? But you arsed it up. You arsed them both up, didn't you, Fine?" Neil's breath was coming in short, hot, little bursts. "I've had enough. One more wrong step and you're out."

Hugo returned to his desk. Tempted though he was to tell Neil where to stick his crummy job, he resisted. Where else would he find something he was qualified to do and that allowed him to look after his son each afternoon? A large part of working parenthood, Hugo had found, was about keeping your mouth shut and your head down. And your mind on matters of expediency rather than bruised ego.

His mobile rang. Raising the instrument to his earlobe, he realized his mistake in assuming the morning could not go further downward. It was Amanda.

"I had a missed call from you," she accused.

"Yes. I was trying to get you last night."

"I was at a perfume launch," Amanda said breezily. "Nothing important, was it?"

"Important? Er, no. Not really." He'd tell her if she probed. If she asked one further question that showed real concern, or that she possessed even an inkling of that maternal telepathy that alerted mothers to the fact their child was in danger.

But Amanda did not probe. She had, it turned out, other reasons for ringing. "Now listen," she ordered Hugo crisply. "I need to arrange a shoot with Theo."

"A shoot?" Hugo was confused for a moment, thinking of Theo in breeches and tweed cap with a gun over his chubby forearm. Then he realized. "You mean you want to take pictures of him?"

"What do you think I mean? For Christ's sake, Hugo."

"But what are the pictures for?" Hugo ignored her last sentence and the fact that this was exactly what he had thought.

"A magazine piece," Amanda snapped. "Now, what's his schedule? When is he free?"

"He doesn't have a schedule. He goes to nursery, he comes back at lunchtime, I feed him, play with him, he has his supper, he plays some more and then it's bathtime—"

"Spare me the fucking details," Amanda yelled. "So basically he's around afternoons, yeah?"

"That's right. But what is this piece about, anyway?"

"It's about me and Theo."

"What *about* you and Theo?"

"About my life as a working mother. How I juggle career and domestic responsibilities. Try to keep working while holding a home life together."

"*What?*" burst out Hugo.

"It's a well-known modern phenomenon," Amanda retorted. "And it's *very* stressful."

"But you *don't* juggle work and domestic responsibilities," Hugo pointed out, determined not to lose his temper.

"Yes I do. It's going to say so in the article: 'Amanda Hardwick: How I Combine Career with Childcare.' It's about how I've overcome the challenges of child-raising to wave a flag for the back-to-work mum."

Skidding to the front of Hugo's mind came visions of himself rushing from nursery to work, increasingly fearful of putting a foot wrong in either; of himself and Theo in the back of the ambulance, Theo with his rash, he in a state of hysterical panic. What did Amanda know about that? Or the more workaday scenarios—Theo yelling with bored fury in the front of a supermarket cart, for instance. No doubt Amanda's idea of shopping with a baby was drifting around Harvey Nicks with a leopardskin papoose, personal assistant at her heels.

"I'm going to be a pinup for working mothers," Amanda announced smugly. "Which is why this magazine wants to do a piece about me and Theo. About my exhausting but rewarding life as a glossy magazine editor and busy mum."

"But you don't have a life as a busy mum," Hugo growled. "You left all that to me."

"Don't start attacking me over my job!" Amanda shrieked. "Have you any idea how it feels to leave your baby behind for long periods simply in order to be able to *work*?"

"What are you talking about?" Hugo clenched the phone, his knuckles white with anger. Her humbug was breathtaking. She had made it clear from the outset that she was returning to her career for her own satisfaction.

"You see! Yours is the typical male reaction!" Amanda shouted triumphantly. "Sexist *pig*!"

Hugo nearly choked at this. By the time he had recovered, Amanda was in full flow again.

"Mine is the classic dilemma of any working mother," she was declaring. "Frankly, you can't win. Either you're seen as a sad sack stuck at home changing nappies, or else as a ruthless careerist hellbent on satisfying your own selfish ambition."

"I agree," said Hugo.

"There you are!" Amanda exulted. "You agree!"

"I agree that that's the classic dilemma of the working mother," Hugo told her. "But I don't agree that it's yours."

"Typical," Amanda snorted furiously. "Women like me just can't win."

"Eh?"

"This was just what I was telling this magazine editor the other day over lunch at Gary Rhodes's. Great place, by the way."

"*Is* it?" Hugo thought crossly of his own lunches, standing up eating Weetabix or SpaghettiOs out of saucepans while listening unwillingly to *The Teletubbies*.

"Mm. Fab champagne list and stunning views of the Gherkin. Anyway, we decided that profiling me as a working mother was more than just interesting, it was *important*. An opportunity to highlight the sacrifices that working women have to make. The compromises that have to be struck. The painful decisions that are necessary before both home and office can be juggled in harmony, blah blah blah—you get the picture. I'll be back in the next few days. I'll let you know."

"You're coming *back*?" Hugo gasped.

"Well, how the hell else are they going to photograph us together?"

Hugo felt sick. He didn't want Amanda to come home. Not in the slightest. He had grown used to her absence. *Un*accustomed to her face. He and Theo were doing just fine without her. The childcare creases were being ironed out and, occasionally, he even felt he knew what he was doing. He enjoyed the sensation that he and the baby were a unit. The boys' club. Father and son.

"Gotta go," Amanda said briskly. "I'm due in a meeting about sea urchins' gonads."

"What?"

"Crucial ingredient in upscale body cream. Christ, Hugo. Don't you know *anything?*"

Ending the call, Hugo found himself looking into Neil's cross red features. He had no idea how long his boss had been standing there.

"Now look, Fine," he blustered. "I'm giving you one last chance here. I need you to do a show-round this afternoon for a flat in a new development called Pride and Prejudice Palisades."

"Right!" Shaking Amanda forcibly from his thoughts, Hugo did his best to look eager and on the ball.

Neil regarded him with a jaundiced eye. "It's a pain in the arse because I was going to do it myself but something else pretty important has come up and I'm going to be out of the office a few days, probably for the rest of the week. Anyway, even you can't fuck this up. It's simple. The people interested in looking at it have practically signed already. All you have to do is turn up at half-past two and open the door for them."

Half-past two. Neil had clearly forgotten that he didn't work afternoons. Dare he remind him, given the earlier scenes? Hugo thought rapidly. Far better to say yes and ring Chicklets in the hope they could hold Theo for a bit longer. Or, better still, he thought, relief swirling his body, he could ring Alice. Hadn't she said he could call her if he needed her?

*   *   *

Alice was sitting reading to Rosa. She was not, however, concentrating on *Peter Rabbit's Touch and Feel Book*. Her mind was on Hugo and the touching and feeling he had been doing.

She had been unable to think about anything else all morning. Hugo's face—handsome, sensitive, tired—had swum before her eyes. Her fingers, turning the pages for Rosa, tingled with the memory of tracing his lips and touching his hair.

"Look at Mrs. Tittlemouse cleaning up those sticky footprints," Alice murmured into the top of Rosa's honey-colored head.

Her mind, however, was on Hugo's aftershave with its pepper-lemon tang. The delicious scent had forced comparison with what Jake smelled like these days.

The bathing issue, which her mother had found problematic all those months ago, had recently got rather more so. Jake now tended to skip not just a day between baths like herself, but entire weeks, which meant he could be a bit rank.

Now, whenever he attempted to hold her his incipient beard scratched her face and her nostrils filled with warm, welling unwashedness. The contrast with Hugo's shaved cheeks and general cleanliness was absolute.

"Ooh, darling, that's the phone. I'll just get it." Carefully, Alice placed her daughter on the floor and turned to the page where Mrs. Tiggywinkle was hanging out a sheepskin rug on her line. As Rosa began to pluck curiously at the fluffy fabric, Alice crossed the room and raised the receiver. Her every vein coursed with hope that it was Hugo.

It was.

"Alice. Thank God you're there. Do you think, possibly, that—"

"Of course," she said smiling, when he had finished.

Alice was not smiling now. Where the hell *was* Hugo? The playground was clearing. As the sun slowly slid down the early spring sky, the last of the mothers packed their toddlers into buggies. Alice watched from the bench as they wheeled them off toward the streetlights coming on at the far side of the park.

He'd meet her and pick up Theo at three thirty, he had said. At the very latest. And what was it now? She looked at her watch. Coming up to half-past *five*.

Up until now, it had been quite a fun afternoon. Theo and Rosa seemed to hit it off well, in that solemn, absorbed way that babies did. Theo, Alice saw, had survived his early parental challenges to become a smiley, happy, adorably cheeky child. And it was wonderful to see Rosa, who rarely encountered other children, interacting so well with a peer. As she watched them, Alice thought briefly and wistfully about Rosa having a brother. Then she put the thought away. Given her age and, particularly, circumstances, it was never going to happen.

The babies' good humor was now starting to dissipate. On Alice's knee as they sat on the bench, Rosa was wailing, waving her pink neon teddy crossly. Theo, in Rosa's stroller, was making irritable, pre-wail noises. Alice looked at her watch again and frowned. It was very unlike Hugo to let her down like this. No doubt there was a reasonable explanation, but she was fast losing the ability to imagine what it could be.

Alice lugged them over to the swings yet again. But even Theo, whose appetite for whooshing through the air in the little cages seemed boundless, had now had enough. His bottom lip was sticking out and his formerly merry dark eyes looked hostile.

Rosa's wails rose sharply in timber as the pink neon teddy fell from her grasp and onto the ground beneath the bench. Hurriedly, Alice bent and picked it up.

Only recently had she liberated from her knicker drawer the handful of toys, including this bear, which was all she had been able to save from the haul Rosa was sent at birth. The rest had been long ago donated to homeless shelters by Jake. Rosa, when presented with it, had fallen on the teddy with a cry of delight and pressed it to her bosom as if it were a long-lost friend. Which, Alice supposed, it was.

Settling Rosa in her preferred position facing outward in her baby sling, and tucking Theo snugly into the stroller, Alice decided to do one last lap of the park.

As she trundled the buggy along the paths she gazed miserably at the asphalt. Her annoyance at Hugo's nonappearance was spiked with savage disappointment. It wasn't just that she wanted to see him to relieve her of Theo, so she could take Rosa home for her supper. She wanted to see him. *Him.*

What had started as pity, then curiosity, then amusement at his ineptitude at fatherhood, had become serious attraction. Last night, after Theo's rash scare, had crystallized what she had not wanted to admit before; the pull she felt toward him whenever she saw him. Hugo was charming, and interested, and funny. His was a dashing, dark-haired handsomeness that even broken nights, food-flinging babies and an obvious inability to iron barely dented; indeed, added a stomach-flipping aspect of vulnerability. She felt a rush of pleasure at the thought of him.

Love? She stopped short on the path. Was that what it was? Or just lust?

But it wasn't lust, Alice reasoned, that made her insides melt whenever she saw Hugo with Theo. Jake, for all his perfect-parent persona, had never been similarly at ease with Rosa. And what else but love, or something like it, explained the tenderness with which she had watched, from the corner of her eye, Hugo silent with agony in the ambulance?

Hugo may have needed help nappy-changing, but he needed no guidance where it really mattered. Theo was quite obviously the center of his life. While the center of Jake's life was—what? Rubbish, basically, thought Alice. He had told her he would be unavailable to help put Rosa to bed this week as he was chaining himself to Dumpsters with Joss and Jessamy in order to urge the council to recycle ninety-nine percent of all household waste. Was it, Alice wondered, possible to recycle that much? Wasn't some waste—well—just waste?

In the center of the park a low bridge crossed a little river. Alice paused on it, leaning over so Rosa could see the rushing water. Rosa laughed and waved her teddy happily. She was fascinated by water, particularly that she saw coming out of the bathtaps. On the rare occasions that this happened.

Theo liked water too, judging from his interested mooing noises. She stroked his head affectionately. He really was a sweet boy. Watching him chuckling as he stared at the water, so happy, so ready to be amused, she felt a stir of amazed indignation on the child's behalf. How could anyone, even Amanda Hardwick, leave this baby behind?

What sort of father too?

Her faith that Hugo would come had now almost completely faded. What on earth was he thinking of, abandoning her—and Theo—here? Had she misread him utterly? Only a moment or so ago she had thought herself in love with him. But was he really no better than his selfish, irresponsible wife?

CHAPTER
23

"H ALL-OOOO!" CALLED HUGO INTO THE DARKNESS. HIS VOICE rolled round in a booming echo. "Hallo! Anybody up there? Oh, sod it. *Sod it.*"

Yet again, he had thought he'd heard a movement. But yet again his ears were playing tricks on him. *Bugger.* What the hell could he do?

Precisely nothing until a resident of Pride and Prejudice Palisades came down to the underground car park in which he had so cretinously locked himself. But how was he supposed to have known that the bloody car park door, which opened simply enough with a handle from the outside, required a bloody *key* to get back out again? A key, more to the point, that he did not have.

Hugo sat on the chilly concrete steps, felt the clammy cold seeping through his pinstriped trousers and brooded on the high price he was paying for professional diligence. He'd got here before the clients to make sure the flat looked presentable. It had. And then, in a moment of over-cautious madness his old London self would have hooted with laughter at, he had decided to check the underground car park. Pick up any unsightly candy wrappers just to be on the safe side. But then had come the clunk behind him and the realization he was a prisoner. The realization that his mobile didn't work underground swiftly followed. Both Alice—in the park with the children—and the office were unreachable.

The clients, he was glumly aware, would have been and gone hours ago. No doubt presuming the real estate agent hadn't bothered to turn up to meet them. Neil, when he found out, would go postal. He would also, Hugo knew, fire him. While he had descended into the car park an employed man, he was unlikely to exit it as one.

Still. Hadn't Neil said he was away for the rest of the week? He couldn't fire him until Monday, at any rate. And there was plenty to look forward to before then. This weekend's dinner with Alice, for instance.

He thought of her anxiously. She must have been standing by the swings for hours now. Christ only knew where she imagined he was.

* * *

Alice was angry. She had, she knew, better start pulling up the drawbridges. She'd given Hugo an inch—although not quite the inch he wanted, thanks to that toy dog. And, typical of his sex, he had taken a mile. Now he was taking her for granted.

"Alice!"

"Hugo. Where the hell . . . ?" Angrily, she shook off the arms trying to embrace her. Theo, recognizing his father, wailed for attention. Hugo immediately dropped to his knees by the stroller, kissing his son and squeezing his chilly little hands. He looked exhaustedly up at Alice.

"Look, I'm sorry." His chest heaved like a piston. Blood thundered around his head. "I got stuck," he explained lamely.

"Stuck?" Alice exclaimed. "For over three hours?"

Hugo had expected her to be cross, but this level of white-hot fury was a shock. He had genuine and dramatic reasons for his absence, albeit reasons he hesitated to tell her about, lest she thought him as much of an idiot as his eventual rescuer, an elderly gentleman who had come down in search of a battered Reliant, evidently had.

His silence annoyed Alice even more. "You're not even going to give me an explanation?" she stormed. "Oh, what the hell does it matter? Here's your son, anyway. Now you've finally deigned to turn up, I'm taking Rosa home."

"Alice, please," Hugo stammered. "I'm sorry. Really, I am. You see—"

But Alice had turned away.

"I'll ring you," Hugo ventured.

"Don't bother."

He was aghast. "Not ring . . . but *Alice*! I've said I'm sorry. Look, it's ridiculous and I didn't want to tell you but I got locked in an underground car park for half the afternoon."

"Is that right?" Alice said disbelievingly, her stare apparently conveying the doubt that even he could be that stupid. "Well, I'm sorry about that. But I'm going now. Good-bye."

"But I'll see you on Saturday," Hugo faltered. "For dinner, remember?"

"Actually, I won't be able to make it."

"Won't . . . ?" Hugo searched wildly for the words with which to plead that she see reason. It wasn't as if what had happened had been his fault. Not entirely. "But I've booked Allingham House," he wailed.

Alice drew a sharp breath. Allingham House. She'd heard of it, of course. Everyone in Bath had. A Jacobean stately home turned wildly expensive hotel in the rolling country outside the city, it was the rural offshoot of a fashionable London club and supposedly the haunt of weekending celebrities. It had a racy, decadent reputation, a cutting-edge spa with upto-the-minute pampering treatments and horizon pools indoors and out. Jake would never in a million years have taken her there. Alice hesitated, sorely tempted. Nonetheless . . .

"I won't be able to make it," she repeated.

Before Hugo could say anything more, something small and pink flew through the air and fell with a plop in the water. It was accompanied by a bloodcurdling shriek from Rosa.

"Shit," muttered Alice.

"What's the matter?" Hugo peered into the river. "What is it? Did she drop something?"

"Her teddy," said Alice agitatedly. "She absolutely loves that teddy. It's her favorite."

Hugo stared down into the water just below the bridge. It was flowing fast and the small, bright teddy, which had initially fallen into a clump of waterlogged twigs, was already working itself free. It would be out and away in seconds. As Rosa shrieked hysterically and Alice tried in vain to comfort her, he realized he had very little choice. Any hopes he had of restoring himself in Alice's affections, not to mention quieting Rosa and the now-wiffling Theo, all rested on one thing. Rescuing that bear.

"Here," he said, shoving his jacket and tie at Alice. "Hang on to these for a minute."

He leaped over the small, white-painted fence that edged the path and plunged across the grass beside the river. It was difficult to see in the fading light but in the water just ahead of him, a small smudge of pink confirmed he was keeping pace with the teddy. As the river prepared to round a bend, Hugo's hopes began to rise that the toy might be driven into the bank by the force. Then he came violently into contact with something hard and spiky.

"Fuck!" cursed Hugo, dancing with pain as he realized he had run legs-first into a three-strand barbed-wire fence separating the park from a neighboring field. But there was no time to feel sorry for himself, or even assess the damage. A bear's life was at stake, a child's happiness, and, almost as important, a relationship he wanted to continue. What were a few scratches compared with that?

Hugo took a few paces back, then shot forward and

vaulted the barbed-wire fence. He landed in a stony clump and twisted his ankle, but the sickening pain of this was nothing beside the agony of no longer being able to see the pink blob in the river. He struggled through the thicket and out the other side to glimpse, to his joy and relief, the teddy bear some distance in front of him, swimming gamely on in what, at this point, was much deeper water.

A less joyful sight altogether was the wall and bridge now looming in front of him. He had reached the edge of the field and was now coming into the town. He could hear traffic on the other side of the wall. By the time he'd battled across what sounded like a busy road, Teddy would be long gone.

Unhesitating before the inevitable, Hugo raced to the edge of the riverbank and leaped in. He yelled aloud with the pain and cold of contact. The shock was almost heart-stopping and the water more freezing than he ever imagined. The current, too, was far more powerful than it looked.

Alice, watching anxiously from upstream, let out her own yell of horror as she saw the distant, running figure of Hugo suddenly change direction and plunge into the water. She felt suddenly sick. She had driven him to this. He had only done it to make amends. To show he was sorry for being late. And that he cared.

Oh, she hadn't meant to be horrible. Really, she hadn't meant it. She'd been tired and cross, that was all. And about what? What did an hour or so's waiting in a park matter compared to a man's life? She had not misjudged him, not remotely; that much was obvious now. Hugo's unhesitating unselfishness in racing after the bear had single-handedly restored all her faith. If anything was an act of love, this was.

As Hugo swirled out of sight under the bridge, his head a dark blob against the foaming gray water, Alice clenched her hands together in agony.

"Hugo!" she bawled. "Just get out. The teddy doesn't matter. Get out of the river!"

But Hugo did not hear. He could hear nothing but the rush of water. Teddy was still ahead of him, though out of arm's reach. Around him, Hugo felt the powerful muscle of water increase its grip and speed. He realized, alarmed, that the anchoring jumble of rocks on the bottom was now far below the reach of his feet. Worse, he and the bear were whirling toward a boiling white mass of water. A weir, it looked like.

Panicking now, Hugo felt, beneath his legs, a tremendous energy forcing him forward upon which his frantic kicks made no impression. Twigs swirled giddily past. The teddy had vanished, and now that the current had disgorged a contact lens, he could barely see anything but spray and water. Or hear anything apart from splashing and his own terrified, painful gulps.

He no longer cared about the teddy anyway. All that mattered now was saving himself. For Theo's sake, if no one else's. He couldn't leave him alone in the world, or with Amanda, which amounted to much the same thing. The image of his son burning in his head, Hugo tried, with one last, enormous, heart-bursting effort, to thrash toward the riverbank.

He felt his foot hit, and then slip off the muddy flanks of safety. One second later he was flailing wildly in terror. The second after that, it was all over.

Something sharp was sticking in his face. Something even sharper was digging into his back and between his legs. Hugo realized, in incredulous relief, that he was impaled on a large tree branch trailing in the river. A mere few feet further on, the water tumbled over into the deadly boiling pot of the weir. The god of parenting had intervened for him.

Or perhaps the god of teddies. Because now, as he heaved great, shuddering, sobbing breaths, Hugo saw that it wasn't only his life the tree had saved. Even with his compromised vision he could see that, crammed soggily between some twigs nearby, was something small and bearlike. And very bright pink.

Shortly afterward Hugo found himself seized bodily, heaved upward and laid spreadeagle on the ground. He blinked up at the group of people—passersby from the bridge, presumably—who had dragged him from the river onto the bank.

"You all right?" one of them asked him, looking quizzically at the teddy bear Hugo held fast in his hand.

One of his legs, he now realized, was burning with pain. He remembered, as if from years ago, the barbed wire fence.

"I've called an ambulance," someone else said. "It'll be here in a minute. Your leg's bleeding quite badly. Best if you go and get checked out."

"Hugo!" Alice's face loomed, startlingly white, out of the darkening blue above him. "I thought you'd . . ." Her breath came short and painful. Pounding across rough ground with one heavy baby in a buggy and another the same size bouncing around her neck had been a physical challenge of the most strenuous nature. Not that she had cared.

Hugo weakly raised the hand from which mud-stained, soggy Teddy dripped dejectedly onto the ground. Rosa gave a crow of delight.

The crowd started to melt away.

Alice bent low over Hugo and kissed him. "I'm sorry," she murmured. "Forget everything I said. Apart from this. I love you."

"Does that mean," Hugo muttered, "that dinner's still on?"

He could not make out her answer. Alice's broad smile, the whole of her face in fact, was swirling like the water in whose pitiless, deadly depths he had so recently been immersed. And then, as they say, everything went black.

CHAPTER
24

IN THE BAR OF ALLINGHAM HOUSE, HUGO FELT SWAMPED BY WEARY familiarity. He felt there was something about the place that seemed to be trying too hard. From the trance music thumping in the foyer to the expectation-defying sports facilities— *blue* tennis courts—it reminded him of London hipness at its most self-conscious and strained. It also, he thought, eyeing the strobe lights sweeping the ornate plaster ceiling and the jellybean machines in a row on the wall, reminded him most uncomfortably of his wedding. There had been jellybean machines there too, at the fashionable Soho club, all of which had been emptied and the contents hurled at him and Amanda.

His eye rolled without interest over the women in caramel leather coats and with thick blonde highlights, or else strutting around in tight black trousers with their bums sticking out. Women like this would have interested him once. But not now.

He rubbed a hand over his tired face and knew it looked very different from those of the other men present. They were all of a certain age—his—and had a certain look to go with it: well moisturized skin, done teeth and short, brushed-up hair of a determined darkness. Had he stayed in London, Hugo supposed, he'd probably be looking like that himself.

Alice was not yet here. At his suggestion, she had arrived earlier in the afternoon and gone straight to the hotel spa.

"But isn't that a bit extravagant?" she had worried. "Won't you have to book a room so I can do that?"

"Yes. But it doesn't matter." Hugo had waved a breezy hand. "You deserve it."

"Deserve it? I almost got you killed rescuing a bloody teddy bear."

"Least I could do. You came with me to the hospital when Theo was ill. You showed me how to put on nappies . . ."

"Oh, please. That was nothing." Alice waggled her hands, embarrassed. "But—this room thing. It'll cost a fortune."

"I don't care." Hugo genuinely didn't. The fact he couldn't afford it couldn't have bothered him less. Since his near-miss brush with death, he had resolved to live more in the moment. What was a few hundred quid if it brought joy to the woman he loved? And who, more to the point, had admitted loving him. He hoped he hadn't imagined that last bit. Given the state he had been in, it was difficult to be sure.

He wondered what excuse Alice had given Jake for her absence. The nature of their cohabitation remained vague. From the little he could gather from Alice, they seemed to have settled into an uneasy mutual living and shared childcare arrangement. During dinner, Hugo hoped, there would be an opportunity to raise the thorny question of their spouses and how to handle them.

For him, it had been relatively easy to arrange the evening. Certain of the Chicklets staff offered a babysitting service and it had been a simple matter to sign one of them up for tonight. Rather more effort had gone into cleaning up Fitzherbert Place to a level passing muster in the eyes of a health-conscious nursery nurse. He needn't have worried, however. From the moment he had showed her Theo's room, the nurse's eyes had shot to the dawn-to-dusk Twinkledreams ceiling and remained there. She had been, quite simply, amazed by it and Hugo doubted she would notice anything else all evening. Except, hopefully, Theo.

As the waiter brought over his drink, Hugo noticed, slumped in the distressed leather armchair opposite, a decrepit heap of flesh that reminded him of portraits of Henry VIII. Except that the slumped and sleeping man, his advanced age notwithstanding, wore a backward baseball cap, a pair of bright orange combat trousers and a camouflage-print nylon T-shirt stretched tightly over his man breasts. His white, veiny feet, in open sandals bristling with Velcro, tapped with aficionado zeal to the omnipresent music. Hope I die, Hugo thought, before I get old. Especially if I get old like *that*.

He sat up hurriedly in his chair. Alice was coming into the bar. Or so he had thought from a distance, but was it her, really? The figure walking toward him had Alice's familiar build and gait but, as it approached, the familiarity receded. Her hair did not hang, poker-straight, to her shoulders in Alice fashion. This woman's hair, shining thick and brilliant, was caught up in a fashionably tumbling manner that framed the long, thoughtful face.

And the face looked different; shaped and dramatized with skillful makeup. The eyes were smoky, the lips painted to a rosy fullness and the high cheekbones glowed. The clothes she wore were infinitely more sophisticated than Alice's usual off-the-dump wardrobe; a clinging skirt in elegant pale blue with a matching tight cashmere top. The high breasts, slim waist and long legs thus revealed were having their effect on the other men in the bar. Even Henry VIII had woken up and was staring appreciatively. The caramel-coated women, meanwhile, were giving Alice an entirely different sort of appraisal through slitted, jealous eyes.

"Hi! Like my new look?" Alice bent over and kissed Hugo on the cheek. A wave of delicious spa smells broke warmly over him from her cleavage.

"Fantastic," he said sincerely. "The spa was good, then?"

"I got a bit carried away." Alice delightedly spread her fingers to display a new manicure. "All those treatments. I haven't had anything like them since I was in New York. I just couldn't resist. I even went to the hotel boutique and bought these afterward." She gestured down at her clothes.

A lump swelled in Hugo's throat. He had always thought Alice was beautiful, albeit in a gentle, understated way. He could see now that he was wrong. Given the right clothes and makeup she was beautiful in the most dramatically obvious way imaginable.

"What's your room like?" he asked.

A faint pastel pink spread over Alice's cheek. She looked at him shyly through her hair.

Hugo was intrigued. "What's the matter with it?"

Alice tucked one of her shining locks behind her ear. She ran a quick, nervous tongue over her lips. "Nothing. Nothing really. It's lovely. Actually, it's quite amazing."

"In what way?" Hugo probed.

"There's just, I don't know, something about it," Alice confessed. "There's a huge mosaic bath just opposite the bed. It's got candles all around it. Then there's a massive shower room with a decking floor and a shelf full of enormous bottles of body lotion. Huge sofas all over the place. The bed is colossal, and surrounded by all these aphrodisiac oils . . ." She began to giggle. "I suppose what I'm saying is that it's not terribly, well, *subtle.*"

"You mean you've never seen so many places to shag in your life?"

Alice squealed with laughter and nodded.

Hugo raised an eyebrow. He'd sold a thousand penthouses just like it and knew exactly the sort of thing. Pretending he didn't, however, could potentially reap dividends. "You know," he said soberly, "I can't visualize it at all. You'll have to show me."

Her face flinched with alarm. "Oh, no. I, er, couldn't."

"I see," Hugo said tightly.

Alice stopped laughing. Her eyes grew round with concern. "You're not offended? I mean, it's wonderful being here. You're so sweet to treat me."

"Well it's *slightly* disappointing you're not entirely happy with the room . . ."

"Oh, I am," Alice said desperately. "Really, Hugo . . ."

He raised a hand to silence her. "But I'll forgive you completely if you take me there and show me what you mean."

"I suppose," he said, ten minutes later, "that it's all meant to be a bit ironic."

There was, Hugo was aware, nothing remotely ironic about the need swelling urgently in his trousers. Nobody, even the most committed post-modernist, had ironic erections. He tried to keep his eyes from Alice's breasts, tried too to stop his mouth watering and his hands shaking. He had so nearly had her before. He felt he would burst if he didn't have her now.

". . . shower head's the size of a trash bin lid," Alice was saying.

He paced toward her over the warmed stone floor. Alice was standing by the bed with her back to him, reaching up for the bottles on a rack just above it. "Just look at some of these names," she was giggling. "Love Potion Number Nine, Eau Erotique . . ."

He felt her stop and stiffen as he wound his arms about her waist. "Oh, Alice." He buried his nose in her wonderful-smelling hair.

Her nipples brushed his hands as she turned around in his embrace. "Hugo." She took his face in her hands and pulled his mouth into hers.

Hugo's hand, under her skirt now, had made a discovery. "You're not . . ."

She looked boldly into his eyes. "Wearing any knickers. I

know. I'd have told you at some stage. Had to get you in here somehow."

He frowned. "You *wanted* me to come in here?"

"Why else do you think I told you about the, erm, facilities?"

"But you didn't want me to see."

Alice raised her eyes, mock-exasperated. "For such a Mr. Sophisticated," she teased, "you know very little about women."

"Hey, hang on a minute . . ."

"Let's not waste time talking," she murmured, leading him toward the bed.

"Steady," she whispered as he tore at her skirt. "We've got all the time in the world. Well, until dinner, anyway."

Sometime later, Alice looked down at Hugo. Radiant with satisfied desire just a moment or two before, her expression was now still and sober.

"What's up?" He placed his hands on the slim hips that still straddled him, feeling his loins stir again.

"You *know* what's up, Hugo. Us. You and me. We're both married. With children."

"Er, yes. Quite. I was going to talk to you about that."

"Good. We need to. What the hell are we going to do?"

Hugo smiled. The dinner was going well. Apart from the food, which seemed to be straining as hard for effect as most of their fellow diners. He and Alice had already sniggered over the reindeer shepherd's pie. Why mess with a classic? As for the lamprey and chorizo brochettes . . .

"Oh well," Alice had said. "It makes a change from mung beans, let me tell you." Yet, despite the laughter, a shadow lay over their table: the fact that, at the end of the evening, they would have to part and return to their responsibilities. Separate families and separate lives. Separate spouses, with only their lunacy in common.

"Oh, Hugo." Alice, face fragile in the candlelight, was clawing at her bread roll with newly manicured fingers. "It's all such a mess. What are we going to do?"

Hugo's mind slid back to the bedroom. The sex had been fantastic, but best of all had been lying with her afterward. It had seemed the most natural, wonderful thing in the world. He wanted to wake with her like that every morning. Or as many mornings as he might have left. Life, as he had recently learned, was shockingly unpredictable and could be very short. There were no guarantees and one had to snatch at happiness where one could.

He reached across the brown sauce bottle and wound her fingers through his. "Well," he said in a low voice, aware of the couples sitting close on either side, "we have two choices. We either carry on like this, seeing each other secretly . . ." He stopped and took a swig of wine. While this was an entirely feasible and indeed time-honored way forward, it wasn't ideal. Neither he nor Alice were cloak-and-dagger people.

Alice's unhappy face mirrored his doubts. "I suppose so," she said reluctantly, crumbling more bread.

"Or," said Hugo, "we break with the mad spouses. We bring it all out in the open, get divorces and start a new life together."

Alice's eyes widened. *"Divorces?"* Her throat contracted in a nervous swallow. "Bit drastic, isn't it? A bit complicated."

"We're in a pretty drastic and complicated situation." Hugo forked up some more of the reindeer shepherd's pie and smiled at her worried expression. "It's not complicated if you think about it. It's actually quite simple. I'm married to someone who's never here and clearly never wants to be, while you're married to a fanatic who'd rather be out chaining himself to Dumpsters or finding new ways to reuse shoelaces. Meanwhile, life is slipping away right in front of us. We've got to grab it a bit more, Alice. Seize the day. Make things happen."

Her face darkened. "That's what Jake said when we first met. He was always going on about having the courage of one's convictions."

"Yes, well." Hugo did not feel this was a particularly helpful example. "*That* was different. You had no idea what convictions he was talking about and if you had you'd never have married him."

"No," Alice said slowly, hoping it was true. It was so difficult, now that the spell was broken, to recall the extent of the fascination Jake had once had for her.

Hugo leaned towards her. "You love me, don't you?"

"Yes. I do. But . . ." She bit her lip.

"But what?"

"But what about the *children*?" Alice burst out unhappily.

He stared at her, amazed. "Well, they'd live with us, of course. Bloody hell, you didn't think I meant we'd be without them?" He felt his eyes sting at the thought. "God, no. We'd all live together. You'd be a fantastic stepmother to Theo."

Alice smiled wistfully. "I was only thinking in the park how lovely it would be for Rosa to have a brother."

"There you are then," Hugo said triumphantly.

"But it won't be easy," Alice cautioned.

"You never know, Alice. I mean, obviously, when most couples split up, that's true. There are all sorts of battles . . ."

When most couples split up. The statistics and likelihood of it happening were, Alice knew, horrifically high. Yet somehow she had never imagined it happening to her. She had imagined that, for her, marriage would last forever. Just as it had for her parents. But it hadn't. She looked down and twisted her hands.

". . . Amanda, I'm sure, won't put up any sort of fight," Hugo continued optimistically. "She'll be glad to see the back of Theo. It's long enough since she's seen the front of him.

She'll be relieved not to have the responsibility." He paused, thinking of the conversation about the photoshoot. That Amanda now seriously considered herself the ultimate working mother did not seem possible, even given her capacity for self-delusion. It was a fad, a front, a publicity stunt. No doubt, by now, she was on to her next incarnation; as what, Hugo couldn't imagine. But at least, in recent days, there had been no further mention of the interview.

"So what about Jake?" he asked.

Alice laid down her forkful of lamprey. "What about him? I hardly see him. If he's working at home, he shuts himself away and doesn't want Rosa or me anywhere near him. And at night he's never in."

"So where is he?"

She shrugged. "Out protesting with the *Get Trashed!* lot."

"*Every* night? You're sure?"

"Pretty sure."

"There aren't any women on the staff?"

Her brow wrinkled. "Well, there's Jessamy, of course. And yes, before you ask, she probably does fancy him. But I'm fairly certain his only interest in her is how effectively she can chain herself to a Dumpster. Or hassle some hairdresser about floor sweepings."

"Really?" Hugo was unconvinced. "What does she look like?"

"She's about six feet tall with bright purple hair and she's a part-time goat psychologist."

Hugo smirked. "She sounds right up his alley, if you ask me. But if you say he doesn't fancy her . . ."

"I do." Alice poked him chidingly. "He's not interested in other women, I'm sure of that. He hasn't got time. At the moment, he's too busy going to burger chains and telling them they should be recycling plastic cutlery instead of throwing it away."

"Christ." Hugo rubbed his eyes. If further proof were needed of Jake's insanity, here it was. Who but a lunatic went out rescuing plastic forks when they could be in with the divine Alice?

"You know," Alice mused, toying with her chorizo, "the more I think about it, the more I just can't understand why he wanted to marry me in the first place. It just seems one of the weirdest things ever. It was easy for me—I was swept off my feet and I wanted a baby. And I thought he did too—he said he did, and that he'd devote the rest of his life to us. But it turned out that he had other priorities." She shook her head and stared at the candlewick glowing in its lick of flame.

"Just like Amanda," Hugo pointed out. "They've both got other irons in the fire that are much more important to them. There's no reason why they'd want to hang on to either us or the children." His voice was hopeful. "So you see, it's just a case of persuading them around to our point of view."

"You forget one thing," Alice said quietly. "Amanda hates me and Jake hates you. Even if they agreed to split with us they'd never allow us to be with each other."

It was a good point and Hugo untastingly finished his pie as he considered it. "I suppose the best thing," he said eventually, "is to do it in two stages. The first is to leave Amanda and Jake and set up house on our own. Separately. And then once they've got used to that and the system is proved to be working, we start to float the idea of you and me being together."

Alice thought about this. In truth, living alone with Rosa would make very little difference to the baby. Thanks to the amount of time Jake spent shut working in the sitting room, or out being an eco-vigilante, Rosa had started to look at him with an obvious lack of recognition.

Hugo bent earnestly over the table. "I know how we should do this. Believe me, I'm a salesman."

"Isn't that a contradiction in terms?" she teased.

Hugo rolled his eyes. "I mean it's my job to sell people things."

"But you sell houses. Houses are different. We're talking about people and their lives."

Hugo shook his head. "Darling, houses are all about people and their lives. You're not selling them bricks and mortar. You're selling an idea about bricks and mortar. A dream of how they could live there. And what we need to sell Jake and Amanda is a dream about how their lives would be easier and better on their own."

"I suppose so," said Alice. It would certainly be no hardship to leave Jake on his own. Despite the incursions of *Get Trashed!* into her savings—incursions which, now she had put a stop to them, had not helped the domestic atmosphere either—she could probably buy somewhere just big enough for a single woman and a baby. Somewhere miles from any reclaimed vitreous enamel or vegetation-sprouting second-hand footwear.

"So that's the plan," Hugo said decisively. "If we handle Jake and Amanda carefully, it'll be fine. The important thing is that there should be no sudden shocks. They mustn't find out what we're up to until we want them to know."

"You make it sound so easy." As Alice, smiling, stretched over to kiss him, Hugo felt a stirring in his groin.

"Well, well, well." The voice coming from behind them had a nasty, victorious note. "The devoted husband and father, if I'm not very much mistaken."

Hugo looked up in horror to see Laura smiling down at him. It was not a nice smile. With her oily trowels of makeup and the light from the candles licking her features, she looked, he thought, like a particularly evil gargoyle.

As she recognized Alice, Laura's beam faded. "And the eco-princess!" she exclaimed. Her eyes slid back to Hugo. "Fancy seeing you two here!"

Her voice was full of bitter triumph. She had obviously seen them kissing. It felt, Hugo thought, like being a mouse in the paws of a particularly sadistic cat.

Laura cocked her head at Alice. "I was right. She *has* scrubbed up well, after all."

"Laura," Hugo said at last.

Her teeth shone sticky in the candlelight. "Fergus is back for the weekend so he brought me here for dinner for a treat. And *what* a treat it's turning out to be!"

Lurking in the gloom behind her was the Henry VIII in the baseball cap he had spotted slumped in the bar. The anti–dog poo guru and consummate wife-neglecter at last, thought Hugo. Any other time, he might have been interested.

Now, however, he felt only a low, thrumming dread. Why had he stayed at Leather, and not run away as soon as he saw her? Only an idiot could not have seen what was obviously about to happen. And why, furthermore, had he ever mentioned therapy? He had not realized that, while hell had no fury like a woman scorned, it had nothing on a woman scorned then told she needed a psychiatrist.

"No need to ask if Amanda's still away then?" He could see, in Laura's eyes, the light of revenge. The dread escalated alarmingly.

CHAPTER
25

A MANDA CLOSED HER EYES AND STRETCHED HER ARMS OUT AGAINST the warm marble. She wriggled her toes in the boiling waters of the Jacuzzi. Some of the jets were directed, apparently deliberately, to give really quite delicious sensations. Her jetlag was fading by the minute.

She looked critically around the room. Those alcoves containing Roman-style oil-burners were a bit ten minutes ago, really. The whole place felt below the standard of spas she knew in the States, notably the one in Utah last week with the electric yogurt body wraps.

Merely having one's meridians rebalanced, the main treatment on offer here, seemed dull in comparison. On the other hand, why struggle on with meridians all over the place? Life for working mothers like her was hard enough as it was. As she planned to tell the newspaper this very afternoon.

"Amazing coincidence," she observed to Laura. "I can't believe you rang and said you needed to talk to me the very second I was getting into my cab at Heathrow."

"Incredible," Laura replied, resplendent in a swimming costume of a pink so hot it made Amanda's eyes ache. "And so great you could come straight to the spa to meet me, rather than going home first."

Amanda wiggled a slender brown foot. Laura's call, as it happened, had fit in quite well. A quick spa session, she had decided, would be just the thing to add extra glow for the camera.

"Especially as you must be desperate to see Theo," Laura added.

"*Theo?* Who . . . ? Oh, of *course,* absolutely . . ." Shit, she'd almost forgotten her own baby's name. Amanda looked warily at the other woman and saw with relief that, somewhat incredibly, she did not appear to have noticed.

Amanda was far from being a sensitive soul, but even she now sensed something not quite right with Laura. Her entire manner was odd. As was her appearance—bloated, bloodshot, spotty and caked in makeup even in the water.

Amanda was smugly aware of looking infinitely better herself. So there was, after all, *something* to be said for flogging herself to death to keep career and family life on track. Perhaps all that effort made the blood flow faster or something. Cleared out the system. Clever her. She could suggest that to the interviewer as well.

"I'll see Theo this afternoon, anyway," Amanda said airily. "Hopefully his looks will have improved since I last saw him . . . not that that was very long ago, of course."

"He must be so excited that you're coming. I imagine," Laura added, choosing her words carefully, "that Hugo must be in quite a state as well."

Amanda breezily examined her nails. "Oh, they've got no idea I'm here. It's a flying visit. It'll be a surprise for them."

She wondered impatiently what Laura wanted so desperately to talk about. She'd better come to the point of whatever it was quickly. Didn't she realize some people had work to do, national newspaper magazines to see?

"Better get dressed, I suppose," she sighed. "No rest for the wicked. I've got a tough afternoon ahead."

"Doing what?" Laura asked, having failed to recognize the nudge.

"Photoshoot with Theo," she groaned. "It'll be exhausting."

"Photoshoot? Sounds like fun," Laura said enviously.

"No, it sounds like work," Amanda corrected her.

"Photoshoot for what?" Laura asked.

Amanda explained. "They want to talk to me about how I combine my busy working life with being a successful mother. While at the same time keeping a happy, flourishing marriage on track."

Laura gave her what, had Amanda been capable of noticing, was a curious look. "Is that right?"

"Uh-huh." Amanda yawned ostentatiously. "So come on, then. What's the problem? You said you wanted to talk to me about a problem you had."

A look of despair crossed Laura's face. "Yes, it sort of touches on what you've just been saying. Being a successful mum. The happy bit especially," she added dolefully.

Amanda smiled with satisfaction. "Oh, I see. You want to know how I manage?" She gave a mock-rueful laugh. "Frankly, darling, I wish I knew how I did it myself. But by all means ask. I'll tell you what I know."

Laura seemed hardly to be listening. "I'm beginning to wonder," she said slowly, "whether or not I should be having therapy. What do you think, Amanda? I mean, you're my friend."

"Er, yes. Yes." Friend? What was Laura going on about? Amanda rarely gave friends a thought. They seemed, on the whole, an irrelevance and inconvenience, always wanting help of some sort or other. She had never had time for them; Laura was an acquaintance at the most. She was of no professional or personal use whatsoever.

"Because frankly," Laura spoke with a sob in her voice, "a friend's what I need at the moment. There's no one else I can talk to. Or who wants to listen."

Amanda cast her what started as a look of impatient contempt. On the other hand, being a friend perhaps suited her.

She could probably do with some anyway; having friends was fashionable at the moment. She'd seen lots of articles about them being the new family and how female networking was the new black. "I've discovered so much more about my *friends*," she pictured herself telling the magazine journalist. "Motherhood has definitely extended my ability to empathize."

"Yes," she said slowly, savoring the curious sensation of uttering the sentence for the very first time. "I am your friend."

"So you'll tell me the truth?" Laura demanded, her eyes searching Amanda's. "Just as I wouldn't hold back if there was something I felt you should know about?"

"Life's just *so* demanding," Amanda continued, taking no notice of Laura's question. "I can't *tell* you how wonderful it is to be here. To have a break, to enjoy a spot of pampering at last. It's dreadful, never having a second to spare for this kind of thing." She raised a smooth, tanned leg, exfoliated the previous week in Utah, out of the water. "But everyone else has to come first—Theo most of all, obviously. And then, at the back of the queue, little old me." She examined her smooth, waxed armpits. "People are always telling me they don't know how I do it." She smiled wearily. "And, do you know something, Laura?"

"Well, yes, actually, I do," Laura said quickly. "Something that you should know as w—"

"*I'm* not sure how I do it either. So goodness knows what I'm going to tell the journalist!" Amanda tittered delightedly.

"I can think of one thing you're not going to tell them," Laura said grimly, climbing out of the water.

Amanda was only half listening. She was observing with satisfaction the patches of cellulite on Laura's thighs. *Serious* orange peel, that. It was shocking how some people let themselves go when they had babies. If she, with her frantic, juggling, crazy, working-mother existence, could manage to keep in shape, what on earth was stopping Laura, who did nothing at all?

"What do you mean, you can think of one thing I'm not

going to tell them?" she said absently, her eyes still on Laura's upper legs.

Laura, midway into her bathrobe, turned. "Well, I'm only telling you this because you're my friend, obviously. Unpalatable truths and all that."

"Of course." Amanda jerked her damp head emphatically up and down. "So what is it? Shoot."

"Your husband's been shagging that eco-hippy from the prenatal class."

It was, Hugo thought, like death. He did not know when the blow would come, only that it would.

His sole consolation was that Amanda might strike from overseas. She had, he knew, been in New York again. And while obviously Laura could and would reach her there to tell her the news, the prospect of being shouted at over the phone from three thousand miles away seemed less appalling than facing Amanda's rage in person.

When he wasn't thinking about his wife, he was worrying about Alice. He had not spoken to her since the terrible night when Laura, eyes glittering, had descended upon them like an avenging fury.

Alice had thrown down her big white napkin like a flag of surrender and dashed out of the restaurant, shoulders rigid with pent-up sobs. He had followed.

Her eyes were wide with fear. "What the hell's going to happen now? What are we going to do?"

"Run away together?"

"And what about the children?" She clutched him with white-knuckled hands. "What about them?"

Hugo swallowed. "Don't worry," he assured her as he helped her into a taxi. "It'll be fine. If it all comes out in the open, so what? It might be for the best. Speed things up a bit."

He knew, from Alice's face, white and unhappy against the

dark plush carseats, that she did not share his optimism. He wasn't sure that he shared it himself.

Life, frankly, Hugo thought, wrestling with Theo on the changing table, was looking pretty shitty at the moment. Literally. As clearing up by conventional methods had proved inadequate, Hugo had just hosed him down in the bathtub and was now attempting to dry his loudly protesting body when he heard someone slam into the cottage. "You there?" a familiar voice bellowed. Hugo froze. *Amanda.* Unexpected, unannounced and obviously back from New York directly on hearing the news from Laura.

Hugo had hoped his being a good father might help ameliorate his sins in Amanda's eyes. But now, struggling with the baby, aware of the half-eaten slop all over the kitchen, and the foam, soiled clothes, wet towels and general chaos all over the bathroom, he knew the game was up. Heart sinking, he listened to Amanda stomping upstairs. His dread increased with her every step.

His wife did not mince her words. "You bastard," she shrieked, stomping into the bathroom.

"Laura told you then," Hugo said resignedly, holding both hands over Theo's ears.

Amanda, he saw, looked extraordinary. Her career as a magazine editor seemed not only to have gone to her head, but everywhere else as well. Her hair was platinum blonde and hung to her shoulders. She wore an arresting outfit involving a black and white patterned miniskirt, matching crop top revealing several feet of belly and, over these a long dressing-gown-like garment of the same material as the rest. Silver high-heeled boots and wraparound shades completed the ensemble. Hugo realized, looking at her, that he had become more provincial than he had suspected. He had completely forgotten that people dressed like this. Theo, meanwhile, was staring at her in amazement.

"Of course she fucking told me," Amanda raged. "She's

my *friend*. She's loyal to me, not that that's a concept *you'd* understand."

Amid his dismay, Hugo felt a jolt of indignation.

"Loyal!" he snorted. "I don't think you'd have thought so if you'd seen her coming on to me the other day. Rubbing herself up against the bedpost, completely nude and pissed as a fart. The woman's insane."

Amanda's eyes blazed. "You sad fantasist sicko. Coming on to *you?* Oh *sure*. Well you would say that, wouldn't you. Anything to get yourself off the hook."

"Eh?—"

"How bloody dare you?" Amanda yelled. "Shagging that mealy-mouthed, career-destroying . . ."

"I don't see that your career's been destroyed," Hugo broke in. "I'd say the opposite, if anything."

Amanda narrowed her eyes and placed both red-taloned hands on her hips. "I wouldn't say anything if I were you," she snarled. "Save it for your lawyer. And the divorce court."

Hugo clutched Theo so hard that the baby yelped. "What exactly do you mean by that?"

"What the hell do you think I mean?" Amanda's voice was raucously triumphant. "What do women—or should I say *mothers*—in my position normally mean?"

He stared at her for several agonized seconds. "*Theo?*"

"Yes, Theo. Quite frankly, now he's so presentable, it's about time he stopped rotting in the sticks and lived somewhere decent. He can," Amanda said decisively, "come to London with me." She swept a withering glance over Hugo's foam-spattered, damp-wrinkled suit. "It's about time I took him in hand. Took him . . . well, everywhere. To premieres. Mother and baby spas. On educational holidays. The Galápagos Islands, that sort of thing. He's got a lot of ground to cover before Cambridge. You can't start too soon."

"The Galápagos Islands . . . ?"

"He needs a proper christening as well."

"But we haven't been near a church the whole time we've lived here."

"Not *here*," Amanda said witheringly. "He'll be christened in London. Obviously. St. George's Hanover Square with a couple of celebrity godfathers, that sort of thing."

"Celebrity g—" Hugo could hardly frame the words.

"As far as his school goes," Amanda added decisively, "I'll call in a few favors and get him in at that prep school where Jude Law's kids go, as well as J. K. Rowling's and Jade Jagger's."

"But Theo's happy here," Hugo objected. "He likes Chicklets. And they think there'll be a full-time place for him soon."

Amanda was not listening. "Great school. Richard Curtis was a human fruit machine at the summer fête last year. We sent a photographer to cover it."

"But you can't . . . just *uproot* him like that," Hugo burst out. "He lives here, not London. *This* is his home."

"Well, it won't be soon," Amanda said lightly. "So you'd better start getting used to the idea."

Hugo's voice was barely above a whisper now. "You mean you're going for custody of him? But you can't. You don't know anything about Theo."

"I know *best.*"

He frowned. "What do you mean, you know best?"

"Because I am, may I remind you, his mother. Mothers know best."

"And I'm his father. I've been looking after him on my own for months."

Amanda yawned. "Oh, change the bloody record, can't you?" She chucked her son under his soft chin with long, hard nails. "Theo's turned into quite a little doll now he's finally got some hair—thank God it didn't stay ginger. We'll look good together. You know babies are the hottest accessory of the moment. He can come with me to the fashion shows and be *Class*'s little mascot."

Hugo was feeling sick for reasons unconnected with Theo's stomach bug. "But you can't—" he began, then stopped.

She could, he suspected. And if things got really nasty . . .

He remembered pictures of fathers in the papers, chaining themselves to cranes, stopping the traffic and throwing purple powder at the Prime Minister. And all because they'd been denied access to their children after divorce. Was that what lay in store for him? Could it really happen? After all he and Theo had been through together?

"Just watch me," Amanda said with bitter triumph. "I'll . . ." But before the unnamed threat could be issued, a noise outside distracted her. She went over and opened the window to see. "Fuck! It's the bloody journalists."

"Journalists?"

Amanda flashed him a glance of furious impatience. "I rang you about it, dumbo. That interview. They want to talk to me about how I combine a brilliant career with a happy marriage and successful motherhood. *Dahhhhhhling!*" she exclaimed, teetering toward Theo on perilous heels. "Are you ready for your close-up?"

Like an eagle with its prey she swooped him up and crushed him closely to her before peeling him off and thrusting him hurriedly at Hugo. "Oh, *disgusting*, he's just wiped his filthy snotty nose all over my sleeve. Here, take him. *Quick.*"

She rushed to the wash basin and dabbed frantically at the damage with a baby sponge. "Doesn't he realize it's crêpe de Chine?" she snarled.

As the doorbell rang, she teetered back from the basin and snatched Theo again. Ripped from his father, the baby started up a thin, tired wail.

Amanda grabbed a pacifier from the bathside and rammed it into his mouth.

Hugo watched Amanda glance in the mirror, check her hair and plaster on a huge showbiz smile before lurching to the stairs under the clearly awkward and unfamiliar weight of a baby. "Careful," he warned.

She paused and looked viciously over her shoulder. "No. You be careful. You'd better bloody play ball with this interview. Otherwise you'll be *really* sorry."

Hugo immediately saw this as a straw to clutch at. Was Amanda saying, albeit unpleasantly, that if he remained discreet, smiling and supportive during the interview she would simmer down and see reason? That there was room for debate, negotiation and, hopefully, the changing of minds?

"Hey-there-how-are-ya-come-*in*," he heard her cry to the group of people at the front door. From the top of the stairs he watched them enter: the handsome photographer with the emphatically tousled hair, his tiny blonde female assistant, the interviewer with her cropped hair, techo-glasses, knee boots and tight-fitting houndstooth-check coat. They all stared unapologetically around.

"This is my husband," Amanda said as Hugo came down the stairs.

The journalist smiled at him glassily. "And aren't you the lucky man? Married to this superwoman!" She gestured at Amanda. "Imagine it makes you feel a bit indequate at times."

"Er, yes," admitted Hugo. Rarely, certainly, had he felt less adequate than he did at the moment.

The journalist made a note. Amanda's expression, Hugo saw, encouraged, was approving.

For the next two hours he fetched and carried cups of tea for the crew while Amanda sat on the sofa with Theo and held forth about her mothering, editing and homemaking abilities.

"You must be *so* proud of her," the journalist gushed as, yet again, Hugo appeared with his tray.

He forced his chin up and down. "Oh, I am." Catching Amanda's expectant expression he realized that rather more was required. "Amanda is . . . *amazing*." That at least was true.

"The way she juggles everything!" the journalist added admiringly.

"It's just . . . unbelievable," Hugo agreed.

"And how hands-on are you?" the journalist enquired. "With the baby, I mean?"

Hugo glanced at Theo, who was playing happily with the photographer's light meter. He sensed Amanda's drill-like stare. "Oh," he said, in an attempt at breeziness. "*Quite* hands on. I try, you know." He gave a self-deprecating laugh.

"But she's a hard act to follow, huh?" prompted the journalist.

Hugo said nothing.

"He's so *good!*" the journalist remarked of Theo. "You really *have* got it down to a fine art." The writer made more notes.

"Thanks!" said Hugo, a split second before Amanda could claim credit. He shot her an apologetic glance, realizing his mistake. Yet it was, for him, a matter of huge pride and yet bitter regret that Theo did not burst into tears or have a tantrum. At one time he would have obliged royally, and put Amanda at an obvious disadvantage. But Theo, as a rule, did not indulge in such behavior any more. As Hugo had relaxed and blossomed into his role as a father, Theo had relaxed and blossomed into his as a baby.

"You're too kind!" prinked Amanda. She held out her teacup to Hugo. "More tea please . . . *darling.*"

"We're out of milk," Hugo said. "Darling," he added hurriedly.

Amanda rolled her eyes at the journalist. "Men! Typical! You ask them to remember *one thing!* Oh well," she added with theatrical brightness. "You know what they say. If you want something done, don't just ask a busy person. Ask a stressed-out, juggling, multitasking working mother!"

As the journalist tittered and made yet more notes, Hugo silently ground his teeth.

"So," he said to Amanda, when, much, much later, the door

finally closed behind the magazine crew, "I did everything you wanted. I played ball."

"You certainly did," she agreed.

"So can we talk about *us* now? About Theo?" Hugo adopted the most reasonable, nonconfrontational tones he could manage.

"If you like," Amanda said. "But I can't see why."

"Because you were talking about divorce," Hugo reminded her pleasantly. "And taking Theo away." He pressed his nose into the warm head of the baby who, as Amanda had busied herself with farewells, he was holding again.

"So what's changed?" Amanda asked lightly.

Hugo wanted to shout with the shock of it. So she had tricked him. She had no intention of negotiating and never had. She had only hinted as much to buy his silence and complicity during a prize piece of personal publicity. He stared at Amanda with loathing. So this was it. This was war.

"You wait," he said in a low, furious voice. "I'll fight you for Theo every inch of the way."

"Well, the best of British in that case." Amanda shrugged on her coat. "You're going to need it. You've just committed yourself to print in a national newspaper saying that I'm a fantastic wife and mother. If you weren't going to lose before, you're definitely going to lose now."

CHAPTER
26

ALICE HAD BEEN WATCHING AND WAITING FOR THE RIGHT MOMENT to discuss the future with Jake. It had not yet come, due mostly to his almost continuous absence from the cottage. His increasing *Get Trashed!* commitments, followed by more and more evenings spent eco-agitating, meant opportunities to talk were confined to first thing in the morning or last thing at night. Neither of which were an ideal time to broach the possible breakup of their family.

She thought constantly of Hugo. Lying alone in bed as, night after night, Jake stayed out late, she relived the memory of his lips on her eyes, mouth, neck and breasts. She ached too to know how he was, and how matters stood with Amanda. But only a fool, in the circumstances, would try something as rash as getting in touch. Matters with Jake needed to be resolved first. And, as Hugo had stressed, in as subtle and sensible a way as possible. She had thought long and hard about their conversation in the restaurant and now felt more optimistic. Given her legal background, her gift for argument, perhaps she could persuade Jake that Hugo's solution really was best for them all.

She had almost fallen asleep the night she heard the front door of the cottage slam hard. And, immediately afterward, heavy, angry footsteps on the stairs.

In the ottoman, Rosa stirred and whimpered. Alice, beneath the duvet, froze even more than she was doing already, given the always inadequate heating.

The bedroom door opened to reveal a crack of light. "Al!" hissed Jake. "I want to talk to you downstairs. Now."

She crept guiltily out from beneath the duvet. He had, she miserably guessed, found out about Hugo. But how?

"Woad!" exploded Jake by way of explanation when she arrived barefoot and shivering in the sitting room to find her suspicions were correct.

"Woad?" Alice clutched her washed-out, oversized second-hand T-shirt about her.

"Woad!" Jake repeated.

"You mean that stuff the Ancient Britons used to wear to scare off the Romans?" How had that helped in his deductions?

"And which is emerging as a viable alternative to the potentially cancerous artificial indigo dyes currently being used for jeans."

Alice frowned. "What? I don't understand."

Jake rummaged in his pocket. "And I didn't, either, when I first found this," he snarled, waving a crumpled piece of white cotton at her.

Alice stared at it, at first bemused and then with heart-speeding recognition. It was the handkerchief Hugo had lent to her when they had met in the bookshop. Jake must have found it in the washing pile. And, of course, it had Hugo's initials on it.

Oh, how *Othello* of her. How *bloody* stupid of her. Alice's fists clenched. She should have hidden the handkerchief immediately. But then, at the time there had been no need. Far from being desperate to see Hugo, as now, she had been anxious to get away from him.

"I couldn't work out who H E D F was," Jake growled, his eyes long and glittering in the light filtering through the ceiling colander. "And then, at the fashion show, it suddenly all made sense."

"Fashion show?" It was all making less and less sense to Alice. What was Jake, of all people, doing at a fashion show?

"London Fashion Week," Jake snapped. "Me and Jess have been there tonight campaigning for wider use of planet-friendly dyes."

"I see," said Alice faintly. "That's where the woad comes in."

"Yes, and that's where I saw that stuck-up trout from the prenatal class. That editor woman." Jake paused. Alice felt a stab of panic.

"Amanda?"

"Who tells me," Jake went on acidly, "that you're fucking her husband." He waved the handkerchief. "Hugo Eric Dennis Fine?"

Now, in the midst of catastrophe, Alice found herself dwelling on Hugo's middle names. He hadn't struck her as either a Dennis or an Eric.

"You know what I could do?" Jake thundered. "Leave . . ."

Hope soared within her. "Well, if you're sure . . ." Him disappearing would solve everything. She had not expected such a simple, quick resolution.

". . . and take Ro with me."

"Take Rosa?" Alice said sharply.

"Don't think I'd leave her with you, do you? What sort of bloody mother are you anyway?" His face twisted with disgust. "That oily bastard of a real estate agent. Al, how bloody could you? How grubby could you get?"

Alice resisted saying that, so far as grubbiness went, both Allingham House and Hugo were cleaner than Jake and the Old Morgue. There were more important points to make. "You *can't* take Rosa," she exploded. "You've got no legal rights to. The courts—"

"Legal rights? Courts?" Jake smiled coldly. "Who needs legal rights? With my network of underground eco-contacts, I could disappear just like that." He snapped his fingers. The sharp sound echoed in Alice's ears. "There's the German beetle camp, for a start."

"Beetle . . . ?"

"A group in Germany who've built a whole city of tunnels under a rare beetle breeding ground they're saving from developers."

Alice immediately imagined Rosa sitting in an underground passage, beetles teeming above and German hippies teeming below. She clamped a horrified hand to her mouth.

"Matter of fact," Jake remarked, inspecting a clod of crud on his grubby red check shirt, "I've been thinking of going abroad for some time, *Get Trashed!* being about to bite the dust and all that."

"Is it?" Alice was aware things had not been going well. But this badly? Had the end of her cash handouts spelled the end for the magazine?

"Unfortunately, yes." He gave her a hard stare. "So pissing off with Rosa rather fits in with my plans."

*　*　*

One of the hopes Hugo was clinging to was that Barbara, one of the mothers at Chicklets, would represent him in the battle with Amanda. He knew she was a barrister, or was trying to be, the struggle between work and children permitting. Once, in the car park, he had heard her sobbing into her cell phone about an incident in which she had turned up to court late because of taking her daughter to the doctor. Her client had been savaged by the prosecution.

Barbara was difficult to approach, mostly because she screeched off at top speed within seconds of delivering her child. As there was no time for subtlety, Hugo decided to be obvious. One morning he lay in wait by her car and begged her to come for a quick coffee. Barbara, however, refused. "I'd love to, but I've no time!" she pleaded. But Hugo was a desperate man. Swiftly, he outlined his predicament. Barbara's tense face relaxed a little. "I can't help you anyway," she explained. "This would be a family case and my specialty is fraud."

Hugo gave a mirthless laugh. "Believe me, this is much more about fraud than family."

Barbara chortled. "Oh dear. But in any case you need a lawyer first and foremost. I can give you the name of a good one. And do, above all, go for counseling."

"Counseling?" Hugo was unpleasantly reminded of Laura. "Bit late for that, isn't it?"

Barbara shook her head. "A willingness to try counseling rather than just giving up on the marriage impresses courts in divorce cases."

"But the marriage is . . ." began Hugo.

"Over? Well of course it is. But what we're talking about here is who gets custody of Theo. The odds'll be stacked against you, you know that?"

Hugo nodded miserably. Barbara rubbed his arm comfortingly. "Don't worry. You've got a good chance. You're obviously devoted to Theo and you're in reliable employment."

"That's important?" Hugo thought anxiously of the underground car park fiasco. Hopefully, Neil could be persuaded to take a lenient view.

Barbara looked at him in surprise. "Of course it is. A jobless father is unlikely to be granted custody at the expense of an employed mother."

"Oh. Right."

"So that plus the therapy will stand you in good stead."

But Hugo's stead, as it happened, stood good only as long as it took to get from the nursery to Dunn and Dustard.

Learning—in glorious technicolor from Shuna followed by a reluctant summary from Hugo—of the occurrences in the underground car park, Neil summarily fired him.

"I'm sorry, Fine. But you're a liability, let's face it," he barked, as Hugo tried desperately to reason with him.

"But, Neil. Come *on*, mate. You don't know what this means. Amanda's divorcing me—"

"Sorry, Fine. You've had your chances."

As Hugo miserably absorbed this, Barbara's voice echoed in his ears. "A jobless father is unlikely to be granted custody at the expense of an employed mother." Especially a self-declared high-achieving, juggling, multitasking mother like Amanda. He didn't have to close his eyes to imagine her in some sharp suit in the courtroom, briefed to the nines, working that dynamically capable chic for all it was worth. And what it was worth, ultimately, was Theo.

The thought of his son being taken from him made Hugo feel desperate. It seemed impossibly unfair that it could happen, and yet, especially now, he did not doubt that it would.

There was, as Hugo saw it, but one option left to him. He pushed past Neil, disappeared into the loos and burst into tears.

*　*　*

Looking back, some time later, on the days that subsequently passed, it seemed miraculous to Hugo that he survived them. In some ways, of course, he had no choice; Theo, at least temporarily, was still in his charge and as exacting a taskmaster as ever. But at night, when the baby was finally silent in his cot, Hugo, in bed, would stare hopelessly into the darkness and try not to think about the even blacker hole that was his future. Whether Alice was still part of that future, he was miserably unaware. All attempts to get in touch with her had met with a wall of silence and on one occasion the closed and unyielding door of the Old Morgue. That had been the lowest point of all.

Hugo had, however, summoned up the resolve to take Barbara's advice and contacted both lawyer and counselor. But after the initial outlay of effort and expense, both initiatives seemed increasingly hopeless. He had lost his job and he had played into Amanda's hands over the magazine article. Through fair means or foul, and her own indomitable will, Amanda would get what she wanted. She always did. Today, for example, in the waiting room of the Northanger Advice and Support Center; he felt he was merely going through the motions.

He heard one of the counselors' doors open, but did not look up. If Dr. Hasselblad was ready, he'd say so. Footsteps came out. Hugo heard the footsteps pause, then change direction toward him.

The shoes were, he noticed, getting nearer. A pair of flat brown brogue toes stopped just under his nose.

"Hugo?" It was Laura's voice. "Is that you?"

He jerked his head up, shocked. *Her!* Sounding as untroubled as if she had spotted him from across the road. Had she no shame?

He looked at her resentfully from under his brows, noting the absence of the usual hot-pink and heaving bosom. Instead she wore a gray polo sweater and jeans almost as sober as the shoes.

"What the hell do you want?" he hissed.

She looked, he saw, nervous. "Er . . . how are you?" she asked. "You look, er . . ."

"Awful?" Hugo prompted sarcastically, aware of his hot, tired eyes and creased clothes.

"Yes," said Laura quietly. "Awful."

He glared at her. "Can't think why. Because I *feel* great, obviously. Never better. My marriage has broken up and I'm about to lose my son. Both thanks in no small part to you. So do me a favor, will you, and piss off."

"Hugo," Laura said, in a low voice. "Listen to me."

"Listen to you? Are you joking? Leave me alone, will you? Haven't you done enough damage?"

"I understand why you're saying that . . ." Laura began.

"I should think you bloody do," cut in Hugo, shaking off the hand she now placed on his arm. He wished desperately that she would go.

" . . . but I wanted to thank you," Laura finished.

"Thank me?" He snapped his head to the side to look at her, so hard he felt his neck crunch. "*Thank me?* You're in the wrong movie, Laura. I'm in the one where the husband who's looked after the child almost all its life loses it on a whim of his feckless egomaniac absentee wife's after her friend tells her he's been having an affair. I'm not sure which one you're in."

Laura met his gaze steadily. "I'm in the one where the hopeless mother goes to therapy on the advice of her friend's husband and finds she's a classic postnatal depressive. And after a few sessions she starts to see where she's been going wrong. With her marriage, with her son and . . ." Laura paused and looked down, "she realizes as well that certain unpleasant and vengeful acts, such as telling her friend about her husband's infidelity instead of talking first to the husband himself and allowing him to make amends, came about out of spite and a wish to destroy. To make everyone else feel as unhappy as she did."

There was a silence. Hugo said nothing. He had some time ago passed the stage of being unable to believe his ears.

Laura's makeup-less eyes flicked earnestly up at him. "So that's why I wanted to thank you. You were the only person who suggested therapy might be the answer. I was furious at first but then I thought about it and I realized you were right. You probably saved my life."

Hugo shrugged. "A moving story," he remarked bitterly. "I'm thrilled for you, Laura, really, I am. I'm so glad you're finding yourself. It makes me feel so much better now that I'm losing just about everything."

"You *were* having an affair," Laura pointed out.

Hugo flared like a match at this piece of staggering impertinence. He rounded on her furiously. "What about you in that hotel foyer with God knows who at Christmas? What about the moves you made on *me?*"

She swiftly dropped her eyes.

"It wasn't just an affair, anyway," he muttered, wanting to

make the point, even to Laura, that his and Alice's relationship could not be bracketed with her own grubby liaisons. "We were going to tell them—eventually."

"Were you?" Laura had raised a disbelieving eyebrow.

He addressed the floor again. "It was a question of timing. We were going to tell them, but not straight away. We needed time, we thought, and they needed time, to help them see what was so obvious. That we were all with the wrong people, basically. Jake doesn't want to be with Alice and Amanda doesn't want to be with me. And neither of them wants to be with their children."

"How can you be so sure Amanda doesn't want to be with Theo?" Laura probed.

Hugo put his head to one side in an attitude of mock puzzlement. "Because she disappeared a few weeks after he was born?" he suggested ironically. "Because she thought ludicrous Hollywood presents—all, incidentally, bagged for free—were the same as being at home looking after him? Because I couldn't get her on her mobile the night I took him to the hospital thinking he was about to die? Because she's prepared to wreck a happy, stable home, albeit an unconventional one, so she can tart him around fashion shows and send him to school with celebrity children?"

He looked fiercely at Laura, who was staring back at him in shock. "I never realized . . ." she stammered. "I mean, it was obvious there were a few self-confusion issues going on there, but . . ."

"*Self-confusion?*" Hugo spat. "Is that what the counselors call it?"

"I'm so sorry," Laura said. "If I could turn the clock back and not have told Amanda, I would. It was none of my business. If I could do anything to help, to make things better, to make amends . . ."

Hugo flicked her a look. "There isn't anything you can do," he said quietly.

"Oh, Hugo, I'm so—"

"I don't care how sorry you are. It's too late. The damage is done."

She was twisting her hands in anguish. "But there might be something . . ."

"There's *nothing* you can do," he snapped. "Except leave me alone. Just *go away.*"

He could hear chairs scraping behind Dr. Hasselblad's door. The protracted session was finally coming to an end. Without another word, Laura got up and left.

Seconds later, Dr. Hasselblad's door opened. Hugo, standing up, glanced casually but curiously at who might be coming out.

It was Alice.

CHAPTER
27

IT WAS VITAL, ALICE HAD RECOGNIZED, FOR HER TO END THE RELA-tionship with Hugo. Whatever her own passionate personal feelings, they had to be put aside for the greater good. Jake was a bottle of marital nitroglycerine, ready to explode with devastating consequences at the slightest unscheduled wobble. Alice was desperate to keep everything as calm as possible. Which meant, so far as was possible, preserving the status quo.

In exchange for promising to give *Get Trashed!* an emergency cash transfusion, she secured from Jake the assurance that he would support her efforts to get their marriage back on track. A lawyer she contacted advised that counseling sessions for them both could be helpful and although, historically, Alice had regarded all therapists as quacks, historically she had not been in the situation she found herself in now. Tired, despondent and above all, desperate. No source of help could be ruled out.

A professional person's view of the matters troubling them might even be useful. If things ever got to court, the fact that the counseling had been her initiative would show a willingness, if not an ability, to make amends.

While she had not seen Hugo since the fateful night at the

hotel, she had rehearsed what she would do if, as was not completely unexpected, she met him in the street. Night after night before sleep finally, belatedly, claimed her, she rehearsed her cool but friendly response with the result that she was almost convinced by it herself. Almost.

What she had never rehearsed for, never expected, was to emerge from a counseling session to see, standing before her, the very reason she was there in the first place.

Not only was Alice unprepared for the sight of Hugo, she was unprepared for what he would look like. Bleary-eyed, wild-haired and as sunken-cheeked as a Schiele drawing. Sleepless black shadows dragged beneath each reddened eye.

A great wave of tender concern smashed powerfully over her head. Hugo looked, she thought, as if he had been under torture. Even his voice sounded broken. "Alice," he said, in a parched sort of way that made her want to gather him to her breast and hug everything better.

"What are you doing here?" she hissed, instead.

His smile was sickly. "Relationship therapy. You?"

She looked away. "Same."

"Jake knows then?" She looked, he thought, so beautiful with a soft pink scarf—surely not from the dump—bringing out the flush in her cheeks and warming her pale sheet of hair.

"Yes. And I gather from him Amanda knows as well."

Hugo nodded. "So basically we're both here to keep our marriages going." He snorted.

Alice, looking at the floor, felt him catch at her hand. A thrill of fear juddered through her as she snatched it away.

"Oh God, Alice, don't do that." He sounded appalled. "It's as if you hate me or something."

"Of course I don't hate you." Her eyes snagged fleetingly on his. "It's just that I don't dare . . . Look, I can't see you again. Ever."

In the ensuing silence, desperate courage flared within him. "You could leave him, you know. Get custody of Rosa."

She shuddered a no. "He's threatened to take her away. I think he means it."

"*What?* He's threatened *what?* Hell, Alice. That's probably grounds for divorce in itself."

She banged clenched fists to each of her sides. "Stop talking about divorce. I don't *want* a divorce."

Hugo felt as if an iron hand had closed round his throat. "You don't want . . . ?"

"I don't want to rock the boat. And I suppose now I feel that I deserve what's happened. I don't want any more upheaval. I want us all to stay together as a family."

Hugo stared, disbelieving. "Oh, for Christ's sake, Alice," he exploded. "You can't possibly mean that. What sort of Calvinistic self-punishing crap is that? You *don't* deserve what's happened. What you deserve is a break."

She twisted her hands. "Well, none of that matters now. What's more important than anything is giving Rosa a happy, secure childhood. With both her parents, like I had."

"Even if one of her parents is a bloody lunatic? You said yourself you had no idea why he married you."

"He seems to be taking to counseling, though," Alice told him defensively. "Maybe this was what he needed. It might make a difference. He might change. He has a bit, already. I think the counselor's noticed the hygiene problem. He's washing again . . ." Her voice was almost pleading.

"You think so?" Hugo said ominously. "Alice, you may be convincing yourself, but you don't convince me. A leopard doesn't change his spots. Even if he washes them."

His skepticism, she knew, was understandable. But, much to Alice's own amazement, Jake really had taken to therapy with enormous enthusiasm. Slightly but definitely, his temper and general attitude had improved since the sessions had started. As had his personal hygiene. Beside washing, he had started shaving again and that lank, greasy look she so hated had finally gone from his hair.

"He's got some moisturizer in the bathroom cupboard, the first I've ever seen him use," she added. "He's even started wearing aftershave, which he never has before."

Her voice sounded almost plaintively deranged in his ears. *"Aftershave!"* Hugo exclaimed, wondering what that had to do with anything. Hastily, he collected himself. "Look, we're wasting valuable time. When do you usually have your counseling? And what time is his?"

"Every Wednesday at nine," she muttered. "And Jake's is at twelve. Why?"

"Mine's usually on Wednesdays at eleven. Today it got moved at the last minute, that's why I'm here now. But Alice, listen, I could move it to the same time as you. Get a different counselor, or whatever. You could keep Dr. Hasselblad—he's been no bloody good to me anyway." He clutched her. "We could see each other then. Before or after. Accidentally, or so it would seem." He swallowed. "What do you think?"

For a second, Alice wavered. Then she shook his hand off. "No," she said firmly. "What would be the point?"

He felt the hope seep out of him, like air from a sagging balloon. "The point?" he repeated. "That we'd see each other at least. Go for a coffee or—"

"We can't."

"Oh, Alice. Please. I can't bear it . . ."

"Well you'll have to," she said sharply. "We'll both have to."

Hugo tried to squash the rising lump in his throat. "You're right," he said defeatedly. "Seeing the people we love in the context of trying to find a way to stay with the people we don't is just . . ."

". . . not the way to keep our children." Alice moved toward the door.

Hugo gave a hollow chortle. "Oh, I've already lost Theo."

This had an electric effect. She whipped round, appalled. "What—has there been a hearing already?"

"No, but it'll be soon. And I'm not expecting to come out

of it all that well. You'll be a witness, obviously." He smiled at her ruefully.

Alice flinched. Witness in a divorce. The other woman. The evil temptress. Not a role she had ever imagined for herself.

"But they can't give Amanda Theo," she protested. "The Children's Act favors the primary caregiver, and that's you."

"I know. But apparently courts always imagine it's the mother. And you know what Amanda's like. She'll put on an Oscar winner of a performance in order to get her own way."

Alice tried to banish the vision of the evil Amanda, Cruella De Vil–like, sinking her red shining talons into the puppylike Theo. "She *can't*. I mean . . . they *won't*. You must have a good chance? With your track record of looking after him. And your job, of course."

"I got sacked a couple of weeks ago. Alice, I don't have a job." He turned up his palms helplessly.

Alice looked back at him in despair.

"So you're probably right," Hugo said with forced flippancy. "There is no point in any of it. This is it then. This is good-bye."

Alice shot forward and brushed his cheek with her lips. "Good-bye, Hugo." She shut the door quickly behind her before he could see the tears.

She sat at the back of the bus all the way home, sobbing quietly into her scarf and feeling as if a razor was twisting in her heart.

She was terrified for Hugo. His fear of losing Theo was probably justified. As she herself well knew, court cases involving Amanda Hardwick meant disaster and nothing else. And he had lost his job in the bargain. Alice groaned. She felt sick and choked, as much by circumstance as by the black fumes pouring out of the vehicle's exhaust.

Home, she pushed open the battered door of the Old

Morgue. Jake, just behind it, shoved at her the whimpering Rosa. "I've got to go out," he announced, clearly in a tremendous rush.

"Oh, right. Where?"

"Counseling," Jake called cheerily over his shoulder, dodging through the vitreous enamel cluttering the path.

Alice fed Rosa and switched on the garish primary-colored cassette player she had recently bought for her song tapes.

Rosa, who loved music, was bouncing triumphantly up and down to "Miss Polly had a Dolly" when the telephone rang. It was Alice's mother.

"How are things, darling?" she asked, more gaily than she felt. As Alice's chief confidante, she was apprised of all recent details, including the threatened kidnap. So far, she had managed to keep her own volcanic feelings on the subject heroically under wraps.

"Oh, you know," Alice said absently, smiling at Rosa, who was pushing up the volume dial with her fat little hands. "Bobby Shaftoe" blared out deafeningly.

"No, darling, I don't know. Tell me."

Alice paused, then it all came out in a rush. "I saw Hugo this morning. At the therapist's." She closed her eyes briefly. "It was . . . horrible. He was so upset."

"And what about you?" her mother probed.

"I was pretty upset too, obviously. But, Mum, I feel so dreadful about the affair. It was wrong. *Really* wrong. I've caused such a lot of trouble. Made such a mess of everything."

"Darling, these things happen," Mrs. Duffield said soothingly.

But not to you and Dad, Alice thought hotly. "Well, they're not happening anymore," she said firmly. "I told him there was no future for us and we were better trying to rebuild the marriages we had."

There was a pause at her mother's end. "Why did you say that, darling?" Mrs. Duffield asked carefully.

Alice felt a prick of annoyance. Was her mother, secure on her lofty pinnacle of unbroken marital fidelity, patronizing her?

"Look, Mum," she said, exasperated, "we've been through all this before. You know it's because I want Rosa to have both her parents."

"You don't think it's a high price to pay? Spending the rest of your life with Jake? After all he's put you through?"

"Honestly, Mum, he's improved. I think the therapy's helping a bit. He's very keen on it . . ."

"Improved?" Her mother's self-discipline finally gave way. "Believe me, darling, people like him don't improve. You're far better off being a single mum, for Rosa's sake as well as yours. Just divorce him."

"Mu-um!" exclaimed Alice. "What are you saying?"

"Only what I've been wanting to say for ages." Mrs. Duffield was now in full, furious flow. "You'd have a case for unreasonable behavior. Jake dragged you back from New York on the understanding that life with him would be just fantastic. And look what happened. He turned you into an eco-prisoner. In ghastly surroundings. Five minutes in your house and any court would come down on your side. The place is a—"

"Bloody bomb site. I know," Alice admitted. "That's just what Hugo said. He said everything you've just said."

"You know, darling, the more I hear about this Hugo the more I like him. Him rescuing Rosa's teddy was just adorable. Heroic."

A pang went through Alice at the memory. "That's beside the point."

"Is it? Why?"

"Because the whole Hugo thing's impossible. I'm staying with Jake and that's that. I've got a responsibility to Rosa and—"

"But the man's a lunatic," her mother broke in. "You said yourself you had no idea why he married you. Don't tell me all that's changed, all of a sudden."

Was Hugo, Alice wondered, actually in touch with her mother? Or were they just employing the same scriptwriter?

"Look," she conceded. "It won't be ideal. Not at first, anyway. And possibly not ever. But I'm not sure I deserve to be enjoying myself, anyway. Not after what I've done."

"But you can't stay with a madman who doesn't love you just to punish yourself. Darling, where's the logic in that? And what good does it do Rosa?"

Alice took a deep breath. She felt tired, defensive and, increasingly, angry. "I know Jake and I will never live up to the standards of you and Dad. But I wanted her to have something like the same security and happiness that I did."

"Your father," her mother replied gently, "is a very special man. But Jake is not, in my view, a special man. Darling, what I'm saying is that I really doubt that you, even with all your good intentions, could make that marriage work after everything that's happened. You're much better off getting out of it."

"Thanks, Mum," Alice said. "I appreciate your support, I really do. Thanks a *lot*." She slammed the receiver down angrily.

CHAPTER
28

HUGO WAS MOOCHING MISERABLY AROUND THEO'S EMPTY NURSERY. He often found himself here these days; it was, he supposed, a way of preparing himself for the approaching time when the nursery was vacant permanently.

He looked at his watch, noting with relief that it would soon be time to fetch his son from Chicklets. The morning, like every morning since he had lost his job, had dragged. After dropping Theo at nursery he had called the lawyer, certain, as always, that the morning post would have brought Amanda's divorce papers and with them the date for the hearing. But as it happened, the post hadn't.

The delay was, Hugo felt sure, another of Amanda's torture tactics. While the date he awaited would obviously mark the end of everything he lived for, he was almost beginning to look forward to it. The limbo he was in was debilitating, a halfway house, a living death.

He should, he supposed, probably be keeping Theo at home with him. He had, after all, nothing else to do and he should make the most of their last few weeks, days, hours, or whatever it was, together. Now he was no longer earning, Chicklets' fees were eating into his dwindling savings as well.

But the thought of his lively, merry baby, used now to the

company of other infants, cooped up with no one but his miserable self and even more miserable attempts at being cheerful was unendurable. Theo deserved better. To withdraw him from Chicklets would, anyway, be to cut the last tie to their old, happy life together. It was not something he felt able to do.

The divorce would obviously mean number four Fitzherbert Place would be sold. No doubt an eager young couple, bright-eyed and enthusiastic about their escape to the picturesque provinces, would buy it and set about it with heritage paints and architectural salvage catalogues. In no time at all they would transform it into a tasteful family home. He hoped they would be happy, whoever they were.

He locked the front door and got into the car for Chicklets, wondering how many of these once-routine, taken-for-granted trips he had left.

Arriving at the nursery, Hugo was almost glad to see the Rottweiler shoot out of her office in trademark style. It brought an element of normality at least.

"Mr. Fine. A word, if you please. In my office."

He followed the nursery head into her lair and looked around at the surprising number of flickering computer screens. It reminded him of an air traffic control center. He had no idea that running a kindergarten was so technical.

"I want to talk to you about Theo," the Rottweiler said, settling herself at the other side of her vast desk.

"Fire away," Hugo said comfortably. For once, he was in no hurry to leave. "It's not the nappies again, is it?"

He had been pulled up short a few days ago about Theo's habit, apparently recently acquired, of filling his nappy en route to the nursery. "Nursery regulations," the Rottweiler had sternly pointed out, "demand that babies are presented at Chicklets with clean bottoms."

Nursery regulations had thereafter seen Hugo stop every two minutes on the way to Chicklets, get out of the car, go around to the backseat, remove Theo from his restraints and lift him up and sniff his rear to make sure all was well. The amused gazes of passing drivers had to be borne, as well as the outraged howls of a Theo recognizing he had been caught.

"No," the Rottweiler said. "It's not nappies. It's about Theo's biting, Mr. Fine."

"Biting?"

"Your son, Mr. Fine, has been biting other children."

"Oh, no." Hugo stared in wide-eyed despair at the surface of the desk. A warm wave of shame flooded him. He remembered how furious and indignant he had been on the few occasions Theo had been on the receiving end of such attacks from his peers. No doubt other mothers and fathers would now be baying for Theo's blood. Thank goodness nursery policy forbade the naming of miscreants.

"I don't understand," he said. "He never bites at home."

The Rottweiler waggled her pen. "Immaterial, Mr. Fine. We need to find out why he is doing it here. And put a stop to it. Sometimes, Mr. Fine, very occasionally, biting can be an expression of anger or frustration about something." She leaned forward, her bulging blue eyes inquiring. "Is there," she asked, "anything that Theo is perhaps reacting to at the moment? Any problems at home, for instance?"

Hugo felt himself shrivel in the intensity of her stare. That the Rottweiler had guessed all was not well was obvious. And unsurprising; he was, after all, the physical embodiment of domestic breakdown. Unwashed, unbrushed, unironed, unpolished. Unhappy.

Even so, for all his personal degradation, he had imagined his efforts to protect his son from the worst of the pre-divorce fallout to have been successful.

So brilliantly successful, he thought bitterly now, that Theo was biting other children to express his unhappiness, even at this early stage. No one had as yet been near a courtroom.

"Oh God," he said, into the hand that had flown to his mouth and was pressing hard against it to stop the howls that wanted to come. He flicked a terrified glance at the Rottweiler, imagining her in the dock supporting Amanda. "I regret to say that Mr. Fine's abilities as a parent were inadequate, if well-meaning . . ." The prospect of social workers and separation orders crowded horribly into his mind. Perhaps he wouldn't have to wait for the divorce to lose Theo.

"Oh God," he repeated to the Rottweiler. "You want to throw him out, don't you? Well, of course you do. Nobody wants a baby that *bites* . . ." His voice broke on the last word.

"On the contrary, Mr. Fine," the Rottweiler said briskly, "we should be very sorry to see Theo go. He is a happy, loving little boy. What we want is to find a solution. Help him through this."

Hugo wondered whether, in his misery, he was hearing all right. He had never suspected the Rottweiler to have an understanding streak. He had always assumed her function was to make parents' lives as difficult as possible.

Across the desk, the Rottweiler's stern features relaxed. "Mr. Fine," she said, in a gentle voice he had not heard before, "while I am unaware of the precise nature of your personal difficulties, I would like to just say this. If there is anything I, or Chicklets, can do to help—an extra hour of care here and there, say—do please let me know. We are here to support you and, of course, Theo in any way we can."

Hugo felt his body slump sideways in amazement. He managed, just in time, to stop himself falling off his chair; managed, even, to stammer out his incredulous thanks.

"You are very welcome, Mr. Fine." The Rottweiler tactfully glanced away from his glistening eyes. "We are, of course, aware of the many difficulties facing the working mother—sorry, *parent*—at Chicklets. And of your case in particular, may I say."

"How do you mean?" croaked Hugo.

"*Ahem*. It was fairly evident at first that you were having—how shall I put it?—something of a challenging time with

Theo. But we all admired the way you overcame those challenges in order to build a really extraordinarily close and loving bond with your son."

Hugo was too surprised to speak.

"In addition, you have always been quick to cooperate with nursery rules and support us whenever you can. You are a model parent, Mr. Fine. Believe me, I wish there were more like you around."

"A model parent," Hugo gasped. *"Me?"*

"Now," the Rottweiler reached for a kettle on a table behind and switched it on. "May I suggest a cup of tea. With sugar," she added, flicking Hugo an amused glance. "I believe," she added with a smile, the first he had ever seen on her lips, "that it's good for shock."

* * *

Theo had recently become extremely attached to a game in which a pile of colored wooden rings was pushed onto a stake. Accordingly, for most of the afternoon following their return from Chicklets, Hugo sat patiently beside the baby in the nursery, cheering and clapping whenever his son managed to re-impale a ring.

"A touching sight," someone observed caustically from the nursery doorway.

"Amanda. How the hell—"

"Did I get in?" She reached into the pocket of her shiny black leather coat and shook a handful of jangling metal. "I've still got my keys."

As she stalked, spike-heeled, into the room, Theo stopped pushing his rings on his stick and stared up at her from the floor, his small face solemn, his big eyes grave. Hugo glanced at him in concern. The baby was soaking up the tension like a sponge. Some poor infant at Chicklets would suffer the consequences of this tomorrow.

Amanda stared at Hugo. "You look like shit," she said frankly.

He noticed her precise makeup and the way her hair shone with the obviously recent attentions of someone expensive. Beside her, both he and Theo, whose face retained ample evidence of the beans he had had for lunch, looked more than a little crumpled.

Hugo edged protectively closer to Theo, whose attention had returned to his rings and stick. He watched his wife warily. Another possibility for her visit struck him. But if Amanda thought she was coming for the baby now, she was mistaken. The courts, as yet, had ruled nothing. They had not even sat. For the moment, Theo's home was with him at Fitzherbert Place.

"Why are you here?" he asked guardedly.

"To talk."

"What is there to talk about?" His first suspicions had been correct, then. "I thought we were talking through our lawyers, anyway."

"I've come to tell you," Amanda said, after what seemed the longest pause in history, "that I was wrong."

Hugo's fingers edged tighter around Theo's warm little side. "Wrong?" he croaked. "About what?"

"About everything." She was still addressing the far wall. Or, perhaps, the chest of drawers against it.

"You mean . . . ?" Hope roared up within him like an erupting volcano. "You mean that you don't want a divorce?"

Brilliant possibilities reeled dizzily through his head. The threat of separation from the baby finally lifted. Theo, him and Amanda, all together again as a family. And while this last was hard to imagine, he would make it work for Theo's sake. He *would*, however badly Amanda behaved. He had a new perspective on that now. The worst, most arrogant and eye-wideningly selfish excesses of his wife were sheer delight compared to the terror he had lived with these past few weeks.

Amanda turned. Hugo's face was blazing so brilliantly with

hope she felt she could warm her hands on it. She shook her head. "No," she said shortly. "I don't mean that. I still want a divorce."

"You do?" The volcano became a chilly chasm.

"You and I were never going to work out. Besides," Amanda added casually, flexing a finger with a big ring on it, "I've met someone else."

Hugo closed his eyes. Just when he felt he could bear the emotional roller coaster no longer, here came another sickening twist. Theo was to have a stepfather. His primary male role model was to be not him, but . . .

"Who?" Hugo demanded. "Who have you met?"

The head of the magazine company, it turned out. "Fantastic guy called Rick," Amanda enthused. "Bald, admittedly, but quite sexy. Shit-hot businessman, though. And as rich as fuck, obviously."

Hugo reflected dejectedly that maybe a shit-hot businessman who was as rich as fuck was rather a good model for Theo. Better than he was at any rate. "And you're going to marry him?"

"Maybe." Amanda gave a coquettish little smile.

"So," Hugo said dully, "what *were* you wrong about then?"

"Sorry?" Amanda said blankly. Her thoughts were obviously still with Rick. Or, more likely, his money.

"You said you'd come to tell me you were wrong. About something."

"Oh, yeah." Amanda ran her hands absently through her expensive hair. "I was wrong," she said, checking her lipstick on one of Theo's cot mirrors, "about *me*."

"You?" He had no idea what she meant.

Amanda started to walk around the nursery again, trying not to skewer the scattered toys with her heels. "I've been thinking about myself," she announced.

"Ye-es?" So what was new? The chances of Amanda ever thinking about anyone else were nonexistent.

"I've realized a few things," Amanda announced. "Things I

never realized before. For instance, while some women are born to be mothers, for others, career is what matters."

Hugo narrowed his eyes. Only to Amanda was that a revelation. He could not imagine what all this was leading up to and the suspense made his muscles ache.

"It's been so tough," Amanda declared, turning tragic eyes on him. "You know, keeping the whole thing going. The job, Theo, you and me. The juggling. That whole hideous working-mother thing."

Hugo felt the familiar fury rise. Not this self-deluding rubbish again.

"You know," Amanda sighed, "one of the worst things of all is that I haven't been able to talk to anyone about the terrible strain I've been under."

Not much, thought Hugo. Only the entire readership of whatever magazine had interviewed her.

"Because, of course, I've never had the time," Amanda continued martyrishly. "Until now. Last night I had a very long talk on the phone with Laura. She rang me. Really *forced* me to open up about everything."

"Did she now?" Hugo said sardonically. It must, he thought, have been like forcing open a box of teabags.

Amanda nodded eagerly. "It was such a relief. We talked endlessly about *me*, for once. About the pressures I was under. The uncertainty I felt. And my frustration, as a perfectionist, at not being able to do everything—work, wife, motherhood—absolutely brilliantly."

Hugo's glance slid to Theo's activity center. Could he, he wondered, batter Amanda to death with it? No wonder he had thought the thing sinister. Had it been a premonition?

"And Laura—you know . . ." Amanda shook her head disbelievingly. "Well, she was *amazing*. I'd completely underestimated her. I had no idea how *wise* she was."

Wise. Hugo could think of many words to describe Laura. That was not one of them.

"She helped me realize what I'd just refused to let myself accept." Amanda's eyes were wide with wonder. "That some women just weren't born to be mothers. But that the journey—having the baby and all that—was a necessary part of the pathway to greater self-realization."

"I see." Hugo's tone was determinedly neutral despite the outraged boiling of his insides. "So Theo and I were a sort of experiment?"

"Exactly that," Amanda nodded delightedly. "Becoming a mother myself was the crucial step to realizing that, actually, it wasn't my bag at all. And Laura's showed me that if that's the sort of woman you are then it's best to admit it and accept your other strengths. That it's a strength to admit your weaknesses." She looked distantly at Theo. "And, you know, I've got so many strengths. I'm a great writer, for a start. Great words person. Great editor. *Class* is doing fantastically."

"Is it?" Hugo thought gloomily of the no doubt also fantastic salary that had mysteriously never made it to Fitzherbert Place.

Amanda bent over the cot mirror again and inspected her mascara. "Rick's desperate for me to do more. Be editor-in-chief of a range of titles."

"Congratulations." Hugo miserably imagined the long days at the aspirational nursery that this would mean for Theo.

"Thank you." Amanda nodded graciously. "But here's the dub, as they say."

"Rub."

"What?"

"Here's the rub. That's the phrase." So much for the great words person.

"Oh, right. Well, anyway, what I wanted to tell you is that Laura helped me *see*."

"See what?" He'd thought Laura was training to be a counselor. Not an optician.

"That I deserved a break, after everything I'd been through.

And that us splitting up was a natural pause, a chance to re-assess the way I wanted to live the rest of my life. A chance to get off this awful pressurized, overachieving mummy-go-round. A chance to start my new life with Rick free of ties and responsibilities. *Hugo*," Amanda said, looking wildly into his eyes. "She helped me to be *honest* with myself."

Hugo was unsure whether to laugh or cry. Or simply scream and jump out of the window. "Amanda, forgive me for being stupid," he said.

"Oh, I forgave you for that ages ago," she replied graciously.

"But just what is all this leading up to?"

Amanda raked her hands through her hair excitedly. "Laura convinced me that taking Theo with me to London would be the worst possible thing for my career. Not to mention complicating the start of my new life with Rick."

Hugo felt as shocked as if a shire horse had kicked him in the balls. "What? She convinced you of *what*?"

"That Theo would be better off here with you. You know, among all the people and places he's used to. The nursery and all that."

Were it not for the fact he was already sitting down, Hugo would, he felt, have sunk to his knees. God bless Laura. She had wanted to help him and she had. And *how*. Bringing her new counseling skills to bear on Amanda's vanity, selfishness and self-delusion, she had twisted them to an outcome suiting everyone.

"So you'll get custody in the divorce," Amanda said breezily. "We can sort out access, alimony and all that crap later on."

All that crap. The kind of crap that routinely ruined lives. Including his own, or so he had expected.

"Alimony?" he queried, the word putting a brake on his rising joy. "You know I'm broke. I lost my job."

"So I heard." Amanda looked at him almost affectionately. "Loser. I'll be paying *you*, obviously. Upkeep for Theo." She looked at her watch. "Shit, is that the time? Must dash, got a lipstick launch at the Grosvenor House later. Bye, darling," she flung absently in Theo's direction, before darting out of the door in her heels.

"Ayiyiyiyi," said the baby triumphantly, sliding the last of his wooden rings onto his stake.

CHAPTER
29

HUGO COULD HARDLY BELIEVE HIS LUCK. THE CLOUDS HAD PARTED. He and Theo were to remain together. Amanda, meanwhile, was to start a new life with her shit-hot businessman who was as rich as fuck. Following the divorce, which had miraculously swung from bitterly acrimonious to almost impossibly amicable, he, Hugo, would be free to marry whomever he wanted.

All that remained to make his happiness complete was to persuade Alice that staying with her husband was a mistake. But this, obviously, was not going to be easy. He had to find a way to help her extricate herself. A way that would appease her obviously rampant guilt while ensuring she did not lose Rosa.

No ordinary display of logic would work, he knew. No normal line of argument would have any effect whatsoever. Not least because she would not allow him to talk to her.

His telephone calls went unanswered. And when, again, he gathered the courage to knock on the Old Morgue's door, it remained, as before, resolutely shut. He had tried shouting through the mail slot, but to no avail. The only life in the place, it seemed, was in the clanging of the garden's bean-can windchimes and the plant-stuffed footwear festooning the house walls.

Only one other possibility of meeting Alice remained. He knew where and when she attended her counseling sessions. He could lie in wait.

When, with an electric jerk of the heart, he saw Alice finally come out of the clinic, he noticed she looked as doleful as the rainy day. Her sessions were obviously just as uplifting as his had been. Among the many joys of his current situation was no longer having to bother with Dr. Hasselblad.

From the warmth of his car he watched her walk down the wet street to the bus stop. Once she was standing there, he started the engine and drove past, slowing down as if spotting her by chance.

"Alice! Want a lift?"

Excitement spasmed across her face at the sound and sight of him. Then, clearly with an effort, she arranged her features into a blank. "I can't talk to you," she hissed, blinking the raindrops off her eyelashes.

"Come on, Alice," he urged. "Get in the car. I've got some news for you. Great news."

"I *can't*." Her eyes flicked about her in terror. "Jake might see me. *His* therapy session is any minute now."

"Alice. Come on. It's pissing down."

"*Please*," she begged. "Just go away. Leave me alone."

Hugo hesitated. He could not drive off without telling her what had happened. It wasn't the best method of communication, granted, still less the most private. But what else could he do?

"Amanda's getting married again!" he roared from the driver's window. "To a shit-hot businessman who's as rich as fuck!"

The rest of the bus queue cheered. "Good for her!" boomed a solid old lady, waving a walking stick in the air.

"She's agreed I get custody of Theo!" Hugo yelled.

More cheers. An emotional fight to the death, meanwhile, was playing out over Alice's face. Her expression was half exultation, half wanting to sink into the pavement.

"So don't you see, Alice?" Hugo bellowed. "Once the divorce goes through I can marry again. I'll have Theo. So all you have to do is divorce Jake for unreasonable behavior and you, me, Rosa and Theo can all live together. Happily ever after."

The crowd at the bus stop went wild. "Go on, dear," the old lady urged Alice. "He looks like such a nice young man. *I* would."

"Well, don't let me stop you," stormed Alice. She turned furiously on her heel and plowed down the street, heedless of the puddles. Heedless himself of the hoots of the cars behind him, Hugo crawled alongside her, shouting and pleading, to little effect. After a few minutes of angry marching, Alice turned abruptly into an alleyway and was thereafter lost from sight.

Hugo continued to cruise round the neighboring streets, but without success. Eventually, accepting defeat, he parked and stared morosely at the steering wheel. So near and yet so far. While a miracle had occurred with Amanda, nothing short of outing Jake as number two to Osama bin Laden would convince Alice there was no future in her marriage.

In fact, did Hugo but know it, nothing could be further from the truth. Alice's hopes for a stable marital future had sustained the ultimate body blow.

Admittedly, there had been clues. He now bathed every day, flushed the lavatory with wild abandon and a number of T-shirts that were definitely new had leavened his otherwise secondhand wardrobe. But it wasn't this that ultimately blew his cover.

Alone in the cottage with Rosa because Jake was out

demonstrating with Joss and Jessamy, Alice had answered the phone to a Joss not only not demonstrating, but clearly unaware he was supposed to be. "Oh right," he said. "So he's out somewhere with Jess, is he?"

"It would seem so," Alice replied tightly.

How could she have been so stupid? So blind? When it had been staring her in the face all this time? Hugo, of course, had guessed the moment she had mentioned Jake's nightly protest outings: *"There aren't any women on the staff?"*

She remembered her denial: *"He's not interested in other women, I'm sure of that."*

Empty days had passed, and weeks begun and ended while Alice fought with herself over what to do. On the one hand, she felt she deserved it, having been unfaithful herself. On the other, they had agreed to stay together for Rosa's sake. Her unhappiness grew. Jake's wardrobe and aftershave, meanwhile, grew ever more assertive. The course of action Alice eventually settled on was continuing to attend her counseling sessions. Perhaps Dr. Hasselblad had the answers. Meeting Hugo at the clinic that morning, however, had only increased the questions.

* * *

Hugo, unaware of any of this, got out of the car and walked toward the town center. There was too much to do. A job to find, for instance.

He had tried most of the big Bath real estate agencies by now. But it was possible an untapped couple of independents lurked in some side street. A smaller agency might be more suitable anyway, being possibly more disposed to accept the part-time arrangement he wanted.

Although Chicklets had offered a full-time place, his afternoons with Theo were, Hugo had decided, too precious to give up. But the fact he wasn't a woman, yet wanted to work mornings only, seemed to confound most of the agencies he approached. "It's an unusual request—for a man," he heard time and time again. Explaining that it was for childcare reasons seemed only to worsen the situation.

Get real, Hugo wanted to shout as he walked out under supercilious stares. Men are parents too. And guess what, it's the way things are going.

Realizing he was about to pass his old employers, Dunn and Dustard, Hugo slowed down. He was unable to resist looking in the window to see if any of the old faithful properties were still there. He was almost certain that they would be. Tarquin's immovable town house, for example.

A number of other people were loitering outside the agency's windows. This was not unusual; the pavement outside frequently hosted knots of daytrippers squinting at prices and fantasizing about life amid Regency splendor.

Tarquin's house was indeed still there. As were the familiar paragraphs accompanying its photograph. "An unparalleled opportunity to purchase this peerless property . . ." Alliteration, Hugo thought, was a wonderful thing. But it still hadn't moved the house.

"Quite honestly, darling, I'm in despair," sighed a camp, nasal voice beside him. "I mean, the Ancient Mariner got off lightly. If he really wanted to know what a serious albatross was, he should have tried selling Firth House. And if only somebody would, frankly."

Hugo was surprised to recognize Tarquin himself. He wore a shaggy gray fur coat, red velvet trousers and an air of comic dismay. Having initially imagined the complaint was addressed to him, Hugo now saw that he was wrong. Tarquin was talking to the tall, broad-shouldered, long-haired man through whose arm his own was tightly threaded. And who bore, Hugo noticed, a powerful resemblance to Jake.

Possibly, he realized, a split second later, because he *was* Jake.

The two of them pulled away from the window and walked

slowly together down the street. Hugo stared after them. Hadn't Alice just said Jake was at counseling?

* * *

That night, Alice had put Rosa to bed and was gloomily descending the staircase when, to her surprise, she heard a rattling at the door. Terror churned in her stomach. Jake was, as usual, allegedly at some demonstration, and no one was expected, also as usual. Was this the moment she had subconsciously feared ever since moving to the English countryside? The moment a madman with a knife burst in and stabbed her to death?

It was not a madman with a knife, however. It was Jake.

"You're back early," Alice remarked.

"Yes."

"Was the demonstration canceled?"

Jake shook his head. His silky hair slid from side to side, shining in the light from the colanders on the ceiling. "There wasn't a demonstration."

"Ah." Much as she had suspected. But why was he admitting it? Alice sensed something momentous was about to be said. Was he about to announce he was leaving her for Jessamy?

"I know I said that's where I was going." Jake's voice was gentle, as if addressing an invalid. "But I wasn't. I was . . ." He looked uncharacteristically uncomfortable. "I was . . . I am . . . seeing someone else."

"I know," Alice said calmly.

He started. "You *know*?"

"Of course. You're having an affair with Jessamy, aren't you?"

"*Jessamy?*"

"Oh, come off it, Jake," Alice snapped. "You've been spending every evening with her for months. You said you were out with her and Joss, but I happen to know that you weren't because Joss called you one night when—"

282

"Jessamy's got nothing to do with it," Jake interrupted loudly. "She's just a friend. A work colleague."

"Is that right?" She blazed him a glance of disbelief.

"Yes." He looked boldly back. "I haven't been seeing her. I've been seeing, erm, Tarquin."

"*Tarquin?* You mean," Alice said slowly, "that you're having an affair with . . . *a man?*"

"Yes."

"Called . . . *Tarquin?*"

"Yes."

"You mean . . . you're gay?"

He did not meet her eye. "It's always been there, Al," he groaned. "And I've always been scared of it. I've tried to suppress it. Get it to go away. But it wouldn't."

Alice's throat was dry. She was so surprised she could barely speak. "But . . . the sex. With me. You seemed to enjoy it."

"I did."

"But if you're gay . . . ?"

"Al, loads of gay men are in straight relationships or even married before they finally face up to their true inclinations. Some of them never do, of course . . ."

"Thank goodness you had the courage, eh?" Alice said bitterly.

"Al, I'm sorry. I really wanted to make it work. I hoped that being married . . . having a wife . . ."

She frowned, working out what he was saying. "That's . . . why you married me? To force yourself . . . to be straight?" She burst out laughing. It was all so unbelievable.

He dropped his head. "Something like that," he muttered.

Alice was not laughing now. "God, of course," she breathed. "I can see it all now." She shook her head. "It must have been so easy for you at Sally's wedding. I was single and desperate, or so you no doubt thought. Easy pickings. Go on, admit it," she snarled, voice rising unsteadily. "Wasn't it like that?"

He sighed. "You were very . . . receptive. And very beautiful," he added quickly.

She ignored the compliment. "And you were pretty full-on. Flying out to New York. Bursting into my office with a million red roses. And then all that perfect father stuff. The prenatal classes . . ." Her throat blocked with fury and she stopped.

He raked an agitated hand through his hair. "I know. I know. I was acting, I admit it."

"*Acting!* Too fucking right. You should be in L.A. polishing your Oscars."

"I thought that, even if marriage didn't work, being a father would . . . I dunno . . . sort me out for good."

His eyes were burning as he looked at her, but burning differently than before. Where they had once been messianic, bullying, they seemed now to be pleading for understanding. "It *had* to work. But it didn't. I knew it as soon as Rosa was born. I realized how wrong I had been and I was terrified. I started making excuses not to be with you straight away."

"Taking my flowers to the addiction center, for instance."

"Alice, believe me, if it could have been any other way . . ."

"But it could have been," she blasted. "You could have been *nicer* to us. Allowed Rosa to go to nursery and me to start some sort of new career. But no. You became a fundamentalist enviro-maniac. Made me"—what had Hugo and her mother said?—"a virtual bloody *eco-prisoner*. But why? What was all that about? What did that have to do with being gay?"

"Everything." As, nervously, he shook his hair, a waft of aftershave crashed into her nostrils. "When I met Tarquin for the first time, I realized what might happen. So I went into overdrive with work. Wouldn't allow myself to think about anything else. Got completely and utterly obsessed with the whole recycling business . . ."

"But who *is* Tarquin?" Alice demanded. "Where did you meet him?"

"Tarquin's an architect. He came to a *Get Trashed!* seminar about sustainable housing." Jake allowed a smile to flicker across his features. "He was extremely interested in the possibilities of grass-roofed underground developments. Or so I thought. In fact, he'd just got out of a long-term bad relationship and was interested in . . . well . . ."

"You?"

He shot her a haunted look. "God, Al—"

"Stop calling me Al."

"You've no idea how I tried to resist him, Alice. But he was very persistent."

Witheringly: "It must have been hell."

"So the more persistent he got, the more extreme the environmental stuff got. I tried to bury myself in it."

"Bury all of us in it, you mean. You could hardly see the cottage for those heaps you started bringing home from the dump. Those loos. And baths. And basins." She stopped as a horrible thought struck her. *The condoms!* she shrieked. "You hadn't, I mean . . . used them . . . on *men?*"

His hair flew about his head in a desperate negative. "No. I promise you. I never had . . . I never thought I would. I was determined not to fall in love with Tarquin."

"My mother knew there was something weird about it all. Why didn't I listen to her?" Alice wailed. "She was right all along."

"I'm sorry, Al," Jake said in a crushed whisper. "*Alice,* I mean. All I can say is that I was confused. Confused, angry and scared. And, yes, I took it all out on you . . . and Rosa."

"You *bastard.* And you made me suffer so much over the Hugo thing. You were going to run away with Rosa."

"I wouldn't have, Al. It was just an empty threat. I was panicking. I would only have been running away from myself."

"Is that Dr. Hasselblad speaking?" Alice asked sourly.

"Ah." Jake raised his eyebrows in a *mea culpa* expression. "The counseling sessions."

In a flash, she understood. "You mean you didn't go to

them? You were seeing . . . *Tarquin* instead?" She pushed a hank of hair out of her eyes. "Jesus."

His voice was pathetically eager. "But Alice, Tarquin's been better than any counseling. He's really helped me get to know myself. Face up to things I never dared to before."

"Like what?" she asked wearily.

"That I'm a bloody idiot, for a start. Tarquin and I were out for dinner one night—"

"Dinner!" Alice's eyes flew open. She and Jake had never been out for dinner in the entire time she had lived at the Old Morgue.

"Yes." He slid her a guilty look. "I'm afraid that we've been having quite a lot of dinners. Possibly when you thought I was out chaining myself to Dumpsters. You see, Tarquin's very fond of good food . . ."

"He's not the only one." Alice said resentfully.

"Anyway," Jake continued, "there I was, telling him about the moral and ethical ramifications of everything he was about to eat. He helped me see I wasn't making the world a better place. I was just annoying people when they were trying to eat."

Alice's stare was steely. "You know," she said with sudden vehemence, "I don't care about any of this. I don't want to know. It's your business. Frankly, you make me sick."

"Alice—"

"You're a bully, a hypocrite and a shameless manipulator. You've messed up my life and not only mine . . ."

"Alice. Please. What I want you to understand is that Tarquin's helped me to think straight. Best of all," Jake added, eyes and voice glowing with sincerity, "he's helped me be *honest* with myself."

Alice was now too angry to speak. How dare he stand there singing the praises of his boyfriend? She felt about for something to throw at him.

Jake, however, sailed on serenely. "He's helped me realize that becoming a husband and father was what I needed to do in order to realize what a completely *useless* husband and father I am. And that the best thing to do now is to just stop pretending. Accept that I'm not Superdad, or ever likely to be."

"I see," Alice's hand had by now closed over a jam jar on a table behind her. Filled with earth from the garden, it was doing duty as a paperweight. She lifted it slowly as she spoke, her voice shaking with anger. "So Rosa and I were a sort of experiment?"

"Exactly that."

Behind her back, Alice raised the jar, preparing to hurl it into his face. *"Experiment!"* she snarled.

"Hey. Don't be cross. It's a good thing. Tarquin's helped me see that if that's the sort of guy you are then it's best to admit it and accept your other strengths."

Her fingers tensed for the throw. "Alice," Jake urged softly, "what I'm leading up to is that I don't think there's any point in trying to keep the marriage going. You and Rosa are better off without me."

The jam jar crashed to the floor and shattered. Earth spilled everywhere. "You mean . . . ?"

He started in shock at the noise and looked in surprise at the filthy floor. "Er . . . yes. You can divorce me for adultery. Or unreasonable behavior. Or both. Or whatever you like. I won't contest it. And you can marry whoever once it's over. Even that oily bastard Hugo." He grinned. But Alice was not yet ready to make jokes.

"Rosa?" Her throat was so full she could barely get the syllables out.

"You'll have custody, obviously. But we need to work out access. I think, at last, I really am ready to be a good father. Properly this time, I mean. And a support to you, as well. *Get Trashed!*'s going much more commercial. Tarquin's got some great ideas. It'll be a proper business. Diversifying in lots of ways. You'll start seeing a return on your investment soon. Oh, Alice, it's been such a bloody mess. But hopefully now . . ."

Alice did not hear the last few sentences. Jake's gabbling had died in her ears. She collapsed on an orange-box chair in a dead faint.

CHAPTER
30

HUGO PEELED HIS FACE FROM THE WHITE-COATED CHEST OF AN EX-ceptionally pretty woman. His rush through the hospital was such that he had failed to consider the possibility that the corner he was heading for might have someone coming round it.

"Sorry," he gasped, mortified.

Dr. Watson, Consultant Pediatrician, recovered her breath. She looked sharply at Hugo. "Don't I know you?"

"We've met before," Hugo admitted, his stomach flipping as he remembered the last time. "My baby son had a rash."

The doctor nodded. "Of course. Nasty-looking one, wasn't it? And how is he now? Walking?"

Hugo nodded, grinning at the thought. Theo thundering about on his fat little legs was a sight of which he never tired.

"So what brings you back here?" the doctor asked.

"A class." Hugo's grin widened. "A prenatal class."

"You're having another baby? Congratulations."

"Thanks."

"Well, I'll leave you to it. You know your way, obviously. Good luck. I might see you on the great day if I'm doing the rounds." Hugo watched the doctor walk off, swinging her great mass of shining black hair.

Actually, he realized, he didn't know his way. He had forgotten. It was almost a year and a half since he had last attempted to find the prenatal classes and the gray-linoleumed bowels of the hospital were as much of a mystery now as they had been then.

He pelted onward down the corridor, then past a couple of bends. It took a further five minutes of rising panic before finally, thankfully, he found the right door.

He knocked and opened it to see Alice smiling back at him from the middle of a horseshoe of people. He stumbled thankfully toward the empty orange plastic chair next to her. "Sorry I'm late," he announced to the class at large.

In the center of the horseshoe stood a thin-faced woman with wire-framed glasses and a bright, toothy smile. "Welcome," she said to Hugo. "Now you are here we can start. My name is Lotti . . ."

It had been Alice's idea to come to the classes on the grounds that she could remember next to nothing of the first ones, thanks to Amanda's distracting, hate-filled stares. He had agreed on the very similar grounds that Jake's nauseous personification of perfect fatherhood had had much the same effect on him.

As Lotti got out the poster of the upside-down baby, Hugo's thoughts wound irresistibly backward. It was now almost nine months since Alice had made that breathless, shouting, crying phone call in which she had confirmed in hysterical bursts Hugo's half-formed suspicions regarding Jake and Tarquin. And, more significantly, the implications of this for their own future together. The fact that they had one, in other words.

The marriages to Jake and Amanda were dissolved, in the end, with little more than a sigh. Shortly after, Alice moved into Fitzherbert Place and a little after that, it was discovered that Theo and Rosa, between who the early promise of friendship had blossomed into near inseparability, were to be joined in the nursery by someone else. When Alice, beaming, had waved the pregnancy tester at him, Hugo felt that his cup of joy hadn't just run over. He felt it was flooding down the street like a fire hydrant.

He had immediately suggested a wedding. Yet Alice resisted. "I made all those vows once," she said. "And I broke them. It's meaningless to make them again." He could not argue with this logic. In his heart, anyway, Hugo felt more than married to Alice. He felt welded to her, with a love forged through the fire of the most abject adversity he had ever known.

Alice, for her part, felt like a horse let out of the starting gate once the marriage to Jake was finally over. She had found work in a local court as a media legal expert and was now much in demand with the battalions of publications and TV companies flocking to Bath from London in search of cheaper rents, less stressed staff and a better quality of life. No matter what the volume of work, however, Alice stuck to her resolve of part-time employment. Never again, she had decided, would her work-life balance get as seriously skewed as it had during her years in New York. She had no intention, moreover, of letting Hugo, who worked part time at his own real estate agency, hog all the children all the time.

Jake's relationship with his daughter and ex-wife was positively flourishing now he was no longer living a lie. And almost as importantly, a steely effort had been made on Alice's part in particular to let bygones be bygones.

Amanda's relationship with Theo and Hugo was equally cordial, although Hugo kept having to remind her that, while her offers of work experience for Theo were very welcome, he was as yet on the young side. "Can't start too early if he's going to be the new William Randolph Hearst," Amanda boomed back.

* * *

"Yugo!" someone foreign-accented was saying. "Yugo!"

Hugo blinked, remembering where he was. Back in the prenatal class with Lotti beaming at him.

"Sorry," Hugo said, startled. "I was miles away. What did you say?"

"I am asking everyone how they feel about having a baby," Lotti explained, blinking earnestly at him through her glasses. "Give the people a chance to air their anxieties, you know? It's goot to do it in this situation, where we are all in the same ship together."

"Boat," smiled Hugo.

"Oh yes," said Lotti. "You are right. Boat. So, Yugo. How do you feel about becoming a daddy?"

Déjà vu swept Hugo. His heart thundered. His gut surged with nausea and his hands twisted together. He opened his mouth and closed it again. Then opened it again. He looked at Alice, who was regarding him with concern.

"Becoming a father?" he forced out eventually from a constricted throat.

"That's right, Yugo. I want you to tell the class how you feel. Any worries you might have, you can share them with us."

Hugo took a deep breath. He reached for Alice's hand and squeezed it. "I feel," he said slowly, "that it's going to be the absolute best thing. The best thing ever in the best possible world."

Also by the
"absolutely fabulous"*
WENDY HOLDEN

 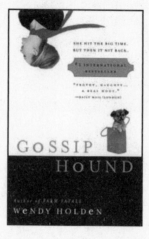 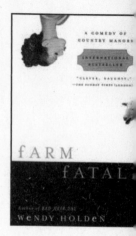

"Holden is very good indeed."
— *The Baltimore Sun*

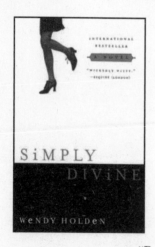 

"Perfect."
— *The Times* (London)